POISON

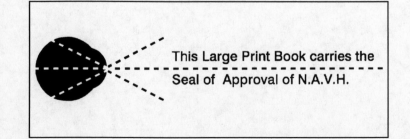

BLOODLINE TRILOGY, BOOK 2

POISON

JORDYN REDWOOD

THORNDIKE PRESS
A part of Gale, Cengage Learning

GALE
CENGAGE Learning®

Detroit • New York • San Francisco • New Haven, Conn • Waterville, Maine • London

GALE
CENGAGE Learning®

© 2013 by Jordyn Redwood
Thorndike Press, a part of Gale, Cengage Learning.

Thorndike Press® Large Print Christian Mystery.
The text of this Large Print edition is unabridged.
Other aspects of the book may vary from the original edition.
Set in 16 pt. Plantin.

LIBRARY OF CONGRESS CATALOGING-IN-PUBLICATION DATA

Redwood, Jordyn.
    Poison : Bloodline Trilogy 2 / by Jordyn Redwood. — Large Print edition.
        pages cm. — (Thorndike Press Large Print Christian Mystery)
    ISBN 978-1-4104-5854-4 (hardcover) — ISBN 1-4104-5854-7 (hardcover)
    1. Dysfunctional families—Fiction. 2. Colorado—Fiction. 3. Large type books.
I. Title.
PS3618.E43538P65 2013
813'.6—dc23   2013007015

Published in 2013 by arrangement with Kregel Publications, a division of Kregel, Inc.

Printed in Mexico
1 2 3 4 5 6 7 17 16 15 14 13

For My True Love: James
Thank you for loving me.

And for Kira and Lindsay
May you also see your dreams
come true.

ACKNOWLEDGMENTS

Sometimes it is hard to adequately express how thankful I am to those who have helped me on this crazy publishing journey. Greg Johnson, my agent and friend, thank you for navigating this road with me and helping me understand things about writing and publishing that I never learned in nursing school. I am blessed to have both you and Becky in my life.

To my experts who reviewed *Poison* for accuracy: Pat Gonzales and Melissa Houser for the psychiatric component and Karl Mai for the police aspects. Thank you for your time and talent. All mistakes are my own and not related in any way to their genius.

I do read a lot of nonfiction for research, so I want to acknowledge those books that I relied on heavily — particularly for Keelyn's expertise as a body-language expert: *What Every Body Is Saying* by Joe Navarro and *The Gift of Fear* by Gavin De Becker. In fact, some of Lee's definitions in the novel come directly from Gavin's book. If you are a woman (sixteen years and up), I do think Gavin's book is required reading. Also, *My Lie: A True Story of False Memory* by Meredith Maran, which delves into how false memories can be created. Maran's book does have subject matter involving child sexual abuse and homosexuality, so a cautionary note to those who prefer not to read on those topics. Also, *The Complete Idiot's Guide to Hypnosis* by Roberta Temes, PhD.

To Susan Lohrer, who I trust implicitly to read my words and help me improve them before anyone else sees them.

For everyone at Kregel — honestly, it is my honor to get to work with you guys. For the editorial staff who help make my books shine: Janyre Tromp, Becky Fish, and Dawn Anderson. Cat Hoort — you are a blessing to me and all the work you do to get the word out about the Bloodline Trilogy is greatly appreciated. Dennis Hillman and Steve Barclift who are always available for my questions. Nick Richardson for your fabulous book covers.

To SE Christian's book club. Thank you for being a faithful group of early readers and helping me see the growth areas my manuscript needed.

A special heartfelt debt of gratitude to Candace Calvert, who has been a mentor to me on my writing journey. Thank you for your guidance and friendship. I'd offer to cook you dinner but I'd rather have you cook dinner for me!

To all my friends and family who support me and pull me back from the cliff just when I'm about to fall off: Marcella Shadle, Jen Loveland, Peg Brantley, Jenni Ackerman, Shellie Brandt, and Crystal Bencken. Thank you for keeping me sane.

And Mom, I'm glad you liked *Poison* better than *Proof*! Hope my readers will, too. Thanks for your love and support and for selling so many of my books.

As always — saving the most important for last. To you, my readers — thank you for your time spent reading my novels. Without you, this whole journey is worthless. I absolutely love to hear from you. Please e-mail me when you've finished reading any of my books at jredwood1@gmail .com. You'll probably hear back from me personally.

CHAPTER 1

Monday

A cool autumn breath whispered at the base of Keelyn's neck and drew her attention to the front door of the busy diner. The man who entered wove through the chairs, unapologetic as he bumped customers along his path. His pale hand laid claim to the red vinyl stool beside her.

"Is this taken?"

Her words caught in her throat as she tried to reply. In the void of her silence, the stranger leaned toward the counter and pushed his scratched, dented silverware into her space.

A clear move to establish territorial dominance.

Heat flushed her cheeks. Heaviness settled in her gut and needled at the peace she generally felt being in the place where she'd shared sweet memories with her mother and sister.

A mother now dead.

A sister estranged.

Keelyn pressed her lips together as she gathered her thoughts. "I'm expecting my fiancé." His eyes pinned her, and she felt entranced by the unusual color of his irises. Like malachite with variegated ribbons of green.

Dark and edgy.

"How about I keep the seat warm for him?" He offered his hand. "Until another one becomes available?"

Keelyn glanced around the diner and saw no other empty seat. She accepted the gesture. His grip tightened around hers, emanating an icy chill that seeped through her skin and thickened her blood. Each heartbeat pulsed at the tips of her fingers. She pulled her hand from his with a tug that unbalanced her on the stool, and he grabbed her elbow to keep her from falling. Once he released her, she swept her hands over her arms to squelch the sensation of burrowing insects.

He seated himself beside her.

Keelyn's eyes landed on the TV behind the counter. She motioned to the waitress to tease up the volume. A mother and her two small children missing — the story consumed Denver local news for days. Rebecca, Bryce, and Sadie, seemingly all kidnapped when she had gone to pick them up from school. No leads yet. Keelyn's heart ached as she watched Rebecca's husband break down in front of the news cameras and shove them away.

It echoed her own grief for those she'd lost.

She pivoted toward the counter and pushed the plate of cookies she'd made for Lee off to the other side, her attention back to the crossword puzzle.

"Hazel," the stranger said.

Keelyn's heart leapt. "What?"

"As in witch or the color of your eyes."

She scanned the clues to the right side of her mostly empty boxes.

"Despair. Four across."

Glancing back at the puzzle, she put the letters in place.

The pen she held tapped against the newspaper. The black print sharpened as her vision crystallized from the adrenaline. What was it about this stranger that caused her nerves to fire? She closed her eyes and sent a silent wish for Lee to arrive soon.

"Unholy. Twenty down."

Keelyn's eyes shot open. He reached around her to point. Did he understand personal space? This time, she didn't engage

13

him and slid an inch to the right, hoping he would pick up on her obvious disinterest in continuing a conversation.

"You're a very confident woman." He leaned forward and peered around her arm. She rotated her chin in her hand, looking at him directly. His deficiency in reading her body language annoyed her. Keelyn worked as a paid consultant interpreting nonverbal communication, and most people intuitively understood cultural boundaries.

"Why do you say that?"

"Because you mark your answers in indelible ink." He traced a finger over her filled-in squares. "You don't think you'll need to change any?"

"Why is that a concern of yours?" Keelyn put the pen down and creased the paper over it. At the footrest of her bar stool lay the loop for her Vera Bradley tote, and she reached to open the bag and slide in the puzzle.

A prickle itched at her ear as she waited for the jingle that would signal someone's entrance from the front door. Hope edged at her elevated heartbeat that Lee would pop through and she would have a reason to ask this interloper to leave.

The stranger seemed unfazed by her question. "Captain Watson has been delayed,"

14

he said. He pulled the tumbler of water the waitress left for him closer and twirled his index finger through the ice. Within the frigid vortex, his finger grew blue.

The tinkle of frozen cubes against the glass sent shivers up her spine. "And you know this how?"

"I know many things about Lee. About you, Miss Blake."

Pressure swelled in her forehead as blood rushed to her head. Her thoughts raced back through their short conversation. Had she told him her name?

She massaged two fingers into her temple to counter the pain. "You're a friend of his?"

"An old acquaintance."

"How old?"

He sipped his water then pulled a purplish finger across his full lips to wipe the droplets away. "I'm surprised Lee lets you keep this little routine." The glass clinked against the counter like a crack in a window. "Being a SWAT guy and all. The two of you meeting at this diner every week is predictable. It allows people to find you. Maybe someone you wouldn't want to meet."

"Is there a message I can give Lee for you?"

He twisted a ring on his right pinky. An eight-pointed star behind an hourglass.

"Who said I wanted to talk to Lee? He's detained because of me, so I could speak to you."

Keelyn's mouth dried. "He's injured?"

"Physically, he's fine. Homicides can have a nasty way of interrupting his day."

"You're responsible for a murder he's investigating?"

"Never directly, of course. Did Lee ever tell you how he felt that day?"

There are instances in a person's life where the words "that day" hold such significance that not another word need be uttered to clarify their meaning. Some of them are collective, like the day two planes took down the twin towers, and others are intensely personal moments.

Keelyn's throat thickened at the mention of her life's moment, but her concern for Lee's welfare and the implications of this stranger's knowledge edged over her sense of foreboding. "That day is something he doesn't talk about."

"You're not curious about it? Such an odd beginning for a relationship. You held hostage by your stepfather. The slaying of nearly half your family. Lee playing a part in saving your life."

Her heart pounded against her ribs.

"You never did tell me your name." Keelyn's voice shook despite her effort to stay calm.

He leaned toward her, a smirk playing across his face.

Cold fear shot through her. Each muscle tensed as his breath warmed her cheek, his lips inches from her ear.

His word whispered malice. "Lucent."

Her heart collapsed as he pulled away. She closed her eyes, the memory always at the forefront even though the incident was seven years past. Her stepfather before her, the black hilt of a knife in his hand as he held the sharp metal blade against her mother's throat. The panic in her mother's eyes as her father spewed hate. Her younger siblings cowered in the corner behind her. The sentence her father repeated like a stuttering vinyl record.

I'm doing what Lucent wants.

Keelyn's body shook as she remembered those few tentative steps she'd tried to take to stay his hand. The phone had stopped him.

A call from the police.

Keelyn swallowed hard. She gripped the counter as she turned toward her nemesis.

"Lucent isn't a person. He's my stepfather's hallucination. I want to know your *real* name. I want to know how you're privy to my stepfather's psychiatric record. Were you in prison with him?"

"So unlike a deer to attack."

"Tell me!" Her words arced above the quiet murmur of the other diner guests.

Several patrons within earshot looked their way. The man, Lucent, smiled and waved them off. He placed a hand on her shoulder, trapping strands of her brown hair and pulling her head into an awkward tilt. When she tried to shake him free, his fingers dug into her skin.

"I've left something here for you."

"Lee is coming. I think you need to leave."

"Raven's daughter."

She shoved his hand away. "That's a sick lie."

He clicked his tongue. "You've never met her. Your niece."

His statement lent credence to who he might be, and Keelyn scoped the diner for a young child. What he'd divulged prior could be obtained from public sources. But the details about Raven's daughter were slim. How did he know this information? How did a hallucination materialize into a person?

Unless he'd been real all along.

After her searching gaze only turned up twin boys tossing ketchup at one another,

18

she turned back to Lucent. "How do you know my sister?"

He skimmed crumbs from the countertop. "Raven and I have been spending time together. That little girl of hers, cute as she is, has been getting in the way. I suggested we find her a new home."

"Raven would never do that. She'd never surrender the child to anyone."

"How would you know how she feels about her little girl?"

A slow ache crawled up Keelyn's back to the base of her skull. The walls of the diner closed in. Lucent's brazen forthrightness stilled her as she considered her options. Turn and run. Punch him in the face. The latter was her preference, but there was a voice within her, a presence that strengthened her.

"Isn't it your duty to take the child in? You found God, as they say," Lucent challenged.

An overwhelming peace consumed her sense of flight. Keelyn felt a calm ease through her like ripples on a lake; each wave steadied her frayed nerves. Her own will battled against the tranquility. Trust was a hard-earned commodity, and the wealth of her faith was poor.

"What is it you want?" She clipped her

words sternly.

"Raven is no longer able to care for her daughter. I've left her here for you. Thought I'd be generous and spare her life. I think you owe Raven this much . . . for what you did."

Keelyn wanted to break free from this man, but his words sank like hooks into her flesh and her resolve wilted under his glare, his accusations a confirmation of her own internal condemnation.

"Why aren't you up out of your seat looking for her?" Lucent asked.

She held his gaze.

"Is it because you wouldn't recognize your niece? Last time you saw Raven, she was pregnant. Two years is a long time."

"What kind of trouble is my sister in?"

Lucent slid the edge of his jacket open. The grip of a gun glinted from the waistband of his black denims.

He pulled her chin up and locked his eyes on hers.

"You need to take what I say very seriously." She tried to pull away, but his fingers squeezed at her jaw like a vise. He leaned closer and lowered his voice. "If you look for Raven, I'll come back and kill you and the child."

Keelyn eased his hand from her face with

shaky fingers. The violent churning in her stomach released a flood of saliva into her mouth, and she swallowed several times to clear it. Was it the greasy smell or his threat that caused her stomach to flip?

"How do I know you're telling me the truth?"

"In the end, it's all about truth, isn't it? And ultimately, the choice you make about your belief in truth. But no matter how heartfelt your belief is, the truth doesn't change. That's what is so fun about humans. They believe they can change truth."

Keelyn scanned the diner. "Where exactly is the child?"

Lucent leaned back and secured his toes under the metal bar upon which he had been resting his feet. "I'm just curious how much you buy into your faith."

"We're done."

"I'm sad we didn't get along." Lucent stood and patted her on the shoulder as though she were a child. "I guess it's to be expected."

Keelyn watched as Lucent left. Her mind begged her body to detain him until Lee came. How could he leave and not tell her exactly where the child was?

As Keelyn sat motionless with indecision, Lee entered the diner. She caught his attention with a quick wave and turned back toward the counter as he approached. His uniform drew every eye like a magnet, and a quiet pause settled over the diner. Lee placed one arm around her, giving her a gentle hug, his service weapon a wedge between them. He pulled back her hair and kissed her cheek. Keelyn raked her fingers through his short blond hair and focused in on the comfort of his sapphire eyes. Could he feel the tremble in her fingers?

"Sorry I'm late. Got a call about someone barricaded in their home, threatening suicide. I hate it when we don't get there in time. Such a horrible day for that family." He scooted onto the barstool Lucent had vacated and looked at her expectantly. "What's wrong? Did I say too much?"

Keelyn placed her hands in her lap.

"Not feeling well?" Lee pursued.

"Can you be sure it wasn't a homicide?"

"Are you questioning my astute deductive reasoning?" Lee waved the waitress off and grabbed the water in front of him.

"Don't drink that." Keelyn shoved the glass away. Water splashed over and onto her hand, stinging like acid.

"What is up with you?"

"I had a visitor while I was waiting."

"Sounds cryptic."

"He called himself Lucent."

The dread in Lee's eyes caused Keelyn's pulse to double. "Lucent? You actually saw him as a person?"

"Yes."

"You're sure?"

"He was sitting right where you are."

"You're sure he was *real.*" The last word was seeded with doubt.

A slow heat built in her cheeks. "Lee, I wasn't hallucinating."

"He hurt you?"

"No."

"Where is he?"

"He just left."

"Is this some kind of joke? If so, it's not funny."

Keelyn inhaled deeply, shaking her head. "It's not a joke."

"What did *Lucent* want?"

"He said he's left Raven's daughter here for me."

Lee settled his hand on his thigh near his weapon. With his other hand, he eased his fingers around her neck and slid his hand under tendrils of her long brown hair and pulled her close into his shoulder. Her skin tingled under his touch. Patrons would observe an embrace between lovers. A seasoned officer could scan a room for threats subversively, and Keelyn knew this was the reason for his public affection.

Cover.

After several seconds, he pulled back and placed his lips against hers in a soft kiss, the warmth dispelling the chill in her bones left from Lucent's visit. His palm cupped her cheek as he broke away to look into her eyes. One of her tears slid down his thumb and over the inked cross tattoo on his inner wrist. She wiped the tear away from the symbol of their shared faith, and she prayed for this gripping horror to pass.

"Keelyn, it's going to be all right. I think this is some freak playing you."

She leaned her cheek into his hand, wanting to melt into his strength. With his free hand, he tugged her open cardigan closed. His insistence didn't ease her nausea. "He knew you were going to be late."

"Sweetheart, he could get that from a police scanner."

Keelyn reached up, placed her hand over his, and held his softened eyes with hers. "He knew about us meeting here."

The dimples disappeared from his easy smile as his jaw muscles tensed. Lee dropped his hand from her face and grabbed a small notebook and pen from his breast pocket.

"I'll need to know everything. What he looked like. We'll need to get Nathan in on this, just to be safe."

"He had blond hair. He was pale, sickly looking . . ."

A woman approached and tapped Lee on the shoulder. "Officer?"

Lee turned, a hint of annoyance in his voice. "What can I do for you?"

"Someone's passed out in their car. There's a child in the backseat. She appears to be sleeping, but I'm worried about her getting too hot."

Keelyn leapt off her stool and took two steps before Lee reached out to stop her.

"I'll go first." He stood and positioned Keelyn behind him. To the woman, he said, "Can you show me which vehicle?"

They walked single file to the parking lot. Gray clouds hovered low in the sky, and the air was thick and musty with the smell of threatened rain. Keelyn huddled herself into her arms, the cool ground further numbing her feet.

The woman pointed to a pearlescent white Highlander parked in a distant corner of the lot.

"Ma'am, can you wait by the building, please." Lee edged the concerned citizen back onto the stoop.

Keelyn wanted to reach out and hold his hand as they approached the car but knew he'd switched into active police persona and stayed three steps behind. The SUV's windows were tinted.

They approached the driver's side. He glanced at her. "Stay back."

CHAPTER 2

Lee grabbed a flashlight from his duty belt as his other hand unsnapped the leather retention strap that held his weapon in the holster, his palm now firm on the pistol grip. He thumbed the weapon's safety off but, without an obvious threat, didn't draw it.

Through the smoked glass, his flashlight revealed a woman slumped in the front passenger seat, her arms limp at her sides. He watched for movement. After several moments, there was a slight lift in her back. Lee stepped closer and placed his flashlight against the window to better penetrate the tinting, the light now bright against the body showed more detail.

Thick red fluid seeped through the left side of her shirt, trails of life flowing over the white leather seat onto the dark floor space.

A cool breeze evaporating the sweat through his military cropped hair caused his scalp to tingle. He inhaled and held his breath to ease the flow of adrenaline. Keelyn's worried gaze mirrored in the glass and burrowed into his back.

He brought his light up and tapped on the window.

"Ma'am, can you hear me?" The door was locked. Seeing no threats, Lee reset the safety on his weapon and snapped the retention strap back into place. No movement from the woman inside the vehicle. The child began to whimper in the backseat.

At least one of them was alive.

He glanced back at Keelyn. She held her position as he'd asked; a look of expectation crossed her hazel eyes.

Thunder boomed and she jumped.

He keyed his police radio.

"SWAT One, copy a medical emergency."

The dispatcher came back. "SWAT One, go ahead."

"SWAT One, I'm in the parking lot of Ruby's Diner. I have a citizen report of an adult female passed out in her vehicle."

"SWAT One, what is the primary medical concern, and do you have a vehicle description?"

"SWAT One, I'm with a white SUV in the northeast corner of the parking lot. I have an unresponsive adult female in the passenger's seat who appears to be bleeding from an unknown source . . . Break."

Training dictated short transmissions so fellow officers in potential danger could get through.

"SWAT One, continuing. I also have a toddler in the backseat, conscious and breathing, unknown further. I'm requesting fire and two ambulances to my location, emergent."

"SWAT One, dispatch copies one adult female bleeding and unresponsive, plus one toddler condition unknown. Fire and medical are en route Code Three."

The dispatcher's stern voice echoed the urgency of Lee's situation.

His resolve came quick.

Lee filled his right hand with the heavy, expandable baton he carried on his duty belt. He raised the device to shoulder level and brought his fist down to his outer thigh in a heavy, forward sweeping motion, with a snap of his wrist at the end. Three sections of the steel escaped the baton's internal retention spring and popped into place. The sound of the steel ball at the end of the ASP baton against the front driver's window was equivalent to a large rock hitting the windshield at highway speeds.

A small pit formed as tiny cracks raced to

the edges of the frame.

One more hit and the safety glass shattered and fell like crystal beads onto the pavement and into the car.

Lee eased his grip on the baton and let the weight of it reverse its position in his hand. Dropping to one knee, he stabbed the steel ball into the pavement, the sound an echo of the thunder that came in increasing waves. Lee looked to the sky and watched for a moment as the sheets of black lines closed in from the horizon.

Lightning flashed.

In his peripheral vision he could see Keelyn with fisted hands over her ears. The wind tangled her long brown hair.

He stood up, reached in through the shattered window to release the electric locks on the Highlander, and opened it. Stepping onto the runner with his right foot, he ducked down and crawled onto the driver's seat with his left knee and reached for the woman's shoulder.

The cup holder collected her congealed blood.

"Ma'am, can you open your eyes? Can you hear me?"

She flopped as he shook. He glanced to the backseat. Dark brown eyes stared as lips quivered around a fully inserted thumb. The adult harness was loose around the child's small body.

"It's okay, sweetheart. You're safe."

He pushed the button to release the unconscious woman's seat belt and eased it up over her body. Exiting the vehicle, he rounded to the passenger's side and motioned to Keelyn for help. With the door open, he stepped up and grabbed the woman under her arms, pulled her from the vehicle, and eased her onto the pavement.

The woman's skin was translucent. As he kneeled, Lee was mesmerized by the spiderweb of veins that laced her face and neck. A crowd of spectators gathered. Sirens whispered tunnel-like in the distance. From a weatherproof pouch on his belt, he pulled two pairs of purple nitrile gloves and gave a set to Keelyn.

"Put these on."

The material was hard to pull over his moistened hands. He missed the powdered latex gloves. Once the barrier was in place, he pulled up the woman's shirt and discovered three holes, two in her abdomen, one in her chest.

His teeth ached from being clenched.

Gunshot wounds?

All three oozed blood. At her neck, he slid two fingers into the shallow groove between

31

the trachea and strap muscles and felt for a pulse. Her skin was cool.

Lee tucked his chin to his shoulder. "SWAT One, copy additional information."

"SWAT One, go ahead."

"SWAT One, I've made entry into the vehicle. Inform medical the adult female has what appears to be three gunshot wounds to her torso. No pulse. Starting CPR."

"SWAT One, I copy. CPR in progress. I'll notify medical. Be advised a patrol supervisor and a district car are en route to your location."

"SWAT One copies. Thank you."

He dropped his hand from the radio and pointed to Keelyn. "I need you to hold pressure on these holes." He stacked his hands and centered them on the woman's chest, pumping hard and fast.

Keelyn knelt beside him and pulled wadded tissues from her pocket, putting them on the wounds to stem the bleeding. Bloodied paper stuck to her gloved hands as she tried to smooth and arrange them in a stack.

"This isn't working." Her words were tight, her breath coming in ragged gasps.

He could hear it in her voice, the resigned despair as this life slipped from their fingers. "Use your hands. Rescue's close. Can you hear the sirens? Babe, stay calm. You're doing great. I'm so proud of you."

Keelyn's fingers stuttered through the tacky crimson layer until the heel of her hand rested on one of the wounds. Small circles of clear fluid diluted the dried red field.

Lee looked skyward. Rain?

A sharp inhalation drew his eyes back to his fiancée. "I can't do this."

No. It was Keelyn's tears.

"Okay, I know."

"I just keep seeing my mother . . ."

"I'm sorry. I shouldn't have asked." He nodded toward the vehicle. "Get the child from the back."

Keelyn rose but did not immediately go for the young girl. Muscles ached along Lee's shoulders as he attempted to push the woman's soul back into her cooling body. Sweat trickled into his eyes as he looked up at Keelyn, her gaze anchored on the dying woman's face.

Sirens cut the stormy day. A fire truck and ambulance pulled into the lot and parked between the crowd gathered at the front of the diner and their position in the corner of the lot. Two police cars blocked the entrance to the highway to control both the scene and potential witnesses. Medics jumped from the EMS vehicles and grabbed bright orange trauma packs. *Why is she just standing there?*

"Keelyn!"

She shook her head and started to sway. "I know this woman."

"How?"

"She was my stepfather's psychiatrist. Lucy Freeman."

CHAPTER 3

Lee rubbed his hand over his jaw and felt the stubble scrape his palm. Through a door in the ER, he watched the medical team give up their resuscitative efforts, and then place a dingy, blood-soaked sheet over the woman's face. A nurse moved away from the bedside, the cap of a needle remaining between her lips as she began to clean the room.

The little girl, in a room to his right, had already been declared in good health by Dr. Lilly Reeves and sat in the arms of a volunteer, her thumb in her mouth as she shuddered at the exhalation of each breath. Her eyes were heavy as the last jags of a crying spell drained her energy.

He looked for Keelyn. She stood in the hall a few paces away, her clothes splattered with blood. He remembered her in the same condition, not so long ago, sitting on the bench in the back of an ambulance, knife wounds inflicted by her stepfather a road map of psychosis on her skin. Eventually, justice had been done, and her stepfather was currently on death row, convicted of the brutal slaying of her mother and two half-siblings. Her eyes met his gaze, and she gave him an unconvincing wave of re-assurance.

Violence had brought them together.

But now it seemed to be pursuing them. Would they ever be rid of it?

He tapped his hand over his heart, and she placed two fingers over her lips. A smile played on his face as he walked the short gap between them. But her eyes had already slid away from him to the glass in front of her.

As he watched the young girl, Lee put his arms around Keelyn. He couldn't help thinking about her half siblings who'd died that day, and as she settled her head into his shoulder, he knew she was thinking about them, too.

He saw Detective Nathan Long walking their way from the end of the hall, his hands buried deep into the pockets of his trench coat. Determination set his jaw. Years of police work creased a constant look of worry into his forehead. Heavy blue eyes full of a sense of responsibility. His wife, Lilly,

36

stopped him in the hall, and he pulled her into a quick embrace. Her lips grazed his cheek as she pulled back and then thumbed the lipstick mark from his face.

Their relationship had been born from violence, as well.

Lilly's fingers combed Nathan's dark brown hair, ruffled from the wind outside, before she turned away. Nathan let his touch linger at her spine until she was out of reach. The love evident between them.

Lee eased away from Keelyn and beckoned Nathan to follow him. Nathan straightened his coat and walked to Lee. They shook hands briefly.

"Captain said you asked for me specifically to handle this case. I'm a little surprised since you weren't too happy with my decision making the last time we worked together."

"People died, Nathan."

Nathan raised his eyebrows. His mouth opened, but he held his comments and shook his head as if to toss the statement away. "Hospital is on my way to the scene so thought I'd drop by quick to get your take on what's happened."

Lee nodded toward the victim's room. "They just declared the woman dead."

"Why ask for me?"

"Seems our past has come to the present to play."

Nathan looked beyond Lee. "Is that Keelyn Blake? Why is she here?"

Lee opened the door to a small family-consultation room. "She was at the scene, too. Let's go in here and sit."

"What's going on?" Nathan asked.

Lee motioned him inside. "There's a lot we need to catch up on."

"Are you and Keelyn together?" Nathan asked as he passed through the door.

"We're engaged."

Nathan's jaw dropped, but he remained silent. Was he censoring what he really wanted to say?

"When did you start seeing her?"

Lee eased the door closed. "About two years ago. After seeing how the department reacted to you seeing Lilly, I thought it wise to keep my involvement with her quiet. Please tell Lilly how thankful I am. She's been very sweet with Keelyn."

Nathan sat on the olive chenille love seat. "Lilly's rape has helped her identify with the trauma of other women. She knows what it's like to be victimized and then have the system fail her."

"I'm glad she was able to get on staff here at Blue Ridge and she's still practicing medicine. The system got it right in the end, and Sage made a mistake in not taking her back."

Nathan gathered up the strewn magazines from the coffee table, tapped them into a stack, and then fanned them out. "When you help put a serial rapist in jail, the justice system tends to be more lenient. Her assault charges were dropped, and frankly, it's nice for her not to work at a place that didn't believe in her integrity."

"I'm curious . . . I noticed she didn't take your name."

"Personal decision on her part. Maybe if we have children she'll do the hyphenated thing."

"Glad things are good for you two."

Nathan clasped his hands together and looked at Lee expectantly. "They are. But my relationship with Lilly isn't why you called me, Lee. What does this have to do with our past? Do you know who the homicide victim is?"

"Keelyn identified her as Lucy Freeman."

Nathan slumped back. His head cracked against the floral wallpaper. "The psychiatrist her stepfather was seeing at the time of the incident?"

"Maybe I should start at the beginning." Lee sat in the wing chair. "Keelyn and I meet every week about this time, if work doesn't keep me away, at Ruby's Diner."

Nathan let out a low whistle. "Not wise . . ."

"I know, but it's special to Keelyn. She used to go there with her mother. It was a place that reminded her of happier times. It helped fill the void of all those losses." Lee tugged at the collar of his shirt. "On the five-year anniversary of that day, I happened by Ruby's, and she was there. We struck up a conversation. It broke me to see her so sad after all that time had gone by. I still felt partly responsible for what happened to her family, so I started meeting her there to talk. We started hanging out, and eventually we fell in love."

Nathan shook his head. "She's younger than you."

Lee bristled at Nathan's accusatory tone. "Four years is not a bad spread."

Nathan dropped his eyes and retrieved his notepad. "What happened today?"

"While she was waiting for me, a man approached her, said his name was Lucent."

Nathan's eyes snapped up to meet Lee's look. He slowly rolled his pen between his thumb and forefinger. "Could it have been? Did we miss him in the house that day?"

A nervous creep coursed through Lee's

chest. "It's not possible. At the time, even Keelyn said Lucent wasn't real. A hallucination. How do you find an apparition?"

"I guess we're going to have to."

Lee cracked his knuckles. "This man told Keelyn he had Raven's daughter."

Nathan leaned forward. "Raven has a child?"

"You didn't know? I was hoping you were still keeping tabs on her."

"Lilly's case tied me up for a year."

"I guess a serial rapist can do that."

"It consumed every spare moment I had. Raven dropped off my radar. I'm just starting to feel like things are normalizing for me and Lilly, and now this pops up. Is the child really her daughter?"

Lee shrugged. "We're not sure. It seems Raven dropped off the map for a lot of people. Last time Keelyn saw Raven, she was late in her pregnancy. Keelyn never met her niece. We're coordinating DNA testing through social services with a local private lab run by a good friend of mine. Should have the results back in a couple of days. Until then, the child will have to go into foster care."

"What's your take on it?"

Lee exhaled slowly, his mind a jumble of possibilities. None of them good.

41

"I'm not sure. I know you feel like I do, Nathan, guilty for those lost lives." Lee edged forward, invading Nathan's space. "You hope for the well-being of those left behind. I know you'd want to help Raven. You're attached to one another. She adopted your nickname for her. For a while, you replaced the father she lost to psychosis and prison. I want to protect Keelyn. This man threatened her."

"How?" The word sounded heavy with the weight of Nathan's remorse.

"Showed her a gun in his waistband. Told her if she looked for Raven, he'd come back for her and the girl. Nathan, I can't let anything happen to Keelyn."

"Lee, we'll get this creep. Could be some sick freak fascinated with Raven's case. That nightmare was just highlighted on one of those news shows last week." Nathan jotted a few notes. "We need to determine Raven's welfare. Has she truly given the girl up? Is the child really a kidnap victim? Is Raven even alive?"

Lee's stomach twisted tighter as acid clawed up his chest. "He may have already murdered this woman — the psychiatrist. What could his motive be?"

"Only he knows right now." Nathan tapped his pen against the pad. "Can you help me with a few things here before you leave?"

"Anything."

"I need the woman's and child's clothes bagged for evidence. Can you coordinate that from here and call a patrol officer to transfer the evidence?"

"Absolutely. Anything you need to get this thing solved."

Nathan pulled out his phone. "After I'm finished at the crime scene, I'll check on Raven. See if that part of Lucent's story holds up. Let me quick call the last number I have for her . . ." Nathan frowned. "Disconnected."

"You'll check for any current missing-persons reports filed that might match her description?"

"Of course, Lee. I know how to do my job."

Lee took a deep breath to bury his response. "What about amber alerts for missing children?"

"There is a current one. Someone nabbed a child off a front porch. Five-year-old male. Doesn't fit this case."

"Have they said if there's anything from the diner's security tapes?" Lee asked.

"A scene officer says there's only one camera from the front of the diner. The

43

SUV was out of video range. All you can see is cars and people coming and going. Nothing looks suspicious. I'll take a closer look at them when I get there. Did you see this man?"

Lee shook his head.

"We're going to need Keelyn to take a look at the footage."

"Do you think it would help to talk to John Samuals about this?"

Nathan considered the statement. "A man claiming to be a manifestation of his psychosis shows up at an off-beat diner and threatens a member of his family. Yeah, we probably need to pay him a visit. Why don't you and Keelyn come by the station later? Let's have Keelyn review the tapes. If this Lucent is not there, we'll have her sit with Tim and get a computer image generated."

"I don't know if she's up to it."

"She's strong."

Lee steepled the tips of his fingers and rested his chin. "She's not like Lilly. Things affect her more deeply."

A pulse of exasperation flared in Nathan's eyes. "Lilly's good at hiding her trauma. It doesn't affect her any less than other victims."

"Nathan, that's not what I meant."

"It took her a long time to get to where

44

she is." Nathan scribbled on his pad, tore the sheet, and handed it to Lee. "See if Keelyn knows anything about Raven living here. It's the last address I have for her."

"When do you need her at the station?"

"Not for a while. Stop and get some coffee before you come in. Take a step back. Things may become clearer for her, and she'll be able to recall details she can't think of right now."

They exited the small room. Lee hung back as Nathan approached Keelyn sitting with her head buried in her hands. Long strands of her hair draped her body — a river of dark waves swallowing her arms and face. Nathan kneeled down, and she caved into him as sobs racked her body. Coming to her aid, Lee eased her into his arms. Nathan gave a quick nod before leaving.

Lee found a small box of thin tissues on a table and pulled a few sheets. Wrapping the tissue around his index finger, he dabbed her face and let the tears absorb into the paper fibers. He had always been fascinated by Keelyn's eyes — the brown center washed into a yellow halo like angelic light spreading into the darkness. "Let's go down to the cafeteria. I'm going to need some caffeine."

He held Keelyn to his side as they made

their way down the stairs. Keelyn took a deep quivering breath as they walked through the cafeteria door. Lee grabbed coffee and doughnuts before they sat. The only sound between them was the quiet squeak of the vinyl chairs. He took several swigs of diluted swill and a couple bites of stale pastry, then brushed the flakes of dried glaze from the table. Suddenly he realized she was studying him.

"I can see you're worried," Keelyn said. "What are you feeling right now?"

"I think you probably know. What I want to know is what's on your mind." She fingered her engagement ring. "You never really told me your side of that day. What it was like."

He sat silent for several minutes, slowly sipping his coffee as he mulled over her request. Before long, his excuse to stay quiet sat as dregs and he crushed the foam cup between his hands.

Lee wanted Keelyn to break the secrecy, what had always been unsaid between them, but he knew it was her nature to let him speak first. She spent her days listening, interpreting body language, the things said between the words. Her silence was a trained response from interviewing hundreds of witnesses. It was a career she had

46

chosen in an attempt to silence her past. And her volunteer work at the domestic violence shelter served as a self-induced penance for not saving her siblings.

"Domestic violence calls are always the hardest."

"I know."

"Yours was the worst."

She caressed his forearm. "Why?"

His lungs burned as his heart threatened to breach its bony compartment, an unwelcome prison for the surge of adrenaline as memories washed over him in a flood of regret. Lee's hand tightened on hers.

"Because we could have gone in sooner, but Nathan made the call to wait. We could have saved your mother and the other kids." The words came out harsh and angry as the sadness sank his soul. He held her eyes. "How can you *not* blame me?"

Lee's voice caught. He set the broken coffee cup aside and massaged his forehead to ease the headache building behind his eyes.

There it sat in the open. What was once unspoken now stood between them like an enormous elephant on center stage at the circus. Keelyn had never said anything about how she felt the police acted. He held his breath as he studied her face. Her eyes now drawn to the speckles on the table.

Why did she agree to marry him when he was responsible for the death of her family members?

Her silence drew his confession. "When Nathan and I came to the ambulance, it was the worst thing I'd ever seen. The three of you sitting there, terrified, wounded, bleeding. Your brother, a baby, nothing but a sharpening tool for your father's knife."

His eyes burned as he willfully quelled tears. Her eyes glistened, a mirror of the memory of their shared horror. By far, her terror was worse than anything he could fathom. Taking her arm, he gently pushed up her sleeve. He traced his finger over the healed ridges of pain, Keelyn's body scarred by her stepfather's illness. "When it became obvious what was happening, we took the house."

She wiped her eye with a knuckle. "What did you see on the inside, Lee? I want to know."

He remembered the heat of that day, and it replaced the chill on his skin. Felt the thick, weeded yard under his boots as he'd jumped from the back of the ambulance and shouted orders through his radio. The concussive waves from the flash-bang grenades hit his chest. Dust and smoke clouded his vision as he crossed the threshold and stumbled over the four police officers who wrestled to pull John Samuals from his spider's nest.

"They were all in the middle of the floor, piled up on each other. Nathan and I pulled them off but —" He choked over the words. "Their throats slit. Raven alive but injured."

Guilt tugged at his soul. He looked at her then, into those hazel eyes that always hid something from him, and he saw pools of despair slip down her cheeks. He held her face.

"I'm sorry." Keelyn pulled his hands down.

"For what?"

"I never want you to think I blame you."

"But how can you not?"

She wiped her eyes. "Because there are four of us still alive. If you'd been inside, you would have understood that there was little hope for *anyone* to live."

"We never even considered Lucent might be a real person."

"The Lucent there that day was not a person. That's one thing I know for sure."

Lee eased back into his chair. "Nathan left the FBI after that. He was the lead negotiator. Did you know he'd been keeping tabs on Raven?"

She dried the last of her tears and straightened in her seat. "Yes, I knew. Nathan was the one thing that held her together . . . for a while at least. What do you think is going on? What does today mean?"

"I think I need to know more about your interaction with this man. What did he look like?"

A cascade of shivers rippled over her body. "His hair was blond, green eyes. Pale. He exuded this confidence that grabbed your attention. It's hard to explain."

"What did he say to you? Start from the beginning."

"First, he knew you were going to be late. He said he was an old friend of yours."

Lee waited as Keelyn paused. He could see the dark clouds brewing in her eyes. A subtle change when she remembered living under her stepfather's illness. Her shoulders sagged like a heavy cloak had been draped across them.

"He knew Raven and I were estranged. That I'd never met my niece."

"That's not too surprising. There was just that two-hour *Dateline* special about your case. Raven said as much in her interview on the show, that the two of you weren't talking."

"Lee, she never talked about her child on the show. Otherwise, I would have discovered she'd had a little girl."

"What else?"

"That he'd left her there. Are you sure that call you went on was a suicide?"

"Absolutely, why?"

"Lucent insinuated it was a murder he was partly responsible for."

"The guy shot himself in the head. The house was locked up tight. No one inside. No signs of forced entry. He'd texted his wife a suicide note."

She pulled her hair off to one side and leaned back in her chair. "He just knew things he shouldn't know."

"Explain it to me."

"It's like he knew how to tap into my worst fears."

"What else did he say to you, Keelyn?"

"He knew it was my decision to break off my relationship with Raven."

"Why did you break it off?"

"I felt her slipping mentally. It's like she wanted to pull me into that craziness with her. Odd things began to happen. She wasn't getting any better with her psychiatrist. She kept saying he was doing something experimental. I begged her to see someone else. She refused. It became this never-ending quagmire."

Lee wanted to push her more to talk about

51

things she didn't want to consider. Was this something they could just walk away from? What was Lucent's reason for involving them in this situation? For himself, Lee knew he couldn't live with the guilt of knowing Lucent was real and he hadn't stopped him years ago. Why had he shown up now? And why was he involving Keelyn? Then there was the girl. Why not just kill her? Why give her to Keelyn? To save her? To torture Keelyn?

"Whoever Lucent is, I think he's crazy," Keelyn said.

"He's more than mentally ill. It's obvious from his history he hasn't been on the good side of things. I mean, whether he was physically there or not, he influenced the murder of three people seven years ago. Maybe another one today."

Lee felt his BlackBerry vibrate. It was a text from Nathan.

He'd verified Raven's last address.

"We should go."

"What about the girl?"

"The hospital staff contacted social services. They're going to arrange a DNA test. You're going to have to give a sample, and we'll see if we can find one for Raven. We'll need to confirm she is Raven's daughter. That she's related to you."

"And after the test?"

"They'll find a foster placement for her."

"What's the point of proving she's related to me if she's going into foster care?"

"It's more to prove Raven is her mother. And if she is, where is she? What's happened to her?"

"I can't live with that," Keelyn said.

"What do you want to do?"

"I feel like I'm . . . we're supposed to take her." She placed her lithe hands over his, a gesture of promised expectation. "I think Lucent is a stone that was dropped in the middle of a big lake that caused these ripples to flow out. I need to have her close."

Lee swallowed heavily and slid his hands from hers. He couldn't have imagined that putting a ring on Keelyn's finger might mean an instant family.

"That's not smart. If he's targeting your family, having the two of you together will put you in more danger."

"It's my job to protect her. I need to do for her what I didn't do for Raven."

"Keelyn —"

"It will be easier to protect us both if we're in the same place."

"I might have to move in."

A smile brightened Keelyn's eyes, and Lee's spirit lightened. "No, no, Mr. Watson.

Not until you say those two simple words at the end of a long aisle and I'm dressed in something expensive and white."

CHAPTER 4

Black clouds roiled overhead as Nathan approached Ruby's in his platinum SUV, and his windshield wipers struggled to keep up with the rain. At the diner's road entrance, two squad cars remained to control the crime scene. Nathan stopped and erased the vapor from his driver's-side window then pushed his badge against it. The patrol officer gave a quick salute of two fingers off his forehead and Nathan proceeded through the barricade of their vehicles at a slow pace.

He parked toward the front of the paint-faded structure and buttoned up his black trench coat. Several additional officers were inside the restaurant gathering witness statements. They would need, at a minimum, their basic information before allowing them to leave.

The killer could be among them.

Nathan exited his vehicle and stood so he faced the corner of the parking lot where the Highlander was parked. The crime geeks were trying to keep a blue tarp over the vehicle, both as protection against the weather and as futile hope against the rain washing away precious evidence.

As he paused to take in the overall picture of the crime scene, he heard the bell of the diner clang against the glass as the door opened.

"Hey, Nathan. Where's your old standby?"

He turned around. The officer, Danny Smith, seated his cap on his head. "Brett's taken an extended leave for a family issue."

"Rumor is the two of you are splitting up as a result of your wife's case."

Nathan pulled his chin up. Brave for a man he barely knew to question an unsubstantiated dissolution of a partnership. "Brett's a big boy. He can admit it when he makes a mistake. His mother is dying. That's why he's not here." Nathan looked purposefully at the diner, then back to the officer. "Anything from inside?"

The young man rubbed an index finger under his nose. "A few people saw the man Keelyn described sitting with her but none of them saw him in the vicinity of the SUV. Of course, we probably haven't caught everyone. There may have been a few who left at the time of the crime. Those" — he shrugged helplessly — "we'll never know about."

"Make sure everyone's comfortable as can be inside. Let me take a closer look at the vehicle, and we'll see about starting to let some of these folks go home."

"Yes, sir."

Ruby's sat in a rural part of the community, just off Colfax as you headed east out of Denver. Arapahoe County was large and the eastern-most part was relatively undeveloped. South of this location, the area was growing, but Ruby's remained a hallmark to the past. Open fields surrounded the restaurant from where it sat off this well-known road.

No hope of another business's surveillance video capturing his ghost killing a woman here.

What was Lucent's relation to the woman?

If Lee's story held a grain of truth, Nathan's life had just become infinitely more complicated. How could he explain a psychotic hallucination coming to life?

The same psychiatrist who told him seven years ago Lucent was a hallucination had been killed here today by someone using that same name. Could this man have somehow been involved with the ghost that influenced John Samuals to kill his wife and two children? Nathan ran the toe of his polished shoe through the water, watching the ripples race toward the edge.

Was Raven the answer? Was she really missing? Was this child her daughter?

Lucent's placement of the vehicle in the lot was clearly purposeful. From Nathan's position near the front door of the diner, the white SUV was to the right and not easily seen from the entrance unless you took a couple of steps out onto the pavement and looked that direction. No other cars were parked close. Nathan paced across the lot.

Was he trampling on the killer's DNA as it floated by in these rivulets of rain and oil?

He approached the CSI van. Owen hopped out of the back, and they shook hands briefly.

"What do you think?" Nathan turned his collar up against the biting wind.

"I think she was shot at this location."

The tall, heavyset man motioned him to follow, and tugged on gloves as he trudged the short distance. They approached the car from the driver's side, which stood open, Nathan presumed, as Lee had left it.

"The VIN and registration confirm this is the good doctor's car. It appears the woman was shot with her back up against the passenger's door. We found a slug near the armrest. Were there any signs of restraint on the victim?"

Nathan shook his head. "Unknown."

"Then I'm guessing the killer met her here. There's a purse with her ID on the passenger's floorboards and what I assume are her keys in the ignition. Question is why she was on the passenger's side."

"They just declared her dead when I arrived at the hospital. I'll have to make a trip to meet with the medical examiner later today. The girl was in the back?"

Owen sniffed sharply with a nod, and Nathan wasn't sure if it was to supply needed oxygen for his large frame or to clear the snot dangling from his nose. The rumbled honk made him lean toward the latter, and he had to resist the urge to grab the handkerchief from his pocket.

Why ruin one of Nana's hankies?

"Where's the car seat?" Nathan asked.

Three officers combed through the waist-high brush that lined the front side of the parking lot. The wind picked up and pressed the rain into a slant.

"Wasn't one," Owen said.

Strange. It would be unlike a woman, especially a doctor, not to secure the child safely. What were the circumstances that brought the three of them together?

"Any luck on prints?" Nathan asked as he leaned into the vehicle, pulling his jacket tight against his chest to prevent contamination of the scene.

"Yeah, lots. We're going to need Miss Blake's for exclusionary purposes. Watson's will be on record."

"How far into processing the scene are you?"

"We've done interior photos, diagrams, and a quick scan for trace evidence."

Rain specked the leather. Owen motioned Nathan back so he could close the driver's door. "There's a pull cover over the cargo space. Just need to quick pop the back gate to make sure there aren't any surprises back there before we seal it up and tow it back to the evidence lot for a more thorough inspection."

"Weapon here!" one of the officers shouted.

Owen lumbered that direction with Nathan a few short steps behind.

"Grab me a few shots before I pick it up." Owen waved to the photographer as he bent over and pulled the dried shoots of grass to the side. "I need an evidence bag over here!" he yelled. Owen laid a hand on his thigh for support as he bent down to grab the revolver. Keeping his beefy, gloved fingers well away from the trigger, he examined the barrel at close range.

"Any blowback?" Nathan asked.

"Not grossly. We'll get it processed. Have more info in a week or so. Maybe sooner if you buy me dinner."

"I can arrange that. Let's take a look in the back. After that, I'll let you get it sealed and towed."

Thunder cracked, and Nathan's heels lifted off the pavement. Lightning flashed clear light into the gray day. His vision spotted with yellow halos.

"Yeah, we're going to have to get the tarp down before we get electrocuted."

Nathan contemplated whether Owen's big frame or the thin metal poles placed him more at risk. He slipped on a pair of gloves himself as they rounded the end of the vehicle.

Booms of thunder concussed the sky, and Owen placed his hand on the latch release. Nathan held his breath. A faint whine sounded in the vacant wake of the thunder as the door rose slowly toward the storm clouds.

A Mexican-style blanket lay haphazardly over a bulky object.

Owen leaned in and pulled away one side

of the blanket.

"Now, who do you suppose this is?"

CHAPTER 5

Keelyn sat on the passenger's side of a squad car in front of the house where Nathan said he'd known her sister to last live. The patrol car's lights flashed ominously into the night, the alternating red and blue a signal that trouble may have passed through. Raven's home resembled an old barn, red brick with a gray slate roof, and was located in an older area of Denver where the houses were small and tightly packed.

Lee and Nathan just completed a search of the home. Raven wasn't there, nor was there any evidence of a child's presence except for one simple book, *Pinocchio,* found on a bookshelf filled with glass vases that no sane adult would have within reach of a cruising toddler. No child's clothing. No child's bed. No child's fingerprints smudging the stainless steel appliances in the kitchen.

Nothing.

Only mystery. Where had Raven gone?

First, the note on her kitchen table: *Sorry about last night, Clay.*

Who was Clay? Did he know where Raven was? Could he be Lucent — the man that had approached her in the diner?

Lee collected a baggie of syringes from the bathroom medicine cabinet, and insinuated that Raven used drugs. Why jump to that conclusion first? It wasn't the stated fact that bothered her but his unconscious covering of his observation.

Was he hiding something? His body language suggested it was probable.

Lee also grabbed Raven's toothbrush for the DNA tests and then led Keelyn into the garage where there were boxes and boxes of Bibles with a stickered bookplate listing information for North Creek Church.

This was particularly mysterious because Raven had sworn off her faith or even the tiniest belief in a loving God.

What anchored like hooks in Keelyn's heart were the unopened letters she'd sent to Raven over the last couple of years. Letters inviting her sister to be with her. To stay with her. All unopened, except the first one. A letter sent long before her child was born. Raven would have been almost fifteen,

64

a constant runaway from social services.

In her hands she still held her note as evidence of the anger her sister harbored for her. The edge of the envelope was hacked open.

Although she already had suffered through it once, Keelyn pulled the note free again. She knew what she had written. Keelyn had been ready for Raven to live with her.

Raven had scrawled two words in red marker diagonally across the face of the note. Large, red dots appeared at the beginning lead of each letter, as if the pen was held there intentionally to let the ink leach like blood into the paper's fibers.

TOO LATE.

Keelyn, a young woman of twenty-three at the time of the incident, had begged her father to take the three survivors of John Samuals's rampage in. He refused. The court stated that since she was an adult, if she proved enough income, she could garner custody herself. Social Security death benefits weren't going to cover full-time daycare, an apartment, and everything that went along with raising three children.

The challenge provided much needed direction. Keelyn had earned a basic psychology degree, but since graduating, nothing had struck her fancy enough for solid commitment. Her father allowed her to live with him and do as she pleased as long as she kept the house straight and his meals on the table.

Then, suddenly, her father died as well.

At first, Keelyn tried minimum wage jobs but the income never provided the amount she would need to care for her siblings. More education was the answer, and she finished her master's in three years. Interpersonal communication with an emphasis on nonverbal patterns. Unfortunately, the two youngest had been legally adopted by their foster families.

Only Raven floundered.

Keelyn leaned against the headrest and closed her eyes.

Her stomach grumbled under her hand — the same sensation she had when she first awoke that fateful day.

Keelyn cracked her eyes open to see Ariana's face peeking around her bedroom door. Not a bedroom exactly — it was nearly empty except for the cot she slept on — but where she slept when she was there. Her half siblings, five altogether, slept in gender specific rooms across the hall. She gave a half-hearted smile and waved the preteen in. Ariana crossed the room and sat on the wire frame, her black hair tangled from last night's sleep, her brown eyes brooding.

"Hungry?" Keelyn asked.

It had been days since any of them had eaten a full meal. A sleeve of saltine crackers shared between seven people didn't go far.

"The police are here."

Keelyn edged up onto her elbow. "What?" she asked, tilting her head toward the door at the sound of a child crying. Was it her three-month-old brother? "Where's Dustin?"

"In his crib. They're saying we have to leave."

A shotgun fired, shaking the whole house. A cacophony of children crying competed for decibels. Keelyn grabbed Ariana and held her close. Who was firing? Were the pellets going out or coming in?

Another boom.

With shaky arms, Keelyn pushed Ariana off the cot and onto the floor. "Get down, get down." She shoved her hand into the middle of Ariana's back and pushed her into the dirty, threadbare carpet, away from the window.

Another blast. Now screaming. A man in pain. Outside.

"Daddy's mad."

They were on the ground facing each other, Ariana's brown eyes dark against pale skin and pink lips. Keelyn threaded Ariana's hair behind her ear, her fingers trembling. "Why?"

"He made me."

Keelyn's eyes locked hers. "Made you —"

The screen door slammed. Her mother, Sophia, pleaded with John between sobs. The words smashed together nonsensically like a bowl of alphabet soup.

Keelyn placed her finger to her lips. "Stay here and be quiet." She crawled to the window, drew the once-white lace curtains to the side, and peeked out.

A deputy's car sat on the front lawn, but she couldn't see the officer. Sirens sounded off in the distance.

John Samuals unhinged . . . again.

Keelyn turned back to Ariana. "Can you help me?"

Ariana sat up, uncertainty crossed her face. "Do what?"

"We need to get the others in here so I can keep you safe." Keelyn thought quickly. It would be easier for Ariana to grab their sisters, since they could walk on their own. "You get Cheyenne and Carissa. I'll get Micah and Dustin."

She grabbed for her. "No! I want to stay here. Stay with me."

Ariana huddled into a fetal position and began to cry. Keelyn crawled back to her position and placed a comforting hand to the small of her back. Ariana reached up and snaked her arms around Keelyn's neck, tipping her forward.

Keelyn lay next to her again. "It's going to be okay."

Now, the sirens were loud. Tires screeched to a halt. Doors slammed.

Cheyenne and Micah piled into her room on their own. Keelyn patted the floor so they would get down. Everyone accounted for except the baby and two-year-old. Where was Carissa? No more crying. Had Dustin gone back to sleep?

For over two hours, they rested there listening to John's ramblings, their mother's pleading and intermittent crying jags. Why didn't the police storm in? Why weren't they helping? Few other sounds came from inside the house. Where were the other children? Why weren't they crying? Were they still alive?

Keelyn's side began to cramp and she shifted her position. Ariana pulled her arms back from her neck and placed a palm against her cheek. "Will you check Carissa?

69

Tell her I'm sorry."

What was she talking about?

Keelyn took her hands in hers. "Of course. Now, Ariana, under the cot and promise me you won't move." Her sister scurried under and turned around, her eyes wide with pleading. There it was . . . the reason Keelyn would never stop coming to this desolate acreage of lost dreams.

"Cheyenne . . . Micah . . . into the closet until I come back and get you."

They hustled into the small space and closed the door behind.

Keelyn peeked out her door. John paced at the bottom of the staircase, twirling a knife in his hand.

A large hunter's knife.

Keelyn stepped slowly down the stairs.

John's voice, steely and hushed. "Please, don't make me. I don't want to kill them."

Her fright over those words caused her to stumble down the remaining stairs. When John heard her footsteps, he snapped the blade up where it rested against his forearm.

A thin line of red imprinted on his skin.

Blood.

Keelyn's stomach squirmed like an octopus trapped in a fishbowl. Its slimy, cold tentacles slithered out and seized her heart and lungs, making it painful to inhale. John

70

backed up, a sneering smile on his face, as he approached her on the landing. Her mother was seated with Carissa, a dingy bundled towel at the child's neck, her brown hair slick with sweat as she whimpered.

"What's going on?" She eyed John first, then her mother. "What happened to Carissa?"

Her mother clamped her quivering lips together.

"I told you to be quiet!"

Keelyn jumped, her gaze bounced back to John who wasn't looking at her, but off to the side where no one stood.

"You know I don't want to. You shouldn't have made me do that. She's just a little girl."

Keelyn stepped into John's line of sight and waved her hands at his blank gaze. "John!"

He focused in on her. "He made me."

"Who?"

"Lucent." At that name, Keelyn's knees weakened. John caressed his belly at the scar line of Lucent's last insistence that he take his own life.

"John, Lucent's not real. Remember? Are you taking your medication?"

He turned away from her, pumping his arms down on either side of his face. "I told

71

you to shut up! I don't want to do it. They're my babies."

Keelyn backed up to where her mother sat on the couch and pulled her sweaty hand away from Carissa's neck. There, a laceration down the side of her neck. "How did this happen?"

Her mother moaned and cried more. Keelyn grabbed the child from her lap and cuddled her against her chest. Exhaling heavily, Carissa closed her eyes, her chest rose and fell against her and faint relief warmed Keelyn's chilled skin.

She began to back toward the stairs, glancing back every so often to make sure she didn't trip over something. To her mother, "You need to get him to surrender."

Her mother shook her head against her words. "He won't listen. Only to Lucent."

Voices penetrated the thin walls, but Keelyn couldn't make out the words. John covered his ears with clenched fists, the knife still tight in one palm.

Then he laid his head back like a werewolf howling at moonrise and the scream wrest from his soul rattled Keelyn's skull. Carissa startled in her arms and began to cry. Keelyn had one heel on the stairs when he lunged at her, grabbing her arms, sending Carissa to the floor where she landed flat on her back, her eyes desperate to draw breath but nothing came from her gaped mouth.

Keelyn tried to pull her arms free but John yanked her close, the stench from his fear-fueled delusion suffocated her. The child on the floor behind her began to wheeze as her lungs risked drawing air again. John now had Keelyn in an embrace, her arms trapped between them, and he drew his blade across her back.

Warm fluid slid down. Then, slowly, as her surge of adrenaline began to wane, her nerves began to Morse code pain signals to her mind. He hummed a childlike lullaby in her ear. Carissa grabbed at Keelyn's pajama bottoms and began to work her way up her leg to a standing position.

"I always wanted to do that."

Above her, the floorboards creaked as the children wandered between rooms — trying to be quiet but failing miserably. There was the soft opening and closing of wood against wood. What were they doing? Why didn't they stay where Keelyn told them to?

John's eyes drifted upstairs. Not his eyes, vacuoles of matted black evil that had snuffed out what little soul he had left. She clenched her eyes closed and held her breath. He pulled her in tighter.

"Keelyn," he sang. Easing her back, he grabbed her wrist and drew the blade down the length of her arm. It stunned her, how little it hurt — at first — and then how painful it became when the blood flowed over cut skin and dripped off her arm.

She yanked back again. His hand tightened around her forearm. "Death or life. Which do you choose?" He settled the knife against her throat.

Carissa was outright screaming behind her.

Keelyn inhaled to sooth her rapid heartbeat. "John, let me take Carissa upstairs. I'll watch the children. Keep them out of your way."

He slithered his fingers up the bloody trail of her arm until his hand clasped behind her neck and he pulled her face close to his, the knife slicing into her skin. With everything in her, she tried to pull back, the muscles of her neck taut against his fingers.

His lips mere inches from hers, he seethed. "I want them all down here."

"Mr. Samuals. John Samuals! My name is Nathan Long, and I work for the FBI."

A sudden tap at the window caused her heart to leap. At first glance, Lucent peered through the glass. She blinked rapidly, and

74

Lee's dimpled smile replaced the malicious leer.

How odd she would see a resemblance between the two.

Lee eased her door open and drew her out of the car then pulled her close to his chest. She collapsed into him, desperately willing her head to stop spinning. "Take a deep breath, babe." His whisper soothed and settled her. Taking a stuttering breath, Keelyn slid her arms around his neck. She closed her eyes and was reassured by the sound of his steady heartbeat.

Ariana was twelve the day John murdered their mother, Cheyenne, and Micah. The scar at Ariana's neck a thick white line of remembrance. When Ariana was in the hospital healing from her injuries, Detective Long had been a frequent visitor and had shared the story of why he nicknamed her Raven — for her black hair and deep brown eyes noticeable from a distance. Ariana adopted the name Raven because Nathan assumed the picture of fatherly love she'd never experienced. Long visited her regularly, made sure she was doing well in school, and brought her gifts for her birthday.

But assuming the name also marked a transition in Raven's life, and despite Nathan's efforts, she slowly enveloped herself in darkness like the blackness of the bird's feathers.

CHAPTER 6

Tuesday

The weather was barely improved from the day before. The air was heavy, and the wind bit as it pulled brown, dead leaves from the deciduous trees that lined the street. Long gone were the shaded hues of gold and red. Winter teased at autumn's last grasp.

Lee drove in silence, trying to read Nathan's reaction through his peripheral vision. Never did he imagine he and Nathan would work on the same force but Aurora Police had made him an offer he couldn't refuse and sometimes geographical distance from a memory served the psyche well.

They'd just come from Chief Anson's office. Lee had asked and been granted permission to step down as SWAT commander for a period of two weeks in order to assist Nathan. Nathan had argued against the idea, stating Lee's close connection to the victim could hinder the investigation.

Unfortunately, the chief threw the argument back in Nathan's face. After all, it was Nathan's feelings for Lilly that spurned his undying commitment to solve her peculiar rape case — risking his job to prove the DNA test from the perpetrator was incorrect. He married the victim. Besides which, Nathan's partner was on leave.

Nathan still looked out the passenger window like a scolded child. Lee could see the man's clenched jaw and stormy blue eyes reflected in the glass. The look could crack stone.

"Are you going to be brooding over this the entire time we're working together?" Lee asked.

Nathan clicked his tongue a few times. "At least for the rest of today."

"Want to explain your beef? I thought you'd be happy for the help."

"That day on the Samuals property was the worst of my life." Nathan turned in his seat toward Lee. "I try every day not to think about it for just one second. Just as I'm starting to find my way around it, with Lilly, you drag me back into this mud pit of hell by requesting that I be the lead on Lucy Freeman's murder. Why do you want me on this case if you think I'm incompetent enough to need a babysitter?"

Lee stopped at a light. "Maybe we just need to get all our cards on the table. I do blame you."

Nathan was silent.

"You were this young FBI hotshot. Your record was spotless. I was new to a position I wasn't quite ready for. Only had a few calls under my belt. Other teams were already committed, and I was called in." Lee thumbed the steering wheel. "I should have deferred less to you and let my SWAT training have a say. I blame you for deciding to wait. I blame myself for not telling you what I thought."

Nathan remained stock-still. Lee turned into the parking lot. He looked over at Nathan, wondering if he'd gone too far.

"I know I'm just as responsible." Lee glanced at Nathan and waited a beat. "Anything you want to say?" he added as he brought the vehicle to a stop and slammed the gear shift into Park.

Nathan opened his door and the wind whipped through the vehicle. "I hope any mistake you make today or tomorrow won't be as vehemently evil as Lucent when it pops back up. Let me point to the speck in your eye yet not notice the log in my own." He exited the truck and slammed the door behind him with a force that rocked the vehicle.

Nathan's mention of the well-known Scripture threw Lee. Why was it that the intellectual parts of ancient Scripture resonated at his core but the practical applications — like forgiveness — were so hard to apply in real life?

Lee exited and walked a few paces behind Nathan. His life's work was built around resolving conflict — albeit with a gun, shield, and several other armed men on hand. How could he turn this situation with Nathan around? Before he could reconsider, Lee grabbed Nathan's shoulder.

Nathan stopped and turned on his heel; his eyes flashed a warning worthy of a dust-filled Western standoff.

"Look. I wouldn't have asked for you if I didn't think you could get this case figured out before anyone else. Let's just agree to not let the past ruin our chances of finding this sociopath. I'm here because I need to see this through. Protect Keelyn. Certainly you can understand."

Nathan grunted, yanked free, and made his way through the door, down the hallway, and into the examination room.

The concrete room lined with steel tables made Lee clench his teeth to the point of pain. He hoped the autopsies from the two victims recovered from the Highlander yesterday were completed and he could get out of the room quickly. One of the reasons he loved SWAT was less time spent here viewing bodies. The medical examiner, Dr. Stratford, was standing beside the woman's open chest cavity, the victim's heart in her hand. She plopped it on the scale for measurement and turned as Nathan's footsteps slapped against the floor. Lee leaned against the opposite table, which supported the male victim found in the cargo space.

"Detective Long, just in time."

"Find anything interesting?" Nathan asked, prepared to take notes.

"The woman is pretty straightforward — gunshot trauma. She was hit in the chest and abdomen with three bullets. One bullet passed through, not hitting any vital structures. The chest shot nicked her right lung."

"Those should be survivable."

"True, but not the third. It transected her descending aorta. Fatal exsanguination."

"How long would it have taken her to bleed out?"

"Not more than two minutes."

Lee stepped forward. "Would that explain the body being warm but having no pulse? We found her not long after she was shot?"

"Likely. The resuscitative efforts will hamper determining time of the shooting, but my guess is she was found shortly after she sustained these injuries. The man is more interesting. There were no signs of external trauma." Dr. Stratford pulled off her gloves and tossed them into a metal kick-bucket and pulled on another pair. "But he did have this unusual cluster of red lesions to the right side of his neck.

Lee leaned in and almost knocked heads with Nathan. "What are they?"

"I'm not sure right now. They resemble hives, but it's rare to have such a confined response. Hives tend to be more of a systemic reaction, but this rash is localized."

Nathan pointed a finger. "There're eight of them. Do they look arranged to you?"

The ME leaned in. "How so?"

"Circular. It doesn't look random to me."

She shrugged. "We have photos. I don't discern a pattern."

"What else could they be?" Lee asked.

"Some sort of simple rash. Molluscum can present as grouped smaller welts like this. It's more common in children, though. It could be anything from rash to bug bites. Some of them appear to be target-like lesions. Could be tick bites, but ticks don't usually group like this, either. Right now, it's curious and unknown. We'll have to look at tissue samples."

"What killed him?" Nathan asked with pen poised over his pad.

Something glistened under Nathan's nose. Lee scratched his upper lip. "Something on your face?"

Nathan ridged one eyebrow up. "Vicks VapoRub. I'd rather smell it than him." He pointed to the corpse on the table.

The doctor laughed. "You know that just opens up the nasal passages, right? You're likely smelling more than if you'd just left it off."

Nathan's jaw clenched. "It's always worked fine for me."

"As to what killed him, I don't know. I'm going to send toxicology reports and tissue samples. There is nothing ominous on gross examination of the body."

Lee stretched his neck until he heard the satisfying pop. "So we have a murder victim in the passenger seat of her own car, shot to death, with a man tucked into the cargo space with no signs of trauma and cause of death unknown. Not to mention the little girl left alive in the backseat with these two, and we have no idea how the three of them are connected."

Nathan grabbed a tissue from a nearby

dispenser. "Any ID on the male?"

"Actually, yes. I should have mentioned that before. A deputy matching our victim's description was reported missing by Teller County Sherriff's office after he missed two consecutive shifts. A check of his residence didn't show any foul play, but they report it's highly unusual for him not to call in if he's ill. They said he's diligent to a fault. Will report himself late if he doesn't show up five minutes early."

Lee smirked as Nathan swiped the tissue under his nose to clear the sticky ointment.

Nathan stuffed the crumpled wad into his pocket. "A cop? From the county where John Samuals took his family hostage?"

The ME flipped through the chart, scanning with her index finger through the information. "Yes, here. Clay Timmons."

Lee's first thought was of the note Keelyn had found on Raven's table. The second thought was from *that* day. He could see the car pull up. The deputy step out of his car, so eager to help complete any task that he'd stumbled through the grass to hand off the food they'd asked for.

Food for the family held hostage.

Lee closed his eyes, waited for the officer's badge to tip out of the sun so he could read his name. Yes, there it was.

Timmons.

Lee opened his eyes. "He was there."

Nathan was busy putting away his note-pad and paper. "What?"

Lee walked closer to the body, bent at the waist to look closer at the face. "Officer Timmons was at the Samuals house. He brought the food from the mini-mart."

Nathan cursed under his breath. "Great. Just great."

Lee could see it in Nathan's eyes. The recognition of how tight this spiderweb Raven had found herself in might be. "The note at her house was signed Clay."

"We need to go back and get that for evidence."

CHAPTER 7

The walkway to the police station was a narrow, cemented path sandwiched between large greened areas. A public library sat on the left. As Keelyn neared the entrance, she passed a memorial to fallen officers. Turning, she paused and lifted up a prayer for those on duty. She checked her watch, tilting the face away from the glare of the sun.

An unusual request had brought her here today. One Keelyn hoped would bring her new business for her consulting work. Interpreting body language was a relatively new art even though scientifically based over the last couple of decades. Thus far, most of her business had been corporate in nature.

Often companies hired her to sit in on contract negotiations — her insights helped head off later disputes and kept her clients out of court.

When she'd first started out she'd been

referred by a college acquaintance whose father owned the company. The man was a stalwart in the industry and couldn't fathom bringing a woman in to observe the legal discussion of a contract whose terms she couldn't understand. She didn't have a background to support any expertise.

Keelyn argued she didn't need to know anything about manufacturing. She dared to say they could be speaking a foreign language and she could still be useful. After all, facial expressions were universal, but gestures tended to be culturally biased. The limbic brain spoke a universal language. One she was well versed in.

He begrudgingly agreed . . . after she offered her services for free. During discussion of one clause of the contract, Keelyn noted one person tightly purse his lips. This signified to Keelyn he was uneasy with the matter at hand. She'd tapped her toe on the company president's shoe, signaling him this area of the contract was problematic.

It had saved the company fifty million dollars.

He'd cut Keelyn a check for one percent of the amount saved, which, even after taxes, turned out to be a huge sum to further her business.

That meeting seemed to be a starting

point. She was now beginning to have difficulty keeping up with the calls plus her volunteer work at the shelter. Her consulting work was starting to show up on the radar of both defense and prosecuting attorneys. One of them had passed her name along to this police district when a particular suspect was arrested. Thus the call to observe the Walter Sidlow interrogation.

A rash of bank robberies had developed west of the Denver Metro area. At the most recent crime, a man had been shot and killed as he tried to wrestle one of the gunmen's weapon away. He'd been wounded from behind by the criminal's partner. Due to the death of the Good Samaritan, this particular crime had saturated the local news coverage and police were under added pressure from the victim's family to bring the band of vigilantes to justice.

A guard from the last bank stood as the lead suspect because video footage inside the bank showed him away from his assigned post. It was theorized he left his position to give the robbers unimpeded entrance from the side of the building rather than the busy street front with four lanes of congested traffic. Public outcry for this man to be convicted added fuel to the flames. The police wanted someone in custody sooner rather than later.

Someone who could offer inside information on the others.

Something about this suspect, however, didn't quite gel. During the other robberies, he'd been working at this particular bank. So essentially, he was at least free and clear of having a presence at the other crimes. Second, he didn't come across as a criminal mastermind. His police record was clean, save a few minor traffic violations. He'd been married for thirty years and active in volunteering at a local youth shelter for runaways. His children were college graduates with busy professional lives of their own.

Keelyn was escorted down the hall to the interrogation suites, her long legs easily maintaining the pace set by the officer ahead. She pulled her shoulders back and smiled as she entered the small room. One officer stood adjusting the recording equipment and another sat behind him reviewing footage of the bank robbery. The one stopped fiddling with the recording equipment and turned to offer his hand.

"Detective Sean Matthews. Thanks for coming on such short notice."

"Keelyn Blake."

"You were able to read over the details?" He released her hand.

Keelyn looked through the glass at the suspect placed behind a table. "Yes. Did you get my request to have him seated so there was nothing in front of his feet?"

Matthews leaned away. Already they were on the wrong foot.

"Does it really matter?" he asked.

Keelyn twirled the gold chain at her neck. "The feet are the most honest part of your body."

"Really." The left side of his lip lifted in a sneer.

"Think about it. From the time we're young, we're told to not give certain looks with our faces. Your mother serves you broccoli and you pout. She says something to the effect of 'Don't give me that face.' "

He placed his hands on his hips. "Never thought about it that way."

"We're instructed to smile at strangers. Tell little white lies to spare someone's feelings while at the same time convincing them what we're saying is the truth. Our faces have had a lot of practice at covering deception."

"Mike has an earpiece. Do you want me to get him to change the suspect's position?"

Keelyn wiped her sweating hands along her navy pencil skirt. "Let's not interrupt him. I can work around it."

Keelyn neared the two-way glass. Sidlow was a slight man. His mug shot showed him to be barely taller than five feet, and she doubted he weighed more than 120 pounds wet. His eyes were wide, the white sclera clearly visible around the pale brown irises, and his shoulders huddled up near his ears, giving him the hunched appearance of a turtle taking cover within its shell. The detective was seated close to the suspect. Leaning in, he closed the gap in the man's personal space. The suspect tried to edge his seat back, but he could only go so far.

Everything set by design.

The detective's voice crackled through the intercom.

"Mr. Sidlow, where were you before the robbery?"

"At my post. You can check the video."

"Where were you during the time the armed men came into the bank?"

Sidlow reached up and pressed his thumb and index finger into his closed lids then let his hand drop, smoothing his palm repeatedly over his thigh.

Eye blocking followed by leg cleansing.

Keelyn turned to Matthews. "There's

something about that question he doesn't like. He's blocking and follows it by using a self-pacifying gesture."

The man's voice quivered through the speaker.

"I'm embarrassed to admit it, but I had to take a bathroom break."

"Where is the bathroom located in the bank?"

"It's to the right."

Yet the man motions with his hand to the left.

"Mr. Sidlow, don't you think it's time to be forthright with the police about what really happened? I mean, don't you find it awfully convenient that the moment you step away from the door, two armed men come in and steal close to three hundred thousand dollars? Did you have anything to do with planning this bank robbery?"

"I swear I did not."

Hands relaxed. Lips exposed. Voice calmer.

Keelyn turned away. "Can I look at the bank footage?"

"Sure." The man leaned to the side. Keelyn bent down to look at the small viewing screen. Walter was at the door, checked his watch, and then walked left.

Matthews glanced up at Keelyn from his seat. "What do you think?"

"He says he moved from his post to use the restroom, which sits to the right. Yet in the interview he signals with his arm to the left. He gestured in a different direction from his spoken one." Keelyn pointed to the footage. "This is supported by the video as well. He goes left."

"So?"

"The only part of the interview he's having a problem with is his location at the time of the entrance of the bank robbers. What is to the left of that door?"

The detective pulled out a set of printed building plans. "It looks like the manager's office."

"That's where he went. You need to explore that line of questioning. Ask him specifically what he was doing in the manager's office."

Sean spoke into a small microphone. Keelyn could see Mike lift his head slightly as he listened to the instruction.

"Mr. Sidlow, how well do you get along with the bank manager?"

"Ms. Richmond?"

"Curious thing happened when a friend of mine reviewed footage of the robbery. You headed in the opposite direction of the bathroom, toward the bank manager's office. It's the only thing in that corner."

Sidlow's eyes narrowed and he rubbed at either side of his thin, pale neck. Keelyn couldn't get the thought from her mind of a chicken's neck across a stump of wood, exposed for the ax about to fall.

"Is that anything?" Sean pointed.

"The neck is aligned with several large arteries and nerves, particularly the vagus nerve. When people rub their necks, in time they will stimulate that nerve, causing their heart rates to go down. It's a self-soothing gesture."

"He's distressed by this question."

"Absolutely."

The tin voice from inside the room continued. "What were you doing in Ms. Richmond's office?"

His hand cupped his neck tighter. His face reddened.

"Is Ms. Richmond involved somehow?"

The man shook his head defiantly. "No, absolutely not."

The interrogator leaned closer. "Then what is the reason, Mr. Sidlow, that you left your post to go to her office approximately five minutes before these men burst into your bank? A man was killed doing your job."

His cheeks puffed as he slowly exhaled. He dropped his hands onto his lap and leaned forward, his head bowed.

"We're having an affair. We'd take . . . some time every now and then . . ."

His breath shuddered as he began to cry.

Matthews cracked open the door and signaled Mike out. "Let's ring up the bank manager. See if she can verify his story."

He turned to Keelyn. "Ms. Blake, I wish I could say I was happy about this, but it seems you just cleared one of my primary suspects."

An hour later, Keelyn sat solo on a park bench. She could see the parking lot easily from this vantage point. Currently, her vehicle was the only one on the blacktop. The sunny morning now a gray afternoon — a typically quick Colorado weather change. Rain condensed on the wooden seat and streamed down the nearby aluminum slide like a waterfall. Her red umbrella did little to protect her from the nearly horizontal rain, and the ends of her floral scarf tugged at her neck as it was sucked into the wind.

What was it with this strange, late-fall weather? Rain instead of snow? Keelyn huddled further into her turquoise raincoat and checked her wristwatch.

Her client was late. Never a good sign

when meeting an abuse victim.

A strong gust pulled at the thin metal rod in her hand, and the umbrella flipped outward. Rain stung her checks as she reached up to pull the wire undercarriage back to its original position. She would have preferred to put it away as the struggle against the wind further frayed her nerves.

But then her client wouldn't know for sure if it was safe and would drive right by.

If she did as she was instructed.

A vehicle came down the road from the left. A red Ford F-250, the water spray from the tires swift. Keelyn tightened her hand around the handle as the wind surged. Her body began to shake.

The truck bothered her. A woman fleeing an abusive boyfriend rarely showed up in something so ostentatious. For one, she likely couldn't afford it. And two, she wouldn't want to draw attention to herself as she ran. No action should draw anyone's attention.

Keelyn thought briefly about lowering the umbrella and throwing it under the park bench. The move might give her plausible deniability.

The truck rounded the corner, a faint squeal as it took the corner too tight. Keelyn slowly closed the umbrella and laid it on her lap. The driver's door flew open. Out popped a man dressed in combat fatigues with a black ski mask over his face.

Keelyn's heart kicked up a notch. She braced her back into the bench. Her mind stumbled over the possibilities of what was taking place.

The man yanked a woman over the console from the front compartment. Her red hair spewed from between the fingers of the man's strong fist that gripped her head like a basketball.

The door slammed. Water splashed from the man's combat boots as he pulled the whimpering woman behind him. He pulled out a gun from the cargo pocket of his fatigues and raised it at Keelyn.

Keelyn inhaled and held her breath, waiting. She set her arms to her side and gripped the cool, wet wood. The man's index finger rested outside the trigger.

"Are you Keelyn?" His voice boomed.

"I am."

"I want to know where you'll be taking her. We have some unfinished business." He tossed the woman forward like a bag of trash. The heels of her hands hit the wet turf first, and she slid forward as she tried to press down for traction but flopped helplessly into the grass. She buried her face in her hands. Keelyn could see her back shudder as she sobbed.

"I can't tell you that."

He placed two hands on the pistol. "I'll follow you there."

Keelyn lifted one hand. "I'm going to reach into my pocket. I'm unarmed."

"What are you getting?"

"An address for you."

The woman brought her face up, wet stalks of grass stuck to her face. A bruise encircled her left eye and cascaded down her cheek.

"Why don't you just tell me what it is?"

"I want you to have something written so you won't forget."

He circled the weapon a few times, permission to let her hand slip into her raincoat. She gripped the small remote and activated the button. It was an emergency beacon to 911 for these very circumstances. This park's location was known to law enforcement. The distress call would immediately send police her way. She pulled the device out and held it between her thumb and index finger.

"What is that?"

"I just called 911."

"Right."

The man stilled as he heard a distant whine.

"They're coming for you. My suggestion would be that you put your weapon down, walk to your vehicle, and place two hands on top so they don't shoot you on sight."

The sirens grew closer. The man twitched and lowered his weapon. "If she doesn't pay, I'll find her and then I'll kill you." He walked backward in quick strides, looked down the street before climbing back into his vehicle. The engine roared as he reversed, swung around, and sped down the street.

Keelyn eased off the bench and crawled on shaky limbs a few feet to the woman. She placed a hand in the center of her back to ease the fear that kept her from looking up. Rain matted her hair to her head, and the temperature was dropping.

"It's okay. What's your name?"

Her voice was barely above a whisper. "Rebecca."

Keelyn's hand paused in the small of the woman's back. The auburn hair. The name matched.

Was it possible the missing woman had just been dropped off at this park?

"Rebecca Hanson?"

The woman lifted her face, pushed with

her hands through the sopping wet grass until she was seated on her legs. The pale green eyes injected with small, jagged red veins stared back.

"How do you know me?"

Keelyn stared at the woman; her mind froze at the implications. "Rebecca, where are your children?"

"What do you mean?"

Keelyn's jaw dropped. The cold air hit the back of her throat and increased the tension in her neck. She shook her head to clear her thoughts and reached for the woman, helping her stand up. "Rebecca, you and your children were reported missing to the police by your husband three days ago."

Keelyn watched the woman's face closely. If Rebecca's children were missing and she'd just found out, her body should be a marionette moved involuntarily by the distress in her mind. The emotion of learning your most precious treasures on the entire earth were gone would have some effect.

Rebecca's face was flat, her eyes dull, not a hint of tears. Had there ever been any true tears? Keelyn grabbed her arms and shook her.

"Rebecca! Where are your children? Bryce and Sadie?"

A police cruiser turned into the lot. An officer stepped out, one hand steadied on his belt. Keelyn waved him over. The woman didn't even turn at the sound of his boots against the pavement.

Keelyn tried to pull the woman toward the park bench. Her hands on those shoulders felt like they were steering cold marble. The woman ran her tongue over her dry, cracked lips, then bit into a hanging piece of skin and pulled off a layer. Blood filled the gap and began to run in a single tract down her chin.

"You okay, Keelyn?"

She turned and recognized the young man. "Joel, we have an issue here."

He took in the young woman. His eyes bulged.

"The kids?"

Keelyn shook her head. The woman tilted to the side. The officer grabbed her by the arm to steady her.

Rebecca began to tremble uncontrollably. She reached into her pocket and withdrew an envelope.

The officer took it from her hand and opened it.

"He said not to open it until he was gone."

Joel lip-synched silently as he read it. Then his eyes fixed into position. He slowly raised

101

his head.

"It's a ransom note for the boy and girl."

"Rebecca, who was the man that brought you here?"

The woman's muscles went lax. She slipped from the officer's grip, then thudded onto the ground, unconscious.

CHAPTER 8

Lee punched in the security code at the door of the domestic violence shelter where Keelyn served as a volunteer. As soon as a fellow officer had relayed the events at the park to him, he'd barreled his way to the safe house. A buzzer sounded, and Lee pushed through the heavy metal door. Nathan followed closely. A second door required a different access number, part of the multiple security measures in place to keep these victims safe.

Or at least as safe as possible.

The first time Lee entered the code at the second door, the lock refused to release. He punched harder the second time, with the same result. Without thought, like speaking louder at someone who doesn't know your language, he began to pound on the frame, his concern for Keelyn's safety overriding common sense.

Nathan grabbed his forearm. "They're going to call 911 if you don't calm down."

His fist ached from slamming into the wood, but his mind crazed at the thought of Keelyn alone with a maniac who could have snuffed out her life with the easy pull of a trigger. Lee pushed away from the door and stepped aside. Nathan thumbed the punch lock, and the latch released. Lee breezed by him. Five steps down the hall and two to the right and he was in her office.

Nathan stopped at the doorframe.

Lee's mouth froze, his words caught with surprise.

Keelyn held the child in her arms, the girl they'd found at the diner. She pulled the toddler close to her chest and swayed side to side. Smoothing her lips together, Keelyn's eyebrows raised in question. Lee took a deep breath and smiled, taking a moment to gather his thoughts.

Cool peace washed over his taught muscles at the sight of her thin frame strong and uninjured. She eased the child down onto her hip and the youngster happily took handfuls of her hair into her fists. The calm smile sparkling in Keelyn's eyes quelled the sick feeling in Lee's gut.

He stammered as he tried to express his relief over her safety and the questions surrounding the toddler she cuddled. Why was the girl here and not in the foster system?

Keelyn eased her hair from the girl's clenched fingers. "The DNA tests came back. Your friend put a rush on it." Her voice was calm and silky as though she were talking to a child to preempt a tantrum.

His mouth dried. Keelyn tightened protective arms around the young child and nestled her face in the girl's curls. Lee turned to Nathan. "Can we have some time?"

Nathan bowed slightly and backed into the hallway. "I'll make some calls to Teller County. See if we can narrow down a time frame on Officer Timmons and get some numbers for relatives."

Lee nodded and closed the door. He eased into the chair in front of her desk.

Keelyn sat as well, her face bright with excitement, nearly matching the day he slipped an engagement ring on her finger. "I bought a car seat. Who would have thought I'd need one of those today? Isn't she beautiful?" Keelyn settled the girl on her lap. "Looks just like pictures of my mother when she was a child."

"What's her name?"

"No one knows right now. They haven't been able to find record of her birth. I guess we'll have to think of one."

He ran his knuckles against the side of his head. "Can we back up ten steps, please? The park?"

Keelyn swayed the child side to side. "That's going to blow up in the news. Did you hear who it was?"

"Yeah, the missing mother. I'm more worried about the other component."

"A violent kidnapper with a weapon? It's not the first or last time that's going to happen with my work here. Boyfriends can be more dangerous than that guy."

"He had a gun."

Keelyn pulled the child's head to her chest and covered her ears. "He never had his finger on the trigger. It was just a big show of bravado. Make himself seem more threatening than he really was."

"Your interpretations are hunches. You were in a dangerous situation."

"I understood the danger. I called for help. What else could I have done?"

"This whole thing doesn't make sense to me. If this is all supposed to be about the ransom, why would he not hold her for money, as well?"

"One, it offers proof he has them. Two, maybe she was becoming problematic. A woman in distress over her children can do irrational things to save them."

106

"The responding officer was concerned he might not drop the threat he made against you. You know, I get twitchy when someone actually threatens to *kill* you."

Keelyn narrowed her eyes. "It's a good thing I have her ears covered. Please, don't say those kinds of words in front of her." Keelyn let her hands fall. "They'll find him. Your friends are very smart."

Lee pointed a finger at her. "He threatened you personally."

Heat rose in his chest. His shoulders ached from the tension. How could he live if he ever lost her? How could she be so calm?

She frowned at his comment and pulled the child's dark curls away from her eyes. "Do you know much about the case?"

"It's not our jurisdiction. I only know what's in the news. Isn't she married?"

"Yes, the husband reported her and the children missing, though he did wait several hours. I believe it was late in the evening. He says he had no reason to worry initially because she'd often been gone with them after school."

"It's your assumption the guy who dropped her off actually kidnapped her and the children?" he asked.

"Yes, an assumption. It must be someone

involved with the crime. MaryAnn is talking with the mom now. Trying to get some info."

"The police are going to want a shot at Rebecca as well. There are still two kids missing. I'm not thrilled with the position you're putting yourself in."

From the desk, Keelyn grabbed a ring that held primary colored plastic keys and handed it to the child. The girl immediately threw it to the floor and whimpered for her sippy cup. Keelyn placed it in her eager hands.

"What do you want me to do? This isn't the safest job. It's why we set up the quick-response system."

"For one, it's not a job. It's a volunteer position. You could give it up anytime."

Keelyn eyed him evenly. "You know that's not an option."

"How about a location for picking up the women other than an isolated park in the middle of nowhere?"

"That location has worked for years. It's actually only a few miles from the District One station. I'm not having a knee-jerk re-action and changing a spot because of one incident. Let's see if this man becomes a problem."

Lee tightened his hands over the arms of the chair. "Keelyn —"

"I think you're right anyway. I don't have a good feeling about Rebecca. There's something there, something she's hiding from us. The whole thing at the park between them felt staged."

How could he make her understand his alarm without coming across as a tyrannical, possessive fiancé? What could he say when his own job held such risk?

"What I'm trying to get across to you is we shouldn't take this man's threat lightly. I don't want you traveling to and from here alone."

She patted the girl's back. "A police escort is going to draw attention. I'm not going to do anything that will put these women at greater risk. I do all the things I'm supposed to."

"What about the child?"

"My niece?"

Lee gripped his thighs, then froze the movement. What did the gesture mean to Keelyn? "You're taking her home?"

"Social services has given me custody until we figure out what's happened to Raven. The DNA tests matched her to the sample you took from Raven's house, and the indexes were high indicating I was related to both of them."

"What if we don't figure that out? What if

we never find her mother? What then?"

"I'll . . . we'll adopt her."

Lee inhaled sharply and closed his eyes. Why was finding the right thing to say so hard? He loved this woman. He was going to marry her. Intellectually, he understood that meant children one day. Their own biological children. He wasn't ready to take on this responsibility now. They weren't even married yet.

Lee reached a shaky hand across hers. "I'm not sure this is smart, Keelyn."

She bit into her lip. His soul crushed under her glare of betrayal. The look on her face made him wonder if he had a chance at changing her mind.

Her eyes glistened. "I would ask why, but honestly, I don't want to know. With a great brother and wonderful parents, it's probably hard for you to imagine how messed up people's lives can get. I know you see it at work, but living it and feeling it are two different things. I owe this to Raven for not being there for her."

"Keelyn, it's not as if you didn't try."

Red splotches rose on her neck. She drew the child closer into her chest in a crushing hug. "It's like swimming to the rescue of a drowning person and they still die. Trying didn't make a difference to her."

Lee's heart pulsed at the guilt he felt for not telling Keelyn the truth about his family. About what he'd done to his own brother. About why she'd never met Conner. If he couldn't care for his own brother, how could he protect this little girl?

"None of us are perfect."

"Then I hope you'll help me do this. Even if it means she becomes your daughter someday."

His chest felt heavy. "I just don't know if I can."

Keelyn's eyes bulged.

There was a sharp rap at the door, and he turned to see Nathan in the doorway.

"I need you out here."

"Can't it wait?"

"No, now." Nathan's eyes challenged him to disagree.

Lee put a palm up toward Keelyn to calm her as he eased from the room and followed Nathan a few paces down the hall.

"What's so important?" Lee challenged.

"I know we're not close, but I'm going to try and help you here." Nathan leaned his shoulder into the wall. "You need to step up and help her."

"This is none of your business," Lee said through clenched teeth.

"Your peace of mind is my business if

we're going to be working together." Nathan took a step toward Lee, his height adding weight to his words. "And if she leaves you because of this, then I have a stressed-out partner in a volatile situation, and that's a bad mix."

"I never wanted to be responsible for other people's problems. Kids from bad situations are always messed up. We see it every day." Lee leaned back against the wall.

"All of this goes with the territory. If you love her, you'll stand by her. If you don't help her now, she is going to leave you, and I'm not going to blame her."

Lee stroked his jaw and looked back at Nathan. "It's a kid, not a puppy. How are we going to manage?"

"I've noticed you often have a book in your hands."

"What does that have to do —"

"It doesn't seem to bother you when the guys rib you about it being literary fiction or the Bible."

Lee shrugged. "Your point is . . . ?"

"I'm wondering if the things you read have any real meaning. If you espouse Christian principles, this is the time to show you mean it."

Lee clenched his jaw and broke Nathan's gaze. Tightness constricted his lungs, and he unbuttoned the top of his shirt in an attempt to breathe more easily.

Nathan continued. "The point is, there's a time when your ideal and real life meet. This is it. The two of you need to figure it out *together.* Loyalty and honesty. It's how Lilly and I survived." He laid a hand on Lee's shoulder. "I need to finish up here. Let's make sure Keelyn knows about what else we found at the scene. Then I'll leave you two to finish your talk."

The two men reentered the room. Keelyn was spreading a coloring book in front of her niece.

Lee cleared his throat to draw her attention. "There's something I haven't told you about the woman from the vehicle."

Keelyn worked to place a blue crayon in the young girl's fist and didn't look up. Instead of taking the crayon, the girl reached up and tugged at Keelyn's hoop earrings.

Lee wiggled his fingers at her. The child returned an easy smile. Why did they have to talk about such dark things? "There was another body found in the car. A young, white male."

Her eyes widened, prey sensing a predator close. "Shot?"

Nathan's phone pinged. He turned to take the call.

"No," Lee said.

"Then what?"

"The medical examiner's not sure. All she found was a rash on his neck. No other findings of trauma. She's going to send tissue samples for micro and toxicology reports, but it could be weeks before we learn anything definitive."

"Do you know who the second victim was?"

He watched for her reaction. "Clay Timmons."

She shrugged her shoulders. No hint of recognition. "You're looking at me as if I should know him." With a sharp intake of breath and sputtered cry, the realization hit full force. The child startled in her lap. A groan uttered from her lips as she exhaled. "The note at Raven's . . ."

Lee edged forward. "He was there that day. Another responding officer."

"Both victims were involved in my family's case?"

"This is why I don't want you caring for her . . . your niece. We don't know who the actual target is. It's probably better if you're apart."

Keelyn's eyes narrowed as a brief look of contempt crossed her face. "I didn't realize it was standard SWAT procedure to split resources to protect people. I don't remember you ever doing that before."

Nathan pocketed his phone. "Keelyn, you're going to need to stop by the station tomorrow to work on a computer-generated sketch of the man who approached you in the diner."

Lee nodded and turned back to Keelyn. "What are you going to do with her when you have to work?"

"There are a couple of older women who come here during the day as volunteers to help look after the children so the women can go to work or school. They've offered to help me. It's a short-term solution until we know what's going on."

Lee turned back to Nathan. "I'll be sure Keelyn gets to the station. Say, ten?"

"I have an officer watching Freeman's residence. We're going to Dr. Freeman's house early in the a.m. and see if that provides any clues. Also, I have an appointment to interview her practice partner around 1700 when he's done seeing clients."

"Lee, I'll get myself to the station. I'd rather you focus on finding out exactly what's happened to my sister."

He pointed to the child, who'd fallen asleep on her shoulder. "Do you have what you need to take care of her?"

"I have a car seat."

He turned back to Nathan. "Looks like I'm going shopping."

"Do you want to touch base with Lilly?" Nathan offered. "Maybe she could help you with a list of what you'll need."

Heat rose on Keelyn's cheeks. "Just because I haven't been a mother doesn't mean I don't know what a child needs."

"All right. Of course. Keep in mind it's always Nathan that doesn't know what he's talking about. I have faith in you. I'll just hold onto her while you install that car seat," Lee said.

Doubt filled her eyes. "Nathan, you do car seat checks, right?"

He shook his head. "Detective, not patrol."

"Well, you can read the instructions for Lee."

CHAPTER 9

It was late. The night was bitingly cold. Small, pellet-like disks of ice fell, melting on the window ledge. Inside Keelyn's house, the light was low. Only a small lamp illuminated the living room. Lee was upstairs, assembling a toddler bed.

The little girl slept on a pad of blankets, curled up with her little legs tucked under her belly, back side up. A small, decorative pillow cuddled her head. Keelyn's efforts to get the child to sleep on her back had failed. When was SIDS no longer a concern?

What could Raven have named her child?

"What am I going to call you?"

As Keelyn softly massaged her niece's back, a faint sigh escaped her tiny pink lips. Peacefulness washed over Keelyn. Of all the girls, Raven looked most like her mother and this child followed that genetic link. "I think, Sophia." Her mother's name. A smile played on Keelyn's lips as she remembered her mother and better times. Keelyn closed her eyes and saw her mother's face as she whisked by on the merry-go-round, her dark hair streaming out behind her.

Earlier, after a solid hour putting together the crib they'd purchased, Lee had put the child in it, and she'd climbed out in two minutes flat.

Strike one in figuring out a toddler.

After that feat of gymnastic ability, she refused to sleep. Lee dismantled and re-boxed the crib and took it back to the store. Then she sat in a corner, wailing. Was she missing Lee? Keelyn wanted to join her, but knew she needed to figure out the issue. When would Lee make it back?

"Not tired. No dirty diaper. What else?" Keelyn sat at the table mumbling and staring at the child. "Food. Food. Are you hungry?" Keelyn jumped up and rummaged through the grocery bags on the table.

Keelyn had no idea what toddlers liked to eat. She guessed the child's age somewhere from eighteen months to two years. Raven looked late in her pregnancy when she last saw her, but it was always difficult to tell how far along a woman was based on the size of her belly. Keelyn pulled out the baby food jars and tiny spoons, hoping they might soothe her. Within ten minutes, the highchair in the kitchen was a splattered canvas of ten different types of pureed fruits and vegetables. Orange mixed with purple mixed with brown. It was a blessing children were unaware of how much baby food resembled certain types of body excrements. Keelyn's gag reflex had kicked in a few times, particularly at the smell of crushed peas.

That's the point when Lee returned from the store, for a second time, with a toddler bed, and his laughter still rang in her ears. At her wits end, she'd grilled a cheese sandwich and cut it up with some quartered grapes. The child scarfed the food so quickly, Keelyn feared she would choke. Keelyn added taking a CPR class to her child to-do list. Just after a visit to the pediatrician.

Clearly, she was past the baby-food stage. Keelyn dropped her head to the table and took a deep breath.

Strike two.

Sophia was sitting contentedly in her high chair, pushing crumbs off the edge, when she suddenly started screaming. About that same moment Keelyn smelled the dreaded stench. And that's when Keelyn hit the third leg of her trifecta of incompetence: finding the right size diapers.

She looked at the two open bags from where she sat on the floor. Both choices had been too small. She didn't have the heart to send Lee back to the store for a few more sizes. Instead, she'd grabbed masking tape from her junk drawer and used it to secure the tabs. Unfortunately, the tape didn't stick well to the cloth-like material on the front of the diaper, but too well to the child's skin. Keelyn dreaded the moment when she'd have to remove it. Would the child's fragile skin tear?

She chewed on her lower lip. Trepidation kept her heart beating at a slightly increased rate. Lee was right. Thoughts of her incompetence pulled her forward like a chained weight around her neck. Clearly, she wasn't prepared to be this child's caretaker.

Keelyn gazed out her front picture window. With the low interior light, she could see stars between the tufts of clouds. The moon nearly full, a faint yellow-blue halo surrounded the gray, pocked circle. It was one thing she shared with Raven — a love of this celestial body. When they were separated, they would often talk on the phone and stare at it together, an object that drew them closer.

Keelyn wished she could go back.

From the corner of her eye, she saw movement to the right of the window. An arm reached forward and quickly disappeared. Doubt convinced her otherwise, and she scooted toward the girl and placed her hand gently on the child's back and felt the slow rise and fall of her breathing.

Was the toddler bed Lee's attempt at reconciliation after he'd voiced concern about wanting to help with the child? Keelyn wasn't sure if she wanted to ask.

Lee's boots on the steps caused her to sit up straight. Keelyn placed an index finger to her lips as he swung around the banister. He stopped and smiled.

"How long's she been out?"

"Not too long. Is the bed ready?"

The doorbell rang, the child stirred but stayed in dreamland.

"Are you expecting someone?"

Keelyn stood, her feet numb blocks as she took a step toward the door. Spindles of fire shot through them. She leaned against the back of her chair to rub the feeling back in. Lee passed her and opened the door.

"There's no one here."

"Probably some kids playing a prank."

"Then what are these?" He reached forward and grabbed a package on the stoop. "Did you call someone and tell them to bring diapers?"

"What?"

Keelyn crossed the distance on deadened limbs and took them from Lee. Size 4 diapers.

"Lee, I didn't pick the right size."

"So?"

"I didn't tell you. Didn't tell anyone. I didn't want to bother you to go back."

"Stay here. I'm going to look around outside." He pulled his weapon from the holster.

Keelyn shook her head in defiance. "Let me call in backup for you."

He pressed his fingers into the middle of her chest and eased her back. "It's probably nothing. I'm just going to check. I'll be fine."

Keelyn clasped his arm, his muscles tense under her fingers. "Someone's following us. They watched us go through the entire store."

Lee nodded and eased from her grip as he stepped outside. Through the last crack, he ordered, "Lock this door."

It was everlasting minutes before he gently knocked. She peered through the side glass to confirm it was him. He shook the sleet from his hair. "There are footprints in the mud to the right side of the picture window. Looks like someone's been standing there for a while. On the edge of the porch are clumps of mud . . . like they scraped their shoes there."

"What should we do?"

"I'll call Nathan. See if he wants to get casts of the prints."

"It's Raven. It has to be. Who else would know?"

"Keelyn, if she's so concerned about the child, why doesn't she just come and get her?"

Chapter 10

Dr. Freeman's home was reminiscent of an old-style colonial plantation. It sat on the outskirts of the general metropolis in a gated community where high-end architects showcased unusual structures on multi-acre plots. Heavy white columns, three on each side of the entry, supported a large shaded porch. Tiled steps led up to the double doors. Lee imagined the doorbell sounded like one that would have summoned Scarlett O'Hara, or her butler at least, to the front of the house.

The weather had turned warmer — a late fall tease before cold weather moved in to stay. Nathan rocked on his heels as they waited for Dr. Freeman's mother to open the door.

Lee tugged at his suit and loosened the tie a few millimeters. He'd never complain about SWAT fatigues again. "Peculiar choice for a house in Colorado."

The massive wood door squeaked on its hinges as a short, frail woman pulled to open it. Nathan stepped forward to push it gently and stepped through the threshold.

"Mrs. Freeman?" he asked, extending a hand. Lee smirked at his intentional exaggeration of his southern accent. Cops, at times, needed to be good actors to garner trust. What could be more genteel than a strong man with a good South Carolina lilt to his voice?

"Detective Long?"

"Yes, ma'am." Nathan motioned for Lee to step into the house. "This is Lee Watson. He's working with me on your daughter's case."

"Nice to meet you. Come, follow me. We'll sit in the sunroom and talk. I'm sure we'll be fast friends. I always think it's better not to let strangers wander freely through your home."

Lee was the last in the line. The woman's humped frame shortened her already small stature. He stretched his neck at the thought of walking hunched over and having to peer up to see where you were going.

Lee waited for the old woman to sit before he seated himself. Nathan walked to the large bay of windows. A well-sized horse stable sat at the back end of the property, nestled in the shade of a cluster of tall pines. The woodsy scent filled the home through open windows, the sheer curtains flapped in the coolness.

Lee leaned forward and placed his hand on the old woman's forearm. "We're very sorry about your daughter, Mrs. Freeman."

She patted his hand. "Thank you for your condolences." Tears flowed down her cheeks. "Do you have an idea who killed Lucy?"

Lee withdrew his hand and grabbed a nearby box of tissue. "It's very early in the case. Isn't there anyone here with you?"

"I'm expecting my much younger brother here later this afternoon." She pulled a tissue from the box and dabbed at each eye. "He's some high-falutin' attorney from New York who thinks he knows everything. But, it will be good to have his help you know . . . for the funeral arrangements. I don't have any idea how to settle an estate."

"Mrs. Freeman, I know this is a very difficult time but are you able to answer some questions about Lucy and her work?"

"I want to do what I can to help find my daughter's killer. Ask away."

"Did Lucy ever talk with you about any of her patients?"

126

The woman inhaled deeply and nestled herself back into the chair. "She didn't really make it a habit with all those crazy privacy laws. Only one case ever troubled her enough to speak about."

"John Samuals's case?" Nathan asked from behind.

"Why, yes, how did you know? Might all this trouble be related to him?"

Lee continued. "We're not sure. The other body found in her vehicle was an officer who responded to the house when John Samuals took his family hostage. Clay Timmons. Ever heard of him?"

"She never spoke to me about any such individual. Lucy, much to my chagrin, was perpetually single, so it would have perked my ears to hear of any man in her life."

"What did she tell you about the Samuals case?"

The woman tugged at her floral silk skirt. "She was never the same after John Samuals killed his wife and children. Can you believe what an awful mess that was? I still can't believe Lucy was involved in an incident that received so much national attention."

Lee dipped his head in sympathetic response. How many lives had changed course because of the actions of one man?

"She moved her practice out of Colorado Springs, just uprooted everything, then built this home here and started all over at a new location."

"What was it specifically that bothered her so?" Lee asked. "I'm sure, as a doctor dealing with the mentally ill, it's not the first time she saw tragedy befall one of her patients."

"No, certainly not. In her twenty years of practice, a rare few have committed suicide. But no one had killed other members of their family. It was those children he murdered that ate her up the most. She went back and analyzed his case for months. I believe she keeps those private files here at the house." The woman eyed Lee conspiratorially. "I'm just an old woman and don't have any need for useless things. Would you like to have them?"

Nathan turned on his heels. "Absolutely, Mrs. Freeman. We'd love to take those useless old files off your hands."

"I thought you'd be so kind."

Lee eased back into the chair. "It was my understanding that your daughter was still providing care to some of John's family members. A girl named Raven."

"John Samuals and his family created a complicated situation that involved more than just her. At first, Lucy's practice took a hit because of the incident. But then, when it became public knowledge John wasn't taking his meds because of financial difficulty and that's what lit the fuel for the incident, the pressure on her eased a bit." The woman clicked at her dentures as she gathered her thoughts. "Then people began to gravitate to her out of sympathy because she had treated John for free. Within a few years, more people were asking for her help than she could handle, and she looked to expand her practice. It took her almost six months to bring someone on board."

"Why so long? Not enough qualified psychiatrists out there?" Nathan asked.

"It wasn't so much that. Of course, she wanted a competent physician with good business sense. Those were easy enough to find. It was more a matter of personality. Lucy wanted to have a partner she liked and respected on a personal level who she felt safe entrusting patients with."

Nathan grabbed his notepad from his coat and thumbed up several pages. "Gavin Donnely was her pick?"

"I don't know if I would say that. More like, he found her, pursued her."

"In a romantic sense?" Lee clarified.

"No, just aggressive. He was young and

129

only a couple of years out of his psychiatric residency. Initially, she didn't seem too keen on bringing him on board. But his credentials were impressive, and he wore her down. Have you met him?"

"We're meeting with him later today."

"He's charming but . . ." Mrs. Freeman glanced out the window as if trying to find the words floating among the trees.

"There's something underneath that's a little unnerving?" Lee offered.

"Exactly." She nodded, turning her gaze back to Lee.

"How did things go between them?"

"At first, fine. Then things began to make her uneasy."

"Such as?"

"John Samuals was no longer a patient of hers. He was in prison or some mental health facility — I can't remember which. My old mind can get fuzzy with specifics. Anyway, their psychiatry staff began to take over his care. She didn't talk about his treatment, but John called her from prison and mentioned to her that Dr. Donnely had been visiting. He wondered if she knew anything about it."

"What did she make of that?" Nathan asked.

"She point-blank asked Dr. Donnely

about it. He simply said he felt sorry for John and his circumstances. That he thought he could be a friend. Not in a doctor-patient capacity. Just provide some guidance. Help socialize him."

Lee leaned on his elbows. "Seems strange for a psychiatrist to do. John is locked up. What's really the importance of socializing him and providing friendship when he's going to spend the rest of his life in jail?"

Nathan took a seat next to Lee. "It's egotistical for a younger man to assume mentorship of an older man. What do they have in common? Donnely's not married, doesn't have children, correct?"

"Right. I think that's what bothered Lucy. Then, over time, John Samuals told her he wanted Dr. Donnely to treat Raven. That she was beginning to have some difficulties he thought Dr. Donnely could help her with. Lucy made it very clear to him she felt that wasn't a wise choice."

"She and Donnely argued over it?" Lee asked.

"Yes. I can't tell you how unusual that was for Lucy. She's a pacifist really. But she was concerned for Raven's safety. Nothing she could put her finger on, mind you, just an instinct. She believed it was crossing a professional line, to befriend a man and use it to garner business. She wondered if Dr. Donnely had been visiting John specifically to get at Raven."

"Did Lucy tell Donnely outright that he was crossing a line?"

"Yes, but she couldn't change his mind. She even considered filing a grievance against him."

"Why didn't she?" Lee asked.

"Well, I don't know if she felt it was so clear-cut. And Dr. Donnely said to her he was simply following in her footsteps by helping this family — that because of Raven's age and due to the fact she was being bounced from foster home to foster home, he wanted to provide his care for free."

"What happened after that?"

"Lucy did make an attempt to keep Raven out of the practice. Nevertheless, she felt she'd said what she needed to say and the decision was going to be his. Things settled down for several years. Then Raven's condition worsened under Dr. Donnely's care. Lucy began snooping behind his back. Reading Raven's chart and making her own observations in a journal she kept here. Just in the last couple of weeks, she said it became crystal clear Dr. Donnely was harming Raven and she was going to report him to the medical board. They had it out one night after work. He refused to leave. Then, I got the call yesterday she . . . was gone. Murdered. Such an —" Her voice broke as tears rolled down her cheeks. "—awful day."

Lee leaned over and grabbed another tissue from the large, gray marbled table and handed it to her. The woman's grief over her daughter's death was a knife to Lee's gut — a visual reminder of the sorrow Keelyn still carried over her own mother's murder. Could his love eventually ease her suffering? "I'm so sorry. About everything."

"Lucy never wanted to be involved with John or his family after that horrid day when he killed his wife and those children." She blew into the tissue. "Somehow, Dr. Donnely snaked his way in and got her involved with it all over again. She didn't have much fight to resist him. When he first came on board, John's trial was coming up, and she was at her wit's end. I think because she felt she'd already taken so much time to decide and she really did need the help, she just gave in."

"Did Lucy ever say why Donnely wanted to keep the partnership together?" Lee asked.

"She guessed it was because of the notoriety. That he was looking to make a name for himself. Every year on the anniversary, the news runs a story about it. I think Dr. Donnely was getting ready to write a book or something. Using Raven to get background information."

"When did Lucy start to become suspicious of Donnely doing something improper?"

"Even though John asked Dr. Donnely to take her on, Raven herself first came to Lucy because she was a familiar face and a woman. She felt like she'd be able to open up more about what was going on. Lucy, however, didn't feel comfortable with the situation. She tried to get Raven placed with a different practice, but Dr. Donnely expressed concern that the state would not provide Raven with adequate care. Raven was sixteen at the time."

Lee nodded. "Did Lucy ever talk about the care Raven was getting? What exactly were her concerns?"

"When Raven first started seeing Dr. Donnely, Lucy rationalized that at least she could keep tabs on the situation." The woman's gaze dropped down.

"What else?" Nathan prompted.

"Raven asked repeatedly to meet with Lucy. Begged would actually be a better term. Lucy said she sounded very distressed, complaining about Dr. Donnely. Lucy worried it could mean a lawsuit and decided it was in her best interest to meet with the girl."

"When was this meeting?" Lee asked.

"About two months ago."

"What happened?" Nathan leaned forward, blocking Lee's view of Mrs. Freeman.

"Raven wasn't getting better. She'd been under Dr. Donnely's care for two or so years, but mentally, she was getting worse. Tormented by violent hallucinations. Depression. She was cutting herself with razors leaving these railroad tracks up and down her arms. Raven claimed she was seeing the same things her father had when he was ill, and this frightened Lucy terribly. That an apparition — Raven called him Lucent — was hunting her."

Lee's mouth dried. "You mean *haunting*?"

"No, hunting. She talked about this presence stalking her."

"Did Lucy believe her?"

"My daughter could see she was a physical wreck." The old woman crossed her arms over her chest. "Were you aware that Lucy was caring for Raven's daughter, Sophia?"

"That's not a good boundary for a psy-

135

chiatrist to have," Nathan said pointedly.

Lee couldn't stop the words as they left his lips. "The child's name is actually Sophia?"

"You didn't know?"

His body felt heavy. "We were unsure. Haven't been able to locate birth records yet. Keelyn, Raven's older sister, just started calling her that. It was their mother's name."

"You're right, Detective Long. It wasn't proper." She turned to Lee. "Keelyn must have intuition about these things. When they met, Sophia was with Raven. Both of them hadn't bathed in days. The child acted as if she hadn't been fed in weeks. Lucy paid for their meal."

"What did Lucy do?" Lee asked.

"She pleaded with Raven to go for inpatient treatment. She refused. Lucy threatened to have her involuntarily committed. Raven said she'd run away. Lucy should have called the police right then. That meeting was the impetus of her thought that it was time to send Dr. Donnely on his way."

Lee locked eyes with Nathan and mouthed the word *motive.*

"Lucy thought that by getting Raven out from under Dr. Donnely's treatment, she'd be able to get a handle on what was really going on, and to see if she needed to be concerned about his other patients."

Nathan looked up from his notes. "Was Donnely aware she was looking into his other patients as well?"

"I don't think she said anything to him, but she began keeping notes about things she thought strange."

"Did she happen to keep those here at the house as well? Another useless file you'd like to dispose of?" Lee asked.

"Oh, I'd imagine she'd have kept that at the office. You'll have to look there."

Nathan made a few notes. "That will be sticky. Getting anything from her office will take a warrant. Hopefully, Donnely doesn't know it exists."

Lee continued. "What happened after Raven refused treatment and threatened to run?"

"My sweet Lucy could never let anything go. I always told her she needed to stop and smell the roses. I wanted her to do something different than be around mentally unstable people. Honestly, she had enough money to do whatever she wanted. Relax . . . travel . . . find a man she could settle down with. But, she saw those marks on Raven's arms, her poor physical condition, and the fact both Raven and her daughter seemed starved. She didn't feel the child was safe.

She told Raven she was going to report her to social services."

"That usually doesn't go over very well," Lee said.

"It definitely caused more arguing. To calm the situation, Lucy volunteered to look after the child."

"From the hostage incident, Lucy had to know Raven had an older sister. Why didn't she reach out to her for help?"

"I'm not sure she felt it was a viable option. Raven was open about the fact she and Keelyn were not getting along. Keelyn had never met her niece. Lucy looked at it as a short-term solution until she could get the situation stabilized."

"Do you know if she and Clay Timmons ever met?" Lee asked.

She shook her head. "I have no earthly idea how the two of them ended up together dead."

"Did Lucy ever think Lucent could be a real person?"

"The whole incident was so odd. Lucy never believed this person was real. Only a hallucination. But then when she met with Raven, her belief began to falter. She wondered if it could be a person. Something she had missed."

Nathan pulled his sport coat tighter over

his shoulders. "Well, if it brings any comfort to you, Lucy's not the only one who may have been changing her mind about such things."

"I'll show you where her office is if you'd like to look through her things."

Lee stood up. "Yes, let's definitely get those files off your hands."

Could it be possible Lucent had been real all along?

If he hadn't been real, then how could he be now?

CHAPTER 11

Parked in her driveway, Keelyn looked behind her at Sophia safely secured in the backseat. A new pacifier gripped between her lips. Two diaper bags sat on the seat beside her. One containing twenty diapers, three packages of baby wipes, three changes of clothes, and an extra snowsuit. The second with assorted toddler snacks and five sippy cups full of various kinds of juice: one apple, two grape, and two white peach. All pasteurized and non-expired. There was also a small medicine bag waiting to be stocked with Tylenol, Motrin, and Benadryl. After reading for several hours about taking care of toddlers, Keelyn had noted those three medicines were mentioned most often. She'd printed off sheets that included the correct dosing based on children's weight.

Had she left the thermometer in the bathroom? Would an adult thermometer work on a child?

That was another problem. Keelyn didn't know how much the child weighed. She'd tossed her broken scale in the trash years ago and never replaced it. If she had to dose Sophia with medicine, it would be a shot in the dark.

One issue to be solved by the pediatrician later today. Another — what to do about her diaper rash?

Keelyn was sure it was too much stuff for a trip to the police station. Her ability to self-edit baby items, however, was in its infancy.

Better safe than sorry.

She let her heavy eyelids close, and the thought of the padded headrest pulled her back. The night was never-ending. Before Lee left, he'd convinced himself a trustworthy neighbor feeling sympathetic had left the bag of diapers on her porch. Keelyn played back the conversation in her mind, and a nagging pessimism began to tug at her sense of security.

Could she trust Lee — this man she loved and had chosen to spend her life with?

It was as if Lee had tried to convince her of something he didn't quite believe himself, just to lessen her anxiety. Something akin to telling a cancer patient there was always hope when the doctor knew full well there was nothing modern medicine could do anymore. That the only hope was heavenly intervention.

Was it better to live with false hope or with the reality of a situation? Keelyn's and Lee's opposing feelings about Raven highlighted the difference between how they approached their respective relationships with God. Her faith led her to believe there was always hope: Raven could be found and redeemed. Lee leaned toward the intellectual aspects of the Bible and logically deducted his way through life's problems: Raven had given up Sophia and had involved herself with a man who would likely lead her to her death. Problems always exploded when hope collided with logic.

These thoughts and the child's restless night had kept her up. Sophia cried for hours. Keelyn's heart broke at every whimpered plea. Close to three o'clock in the morning, both had drifted into a fitful sleep. Keelyn felt the indentations of the carpet nubs that dimpled her skin in the morning.

The child's voice brought her eyes open. Keelyn's vision blurred, and she blinked several times to clear the sleepy haze. How long had she been asleep? Her watch verified ten minutes had passed. Cool air drifted through the interior compartment, fanning the right side of her face. At first, she relished the breeze as it cleared the shadow of cobwebs that fuzzed her thoughts, but then her mind questioned its source. She glanced back and right and noticed the rear passenger door was open.

Had she been so careless as to leave the child's door open?

Then she noticed it, a stuffed rabbit sat next to Sophia on the seat. A note pinned to its chest. Sophia caressed the animal as she pulled the gray-and-pink stuffed ears through her small, chubby hand.

Keelyn quickly glanced in all directions. No one in sight.

"Hey, sweet girl." Keelyn let a few seconds pass to ease the high pitch of her voice. "Where'd you get that bunny rabbit?"

Sophia plucked the pacifier from her mouth, held it between saliva-coated fingers, and pointed outside.

"Mama."

It felt like fire shot through Keelyn's veins. She fumbled at the clasp of her seatbelt, the red plastic button stubborn against her efforts to release it. After several frantic attempts, it gave way. She whipped the nylon strap aside. A sharp crack pierced her ear as the metal buckle flung into the window. Pulling the handle, she shoved the door open, her knees so weakened by her trembling they buckled beneath her. She steadied herself on the door frame and took several deep breaths to calm her racing heart. She straightened up and walked to Sophia's side of the car, scanning the houses surrounding hers for any sign of Raven.

She stood for a few moments, seeing nothing. "Raven!"

A garage door opened several houses down, a red Corvette pulled from the open mouth. Keelyn watched it drive by. The tinted windows hindered her view of the driver. She hated not being able to see inside. Just another form of deception that seemed to mock her as it passed by.

She leaned into the car and took the animal from Sophia. Brown dirt caked the fur, and it reeked of cigarette smoke. Tufts of cotton batting peeked from where its button nose should be. The safety pin dug into her thumb as she unclasped it, and the wind lapped at its edges as she opened it.

In heavy black scrawl were the words: "Stay away!"

Breakfast curdled in her stomach, and she shook. Sophia began to cry for the toy.

Was it a favored toy, as she suspected, or a nefarious sign of something else? Keelyn wanted it gone. Alligator tears welled up and slipped down Sophia's cheeks. She whipped her head side to side, brown locks slapped at her face.

"Whiskers!"

Keelyn handed it back and Sophia clutched it to her chest. "Shhh, okay, okay. You can keep it."

For now.

She eased the child's door closed.

Should she lock the child in the car and look for her sister? Or was that the plan — to draw her away from the child so Raven could take her back? Her mind ached to call Lee, for him to come and offer his sure and steady calm. She craved the feel of his arms around her body. Would he believe her or chalk it up to the hysterical musings of a worried aunt?

She pulled her hair behind her and held it clasped in her hand to keep the playful breeze at bay. She returned to the driver's seat, buckled, and backed out, scanning the houses as she drove by.

No signs of a solitary figure anywhere.

District 2 Station was in the center of Arapahoe County in an older part of Aurora. Keelyn parked near the municipal building and walked the narrow sidewalk with Sophia on one hip. The two diaper bags pinched her skin under their weight as Sophia still clutched the acrid Easter toy. She struggled at the door until a young, olive-skinned man, each finger tattooed with an acronym she didn't understand, reached forward to hold the door open for her. She proceeded through and walked the tile hallway to the glass-encased, she assumed bulletproof, phone center.

"I'm here to see Officer Brentwood."

The man looked up. His tin-like voice cracked through the speaker. "You moving in?"

She smirked. "Is he here?"

"Yes, Keelyn. He's been waiting for you. Any more trouble from that crazy man from Monday?"

"Not yet, but you haven't found him, have you?"

"Just keep your eyes open."

He walked around to let her through and motioned her to follow. After several twists and turns, they came to a small room. The officer at the desk stood and took the heavy bags from her shoulder.

She settled into the cozy desk chair, turned the child around in her lap, and set out a coloring book and crayons for her to doodle with.

It took hours to get the composite right.

The image that stared back from the computer screen was close but not perfect.

"He has a mark, maybe a mole, that sits just outside his left eye."

"How does this look?"

Keelyn's neck was slick where sweat had collected between the sleeping child's cheek and her chest at the open V of her pink sweater.

"Good. I think that's as close as I'm going to get."

Keelyn could hear Lee's voice at the door. Two quick knocks and he pushed through, Nathan a few steps behind. She swiveled the chair but remained seated. His dimpled smile warmed her tired spirit.

"I didn't expect to see you here," Keelyn said.

"We just got back from interviewing Lucy Freeman's mother."

"Anything interesting?"

"Just that you might be psychic."

"What do you mean?"

Lee pointed at the sleeping child. "Her name . . . is really Sophia."

Keelyn instinctively huddled her close. Maybe she understood Raven more than she thought.

"By the way, I thought you were going to leave her at the shelter."

Her joy iced over. "I didn't feel right doing that. Her life is unsettled enough right now."

Lee walked around and neared the computer. "This is Lucent?"

Keelyn nodded. "At least the person who calls himself that."

Nathan fingered the mole on the composite. "You recognize this person, Lee?"

As he leaned toward the screen, Keelyn studied his reaction to Nathan's question. It was there. She couldn't deny it. A slight lift of the eyebrows as his breath stilled. His tell when he would withhold information from her. Typically, she noticed it when she would ask him about SWAT calls. Her stomach cramped at the thought he could already know this person who'd been involved in murder. Someone he'd arrested? Someone he'd helped convict in the past?

He shook his head and stood up. "No one I know."

"You sure?" Nathan pressed.

Keelyn eyed Nathan. His gaze fixed on Lee. Unwavering.

He sees it, too.

"I told you, I don't know who he is."

Nathan looked back at Keelyn and shrugged it off. "Lee, we best be off. It's late, and we have to meet with Dr. Donnely.

Thanks for coming into the station, Kee-lyn."

Lee leaned down and kissed Keelyn on the cheek. He placed a protective hand on Sophia's head. The little girl stirred under his touch.

"I'll stop by later."

She bit her lower lip as he left. There was something disingenuous in his demeanor. Keelyn was sensitive to the disparity between what a man said and what he did. Lee's statements were far from what his body language portrayed.

He was lying.

He knew the man in the sketch.

CHAPTER 12

The scenery passed unregistered as Lee's mind whirled at the implications of keeping the information from Keelyn, from Nathan, from the chief of police. The remnant of the man he used to be still haunted him. The one he'd tried to bury more than twelve years ago threatened to breach its crypt. He imagined the deception materializing like fingers wrought with decaying flesh as they broke through the dirt that kept them hidden.

He wanted to vomit.

"How's your brother been?" Nathan asked as they sped toward Gavin Donnely's office.

Lee swallowed hard. "Why do you ask?"

Nathan flipped the turn signal and positioned the vehicle in the left turn lane. "I seem to remember he was in some trouble a few years back."

"You know" — Lee's voice cracked and he cleared his throat — "we don't talk anymore."

From his peripheral vision, Lee saw a nod of contemplation. "Do you know where he's living?"

"No idea."

A cool stalemate remained between them. Nathan seemed resigned to the fact that Lee was sticking around and at least worked to be pleasant. The building was a short distance after the left turn. Nathan parked and laid his hand on Lee's shoulder.

"I'm sure in SWAT, trust is primary. Am I right?"

Lee's ability to act nonchalant during this conversation was fading fast.

"Truth first," Lee confirmed.

"It's the same thing for me. If I can't trust you, we won't be working together. This has nothing to do with what you told me yesterday. Can we agree?"

"Yes, absolutely."

Nathan eased his hand off and opened his door. "Just want to make sure we're on the same page."

The building was a short, three-story brick structure. The offices of Freeman and Donnely were on the third floor. Dim hallway lights guided their way to 307, through the door, into a cozy waiting room void of patients. The receptionist's desk sat empty.

"Dr. Donnely?" Lee called, his voice small in the large space.

Nathan fanned out a pile of magazines. *People, US,* Oprah's flagship publication. Missing from the stack were *Field and Stream* or magazines for cars and trucks. "Let's head to the back."

Light spilled from a cracked office door. Lee neared the door and pushed it open a few more inches. "Dr. Donnely?"

Still no answer.

A lamp at the desk provided solemn light. Large shadows cast into the center of the room resembled gargoyles waiting to pounce. Lee stepped into the office with Nathan close behind. There was a small hallway to the back left corner of the desk. Lee motioned for Nathan, his hand on the hilt of his service revolver.

Another door, open slightly. Lee snuck up and peered through.

He couldn't fathom what he was seeing. Donnely, he assumed, was bent at the waist spraying something with what appeared to be a can of compressed air. Next, he grabbed a small probe, a small blue spark appeared, electricity arcing. A scene from *Young Frankenstein* played in his mind. Lee knocked louder at the door.

Donnely stood up and turned around.

"Detectives! Come on in. Sorry, I get concentrating on my hobby and it's hard for me to hear people enter the office."

Lee walked in. "Thank you, Doctor, for agreeing to see us today. I'm Captain Lee Watson. This is Detective Nathan Long."

Donnely's hair was brown and his eyes, a shade lighter than his hair, were set deeply into his skull. His cheekbones would be the envy of any male model, and the strong jawline added to his tough exterior.

A faint smell of burned flesh hovered in the room. Lee neared the doctor's work station. In a small vice was a shiny, eight-legged spider. Donnely returned to his prisoner and sucked venom from the microscopic fangs into a glass pipette. A prickled heat rose on Lee's arms.

"What are you doing?" Nathan asked as he took position on the other side.

"Harvesting this little guy's venom. *Latrodectus mactans.*"

"The black widow spider."

Nathan eyed Lee quizzically. "How would you know something like that?"

"Science nerd. I loved bugs growing up."

Lee's heartbeat touched up a notch at the ease with which the lie slipped off his tongue. How far down this muddy slope had he slipped back into his old ways?

153

Could he climb back up?

In truth, he struggled to cover the fine tremble in his hands. An ache smoldered from the scar in his right side where the venom from a brown recluse had necrotized his skin into the muscle. Since that junior high summer day when the fangs of a fiddler bit into his skin, any sight of the eight-legged fiends caused his knees to weaken with dread. His knowledge of their ways was a defense mechanism for control.

He studied them like one would study an adversary.

"Why are you collecting the venom?" Nathan asked.

"I've been researching different types of neurotoxins. After all, botulism is a neurotoxin, and we doctors use it for cosmetic purposes, among other things. It is also used for certain medical conditions." Donnely winked and sniffed hard. "Small doses may be beneficial. That's what I'm trying to figure out. If I could come up with an application like Botox, I'd be so rich I could retire at fifty."

"Isn't your background psychiatry?" Nathan stepped back.

"Of course, but I am a medical doctor first and foremost. These creatures have always fascinated me." He turned to Lee. "We would have been great childhood friends. Let me put this one back, and I'll meet you in my office."

Nathan seemed thankful for the excuse to leave. Lee struggled to stay as he watched the doctor place the anesthetized spider back in its case and thought back to Donnely's last statement.

We would have been great childhood friends.

Forced teaming.

It was a technique he learned as part of his SWAT training. Subtle clues a stalker might give early in a relationship to build rapport with the victim. When he interviewed women, he would often evaluate for these types of interactions. This particular strategy on the part of the criminal involved using the word *we* to establish premature trust.

Had the psychological game begun? If so, why?

Lee hung back to examine the piled myriad of specimens. He felt the tiny ends of eight spider feet climbing up his arm to his shoulder, and he swiped at the bug, meeting nothing but air.

"You're sure you're a fan?" Donnely's voice was low, insulting.

"Absolutely." Lee swallowed hard.

Clear plastic cases, at least one hundred, were stacked on the wood shelves. Each contained an arachnid variant. Most of them black widows.

"You use these for any other purpose?" Lee asked.

The doctor latched the lid in place. "I use them with people who have a paralyzing fear of spiders."

"Exposure therapy. Isn't it outside the norm to use actual, poisonous specimens?" His mind raced back to one doctor's visit as he sat stock-still while holding a photo of a large tarantula. The pain in his chest so overwhelming he thought he'd had a heart attack. He couldn't fathom the real thing crawling up his leg.

"You're familiar with the concept?"

Lee crossed his arms over his chest at the mild upswelling of pressure. "We cops aren't as dumb as we look."

Donnely paused, a little longer than Lee liked. "Never assumed that."

"To me, the concept is counterintuitive."

"Usually people with a deep-seated fear will say that."

Lee fingered the cases as he walked by. Did the maneuver convince the doctor he was comfortable? He lingered, his nose close to a case. Pain replaced tension as it crawled into his mid chest, spreading into his shoulders.

There it sat.

Loxosceles reclusa.

The brown recluse.

The fiddleback spider.

His scar burned at the sight.

Donnely came beside him, took the case from the wall, and opened the top. He tapped his index finger against the spider's web. The creature spun at the vibration of the silk threads. "Facing our fears is the best way to overcome them. Do you have any fears, Captain?"

His gaze pinned Lee like a bug to foam board. "Not many." Lee turned and eyed him evenly. "You?"

Donnely shrugged his shoulders and placed the fiddler's case back on the shelf. "Perhaps. But all of this is not really why you're here. Perhaps we should join your partner."

The tension leached from Lee's body with his foe imprisoned and back in its proper place.

At least one of them was.

They entered the main office. Donnely motioned them to sit in the overstuffed, posh leather seats.

Lee watched the fine doctor closely. "First

of all, we're so sorry about Dr. Freeman. This news must be very upsetting."

"Yes, it's strange not to hear from her for three days. Very unlike her not to show up for work."

Lee opened his mouth to speak, but Nathan gave a slight shake of his head to stop him. He assumed Nathan had told Donnely about the murder. How could he not know? Did he not watch the news? "She's not been here for three days?"

"Well, Monday. She didn't show up for work." Donnely's eyes widened slightly, sensing he'd made his presence known at the edge of a web Nathan built. "Her patients were quite distressed."

Lee tapped his thumb against the leather. "I'm sure it will be hard for everyone to learn of her death."

The ticking clock marked off the seconds. A full thirty passed. They waited for the doctor to speak.

"She's dead?"

"Murdered, actually," Nathan offered.

Lee stepped in. "I'm surprised you don't know this. It's been heavily reported in the news."

"When was she killed?"

"Monday."

"Well, before you pin me as a suspect . . ."

"Why would we do that?" Lee asked.

"Let me explain. Dr. Freeman —"

"You seem to address her very formally for a partner in a business. You're not friends?" Nathan asked.

The doctor shoved back from his desk and slumped in his chair. "If I could simply finish one sentence, you might be more apt to get some useful information." He inhaled deeply. "Lucy works part-time. She didn't show up for work on Monday. She normally sees patients on Mondays, Thursdays, and Fridays. So one day of missed work is hardly anything to write home about."

"Did you call to check on her?" Lee asked. "Considering the distress of her patients?"

"My secretary left several messages. Again, it was just one day."

Nathan eased his notepad from his coat. "Are you friends?"

Donnely shuffled through a stack of manila folders on his desk, fidgeting. "Detective, you're not dumb enough to play this game."

Typecasting. An aggressor's use of a demeaning label to compel an opponent to defend himself against the remark in an effort to prove it's not accurate. If onto Donnely's game, Nathan should respond as he was.

159

With silence.

As if the insult had never been spoken.

Donnely swiveled the chair. "We're not friends."

"Why?" Lee asked.

"We don't have much in common."

"Did you have disagreements on how the practice should be managed?" Nathan asked.

"Not at all. She had her treatment philosophy, and I have mine."

Lee edged forward in his seat. Nathan took his signal to lead the questioning. "This difference . . . did it concern more than one patient?"

"It's not unusual for doctors to vary their treatment style. Just because my treatment style may be slightly different from mainstream psychiatry doesn't mean it's harmful to the patient."

"What treatments did Dr. Freeman express concern about?"

"She wasn't a fan at all of hypnosis." Donnely brushed at nonexistent particles on his desk pad.

Lee smoothed his hands over his knees, mirroring Donnely's movements intentionally to gain his trust. "Why not?"

"She was concerned about its potential

for leading patients to develop false memories."

"You don't have this concern?"

Donnely crossed his arms over his chest. "First, let me speak to how useful hypnosis can be. In documented cases, it has helped with smoking cessation, weight loss, and a myriad of other conditions."

"But you're not using it for those situations exclusively."

Donnely squirmed in his seat. "No, but it's not harmful."

Nathan tapped his pen against his pad. "Did Dr. Freeman accuse you of harming patients?"

Donnely frowned. "I don't know if I'd use that term. She and I discussed how some of my modalities concerned her."

"What specifically concerned her?" Nathan said, pointing his pen at Donnely.

Gavin batted his hand in front of his face as if the pen was mere inches from his nose. "Freeman was stuck in the frame of mind that all hypnosis is bad. That's simply not true."

"Are some people harmed by hypnosis?"

"It depends on how you classify the word."

"What was Dr. Freeman's concern?" Lee asked.

"If you remember back into the nineteen

eighties, a fair number of people were falsely accused of harming children. It came out that some of these supposed victims created false memories during therapy, becoming convinced they were harmed when no crime had actually occurred. Some adults were sent to prison based on these false accusations."

"And hypnosis was involved in some of these cases?"

"Yes. But much of it surrounded recalling repressed memories. There was a thought at the time that some manifestation of psychiatric illness meant you were repressing memories of earlier traumatic childhood events and, if you were helped to remember those, it could provide healing in your current situation."

"Help remembering through hypnosis?"

"Yes, exactly."

"Isn't it usually the forgetting part that's the problem?" Nathan asked.

"In what sense?"

"My wife was a victim of a violent crime. Her problem is forgetting what happened. Most victims I work with are plagued with remembering."

"Post-traumatic stress. That's one end of the spectrum. Repressed memories would be the other end."

Lee leaned forward. "So you say this phenomenon does exist?"

"And you use hypnosis as therapy for such a condition?" Nathan added.

Donnely's head pivoted as if watching a tennis match from a Court-level seat. "I think it can still be useful."

Lee stood from his seat and walked toward a line of medical texts near the doctor's desk, a maneuver to close the gap and impinge on his personal space. "Did this conversation also surround a particular patient, Raven Samuals?"

Donnely pushed his tongue into the side of one cheek. "Possibly."

"You are providing care for her, correct?"

"Ethically, I shouldn't even disclose that, but my guess is you already know. Yes, Raven is a patient."

Lee's eyebrows rose at the confession. He'd assumed Donnely would try to hide it. "Are you using hypnosis as part of her therapy?"

"Honestly, I've said too much already, Captain. You know I won't be able to get into specifics about her care. Not without a warrant or her consent."

"Can you account for your whereabouts on Monday?" Nathan asked.

"I was here. Came into the office about

163

five o'clock in the morning. My secretary arrived shortly after."

Lee sidestepped a few feet closer to the desk. "Isn't that awfully early for office hours?"

"It works well. That's an early day. Patients start coming in around six thirty. You know the harried business executive that can't make it through the day without touching base with his psychiatrist."

"That feels a little derogatory coming from you as a physician."

Donnely backed a fingernail over pens sitting in a decorative cup on his desk. "Statement of fact. And they're lucky to have me as only a handful of psychiatrists even do psychoanalysis anymore. What would I do without mental illness? It's the bread and butter of my practice." He swiveled in his chair and slid a few inches away from Lee. "Just because I call something what it is doesn't mean I don't care deeply for my patients. How excited do you think a surgeon is after he takes out his five hundredth appendix?"

"In my experience," Nathan proposed, "doctors with harsh attitudes toward their patients are usually hiding something. Something sinister."

Donnely waved it off. "You're reading too

many crime novels."

Lee stepped next to the doctor's chair, placing one hand on the back. "One thing I'm curious about is the question you haven't asked us."

Donnely folded his hands on his lap, perhaps making himself a smaller target. "What would that be?"

"How Dr. Freeman died. It's usually the first question. An inquiry as to what happened."

He huddled tighter. "Like I said: we weren't close. Why would I want to know the gory details?"

Lee leaned down like a compassionate father to a disobedient child. "It's human nature to want to know. The only people who don't ask are the ones who committed the crime or are sociopathic enough not to feel any compassion about it." He leaned closer. "Either of those describe you Dr. Donnely?"

CHAPTER 13

Keelyn had worn a path from her living room, to her kitchen, and back again. Sophia tore at her hair, her face red from her hour-long scream fest. Though Keelyn would never consider harming the child, she began to understand the line between good and bad parenting may be thinner than she'd imagined.

Lee was unavailable. Often when her calls went unanswered, he was out on a SWAT call. She'd been too tired to truck up the stairs to check the scanner.

No news was good news.

Even though he was working with Nathan, Keelyn knew the call of his heart was the SWAT team, and if they needed him, he would go. That prioritization had never bothered her before, but would it be different when she was a mom? Would it still be okay to come second then? Would it calm her spirit to see him walk out the door to serve the police when she needed him to support her during these moments of sheer frustration? Could his priorities change? Would his love for her be an impetus for change?

And what if he didn't change? Could Keelyn handle the loneliness and stress?

Would she meet the same fate as her mother?

A depressed, solemn shell of the woman she was now?

The stress of the moment brought back thoughts of her mother's life. How the separation of living isolated on those acres had stripped the woman of her once faithful and optimistic spirit. Early in Keelyn's childhood, her mother had planted the seeds for her faith by giving her a Bible and reading it to her. Keelyn's cherished pink Bible with a white lamb on the front still sat on the bookshelf in easy view. It had been her prayer for years that her mother would find the strength to leave John Samuals and rescue her half siblings.

Instead, her prayers for deliverance were met with the death of those she loved most.

After that, Keelyn's faith strangled under the assumption that possibly God didn't have time for the prayers of those who called him Father. Her mother's funeral had been more than she could bear. As a young woman, she'd sat with that pink Bible clenched in her fists on the plush, red velvet seat as the coffin lid closed on her mother's finally peaceful face.

When the trembling paralyzed her, keeping her from walking to the car for the funeral procession, and the funeral director had come to her aid, the Bible had fallen to the floor, and a piece of paper popped from between the tissue-thin pages. She'd grappled for the note like a drowning person for a life preserver.

God never abandons his children. Faith is the hope for reclamation.

When had Sophia written those words?

That message helped Keelyn not blame God for her mother's death and was the foothold for the faith she had now.

Her lifeline.

The girl screamed again and slammed her head into Keelyn's chin, effectively pulling Keelyn back into the present. Keelyn plopped on the couch with the young girl and cupped her face in her hands. "What is it? I don't know what's wrong."

She eased back into the pillows of her couch. Sophia began to jump and claw at her arms. Keelyn pulled her close and swaddled her tightly with her arms and began to cry herself.

How did she ever think she could do this? Care for a child?

The stress of the last few days broke the dam that held back her emotions. Keelyn's eardrums pained at Sophia's high-pitched screams. The isolation of her life began to bubble up through the tears that slid down her face. Her mother and father were dead. Her stepfather imprisoned. Female friends? None she could rely on in a situation like this. They were young, unmarried, without a care in the world.

The heaviness of her past was a shroud that kept people out. Was that by her design? A vibe she gave off that said *keep away*?

Lee was her only lifeline. That couldn't be healthy.

Dear God, please help me.

A soft knock at the door stilled her. She fought the urge to cover Sophia's mouth with her hand to quiet her screaming. Had she imagined it in her desperation?

Three hard pounds at the door. Her name called by a muffled voice.

Keelyn gathered Sophia and neared the door. Surely, any nefarious character would run full tilt the other direction as soon as she opened the door and he saw the child in the midst of a nuclear meltdown.

Without eyeing the visitor through the peephole, she flung the door open, almost welcoming the diversion of reckless abandon to free her from this drama. Her mouth dropped open as she saw Lilly Reeves standing there, a basket of supplies hooked in the crook of her elbow.

Keelyn stepped onto the stoop and hugged Lilly tightly with one arm. "How did you know to come here?"

Lilly hugged her back. "Here, let me take her." She pulled Sophia from Keelyn's grip and eased Keelyn back inside and locked the door in her wake. "Lee called me."

The relief at having reinforcements brought a new tide of jumbled feelings. Keelyn shook uncontrollably and sobbed into her hands. Lilly guided her back to the couch.

As she sat, the quiet calm Lilly exuded comforted Sophia. Keelyn looked up and could have sworn she heard the alleluia chorus of angels singing. Though not completely happy, Sophia rested heavily against Lilly's chest, whimpering softly.

"How did you do that?"

From her basket, Lilly pulled a box of Kleenex and handed one to Keelyn. "First thing to know about kids is they are very tactile creatures. The more stressed out you

170

are, the more stressed out they'll be."

Keelyn dabbed at her eyes with the tissue. "Is there a book somewhere that tells you that?"

"Probably hundreds." Lilly reached back into the basket and pulled out a large fountain drink from the local gas station. "Lee said Coke was your favorite. Fully loaded."

Keelyn accepted the cup from Lilly. The uber-cold effervescent bubbles were like Valium to her frayed nerves. "Better than liquor for me."

Lilly smiled. "Good. Let me take Sophia upstairs with my basket of goodies and see if there's anything causing this crying spell." She eased off the couch, turned on the TV, searched through Keelyn's DVDs, and inserted one. "*While You Were Sleeping,*" she said with a grin.

"My favorite."

"Mine, too. Take a break and I'll be back."

Keelyn's eyes flipped open, and she nearly dropped the drink she'd cradled in her hands. Lilly was tugging at her shoulder. The quiet relief had apparently lulled Keelyn into a quick sleep.

Almost an hour had passed.

Looking up, the remaining stress eased as

171

she saw Sophia's happy face beaming back. The child reached for her, and Keelyn's heart pooled in the sweetness of her smile.

"You're a miracle worker."

Lilly sat next to Keelyn on the couch. "I wish. It's an ear infection."

"Shouldn't I have known that?"

"Of course not. She can't verbalize to you exactly what hurts. I gave her some ibuprofen. A pediatrician friend of mine had some Amoxicillin samples on hand. Is she allergic to penicillin?"

Keelyn shrugged. "If only I knew." Sophia settled against her and took eager gulps of juice from her sippy cup.

Lilly pulled an oral syringe of the pink fluid from her pocket. "Well, let's try it. I'll write you a script for the rest. I'll sit with you a bit to make sure she doesn't have any life-threatening reactions. If nothing happens in a couple of hours, she'll probably do fine with it."

The fluid dribbled down her chin. Keelyn swiped it with her thumb. "I made cookies today. Can I offer you some? Would you like my house?"

Lilly laughed. "Nathan and I may take you up on that. It's a beautiful place."

Keelyn clasped Lilly's hand. "Honestly, you saved my life today."

"I have a debt to pay to those who care for others' children."

Keelyn was aware of Lilly's history, of the twins she'd given up for adoption as the result of a sexual assault. "I know I should have something amazing to say, but I just don't. I can't imagine having gone through what you did."

Lilly offered a warm smile. "I wish other people would be as honest as you rather than offering platitudes that come across sounding fake."

Keelyn dropped Sophia into the crook of her arm like a newborn. "For me, honesty is the most important thing."

"I really am fascinated by your career. How did you become a body language expert?"

"Unfortunately, real-life experience. Growing up exposed to a hostile family situation, I had to learn to take a read on everyone's emotional state. Kept me out of trouble."

"It probably saved your life that day."

"Maybe. Being able to detect deception could save a lot of lives. During my schooling, I came across a story about Hitler meeting with Chamberlain where he baldfaced lied to him and said he didn't have any plans for invasion. If the prime minister could have picked up on that, imagine how different the world would have been. All those lives could have been spared."

"There's probably more than that, though. It seems more personal to you than some anecdotal story you ran across."

Sophia slept in her arms. Keelyn's stress fell away at the peaceful look on her face. "My father became ill with depression. Started having suicidal ideation. He'd been in and out of treatment, and I thought things were getting better. I'd always ask him before I left for work if he had any plans to hurt himself." Keelyn swiped a tear from her eye. "The last time I saw him, he had the sweetest smile on his face, kissed me on the cheek, and promised he'd have dinner waiting for me when I got home."

Lilly handed her more tissues. "I'm guessing that's not what happened."

Keelyn sniffed hard. Sophia stirred and Keelyn pulled her closer and rocked gently. "He shot himself. They thought probably right after I left." She tore the tissue into small bits. "Then I was so mad at him for leaving me to clean up the mess. For leaving me . . ."

"I'm so sorry you had to go through that."

The pressure of Lilly's hand on her shoulder calmed her sorrow. There was a light-

174

ness in her eyes, a warm touch of shared experience. "See, you do know the right things to say."

Lilly's eyes twinkled. "I get more practice in my job than you probably do."

Keelyn gathered up the tissue and clenched it in her fist. "What people don't get is that it's the lying that kills you. No matter what it is, if you know the truth you can deal with it." Sophia's breath shuddered. Keelyn stroked the little girl's arm.

"Lilly," Keelyn looked up through her lashes. "Have you ever felt like Nathan was lying to you?"

"One thing about Nathan: he's honest to a fault. If he causes a minor scratch on someone's car, he leaves them a note about it."

"So, you've never felt he was hiding something from you."

"Are you having these feelings about Lee?"

"It's just a feeling like he's holding something back."

"What are his thoughts about Sophia?"

"That he's been completely honest about. We've talked a lot about having children. I knew from the beginning he wasn't keen on adopting older kids. He's seen so many troubled ones that he wants to be in their lives from the beginning. After a year, he

175

considers them . . . I don't know . . . spoiled goods in a way."

Lilly tucked her hair behind one ear. "One thing I've learned about God is he has a way of disproving you in the most obnoxious ways sometimes. Painful ways — to break you and draw you closer. Show you where your imperfections are. What would you do if there came a time when Sophia needed a home and it was you or foster care and Lee said no?"

Keelyn curled Sophia's fingers around her thumb. "My choice would be clear. I'd have to choose her."

"It wouldn't surprise me if this is more of a test for Lee than for you. I know you're strong. You could do it by yourself. The question is, will Lee put his love for you aside and let you go it alone."

Keelyn took a deep breath as fresh tears pushed their way into her eyes. "If he did, then he probably never truly loved me."

Chapter 14

The drive from Aurora to Florence took two hours. Keelyn sat with her chin on her hand and watched the scenery pass. Evaporated thunderclouds left thin white threads against the soft blue sky. Sunlight warmed the glass of her passenger window, and she leaned her cheek against it, hoping it would thaw the gloom hovering over her spirit. Miles of reddened dirt pushed at the base of the Rocky Mountains, seemingly shoving them out of reach. The solace of mountain pines and cool river streams often made her feel so close to God. It was the one place she felt swaddled in his comfort.

Now both the mountains and God seemed unreachable.

"You're so quiet."

She turned to look at Lee. He sat with one hand on the steering wheel and the other hand around a travel mug.

"Is there something you want me to say?" Keelyn asked.

He tapped his fingers against the cup. "There's nothing I want you to say. But could it be the other way around?"

Chilled bumps raised on her arms despite her shirt and sweater. Did she want to get into this now? On the way to see her stepfather in prison?

Lee eased the car into the passing lane. "You've been pretty quiet of late."

"I have a lot on my mind."

He nodded. "Has Nathan spoken to you?"

Her suspicion grew at the question. "About what?"

He shrugged his shoulder as if unconcerned, but the fact that he left it raised betrayed the tension he felt. "About anything."

"Is there something he'd ask me about?"

Lee looked away from her out the driver's window.

Hiding his reaction?

"I don't know. You can never tell. He's been known to have some peculiar theories about things."

"Theories proved to be true in the end, right?" Keelyn studied Lee. He stroked at the muscles in his neck. What did Nathan know about Lee that worried him? Did he suspect something about him as she did?

"You must be nervous. Seeing your step-father and all."

Topic change. Another tell. He didn't want to be pushed on whatever the subject was. Keelyn turned back toward the view out the passenger side. They passed a rusted blue Chevy truck. "I'll do what I have to do for Raven."

Even as the words fell from her lips, her ears could hear the hollowness in them. After all, she hadn't done all she could. If she had, wouldn't Sophia still be with her mother?

"Are you ready for this?"

"As ready as you can be to talk with your mother's murderer."

"You need to be mentally prepared. It's not a spa, Keelyn. It's a harsh environment. We're just lucky he's out of supermax."

The Alcatraz of the Rockies. A prison in a sea of desert red clay. An individual water drop or particle of sand rarely provide a barrier. But their collective force can be daunting. A violent, churning bay. A harsh, dry desert.

Where John Samuals was confined.

Keelyn saw the prison structures in the distance. They passed a sign that warned, "Do Not Pick Up Hitchhikers."

From the sky, ADX Florence appeared like a fan-shaped structure, a mock salute to the heat that accumulated between the desert and the sky in stifling waves during hot days. Redbrick buildings with harsh metal watchtowers.

The trial of John Samuals had been easy fodder for the cable TV court shows. He was a murderer and a domestic terrorist. The new catchphrase of the twenty-first century.

It wasn't just his attack on Keelyn's family that had gotten Samuals into trouble; it was the biological experiments in a home-built lab. Law enforcement theorized he was creating a bioweapon. Discovery of his lab made an insanity plea over his hallucinogenic murder spree difficult. After all, how could a man be truly insane if he could maintain and function a well-designed lab stocked with toxic neuroagents and not infect himself? Prosecution lawyers pointed to that as the product of a well-functioning mind.

In addition, at the time of John's arrest, drug levels for his antipsychotic medications were at therapeutic levels, which surprised many involved in his case because it was presumed financial difficulties had prevented him from buying his medication.

Had Lucent been a ruse by an intelligent man for the insanity defense? Had an evil mind, not a psychiatric illness, driven him to slaughter his family? Medical records provided historical proof that when these drug levels were normal, John's hallucinations were kept at bay.

The proposed theory was he'd used Lucent as a scapegoat for the murder of his family so he could continue his experiments unimpeded. No one really knew what had been in the man's head, but everyone agreed he was dangerous.

He had been convicted under federal law.

That gave him a free pass to the supermax. Fellow inmates included convicted Mexican drug lords, white supremacists, and the Unabomber.

Reportedly, the rooms were nine by six with concrete furniture and a polished steel slab for a mirror. Every prisoner was under administrative segregation. When they exercised, they were singly caged to prevent them from killing one another. Television and radio were present but inaccessible to the inmate, given as reward and taken away for punishment, the jailors as proverbial gods.

That this prison was a cleaned-up version

of hell might well be an accurate description.

John Samuals remained on death row.

Normally, John would be allowed visits from his lawyer or special investigators. Lee had to request special permission from the Department of Justice and the Federal Bureau of Prisons to allow Keelyn this visit.

The only reason she'd agreed was John's insistence that he would only share information in her presence.

In consideration of the two murder victims, a missing woman, and an abandoned child, the agencies had approved her visit.

Biologically, Keelyn and John were not related. What did she owe a man, her stepfather, who'd brutally murdered her mother and half siblings?

Nothing, raged through her mind.

But the Holy Spirit quietly nudged her on the road to forgiveness. And as she walked toward the structure, her steps hesitated as her old nature warred with the quiet voice within.

After presenting their IDs, Keelyn and Lee were scanned and escorted through several security points before they came into a small room. Her stepfather sat alone, shackled to metal loops secured into the concrete floor behind a wood table. His head was Mr. Clean bald, and his eyes were cloudy and dark. The hollow gray of his irises bled of life. Keelyn wondered if the stress of the trial and prison had caused the changes in him. He was a low flame that struggled at the last vestiges of a wick before the wax choked it out.

Hopeless.

John Samuals hadn't always been a dark figure. The change was slow, maybe unnoticed by her mother as she was by his side every day, but detected by Keelyn during her visits. On Easter one year, it was an antigovernment tirade at dinner. When she came the following year during summer, several large plywood signs sat on the edge of the property, touting freedom from taxes and supporting the right to bear arms. Others were more ominous:

No Trespassing!

No Government Agents Allowed!

If You Can Read This Sign . . . You're Within Range.

The slogans were spray-painted in red and black, the color dried in dripped black lines like her mother's mascara down her tear-stained face. One of the last times Keelyn had visited, she remembered looking back at a new glint off the wood fenceline. The top edge newly covered with barbed wire. It was during the same visit she'd noticed the house numbers missing. Darkened brown rectangles left next to the faded, chipped siding.

Next Christmas, the mailbox was gone. How would she get her Christmas cards? Instead of the usual pine tree Keelyn loved to decorate, cut from a local tree farm, sat two long-arm guns and an archer's set, complete with quiver of arrows. To demonstrate the weapons' danger, John had taken her hunting and killed a rabbit. To say there was nothing left after the buckshot tore apart the creature was an understatement.

It had evaporated into a haze of red mist.

At least, that's how her young eyes remembered it.

Keelyn didn't know how long she stood still, trapped by the memories, but she jerked to the present when she felt Lee's hand on the small of her back nudging her forward — into another, current nightmare. Her heart stammered in her chest as her mind recalled John's maniacal look the day he'd slaughtered her family, and she pressed her toes into the floor to prevent the forward motion. Closing her eyes, she began to pray for deliverance.

Once she dared open them again, John

looked docile, shrunken.

Lee pulled out one of the metal chairs on the opposite side of the table, and the sound scraped her nerves. The word *Papa* hung unspoken on her tongue. What she used to call him as a child. As she grew older, the name didn't seem to fit who he'd become and she began calling him by his first name. Why did her mind revert back to the more innocent times?

Now, she couldn't bring herself to say it . . . or anything else.

Keelyn felt Lee's hand on her shoulder as it pushed her into the seat. The coolness of the metal saturated her jeans like the crystals of frigid indifference hardened her heart. She held John's gaze. He looked down.

Lee rustled his hand over the wood. "Mr. Samuals. Thanks for agreeing to see us today."

John looked up and his gaze locked onto Keelyn's eyes. She reached beside her and gripped Lee's thigh. He covered her shaky hand with his.

"I've missed you, Keelyn."

A slow heat built in her chest. "How about I'm sorry?"

"Keelyn, maybe this isn't the way to start," Lee warned.

She pulled her hand away from his protec-

185

tive clasp. "You don't get to decide what I say." She turned back to John. "Really, that's it?"

He leaned forward, the chains strained at his wrists as he reached for her. "Would you have been happy with anything I said?"

The spark of defiance in his eyes threw her vengeance off-kilter.

John offered up his palms. "An apology would be worthless. My sorrow over what I did, hollow to the loss of those people in your life. Would it make you feel any better about what I did to your mother?"

Her voice broke over a covered sob. "Why did you want me here? Insist on it, if not to apologize?"

"I wanted a glimpse of Sophia. You always had her eyes."

Keelyn stood but Lee grabbed her hand. "We're not going to solve this today."

"I'm not going to stay to help some sick freak remember the woman he murdered."

Lee's lasso around her wrist pulled her back into the chair. "We're here to ask about Lucent. We'll work toward family counseling later." His blue eyes, a calm lake, implored her mind to reason.

She swallowed as images of her sister and niece came to mind. Taking a deep breath, her heart slowed. She would do this for Raven.

The chains slid over the wood as John eased back into his chair. "Why ask about him? He doesn't bother me anymore."

"A man, claiming to be Lucent, has threatened Keelyn's life."

"That's not possible. He was just something my mind made up. A chemical imbalance."

"Raven is missing," Keelyn said.

"How?"

"This man says she's with him. Did you know she had a little girl? Your granddaughter?" Keelyn asked.

"Raven and I don't keep in touch."

"Is Lucent a real person?" Lee asked.

John pulled his hands toward his stomach. The metal links rang like ten children each hitting a musical triangle. "For a long time, I thought he was real. Now I know he wasn't flesh and blood like you and me. Just a demon."

"When did you stop having the hallucinations?"

John bent his head to his cuffed hands and wiped his nose. "The prison loony docs seemed to come up with the right drug combo to put him in the grave."

"Your medical records show you had

187

therapeutic drug levels in your system on that day. You shouldn't have been seeing him at all."

"Perhaps it wasn't just the drugs but a combination of other things." John tapped his wrist. "I see your fiancé may know what I'm talking about."

Keelyn looked at Lee's wrist. His cross tattoo. "You're claiming God saved you from Lucent?"

"What I know is when I learned about him, Lucent stopped coming. Call it new drugs. Call it whatever you want. I can tell you this happened. Part of that came with the realization of what I had done. The ramifications of it. Lucent was something evil my mind drew power from. I struggle with what the Holy Book says. I don't think forgiveness for me is possible."

The admission caused his body to sag; his neck bent as if it pained him to look up. Keelyn's heart felt a pang of compassion. The weight of his actions evident.

Is remorse better than an apology?

"You need to read more of that book, then. Forgiveness is possible for everyone. What you believe is a lie," Lee said.

Keelyn glanced sideways at Lee. Could he counsel another about such a truth and still be hiding something from her? She folded her hands and placed them on the table. "I thought Raven was writing to you."

"She was for a long time. But the letters grew strange and then stopped."

"What bothered you about them?" Lee asked.

John placed his cuffed wrists onto the table and sawed with the chain into the edge for several unspoken minutes.

The sound grated at Keelyn's nerves. "John?"

He stopped, one link of the chain caught into a crevice in the wood. An image of John's knife edge buried into the skin of her mother's throat flashed through Keelyn's mind.

"She said he was stalking her."

Keelyn swallowed. Her spit a thick gel that dried her tongue in its wake. "Lucent?"

"So, he was a person to her?" Lee asked.

"Physically, yes."

John traced scratches in the tabletop with his fingers, the sound of the trailing metal links discordant. Keelyn arched her back as if he'd laid the cold silver rings against her spine.

"At first, she wrote that he came to her in her dreams, and she wanted to know if that's how he first came to me."

"Was it?"

He shook his head. "For me, at first he was just a voice. Like a low hum my ears could never clear."

"And then?"

"Darkness. A shadow passing in my field of vision."

"When did he start to talk about killing us?" Keelyn asked, folding her arms over her chest to cover the chill that rose on her flesh.

"Until that day, Lucent was never commanding. It was subtle. A suggestion for how free I could be to do the work I needed to do."

"What *was* that work? You've never been forthright with law enforcement about what you were doing with that lab on the property," Lee said.

"The lab was always about redemption. About fixing a mistake from my past. I wouldn't have hurt anyone."

Keelyn leaned forward and held his eyes like she'd cup a child's chin for reprimand. "You must see how empty that sounds after what you actually did." Tears pooled in John's eyes, and he blinked them away, once again studying the table between them.

"Did you and Raven ever talk about Gavin Donnely?" Lee asked. "Even a demon has a master."

Tiny ghost fingers caused Keelyn's flesh to crawl. "What's that supposed to mean?"

"Lucent wasn't a problem for Raven until Dr. Donnely began to care for her."

"You knew he was treating her?" Keelyn asked.

"Yes. I was the one who asked Gavin to take her under his wing. But now I see that was a mistake."

"What kind? John, speaking in these riddles is not helping Raven."

He threaded his fingers together and cracked his knuckles. "I'm still Raven's legal guardian. My parental rights were never severed."

"What does that have to do with anything?"

"You need to look at Raven's psychiatric records. I'll sign the release so you can get them."

Lee dug his fingernails into the wood. "That's a little sticky, John. Raven's not a minor anymore. She'd have to give her consent, and she's missing."

"There must be something you can do, Captain Watson, to take a look at them."

"We're probably going to have to get a warrant. I'll check into it. I may need you to provide a written statement to persuade the judge those records are going to be valuable in finding her."

"John, this is your offer? To sign a medical release for a woman you no longer have any control over?" Keelyn asked. "This big trip was for you to tell us to go get her psych notes?"

John placed his folded hands against his lips. Was it a prayer?

"It's the one thing I can do to save Raven's life. You see, if Lucent has found her, you'll need to know how he came to life in her mind. That record will reveal his creator."

CHAPTER 15

Friday

Lee pulled his watch close, and his breath misted the glass. After he checked for the umpteenth time in a few short minutes, he pulled the cuff of his fur-lined leather glove over the silver-edged face. He huddled deeper into his ski jacket as he edged into the corner of the building. Crumbles of brick fell into the puddle next to his shoe. He tried to ignore the other trash in the alley, like cellophane bags empty of their homemade pharmaceuticals.

Technically, he was off duty . . . if there ever was such a thing in law enforcement. His phone vibrated in his pocket nearly as often as he checked the time.

He was ignoring a page from the chief of police. Never a smart career move. He couldn't fathom what was so urgent to require his immediate attention. The police radio had been quiet so he concluded it wasn't SWAT related.

Which worried him more.

A man approached from the end of the ally and walked purposefully toward him. Lee shoved off the building and stepped a few feet into view. Closely, he watched for any mannerism that would lead him to believe the man had any intentions other than holding a simple meeting.

Using another officer's confidential informant was frowned upon. Those relationships took years to cultivate at risk to both the officer and the whistle blower, community watchman, righter of evil deeds . . . or whatever politically correct term chosen to call someone who ratted out his friends.

Even if those friends were criminals.

However, this man wasn't. He'd been wrongly convicted of his brother's crimes and offered a job but decided he was better suited to do undercover, off-the-books, paid work on his own schedule without a boss looking over his shoulder.

He'd done time and now sought to clear other innocents.

That's why Lee needed him.

The man held out his tattooed hand. A child's tear-stained face memorialized on the thick, tan skin.

"Thanks for meeting me, Drew. Someone

you know?" Shaking Drew's hand was like brushing up against coarse sandpaper.

Drew released his grip. "We could have discussed my tattoos over a beer at the bar."

"Right." Lee pulled the zipper of his coat down and pulled a photo from an inner pocket.

"I need you to find this man." Lee handed the snapshot to Drew.

He studied the image. "Who is he?"

"My brother. Conner Watson."

Drew's thumb traced over Conner's face as if scanning the image into his memory. "What kind of trouble is he in?"

"That's what I want to find out."

"When's the last time you saw him?"

Lee sighed. "It's been awhile. Conner has a drug problem. I finally did the tough-love thing and kicked him out about three years ago. I haven't seen him since. I hear things every now and then about him living on the streets in downtown Denver."

"Why the push to find him now?"

"Do you know anything about Nathan's current case?" Lee asked.

"He mentioned something about chasing ghosts from a hostage situation gone bad when he was with the FBI."

"One of those hostages is now my fiancée."

"Okay."

"Someone approached her at a diner where we meet. He threatened her life."

"And what does this have to do with your long-lost, drug-infected sibling?"

"The police sketch based on her description of this man looks just like Conner."

Drew studied the picture. "Nathan know about this?"

Lee shook his head.

"Why not?"

"The good detective and I are not on the best terms. I was with Nathan on that day. We disagreed about the timing of the response. People died."

"Yet you're working together now?"

"Even adversaries can have a common goal," Lee said. "We're operating under a cease-fire." Was that what he considered Nathan? An enemy?

"Where do you think Conner might be?"

"I have one address from a place downtown. I'd probably start there and work my way out."

"Are you sure he's still alive?"

"I check hospitals and the morgue at least once a week." The emotional relief and sorrow at not finding Conner tugged at Lee's soul. He sighed. "No one matching his description has been admitted."

"You sure you don't want to do this yourself?"

Lee shook his head. "If I suddenly start taking hours upon hours to find Conner, people will wonder why. Especially Nathan. I don't want to draw any suspicion. If you locate him, you call me so I can talk to him first."

"To get him to turn himself in, right?"

Lee shifted his foot through the trash. "Something like that."

Drew tucked the picture in the back pocket of his jeans. "I'll see what I can find."

CHAPTER 16

Keelyn browsed the pharmacy aisles with the list of recommended medications in one hand. Sophia held onto the fingers of the other hand, her attention held by all the colorful packaging.

The pediatrician's appointment had been interesting. Keelyn spent most of the short visit peeling a panicky, screaming Sophia off furniture long enough for the doctor to look at the child. Keelyn had no idea whether Sophia was up-to-date on immunizations, and all the other details the doctor supplied had given Keelyn a migraine. She'd hoped Lee would come to offer another set of hands. But he was MIA, even though it was his day off. It wasn't unheard of for him to spend time with other friends, but he'd never avoided her before.

Keelyn continued to suspect Lee of hiding something from her, and in the absence of information, her mind began to fill the void with possible reasons for his obscurity.

None of them were fun to think about.

The pharmacist had told her it would be twenty minutes to get the prescription filled for Sophia's rash. Another five minutes to spare. Letting go of Sophia momentarily, Keelyn pulled the red plastic basket toward herself to double-check the list.

Tylenol.

Motrin.

Benadryl.

A cascade of Strawberry Shortcake Band-Aid boxes dropped on her feet. Looking down, Sophia pointed to the area where the bandage on her leg was covered by her pants, a wound from her injection site.

"More?" the toddler asked.

The pediatrician mentioned Band-Aids could cure a lot in this age group. Keelyn placed two boxes in her basket. "How did you know those were on my list?"

She gathered the remaining boxes and stood to restock them on the shelf. From her peripheral vision, she saw a woman hovering a few feet away. The same woman who seemed to be in several other aisles Keelyn had shopped in.

Her suspicion overtook her wariness. "Can I help you?" Keelyn asked.

"Is your name Keelyn?"

Keelyn bent over and picked Sophia up. Searching the woman's face, she tried to recall if they'd ever crossed paths before. But then again, an acquaintance would know Keelyn's name and not have to ask it.

"Yes."

The woman took a few tentative steps in her direction. Keelyn huddled Sophia closer.

"A man leaving the store said you dropped this."

She held out the brown-paper, lunch-size sack. The bottom hung heavy. Keelyn's name was printed on the front with thick, heavy black marker. A smiley face folded into the top.

Keelyn reached forward. "What did he look like?"

"Older. Brown hair. Brown eyes."

Keelyn peered around her to the front of the store. "How long ago?"

"Maybe five minutes."

Keelyn pulled the staples free and looked inside. A small white tub with green lettering sat at the bottom. Reaching into the bag, she hoped it didn't cover up something else. Was she grabbing for something that would blow her hand up or poke her finger with a contaminated needle full of HIV? She pulled the item out.

Diaper cream.

"He said you'd definitely need it for the baby's rash. That you'd dropped it out of the diaper bag."

"How would he know what it was if it fell out of my bag and was stapled closed?"

"All I can say is he seemed to be in a hurry. Like he didn't have time to try and find you in the store."

Keelyn stepped toward the woman. "Are you sure you don't know this man? Was it Raven who sent you?"

The woman began to back away. "Now that you have it, I'll be on my way."

"Are you sure you don't know him?"

The woman turned.

"Wait. Please." Keelyn reached into her purse to dig out Lucent's picture when her phone signaled. She grabbed it. A text that her prescription was ready. When she looked back up the woman was already out the front doors of the pharmacy.

She blew the stray hairs from her eyes.

Why was Raven taunting her like this? Why didn't she just talk?

After checking out, Keelyn secured Sophia in her car seat, then consulted her list for her next stop. Just a few blocks from the drugstore. In the seat next to her were several printed flyers of the man who'd approached her in the diner.

She called Lee again. No answer.

Seemed like a lot of his responses were silence these days. Heaviness grappled with her spirit.

The drive to the church was short. Keelyn stood in front of the building, balancing Sophia on her hip, diaper bag dangling from the other shoulder. After triple-checking the address, she shoved it in the diaper bag, beside one of the Bibles from Raven's garage, and made her way through the front door.

She'd hoped Lee would accompany her on these errands. When they touched base before Sophia's scheduled pediatrician's appointment, he'd claimed other plans but didn't volunteer what they were.

Why couldn't he tell her what he was doing? Or was Lee just avoiding becoming part of Sophia's life?

Yet here she was, trading secret for secret. Was a lie of omission still a lie? She knew Lee and Nathan had planned to stop and talk to the minister. But Lee was off, and she knew Nathan wouldn't let her tag along. Perhaps the minister would be more forthcoming with information to a concerned sister over a snooping detective, anyway.

She entered the door. The hall carpet was red and threadbare. A thick, musty odor hung heavy. Sophia squirmed to get down.

"Just a few minutes, sweetheart." Keelyn rummaged through the diaper bag and eased a pacifier into the child's mouth.

She entered an office on her left. The receptionist's desk sat empty. As she leaned over to grab a pen and notepad, a deep voice from behind startled her, and she nearly dropped Sophia. Her loosened grasp caused the toddler to slide a few inches down her side. She clenched her arm tighter around the child, squeezing a few inches into the puffed coat before she felt she wouldn't drop her. She turned around with Sophia dangling. A tall, muscular black man stood a few steps away, his hands up in silent surrender.

"Sorry, didn't mean to scare you. Don't get many people passing through on a Friday since the office is generally closed."

He was dressed casually in jeans and a sweater. His eyes so dark she couldn't differentiate between iris and pupil. Small craters pocked his cheeks. The scars gave him a rough edge even though his voice was low and smooth.

Keelyn hoisted Sophia back up. "I should have set up an appointment." She extended her hand. "Keelyn Blake."

He gripped it tightly. "Russell Atkins."

"The minister?"

"You could call me that. Most just call me Russ."

"Do you happen to know a woman by the name of Raven Samuals?"

Darkness passed over his face as his curious expression changed to one of reserved expectation. "What's your relation?"

"I'm her sister."

His eyes cinched with the finest hint of suspicion. "She said her family was dead."

Keelyn's strength seeped from her knees. Sophia pushed hard against Keelyn's chest and swung her feet wildly. She bent to put her on the floor but kept hold of her hand. "Is there someplace we could talk?"

If Sophia had not been with her, Keelyn doubted she would have gotten much further with this man. His forehead creased; his eyebrows drew closer in thought. "Let's go to one of the Sunday school classrooms. It will give the child something to do."

After settling Sophia with a few puzzles, they sat at a nearby table on pint-sized seats. Keelyn reached into the diaper bag and pulled out the Bible from Raven's garage. She opened the front cover.

"This is how I found you."

Russ picked at a corner of the sticker with his nail. "What can I do for you?"

"Raven is missing. I'm trying to locate her."

"What makes you think I can help?"

"I thought you might have had some sort of relationship with her, since I found several boxes of Bibles in her garage with these stickers in them. Possibly you had a reason for them being there?"

He thumped his fingers against the chipped Formica tabletop. "How can I be sure you're related?"

Keelyn closed the Bible and pulled it toward her.

Why did this man act so guarded?

"You can't. You can only take my word. Who else would come looking for her?"

The man ran his thumb over the engorged veins in his hand, shoving out the blood and watching them fill. Slowly . . . methodically.

An odd pacifying behavior Keelyn hadn't seen before.

He stopped and rested his hand loosely over his upper arm. "I met Raven about two years ago. She came to me, asking to do some outreach ministry. We have several groups serving the homeless in downtown Denver."

Sophia toddled over and laid a wooden puzzle piece in Keelyn's hand. "Bunny!"

She handed the piece back. "Find me an

ostrich?"

"I don't think there is one of those," Russ said.

"That's the point."

Now he rested his arm on the table and fidgeted in the toddler chair, unable to find a comfortable position physically or mentally. Was what he knew about Raven that unsettling? "I asked her why she was interested. She said she felt alone and thought by serving others, she could ease this isolation she felt. Is it true that your father killed your family?"

A tremor shook Keelyn's legs and matched the butterflies flinging themselves against her stomach. She leaned her elbows onto her thighs. "Yes, half of them died. My mother and two siblings."

"Were you there when this happened?"

Another wooden puzzle piece set on the table. "Birdie?"

Keelyn slid the piece back to the young girl. "Yes, you're right. Find a bigger one." Keelyn tickled at Sophia's belly and sent her scurrying off, her laughter light in the dark room. Through the blinds, Keelyn could see it start to snow.

"It's just you have the same look in your eyes as she did. A weariness. Like you're always being tracked by something."

"Something evil?" Keelyn asked.

The minister tilted his head to his left shoulder — a thoughtful consideration of her question. "She was so young. Considering her story, I told her to start coming to church and sit in with the women's Bible study. Usually, a request like that will wash out people who aren't very serious about serving. It's hard to train up people, then have them walk out in a week. Working with the homeless isn't an easy task."

"Did she do as you asked?"

"Following direction was never Raven's problem. A couple of weeks after starting the study, one of the women approached me, concerned about some of the things Raven was sharing with the group. Wondered if she might need professional help."

"What did she share?"

"Issues of depression. Having nightmares. She alluded to having hallucinations, but when flat-out asked, she denied it. Claimed she always felt like someone was following her."

"What did you do?"

"I pulled her aside. Told her it might be in her best interest to see a doctor."

"And you found out she already was."

"I don't know which was more disturbing. That she was getting help or that she seemed to be worsening under that help."

"What did you do at that point?"

"Since she was already seeing a psychiatrist, I figured we could offer her additional stability. Bring her into the fold as they say. Show her true Christian fellowship."

"Get her involved in some groups?"

"She continued to push to get involved in outreach ministry. At first, Raven seemed up to the task. Showed up for meetings. Got the training. Donated a bunch of money to buy those Bibles and pass them out on the streets. Most people aren't all that comfortable visiting what they consider to be castoffs from society. Even though those castoffs are people."

Keelyn glanced behind her. Sophia remained busy with her puzzles. "It didn't bother Raven?"

"Honestly, she seemed to revel in it. Delight in hearing their stories of how far they'd fallen."

He covered his face with his hands then slowly released his eyes from the veil of his fingertips. "Then, it became obvious she was pregnant."

"Do you know who the father is?"

He shook his head. "Some of the women tried. She was pretty closed off when the topic came up. We just felt that meant she needed us more." He broke off as if collecting his thoughts.

Keelyn couldn't take the silence. "Do you think she . . . *believed*?"

A subtle shake of his head in the negative.

He opened his eyes. "Raven was very good at the mechanics, the intellectual component of Christ's message. She could quote the Bible like a seminary student. Unfortunately, her evangelism came across like she was reading a phone book. There was no depth, no feeling. I would dare to say possibly she didn't truly understand God's grace. Of course, only the Lord ultimately knows if her conversion was real."

"Did you ask her to stop witnessing?"

"I took Raven aside and expressed my concern. Tried to get at her heart. See if there was an emotional connection with the relational value of being a Christian."

Sophia came alongside Keelyn, her arms raised high. Keelyn scooped her up onto her lap. "And?"

"There was nothing substantial there. Initially, all I got was a vacant look in response. Then there was indignation that I questioned her salvation. Ultimately, it's not my place to determine whether or not another person has a genuine relationship with Jesus Christ."

"So she stayed on the streets?"

"The only change I insisted on was that she have a partner with her. Someone who was good at explaining God's love . . . his sacrifice. The relational aspect." He inhaled deeply. "That's what never came through when she shared. God's essential character of love. It seemed beyond her understanding."

"Was it better after that?"

"For a short time, the setup seemed to work. The downside was that it was hard to get people to volunteer to go with her. There was something about her that made them uneasy."

"Like what?"

"A vibe is the best way I can explain it. Sometimes Raven liked to focus on what we would call the downside of Christianity. Some would call that particular evangelistic approach 'selling fire insurance.' Talking too much about the devil and his work. To her fellow volunteers it felt like she even glorified Satan's power."

Keelyn's stomach knotted. "These possible hallucinations you mentioned before. Did she claim they were of an individual?"

The man's pulse thumped at the side of his neck. "To one young woman, she called

210

him Lucent. To me, she never said anything."

The pain in Keelyn's belly intensified. "Was there an end to your connection with her, or was my bringing the news of her missing a surprise?"

"There was a falling-out of sorts."

"What happened?"

Pastor Atkins leaned back in his chair. The plastic creaked under his weight. Even Sophia stopped at the eerie noise in the almost-vacant room. "Things were always DEFCON 4 with Raven. She had the baby and seemed to be just holding it together. Several of us thought maybe she should spend more time with the baby."

"There seems to be more."

He tapped his fists on his knees. "Raven was working pretty hard with two individuals on the streets. She always sought them out. One day, one of them turns up dead. Police come by here and question the staff because several of this individual's street buddies talked about members of our church being with him. Then the police mention this other young man has gone missing."

"Did you know these two men?"

"I would accompany the group once in a while. I'd know a first name, if it was a first name, and face. That's all you're likely to get."

"Was the death of this man suspicious?"

"Not necessarily. But it did strike me that the police seemed to be paying particularly close attention to it."

"Why do you think they were?"

"There were some reports on the street he'd gotten a bad mix of drugs. A woman was seen with him a few hours before he became symptomatic and ultimately died."

"Did this woman resemble Raven?"

"Nothing conclusive. Some yes. Some no. Nothing consistent took hold."

"What did Raven do after that?"

"After the police spoke with her, she didn't come around anymore. That was a couple months ago."

Keelyn shifted Sophia back to the floor and pulled the diaper bag closer. She rifled around until she pulled the computer image of Lucent free from one of the inner pockets. Opening it, she smoothed the creases, sliding it over the tabletop toward Russell. He leaned ever so slightly away from it.

"Do you recognize this man?"

"Where did you get that picture?"

"It's a computer-generated photo. It's my rendition of a man who approached me in a diner, threatened my life, and possibly murdered a couple people."

He tapped his finger over the image. "This is CW. The man who's been reported missing from the streets. One of the men they asked Raven about."

CHAPTER 17

Every eye followed Lee as he made his way to the chief's office. He felt as if he'd just been sent to the principal. He tried to smile and wave like nothing was amiss, but the probing eyes gave off tense vibes as he placed his hand on the metal knob. He held steady for a few seconds, gave two quick knocks, then heard a muffled "Come in" from the other side.

As he opened the door, he saw Nathan standing off to the side. Not good.

"Have a seat, Lee," the chief ordered.

Lee held his tie close to his chest as he rounded the chair. He kept his legs steady only with concentrated effort. It felt like his bones had liquefied. Nathan's eyes locked on him.

"I've been trying to get ahold of you for several hours," Anson said, opening a manila folder on his desk. "Want to explain why you're ignoring your pages?"

The chief was well respected and known to take a hard line at times when his underlings began to drift off course.

Now Lee seemed to be one of those strays.

"It's my day off. I was running errands. Didn't have my pager on."

Anson settled one hand over his other wrist, almost clenching it. Lee wondered what Keelyn might say about the postural change. Now he wished he'd listened to more of her musings about body language.

"That's not like you, Lee. You're still head of SWAT."

"I'm not functioning with SWAT right now. That was part of the deal. To try and give Holmes a chance to lead the team. So there'd be more than just me at that level."

"I'm pulling you off Lucy Freeman's case."

Surprise flowed through his mind. "Why? Is this because of Nathan?"

Lee refused to turn and look at Nathan. It might give Nathan the satisfaction of seeing the betrayal Lee felt in his gut. Of course, did betrayal occur between enemies? Or was that just the nature of the relationship?

"Actually, Nathan was not involved with this decision. I brought him in so we'd all be on the same page."

Anson sorted through a few papers on his

215

desk and pulled a report, stood up, and leaned to give it to Lee.

A ballistics report.

"Is this supposed to mean something to me?"

"You should read through that before coming back at me with some wisecrack."

Lee scanned the page, which detailed the information on the gun found at Ruby's Diner. The weapon was a match to the slugs found in Dr. Freeman's body.

Lee snapped the sheet with his fingers and laid it back on the chief's desk. "Great. We know for sure the gun found at the scene was the one involved in the crime. Should make the prosecution team happy once we find a suspect."

"Perhaps you should read through the report more closely. Bottom paragraph."

Lee pulled the report again. As he read it slowly, word for word, he began to understand the contemptuous look on Nathan's face, the subtle anger seething from the chief.

His chest caved. "It's not possible."

"The only reason I'm not suspending you is because you reported this gun stolen from your residence three years ago. That saves you from immediate suspension and an internal affairs investigation."

Lee's heart hammered in his chest as sweat leached from the tips of his fingers, soaking into the paper now clenched between the vise of his thumb and forefinger.

Anson stood, the wheels of his chair squeaking as he pushed it against the wall. It tipped, almost fell over as it came off the wood slab designed to protect the carpet. He sat on his desk, hovering over Lee.

Lee tried not to cower. With the threat of his secret becoming exposed, it was all he could do to keep his mind focused. Something Keelyn said came to the forefront.

A suspect can only hide so much. Part of your brain is always awake. Always working. Always telling the truth.

"Lee."

Nathan's voice. Lee focused his attention back to the chief. Nathan's voice softened. "I'm not assuming you're involved in the crime, but I need to know who may have stolen that weapon. Let's just say you weren't exactly forthright in your initial report."

Lee's vision flared red. "That's because I didn't know who took it."

Nathan stepped forward. "Wasn't your brother living with you at the time?"

"Yes."

"You don't think he's a viable suspect,

considering his difficulties? His drug habit? His other warrants for petty theft? The shoplifting —"

"All right, I know how it seems. But Conner would never do anything like that to me."

Anson knocked at his desktop like a judge tapped a gavel, drawing Lee's attention away from Nathan's inquisitive stare. "Lee, your brother has always been a blind spot for you." Anson's voice was quiet and as gentle as Lee had ever heard. "You've been to drug house after drug house. Criminals have no honor. It doesn't matter who they're related to. They'll steal from anyone. Including a brother."

"It's always the ones closest to them they'll hurt the most," Nathan ventured. Lee purposefully quieted his hands and looked steadily into Nathan's eyes. Lee saw compassion but knew Nathan was a top-notch interrogator and the look was likely an act — he was playing good cop.

"Has Conner been in touch with you?" Anson asked.

"No, I haven't seen or heard from him in a long time. I don't even know when the last time was."

"Are you trying to look for him?" The tone in Nathan's voice made Lee wonder if Drew

218

had given him up.

"No, I'm not trying to look for him."

A partial truth was still accurate, right? He could probably pass the lie detector, as he'd done before, if asked that same question.

"If Conner has any contact with you —"

"Listen," Lee said, putting his hand up. "You're assuming a lot at this point. You're assuming he stole the weapon, has held onto it for a couple of years, and now has used it in the murder of a psychiatrist he has no known tie to. Even a prosecutor is going to find this a very thin case. Are his fingerprints on the weapon?"

"There is a set on the weapon. Fingerprinting is a little backed up right now."

"Is this Nathan's theory?" Without glancing behind him, Lee felt the heat of Nathan's gaze.

Anson crossed his arms. "I'm not saying there's not more work to be done. But in light of the current circumstances, I've instructed Nathan to go full tilt on finding Conner. The sooner we clear him, the better it will be for you. For now, I will let you resume your duties with SWAT. In fact, there's a current call Holmes could use your help on."

"I'm not scheduled to work today."

"Consider it my way of keeping you out of trouble." He pointed a finger. "Keep your nose out of Nathan's case."

Lee stood and turned on his heel. The five short steps seemed like a mile. He exited the door like a diver breaching the water's surface for a sharp intake of breath. But relief from the pressure in the chief's office was momentary. Lee felt like he was drowning.

CHAPTER 18

The air condensed as the temperature dropped. Puffs of vapor spewed from Nathan's nose as water droplets formed at the tip. He took his ironed, folded hankie and cleared the drainage. The coming storm, and possibly a head cold, weren't the only things brewing.

Thoughts of his meeting with the chief and Lee churned like rain-deluged whitewater. Nathan knew about secrets. Knew keeping secrets could be deadly.

Lee was keeping a secret. Likely about his brother. Who would that secret be more costly to? Someone on the police force? Lee himself?

Keelyn?

Was Keelyn a potential casualty of what Lee was hiding? Nathan studied the old photo he'd snagged from Conner Watson's file then put it back in the inner pocket of his coat. There were some eerie similarities between Conner's photo and the mysterious Lucent. Definite differences, but still.

He noted the time as he leaned against the coarse brick of Gavin's office building and drummed his fingers against the stone. The psychiatric consultant he'd requested to accompany him on his visit had two minutes to arrive before he was late. The small movement of his twiddling appendages was not enough to dispense his eagerness, and he pushed away from the wall and pulled the warrant through his fingers as if he were sharpening a knife. They were authorizations for copies of full records of both John's and his daughter's psychiatric treatment.

The purpose of the consultant was to ensure the medical records were given in their entirety, so the suspect wouldn't surreptitiously hide a few sheets from the police. Nathan had worked with Dr. Derrick Vanhise before and was looking forward to his expertise on the Samuals cases.

A red Corvette pulled into the lot, a perfectly fine car, except under the common Colorado winter maladies of icy roads and flying snow. Though a fine clinician, Derrick liked to display the accoutrements of his success, and a red car against white snow definitely drew eyes.

Vanhise emerged from the car. The double beep indicated his car alarm was set. He was the picture of Ivy League elite. Average height, thin build, black hair with graying beard. All he needed was a pipe held in one hand to complete the picture.

That and maybe a suit.

The Hawaiian shirt, torn jeans, and Teva sandals didn't lend much to his credibility in light of the weather. However, his demeanor and dress fit the typical Boulder residential profile. An area of Colorado well known for its more liberal residents who liked to go against the grain. Even in cool weather, it wasn't unheard of to find some Coloradans dressed in shorts and tanks.

Nathan extended his hand. "You couldn't have dressed up to help me serve the warrant?"

His hand was warm and strong. "I love raising the ire of my most obsessive detective."

Nathan released his grip. "I don't know if Gavin will buy into the fact you're a much-sought-after expert witness."

They neared the building. "My dressing down will make him feel superior, and he might let something slip. From what you've told me so far, I get the sense he likes to operate outside normal psychiatric boundaries. He'll want to explain how current psychiatric practices are out of vogue. His and Lucy's setup is a conundrum in itself. It is very unusual these days to have two psychiatrists providing continued psycho-analysis in today's health care climate."

Nathan hit the button for the elevator. "Maybe they have a lot of Self-pay clients. Do you even own a suit?"

"One. For funerals."

Down the hall, a few quick turns, and they were at the receptionist's desk. Nathan had planned to be there five minutes before the top of the hour to limit Gavin's excuses for delaying their ultimatum.

"We need to see Dr. Donnely."

"He's about to see his next patient."

Nathan tapped the papers on the counter. "He'll want to see us." He leaned down to whisper. "Unless you'd like me to announce loudly to this gentleman here he's being served with a warrant."

Her eyebrows lifted. "For murder? I thought he was gone a little too long for lunch of Monday."

Nathan eased back. These utterances could be very telling. Nothing had been mentioned about an *arrest* warrant. Sounded like he'd have to bring her down for questioning. He pulled a card from his pocket. "I would like to speak with you later. What time do you get off work?"

She pulled the card from his fingers and tucked it into her leopard-print purse. "Four o'clock."

"Meet me at the station after work. I'd like to ask you a few questions."

There wasn't a distinct affirmation of his request, but he could see the heavy sense of civic responsibility on her face.

Or perhaps worry over working for a murderous leach.

"I'll get Dr.Donnely for you."

Moments later, Gavin made his way down the hall, escorting them into his office. In the two days since Nathan's last visit, Donnely's physical appearance had deteriorated. The once metro-chic male looked barely above bum status. His clothing appeared wrinkled and unkempt. Oil caked his hair into stiff rows like crops for harvest. Coarse facial hair was matted and patchy. Instead of sliding smoothly, his eyes ricocheted.

A classic sign of being under the influence.

He sat heavily behind his desk. "What brings you here today, Detective?"

His words were clear. Either there was another reason for the nystagmus or he was

225

a professional drinker on the downslide.

"I'd like to introduce you to Dr. Vanhise. He's a psychiatrist who does some consulting work for the police department."

"You still haven't answered my first question — the purpose of your being here today?"

Nathan stepped up to the desk. "We have a warrant for evidence. I'll need copies of the medical records for John Samuals and his daughter Raven."

Donnely looked off-kilter, as if a seizure was getting ready to ensue.

"I'm not releasing those. That's a violation of doctor-patient confidentiality, and Samuals is a federal prisoner."

Nathan stepped behind the desk and tucked himself up against Donnely's chair, his invasion of Gavin's personal space intentional to establish dominance over his whiny objections. "Doctor, being a federal prisoner doesn't have any effect over the control of his medical records or the validity of the warrant."

"Why are you aiding John Samuals?" The room stilled at the rise of his voice. Donnely huddled himself into the chair.

Nathan crossed his arms. "We're not helping him. We're trying to find Dr. Freeman's murderer."

"But how can these medical records possibly help?"

"Someone is using the name Lucent and causing trouble. As you're aware, this name is significant."

"I don't see how their medical records could be of any help."

"What surprises me is that you're not anxious for us to find out who murdered your partner. What if you're the next target? Or are you trying to hide something?"

Donnely stood from his desk and pointed a finger in Nathan's face. "I'm only trying to protect my patient. John Samuals is not the man he pretends to be."

Nathan could feel the tingly rise of adrenaline but maintained his position and placed a bored look on his face.

Gavin's statement seemed to perk Vanhise's interest. The man leaned back and crossed his legs. "From what I understand about the circumstances, you willingly got involved in Raven's care."

Donnely turned to face him. "Yes, for her. Imagine the trauma of living through those circumstances. Of being raised by a cold, calculating murderer."

"That's not exactly an unbiased opinion, is it?" Vanhise pulled at the torn shreds of his jeans.

Gavin crossed his arms tightly. "I only speak what I know to be true."

Vanhise kept his gaze on the man. "I mean professionally. It's well-documented in public sources that John was suffering under some pretty horrific hallucinations. That these directed him to do his murderous deeds."

"Are you aware his drug levels were normal at the time of his arrest?" Donnely asked.

Vanhise waved it off. "It doesn't mean those drugs were keeping the hallucinations quiet. Clearly, John Samuals is one of the few who committed murder as the direct result of a serious psychiatric disorder. The curious part is why the defense didn't use that fact to clear him. Why isn't he in a mental hospital?"

"I can't answer that. You'd have to ask his attorney."

"Do you have a personal vendetta against John Samuals?" Nathan asked.

"Of course not. Why would you ask?"

"Because you don't have any sympathy for his state of mind when he was clearly mentally ill."

"I was not directly involved in his case. My concern is only for Raven as my patient."

Nathan leaned closer. "Then help us help her. If we can understand more about her, maybe we could find her and return her to her child. Besides, I have a court order. Either way, I'm leaving with those files. So you can either turn them over voluntarily, or I can get a couple of officers over here to search for them. They tend not to be as neat as me."

Despite his words, Gavin seemed to acquiesce not out of concern for his patient but because he was backed into a legal corner. His eyes ticked between Nathan and Derrick. He took two steps away from Nathan and turned to a wooden file cabinet. He pulled out one thick file folder and handed it to Nathan. After giving it a cursory look, Nathan handed it to Vanhise.

"My secretary will make a copy for you on your way out."

"Where's John's file?" Nathan asked.

"John was Lucy's patient. I'll have my receptionist look in her office."

"This appears to be in order." Vanhise slapped the pages closed.

No further records were garnered from Dr. Freeman's office. Nor did they find the doctor's journal Mrs. Freeman had mentioned. As the receptionist handed them Raven's copied file, she looked at Nathan like an orphaned puppy needing a home. He motioned to her with his hand formed into a phone to his ear. She nodded in return.

Nathan and Vanhise stopped at a nearby Starbucks. Nathan wanted some cursory thoughts.

They'd been sipping coffee, Vanhise flipping slowly through pages, as Nathan watched the fog solidify into flakes.

"Find anything of interest?"

"The whole record is intriguing. I'm just not sure what to make of it yet."

"Does he have notes about his use of hypnosis? The investigation thus far has shown this was a point of contention between him and Dr. Freeman. She wasn't a fan."

Vanhise flipped through several pages. "Yes, he has several sections about hypnosis sessions."

"What's your take on hypnosis as therapy?"

He set the folder aside. "Honestly, clinically, it can be helpful. But I think its use is limited. It's been shown to be effective for things like weight loss and smoking cessation. A girl suffering from depression and hallucinations is an entirely different ball of wax. In that situation, I can't see how it would be helpful. It's definitely not on the list of evidence-based modalities."

"Why do you think he was using it?"

"At this point, I don't know."

"What's your guess?"

"I don't even have a good one." He twirled the cup on the table. "You know memory is not infallible. What we believe about something can be highly suggestible to outside influences."

"Like eyewitness testimony."

"Exactly. I'm sure you've been in situations where you've done a lineup and the victim would have bet his last dollar that the man he identified committed the crime. Then some other evidence comes forth that conclusively clears that person."

"Yes, I've seen it happen." Nathan took a swig of his own caffeinated pick-me-up.

"The issue with hypnosis is that it puts the mind into a suggestible state and what comes out may not be the truth."

"A false memory."

"I read a biography once of a woman who was a journalist. She was doing a lot of stories about sexual abuse. I think that saturation of information, the things she was writing about, caused her to overanalyze very innocent things in her own family."

"Doesn't sound like it has a happy outcome."

"She ended up accusing her father of molestation. Later, through a series of events, she determined these were false memories. Her relationship with her father never fully healed."

"Do you think someone could use hypnosis to attempt something detrimental to the patient?"

Vanhise shuffled through a few more notes. "Like what?"

Nathan tipped his cup back and forth. "I don't know. These weird theories pop up in my mind. Sometimes they don't hold much water."

"I don't think you'd have the reputation you do if you didn't think outside the box."

"Did you find it strange . . . his concern that we were helping John?"

"Many people find helping convicted criminals distasteful."

"True, he had the same face I see sometimes with families when a criminal goes free on some technicality. Yet why would he visit John in prison if he found the idea of helping him so loathsome?"

"I agree that seems contradictory. Have Gavin's and John's paths crossed at some point in the past? If he truly doesn't like

John, why would he want to help his daughter?"

"Sometimes the best revenge is not killing a person but psychologically torturing them."

"And how would he do that?"

"By tormenting his already troubled daughter." Nathan stood from the table. "Take a good look at that file, Derrick. I think I need to start looking into Dr. Donnely's past."

CHAPTER 19

Lee exited the roof access of the building that sat across the street from the bank. Despite the chill in the air, Lee's body temperature rose in his SWAT uniform. The weight of the vest usually comforted his psyche, but today it felt wholly constricting and he wanted to peel it off and toss it over the side of the roof. He had trouble discerning if it was his anger or his consternation that caused the increased heat. Sweat pooled at his armpits and at the small of his back. He swiped at a trickle that slid down the side of his face.

Holmes had assigned him to be a spotter for the roof sniper, whose world consisted only of what he could see through the scope, leaving him vulnerable to everything in the periphery. Lee would have the advantage of seeing the whole picture, backing up Holmes if needed.

Officer Ryan Zurcher was setting up his

rifle and scope. He was a lateral transfer from Lee's old department, one he was glad to have on board.

Another person he could talk with about that day, as Ryan had lived through it with him as well.

Unfortunately, Ryan's transfer was under duress. His parents were older and in poor health, and the drive from Colorado Springs became too arduous for him to keep up with their needs. As any good son would do, he moved close by them. Sometimes, Lee wished he could find an outlet for the constant stress the younger man was under.

Lee patted his shoulder. "Ryan, looks like you're stuck with me over the next several hours."

"Couldn't think of a better man."

Lee adjusted his vest and grabbed the binoculars. As the temperature dropped, an eerie fog gelled and hung low over the area in a thick haze. At the front of the bank, all the blinds were closed. The end of a weapon poked through the thin metal slats with a set of eyes next to it peering out to see what the police were up to. Gray sweeps of hair curled in front of one eye.

The Granny Gang was what the press had dubbed them for dressing in oversized floral dresses complete with drooping bosoms and wrinkled, elderly masks. This was their first visit to Aurora.

"Looks like today will be the end of their run." Ryan set the scope on the roof and settled on his abdomen. Suddenly, he turned on his side and gasped in pain, as if he'd settled on something sharp.

Lee kneeled next to him. "You okay?"

The younger officer wiped the sweat from his brow. "Yeah, just some weird belly pain."

Even though SWAT uniforms trapped heat, the amount of sweat that poured from Ryan's face was unusual.

"Are you sick?"

"I had an interesting night."

Lee heard a command crack through his earpiece. "SWAT Two, do you have line of sight inside the bank?"

Lee stood and double-checked the hostage taker's position. No change. "SWAT One, that's negative. Getting sniper into position." Lee turned back to Ryan. "What happened last night?"

"Met a girl."

"Yeah?"

Ryan chambered a round. "She was into some strange things."

"You didn't do anything you'll regret, did you?"

The officer shook his head and leaned

back into the scope. "Wish it would have been more fun for me. I have horrible allergies. Took a dose of allergy medication and was dead to the world. When I woke up, she was MIA."

Lee settled next to him and took another view. Things had escalated inside the bank. One window now had an open view inside, the blinds askew, the cords swung wildly as if someone had pulled them and been yanked back from their position. He could see one of the gunmen shouting. He had a woman pulled up against his body, his arm clenched tight around her neck, the barrel of the gun at her temple.

Violence from a distance, without the sound or feel of the energy from those on the ground was like watching a silent movie.

"Got a lock?" Lee asked.

No response. Lee looked down. Ryan used the back of his hand to mop up the sweat with his glove. The end of the rifle shook, unsteady.

Before Lee could suggest Ryan set the weapon down, the young man convulsed, his finger jerked against the trigger. The unexpected, explosive concussion of the high-power rifle stunned Lee's senses. The instantaneous noise of the bank window shattered by the supersonic round sounded like it was coming from a room down a distant hallway. From that same distant place, Lee could hear Holmes's voice in a controlled rage.

"Who fired! Who fired!"

Lee keyed his mike. "SWAT One, accidental discharge. I say again, accidental discharge."

"Hit now! Hit now!"

There was a series of concussive booms as flash-bang grenades went off inside the bank and fellow officers rushed in.

Ryan's screams nearly drowned out Holmes's voice in his earpiece. Lee crouched to the roof. "Ryan!"

The man had rolled away from Lee, the rifle tight in his arms. Lee belly crawled to his position. A chunk of ice fell from the sky.

Great, hail.

"Ryan? Can you hear me?" Lee latched a hand onto the man's arm to keep him from rolling, stopping him facedown, the rifle pinned under him. The man's howls echoed in Lee's memory like the wolf he'd once stumbled upon caught in an old steel trap.

He's dying.

"Just let me do all the work, buddy."

Lee seized Ryan's right hand, ensuring control of his trigger finger, and pulled it straight off the rifle. Then, he placed his free hand under the sniper's armpit and carefully rolled him off the weapon.

"I'm going to move this, Ryan, just relax." Lee eased the weapon from his hands.

The man clutched his belly, writhing like a worm caught on a fishhook. Lee wanted to clasp his hand over Ryan's mouth to drown out his violent shrieking. More shots sounded from the bank. Chunks of ice danced on the roof. Lee shielded the man's face with his body.

"Ryan, you've got to tell me what's going on."

Ryan only screamed through gritted teeth. Keeping a steady hand on Ryan's shoulder, Lee peeked over the roof's ledge. Two men were facedown on the sidewalk, their arms cuffed behind their backs, guarded by two officers with weapons trained at the ready. Ex-hostages were grouped to one side. Several officers had notebooks flipped open, taking statements.

Holmes came over the radio. "SWAT Two, send SWAT Seven to the command post immediately. I need you to remain in place and secure your position as a crime scene."

"Command, this is SWAT Two, stand by. We have a problem up here. Come to my location."

Ryan grabbed at his legs and began to roll side to side.

"Try to stay still. I need to secure your rifle."

Lee stood and took one large step away from Ryan. He activated the safety and opened the bolt, locking it to the rear. The empty brass cartridge ejected into the air and Lee watched gravity work in slow motion as the brass spun end over end, the familiar *tink-tink* an exclamation point to Lee's current thought.

Hell in a hand basket was an understatement for this day.

Lee released and let the magazine slide out into his palm and placed the weapon on the roof with the bolt open and the empty chamber visible. He placed the magazine by the butt of the weapon so it would be obvious to upcoming officers that the rifle was clear and safe. He picked up the spent brass and laid it next to the rifle.

Returning to Ryan, Lee worked to undo his vest. The color drained from Ryan's face, as sweat continued to pour from every conceivable pore.

"Ryan, did you take something?"

He flung his head side to side. "Make it stop! I can't take the pain!"

At first, Lee thought Ryan was seizing. All

his posterior muscles pulled taut and yanked his back to an arched position to the point only his head and heels touched the ground. Ryan's eyes widened and a scream peeled from his lips louder than the hail falling around them.

Then he went limp and fell against Lee, his lips silent and slack.

His eyes rolled back into his head. His breathing slowed.

"Officer down! I repeat, officer down! I need a medic team on the roof."

CHAPTER 20

Lilly Reeves waited just inside the trauma bay for the ambulance to arrive. Night had fallen, and the eerie late afternoon autumn storm infused a slow paralysis over the city. Colorado weather was known for its rapid changes, but this was beyond anything she experienced before. Fog, then hail, and now a blizzard.

It was the moment every police wife feared. The harried report of a fallen officer being transported to the ER.

Lilly took a deep breath in an attempt to steady her breathing. She hadn't heard from Nathan all afternoon . . . and what made it worse was that she was the receiving ER physician.

The sound of the wind deafened the approach of the sirens. The first hint of their arrival was odd white lines unhinged from any person, the reflective stripes of the EMS uniforms as they neared the well-lit trauma bay.

Within seconds, the glass doors parted, and the screams propelled Lilly from the wall. Then she recognized Lee in front of the medical team. She found herself staring but unable to move farther.

"Is it Nathan?" She desperately needed to know and didn't want to know at the same time.

Lee shook his head. "SWAT call."

Lilly felt weak with relief. As the gurney passed, she placed her hand on the young man's chest; his muscles were rigid, his skin soaked.

The SWAT medic began his report as they turned into the trauma bay. "Ryan Zurcher, twenty-eight-year-old male with complaints of severe generalized muscle pain, chest and abdominal pain. Blood pressure 170/100. Heart rate 140. Respirations 32. Patient is pale and diaphoretic. No known injury."

He was transferred to the ER gurney. Several nurses began connecting the young officer to medical equipment. In her peripheral vision, Lilly could see his ECG tracing appear on his bedside monitor. The normal buzz of the blood pressure cuff cycling barely registered above her patient's screaming.

She saw Lee hovering in the corner, his

large frame pushed in as far as he could wedge it.

"Lee, what happened out there?"

His eyes were wide, his lips quiet.

"What did he tell you before he became sick?"

He stepped toward her. "Lilly, there was nothing. He began to complain about his stomach hurting. Then it just . . . cascaded quickly into what you see. The pain . . . it's just intense. It's worse than anyone I ever saw who's been shot."

"Did he take something? A drug? Contact with a poison?"

"I asked him. He denied it."

Lilly turned back to her patient. It was as if his skin was on fire and his body was using his cooling mechanism to drench it. To stick his monitor patches in place, the nurses had dried off his chest.

It was already slick with sweat again. The nurse dropped the rag and quickly bent to retrieve it. The officer's screams were unbearable, and Lilly could see her nurses were on edge. Rarely did they drop things or seem clumsy.

This was different.

Lilly herself fought the urge to pull her head into her shoulders at the young man's death throes.

Emergency personnel were used to seeing patients in pain, and they could easily differentiate types of pain. The drug seeker wanting a narcotic fix. Pain from fractures. Ischemic pain as the heart protested a lack of oxygen from clogged arteries.

Zurcher's pain was an ear-splitting brew of torment. Hopelessness that they couldn't stop what was happening.

"Ashley, start him on high-flow O2. Let's get an IV in."

Her mind filed through several diagnoses, none of which fit his clinical picture. What could possibly cause such intense, whole-body, muscular contraction? High blood pressure? Diaphoresis to the point he sweated off every piece of tape they placed on his skin?

One thing she knew through every worried eye looking her way was she needed to show direction.

A game plan.

Now.

"Denise, let's run a twelve-lead ECG. Cindy, let's get these labs. Blood counts, complete metabolic panel, inflammatory markers. Let's check his cardiac enzymes. Grab a blood culture."

When the answer wasn't clear, a broad attack was necessary. Some equated it with

245

throwing noodles at the wall to see what stuck. Hopefully, something would pop up and give a clue as to what was killing the patient.

Normally, it wasn't such a shot in the dark.

"He's not even thirty," one of the nurses commented.

Lilly pulled her bottom lip between her teeth. "It won't be the first heart attack we've seen in a young man. Next, I want him in radiology. Let's get a CT of his chest and abdomen."

She turned back to Lee. "Does he have family?"

"Yes, but they're not exactly mobile."

"I need someone to go get them. Send a car."

"Is he . . . ?"

It was the unasked question friends and family dreaded but found hard to verbalize. Death. The angel that waited for every person at some point. Yet people were often blasé about their thoughts of God and what that belief meant for them in the end.

Denial as a safety mechanism.

"I don't know. I need more history. Maybe they'll know something."

Lee exited the room. She could see him framed by the window. It wasn't unusual to have a number of officers at the hospital if one was injured. Considering this seemed more medically related, Lilly wondered why they continued to hover.

"I've got the labs," Cindy stated. "What are we going to do for his pain?"

"Let's try Valium, two milligrams, and fentanyl, one hundred micrograms, IV and see what it does. Any word on CT?"

"They just called. Should be ten minutes. They had a stat from intensive care that pushed him back."

"Here's the twelve-lead."

She took the pink-and-white-graphed paper in her hands.

The cardiac waves looked normal. It was fast, but anything could cause simple tachycardia. Pain, anxiety.

Check. Check.

"What was his temperature?"

"Mildly elevated. One hundred point two."

Not high enough to affect his heart rate.

He didn't show classic signs of a heart attack. Theory one down the drain, although more definitive data would come from the blood work.

The cluster of painful areas could fit a dissecting aortic aneurysm, where the layers of the large artery began to split apart. She listened with her stethoscope again to his abdomen, checking for the classic bruit, a harsh sound like a murmur, which would indicate turbulent blood flow.

Silent.

She continued to assess for this condition. Feet normal color. Good pulses at his ankles. He didn't seem to have any of the other risk factors other than he was male.

Normally, this would be more likely in men over fifty.

Lilly slid her tongue on the inside of her cheek. His symptomology didn't fit anything originating from a medical disease in her mind. It had to be something toxic. Either ingested or given.

Her mind flipped through several toxidromes, classic groupings of signs and symptoms indicative of a particular poison.

The young man didn't fit any of those groupings either. Though not a classic presentation, Lilly sensed it was an avenue worthy to explore.

His illness wasn't contrived.

"Ladies. I want his clothes stripped off. We're going to place a catheter and send a urine drug screen. I want to look over his skin and see if there're any odd markings. Track marks. Bite marks."

"Human?"

A faint smile tugged at Lilly's lips. Dark humor was the ER staff's way of releasing stress. Few others understood its use when someone was suffering. Lilly knew this man's case hit an instinctual reflex in all of them that something was beyond the norm. Something they needed to find.

"I was thinking more six-legged," Lilly quipped.

The silver blades of trauma shears flew. No one could undress a man faster than a team of ER nurses. Within minutes, the tube was placed, he was placed in a gown, then covered with a thin white sheet. Already pockets of sweat darkened circular areas.

Lilly stepped next to the bed. First, she picked up an arm and checked the surfaces nestled against the covers. She ruffled her fingernails through the coarse hair of his forearms, looking for hidden needle marks. Methodically, she looked at the other arm. Turned his head side to side, she examined closely for anything out of the ordinary.

Nothing.

"Let's turn him up on his side."

After the pain medication, his screams had quieted to whimpers.

Two nurses laid gentle hands on the man's body and pulled him away from her. The medications she'd given thus far made little difference in easing his muscular contractions.

She placed two fingers along his spinal column, feeling the tips of the vertebrae. Not really expecting to find injury but thinking with each sense her fingertips communicated. "Let's repeat the Valium. He'll need to be still for the CT."

When Lilly edged his gown aside near his iliac crest, she found what she was looking for. It was a marking, but not like anything she'd ever seen.

An hourglass had been sliced into his skin near his left flank. Eight small wounds, possibly injection sites, hovered around the hourglass like orbiting moons. The skin was blanched around the tiny, reddened dots. Red streaks groped away from the hourglass into untouched skin.

An infected tattoo?

Lee entered the room and neared her side. She glanced his way while pointing, directing his attention to the marking.

"Any idea what this might be?" Lilly asked.

A slow crawl of recognition hinted of something in his eyes.

"What?" Lilly pressed.

Lee cracked his knuckles. "He mentioned an interesting date."

"Anything specific? Did they take something?"

"He made it sound like he faded out. Took some allergy medication and fell asleep. In the morning, she was gone."

"Did he say for sure the pills he took were his?"

"You think she might have given him something?"

Lilly shrugged as the possibility crossed her mind. "Something to knock him out enough to do this? If a man can do it, why not a woman?"

She motioned to her team to ease him back. When his skin made contact with the bed, he screamed as if they laid him on a shallow pool of lit gasoline.

Whatever those marks were, it could be a source of infection. A source of whatever was ailing this young man. Even sepsis didn't quite fit his clinical picture.

"CT called. They're ready."

The nurse repeated the pain med. The young man had his arms clasped into his chest, shivering through clenched teeth. His lips bled from where he'd bitten into them.

"Let's get him over there."

CHAPTER 21

The snow swirled around Keelyn's entryway as she struggled with holding Sophia and getting her keys in the lock. Sophia began to cry, matching the sound of the howling wind in her ears. Just as she reached to turn the knob, the door released in front of her. A small gasp escaped her lips before she realized Lee's frame filled the doorway. He took Sophia from her arms and pulled her up into the foyer. The wind whistled through the narrowing crack as he eased the door closed. With his free hand, he pulled her into a tight hug and nestled his face against her cheek. Her mind hazed at the scent of his woodsy cologne; the warmth of his skin against hers tingled her nerves.

A moment she wanted to hold onto forever. Happy. Sweet. Peaceful.

"Didn't you see my truck on the street?"

She frowned and pulled away, knowing any answer she gave would raise his hackles.

Keelyn was never as observant as Lee wanted her to be, which infuriated him, considering her chosen profession. Focused observation was her specialty. The periphery was a different skill.

"I'm sorry. With the snow, Sophia crying —"

"Don't you test the knob to see if it's locked before coming in?"

Carrying Sophia, Lee walked to the kitchen table and sat. Sophia danced briefly before she sank into his muscled arms and snuggled her face into his neck. Lee nudged at a pile of disks with his finger. "Why are all these DVDs from Boulder police here?"

"Do you remember the woman in the park?"

"The one with the missing children?"

"Yes. Well, they're not so sure Rebecca's not involved. They've asked me to review some recordings and help with her interview tomorrow afternoon." Keelyn eased her coat off her shoulders. She could see the worried cracks harden his face as he rocked the child side to side. "Do you want to talk about it?"

The news had been heavy about the bank incident throughout the evening. Lilly had texted her when she knew the officer's identity, knowing Lee would be tied up with the sickened officer and the subsequent internal affairs interview.

He shrugged haplessly. "It wasn't the best day."

"Why were you even at the incident? I thought you were working with Nathan on Freeman's murder and when you figured that out we'd know where Raven might be."

"I got pulled off the case."

Her mind whirled with suspicion. What was the reason? This would be an unusual move for the chief unless something extraordinary was going on. Lee was a well-respected officer with several commendations.

Did this have something to do with what she felt he was hiding from her?

Keelyn sank into the chair opposite him. In the center of the small farm table was a wicker basket with several toys. She pulled it toward her. Her heart swelled at the thought that Lee had taken time to shop for Sophia. Maybe he was beginning to see a life with all of them together.

"It seems a weapon I reported stolen about three years ago is the same gun used to kill Dr. Lucy Freeman."

The happiness fleeted as dark shadows of uncertainty clouded her mood.

"How is that possible?"

He shook his head and resettled Sophia,

cradling her like an infant. "I wish I knew."

"Who stole the gun?"

"I don't know."

"Meaning you won't say who the most likely suspect is."

Lee busied himself tracing his finger over Sophia's cheek, his deep blue eyes downcast. His jaw tensed, and he closed his eyes. The wave of tension set Keelyn's heart rate higher. Finally, he turned to her. "There's something I've never told you about my brother."

"What is it?"

Why did it pain him so much to disclose this information to her? Should there be any secrets between two people pledged to be married?

Lee traced lightly over Sophia's closed eyes. "Conner has a drug problem. He lived with me for a while, but things got pretty rough between us and I kicked him out. To you, I'll admit, Conner probably took the gun, but that's a far stretch from saying he murdered someone. Maybe two people."

Keelyn's gut was heavy with his revelation. He'd lied about his relationship with his brother and that utopian relationship had given her additional guilt about Raven. She put her shaking hands under her legs and turned back to Lee. She wanted to question him for more information, but he had physically turned his body away from hers, his shoulder now in direct line with her chest, a nonverbal shout of his mind closing down this topic of discussion.

How far could she push him? "What's your theory, then?"

"That he took it and sold it for either drugs or money for drugs. It's not unusual for stolen weapons to cross through several people."

"What's Nathan think?"

"Nathan and I aren't on the same page. Conner is his number one suspect at this point, and the chief is on board. He wants to keep any complaints about conflict of interest at bay." He bent and placed a light kiss on Sophia's wispy dark curls. "But enough about my miserable day. How was yours?"

She pulled the wooden mallet for the xylophone from its holder and clapped it against the rainbow-colored metal. The metal notes caused Sophia to lift one eye open and she clenched the mallet in her fist.

"I went to the church identified in the Bibles we found at Raven's home. I spoke to the minister."

Lee's head snapped up in surprise. "You went there without Nathan?"

Keelyn nodded without looking up from the wicker basket.

"Find out anything?"

"It's hard to know where to start."

"The beginning is always best."

"The minister, Russell Atkins, had a mentoring relationship with Raven. He was very concerned about her."

"About her mental stability?"

"That and more. He said she was having trouble with depression. Claimed to another member of the church she was having hallucinations. Called him Lucent." She fingered through the toys in the basket. The wind knocked at the closed windows. "She worked with a group of people who did outreach ministry with the homeless."

"Sounds like she was doing very honorable work."

"One of these homeless individuals she was evangelizing turned up dead. Another one is missing. Someone who goes by CW."

Lee pointed one of his feet in the direction of her front door. A classic sign for wanting to end the current interaction and leave. In a normal interview, she would dive into the subject matter immediately preceeding that indicator as the individual showed an area of agitation.

His voice was a pitch higher than his

normal resonance. "CW?"

She softened her voice. "Do you know who this person might be?"

Lee shook his head yes but responded, "No idea."

Directional conflict. Just like the bank guard. "You're sure."

"Yes, absolutely."

"You seem stressed out."

"Just thinking about Ryan." He leaned toward her to surrender Sophia.

Keelyn took the sleeping child into her arms and settled her upright, fingering the stray curls of her hair. "Is there something you're not telling me?"

"He was there."

"What do you mean?"

"Ryan was one of the entry team. Pulled your father out of the house."

"And you're concerned now because that's two suspicious circumstances sur-rounding men who were there that day."

"Yes, one dead and one ill."

"But you don't know what's wrong with Ryan. It could be totally unrelated."

Lee massaged his thumb into his opposite palm. "I don't think what's happening to Ryan is all that benign."

"Why?"

"Lilly found marks on him. They looked

fresh. An hourglass surrounded by these points."

A chill washed over Keelyn. She turned to see if the front door had opened. It remained closed. "Like a star?"

Lee considered her question. "Could be. Why do you ask?"

"Because Lucent wore a ring like that. An hourglass in front of an eight-pointed star."

Lee stood up. "Why didn't you tell me before?"

Keelyn looked up at him. "Honestly, I didn't think it mattered what kind of weird jewelry he was wearing."

"I need to make some phone calls. I'm going to call El Paso and Teller County to get run sheets of everyone who was there that day. Check on their welfare. See if they've seen this young woman."

"You think there's something to what Russell Atkins is saying?"

"I don't know. It seems thin. All I know is Ryan had a date last night he called 'interesting.' He's sick the next day. Your sister might have been involved in these other cases."

Keelyn swallowed hard. "How would she have ever met Ryan?"

He leaned forward. "Maybe she pursued him. She's the common denominator at this point. She was there the day your father —"

"Stepfather."

"Whatever — goes haywire. Two men have come upon some unfortunate circumstances. Now, the church where she was doing mission work has another two men, one dead, one missing. I'm saying we can't overlook this aspect as a possible explanation."

"You're willing to string my sister —"

"Half sister —"

"Up as a killer, yet you have no thoughts about this concerning Conner?"

He exhaled sharply. He eased her up from her chair and wrapped his arms around her, careful not to startle Sophia. "I don't want to fight. It's probably nothing. I'm just stressed out, like you said."

Keelyn backed out of his arms and offered a gentle smile. "Okay. I know it's been a long day. For both of us. I'd offer to make you dinner, but I need to get Sophia settled. Why don't you head home and get some sleep? By the way, thank you for all the toys. That was very sweet of you."

"What are you talking about?"

Keelyn motioned to the basket of toys on the table. "These. When did you have time to get them?"

"Keelyn, I didn't bring those for Sophia."

Her stomach and heart collided. She began to step back from the table. Lee reached for her.

"What is it?" he asked, his hand firm on her arm to steady her shaking.

"If you didn't bring them, then someone else has been in here. Someone broke in and left them. Was the door unlocked when you got here?"

Lee rushed forward, grabbed her jacket from the chair where it had been tossed, and loosely wrapped it around her and Sophia. He hurried her to the door.

She pushed back against his chest. "What are you doing?"

"I'm going to search your house."

"Lee, it's freezing outside."

"It won't take me long. Go to the neighbor's house. I'll find you."

Out on the front step, the wind howled as it blew around the house. She put the coat on backward to shield Sophia from the cold and glanced right and left. Both homes were dark. The child slept heavily and barely stirred so she settled against the door to wait.

What is happening? Who is leaving all these strange gifts for Sophia?

Common sense would suggest it was Raven, concerned for her care, possibly using them as a way to reach out to Keelyn. Did she not know she could just show herself and stop these silly games? Something prevented her from doing just that. What could it be?

The door gave way behind Keelyn. Unable to get her footing, she began to fall into the doorway until Lee's sure hands caught her from behind and helped her stand.

"All clear."

"Find anything?"

"Is she still sleeping?"

He eased the coat off her arms. Sophia let out a contented sigh.

"I'll put her to bed."

"Good. I can make those phone calls. Bring down a couple of blankets. I'm staying here tonight."

Keelyn took the stairs one heavy step at a time. The volunteer at the shelter had given Sophia dinner, a snack, and dressed her in her polar bear footie pajamas. After tucking her in, Keelyn kissed her forehead. With two blankets in her arms, she returned to the living room. Lee had the fireplace on and some tea on the table.

"Let's get you warmed up."

Keelyn sat beside him. Lee pulled her into his side and wrapped his steely muscles around her shoulders. With the blanket unfurled, he covered her legs and handed her the hot mug. She held it under her nose, the scent of cinnamon and vanilla with sweet cream quieted her mind.

These were the moments with Lee she relished. Feeling cared for and safe. As she settled beside him, his muscles relaxed and he played his fingers through her hair, easing out the windblown tangles. A hint of his cologne, like a low fire in pine trees, brought back memories of past camping trips huddled in a tent in the woods as they would watch the stars move slowly above the open flap.

She wanted this every day and twirled the promise around her fourth finger.

"I'm glad you'll be here."

He pulled her closer. "Me too. I did find something."

"What was it?"

"A note in the bottom of the basket."

"Are you going to tell me what it said?"

He pressed his lips onto the top of her head. "I don't know what I'd do if anything happened to you."

Darkness clouded her mood. And Sophia?

He eased back. "It said, 'Someone you perceive as a friend is really your enemy.' "

The blackness squeezed tighter. "Maybe

they read Shakespeare like you do."

"Veiled threats should not be taken lightly."

As she sipped, Keelyn's tea scorched her tongue like she imagined the hemlock burned Juliet's throat when she drank in the despair of her lover she thought dead.

Lee flipped on the TV and began to channel surf.

Keelyn gripped his knee as a news piece with Rebecca and her husband flashed on the screen. "Go back. Channel 7."

Rebecca was standing next to her husband. She was almost a full head shorter than he. During the interview, the husband kept admonishing the press and police for considering that his wife could be a suspect in the disappearance of their two children. His support was clear and unwavering. Rebecca looked only at the camera or down. Never up at her husband. Never nodded her head in agreement to his statements that she wasn't involved.

"If I had to place my bets, I think she's done something to those children."

Keelyn nodded. "Yes, she's definitely hiding something."

CHAPTER 22

The snow had stopped, and the dim lights of the parking structure gave patchy comfort as Nathan jogged across the lot into the hospital's foyer. Word of the fallen officer had spread through the framework of the police department. He was peripherally aware of Ryan's circumstances and, because of his relationship with the attending physician, the chief had asked Nathan to go to the hospital to check things out. Possibly he could even offer some assistance to the parents.

Question Lilly for inside info.

After making the rounds with the other officers who milled around the waiting area, entered the ICU and neared Ryan's room. Lilly stood at the bedside in discussion with another physician.

Lilly motioned him in. Mrs. Zurcher was confined to a wheelchair. Her hair thin, muscles wasted, her color sallow. As a teaching note for his work with the public, he remembered Lilly saying that a yellow tinge to the skin often meant liver failure and he should be aware of this among those who possibly imbibed special spirits on a regular basis — though Mrs. Zurcher didn't strike him as having a problem with the bottle and there were likely dozens of issues that could cause jaundice. Did that explain the rash of bruises that spotted her skin? Her weakness? Could she slide right out of her chair?

Mr. Zurcher seemed marginally better. At least he could stand, though he leaned heavily on his cane. Nathan placed a comforting hand on the old man's shoulder.

"I'm so sorry about Ryan." He eyed Lilly. "Do we know anything yet?"

The old man dropped his head lower. "Don't understand much of what's going on."

Lilly stepped nearer to the couple. "Is it all right if I discuss Ryan's case in front of Detective Long?"

"If you think it can help."

"Maybe. There's something that might interest him."

Nathan eyed her conspiratorially. They walked to the head of the bed. Ryan had a tube plugged into every orifice and Nathan cringed at the thought of what was unseen.

A tube in his mouth connected to a ventilator. One snaked into his nose that sucked thick, green bile from his stomach. Chest leads monitored his heart. A lit probe on one finger measured his oxygen level.

Lilly had been a good teacher about these things.

"What's wrong with him?" Nathan asked.

"Did you talk with Lee at all?"

Nathan unbuttoned his coat, eased it off, and tossed it to a nearby chair. "Lee's probably not in the mood to talk with me."

"Aren't you working together?"

"He's off the case."

"What? Why?"

"I'll tell you later. Let's get this young man's situation figured out. You heard about the accidental discharge?"

"On the news, but the details are fuzzy."

"The chief is very interested in finding out a cause that's not negligence. What's wrong with him?"

Lilly glanced at the Zurchers, who seemed entranced by *Wheel of Fortune*. She lowered her voice. "No one really knows."

"How is that possible?"

"It's not a clear picture medically. He presented with intense pain, sweating, and a fast heart rate. Nothing really showed up on any of his labs. His scans were clean.

Surgery was so baffled, even in light of the negative scans, they took him to the OR to look inside his belly."

"I thought CT could find anything."

"Not always. Sometimes certain organs are harder to see than others. His appendix wasn't visualized, and his abdomen was painful and rigid. Surgery thought, in light of those results and his excruciating pain, that it at least warranted a look."

"But nothing?"

"No."

"Then what?"

"I want to show you this. I'm going to turn him on his side."

Lilly pulled the sheet off his body. He was dressed in a thin, pale blue gown. After she placed a hand on his shoulder and hip, she eased him up onto his right side. "I need you to slide his gown up."

"Lilly —"

"Come on. There's a good reason. I'm holding him and watching all these tubes."

Nathan eyed the hall. No one seemed turned his way. All he needed was endless razzing about him undressing another man. He lifted his nose as he eased the fabric up.

An hourglass shape had been carved into his skin. Small red dots orbited the marks.

"It looks infected."

268

Lilly eased Ryan down and draped the sheet back in place. "Maybe."

"Could it be why he's sick?"

"His symptoms don't fit the clinical picture of blood-borne sepsis very well. Cultures won't be back for a couple of days."

Nathan shrugged it off. "It's not unusual for these guys to do some type of unique branding. Maybe it's a SWAT thing. They're essentially paramilitary. Did you ask Lee about it?"

"Yes."

"And?"

"Nathan, you're usually very intuitive about these things."

He ruffled his hands through his brown hair. She was right. He was far from thinking clearly. Exhaustion had put his neurons to sleep.

"Help me with this one."

"The autopsy you went to?" The lilt in her voice a friendly tug to his memory.

"Yes."

"You mentioned an odd rash the ME found."

"She didn't know what it was."

"Remember how many dots there were?"

"I didn't want to appear to be lingering."

Lilly rolled her eyes at him. "There were eight dots. That's what you told me."

269

"Okay, so they both have eight dots of unknown origin. What am I supposed to put together?"

"I don't know. That's why you're the detective. But don't you think it's odd that two officers who were involved with the John Samuals hostage situation have fallen under peculiar circumstances and on their bodies is a collection of eight puncture-type wounds? One is dead from an unknown illness, and the other is sick and we don't know why."

Nathan felt the fatigue of the day drain his last bit of energy. "I don't remember him being there. Did Lee tell you that?"

"No."

"Then how do you know?"

Lilly motioned to the nearly comatose couple. Mr. Zurcher had taken a seat and fallen asleep against his wife. Her wheelchair gave her enough height to rest her head on top of his. A weird vision of a totem pole popped into Nathan's mind.

"Ryan's parents are very proud of his accomplishments. They talked about the highlights of his career thus far. About how Ryan was one of the men who entered the Samuals home to save those children."

"So now I have a murdered psychiatrist, one dead officer — reason unknown. I have an ill officer — reason unknown. This young man has a body marking possibly similar to the dead officer. And I have a missing woman. All were involved in that one hostage event."

"Don't forget the hallucination that materialized and visited Keelyn."

"Yeah, there's that, too."

"What are you going to do?"

Nathan slid his toe over the linoleum. "I'm going to have to go back. I don't want to go back."

"Maybe through this, you'll forgive yourself for what happened."

"How can I when people are still dying?"

CHAPTER 23

Saturday

Keelyn sat with Sophia at the base of her bay window, tracing patterns in the condensation fogging the small sectioned panes. Then Sophia found great joy in furiously wiping through the design with her index finger. Her belly laugh pulled back the shadowed gloom, and Keelyn found it hard to resist a smile as she nuzzled her face in her niece's neck and took in the lingering sweet scent of her lavender body wash.

"Heart?" She placed her pudgy hands on Keelyn's cheeks and pushed her mouth into pucker position.

Keelyn spoke through the fish-lips. "You want me to draw a heart?"

This sent Sophia into a spasmed frenzy and she threw her head back as squeals of laughter overtook her. Keelyn gave her exposed tummy a raspberry, and Sophia rolled away from her. Righting herself, she plopped back onto Keelyn's lap.

"Help?"

Keelyn placed her hand over her niece's, extended her index finger over the small child's, and drew a heart. Small drips formed at the edges of the picture, and despite Sophia's exuberance, the sentiment echoed what she felt in her own heart.

Sadness.

She'd hoped Lee would stop by today, but he claimed he needed to go to Ryan's apartment to pick up some things for the family. Did that need to take all day? There was something he wasn't sharing, something big he was keeping from her. Then again, maybe it was her fault their pasts were such a blank canvas. Why dredge up such unhappiness? Lee had basically said the same thing, so their troubled pasts generally were left untouched in conversation. It had been enough to know they loved one another and wanted to build a solid, happy, fruitful life together.

Now, what had been buried, kept quiet, seemed to trail them, until the secrets were beginning to suffocate what they had built, weakening their foundation.

She snuggled Sophia. "Want to watch a movie?"

She wiggled off her lap. "Blocks?"

Keelyn patted her bottom in the direction of the small play area. "OK, sweet girl. You play over there, and I'm going to watch TV."

She waited for Sophia to get settled as she loaded one of the DVDs sent to her from the Boulder police. She sat still, the remote poised in her hand but the television still off.

These moments of complete silence were now rare.

In about one hour, Mrs. Linwood would be by to watch Sophia so Keelyn could continue her search for the enigma otherwise known as Lucent. Until then, she was going to immerse herself in Rebecca Hanson's home movies to prepare for the interview.

She could feel the difficulties in her life beginning to overwhelm her.

Caring for a child, Raven missing, Lucent's unknown whereabouts, and the string of odd events kept her up at night. Add the murdered psychiatrist, the sickened officer, Lee getting booted off the case that could have been the answer to Raven's whereabouts . . . it was all beginning to be too much.

The anticipation of helping with a highly visual case and what it could do for her company had set her heart into an elevated rhythm for days. She needed this. The income would not only pay her bills, but might be required to support a child for the long term. She couldn't quiet her mind at night, and all of that, combined with little sleep, caused her to doubt the wisdom of the cup of coffee she grabbed from the table.

She closed her eyes to settle her stomach.

One step at a time. Lord, give me wisdom. This is what I can do for now. Help me focus and see the things I need to see to help these children be found alive.

Keelyn waded through the known facts of the case. The day Rebecca had gone missing, her husband stated that when he came home from work around four o'clock in the afternoon, she and the children weren't home. School let out at three o'clock, and she normally would walk halfway to meet them.

Why halfway?

Keelyn thought back to the husband's police interview she had also viewed. In response to that question, his hands were settled in his lap. His feet firm on the floor, facing the detective, not the door. He was still and calm. He'd stated that Sadie and Bryce expressed a desire to exert some independence and walk themselves to school. Rebecca agreed to meet them in the

275

middle as a compromise of sorts.

"When did that start?"

"About one month ago, a few months after the start of the school year."

Finding the home empty did not initially concern the husband. It was Rebecca's practice, at times, to run a few errands with the children before dinner.

"Did she leave a note?"

"No."

"Did she usually?"

"Yes."

That was the first thing Keelyn clipped in her mind's eye. The first deviation from normal practice.

"How is your marriage?"

He smoothed his palms together. A pacifying gesture. "Good. We have our normal ups and downs."

"Any financial trouble?"

His hands paused. "In this economy, who isn't having money trouble?"

"Does Rebecca work?"

"No." He ran his fingers through his hair. "I guess that surrounds some of our issues. I had to take a thirty percent cut in pay to keep my job."

"How did she respond to that?"

He shrugged. "It doesn't really seem to bother her. She's still buying herself all she wants whenever she wants."

"So, you're going further into debt?"

He leaned back in his chair and eyed the detective squarely. "To be honest, I don't know where she's getting the money."

The husband's interview continued running through Keelyn's mind.

Dinnertime came and went, and the husband's anxiety concerning the situation increased. He'd called family, friends, and neighbors to ascertain her whereabouts. He'd walked the route to school and any alternative routes he could think of. After his calls and search came up empty, he'd called the police. Keelyn's sense from watching the husband was he was very forthright about what had happened.

Currently, Rebecca's story was not on solid ground, and public support of her was beginning to waver.

Problem one: Rebecca stated she was pulled into a van as she walked to get the children from school. That she'd been kept in a basement as a hostage until dropped off at the park. A woman who called herself Rebecca had called the shelter where Keelyn worked as a volunteer for intake, which is why Keelyn was there to meet her. The real Rebecca claimed otherwise.

Voice analysis suggested that Rebecca

Hanson was the one to call the shelter.

Problem two: Three women had come forward claiming they'd seen Rebecca meet up with the children in their usual spot but take an alternate turn away from their home. This stuck in one lady's mind because Rebecca was usually quite rigid in her dealings with the children, and she found it atypical that they'd be "walking a different way home."

Rebecca denied this ever happened. She claimed the women never liked her and were setting her up to take the fall for her missing children. To Keelyn, this seemed like a big stretch for a personal vendetta, setting someone up for potential criminal prosecution and jail time out of general dislike. Could PTA disagreements actually lead to someone framing another for a crime?

Problem three: The partial license plate number Keelyn provided to the police. Not enough information. The truck and the man had not been located. Keelyn couldn't provide a description of the man because of the ski mask he'd worn. All Rebecca would say was that he was the man who had grabbed her and held her prisoner. She stated he'd rarely talked to her, just provided food at times, until the day he'd dragged her to the park.

278

Keelyn cued the player. Voices from the home movie started, and Keelyn grabbed her pad to take notes. The first disk she'd plucked was the most recent. It was video of Bryce's ninth birthday party a few weeks ago in mid-October. Their backyard was a heavily treed lot and strung between the oaks were orange-colored pumpkin lights with large white lanterns hooked onto the string. One could easily mistake it for a basic Halloween party if not for the view of the birthday cake with a wax number candle denoting the child's age shoved in the center.

Keelyn stilled the frame and leaned forward to examine the cake more closely. All reports of Rebecca indicated she was a Martha Stewart wannabe. Friends of hers interviewed by the police commented on how well taken care of her home was, the children always had these overdone special parties that were the envy of working parents everywhere. One had a Candy Land theme where the children actually participated in the game with a ropes-and-ladder training course to simulate the ebb and flow of the game.

This cake was messy. The wax candle was half buried as if pushed down in anger.

Smothered.

Red gel letters — "Happy Birthday, Bryce" — bled into the white frosting. Keelyn grabbed a few photo albums that were stacked beside her. She flipped quickly through the pages until she found Bryce's eighth birthday party photos.

A medieval knight theme. The photos of the cake were meticulous in and of themselves. Shots from every angle. The detail on the castle was intricate. It looked covered in small, gray glass bricks.

Keelyn restarted the disk. Several adults were seated at a picnic table eating a barbecue-style dinner. A light breeze lapped at the edges of the classic red-and-white-checkered tablecloth. Rebecca sat on the end across the table from a gentleman Keelyn didn't know. Steven, the husband, sat at Rebecca's right. Keelyn was pleased with this positioning because she could easily see Rebecca's entire figure. Particularly from the waist down, the area that hadn't been taught from birth to lie.

Even though there was ample room to sit comfortably beside her husband on the bench, she was perched almost precariously on the edge, and leaned as far away from him as possible. Her upper body turned diagonally to block him. He would touch her arm, and she would pull away. Generally, the closer the arms were of couples, the more comfortable they felt about the relationship.

If Keelyn hadn't already known Rebecca and Steven were married, she would have guessed them to be strangers. And he clearly irritated her.

The curious thing was the gentleman who sat in front of her. When he spoke, she would lean in. She'd playfully twirl her necklace when she laughed at something he'd said. But it was her foot that gave the telltale signal of how she really felt about this stranger. Each time he spoke, her high-heeled silver shoe would playfully tip from the end of her toes. Movement draws attention, and she wanted this man to notice her. It was an orienting reflex. But when her husband leaned in, she would slap the shoe back on her heel.

Whoever this man was, he was the one she truly wanted to be with.

After another twenty minutes of this behavior, young Bryce came up to his mother as the adults were clearing the table. She leaned down to hear him speak over the milling voices of the partygoers. Rebecca then gave a half-hearted pat on his back, her smile icy at best.

Keelyn edged the scene back, paused it,

and forwarded it frame by frame.

Not an icy smile, a sneer.

Sneering was a clear sign of contempt. What Keelyn saw was not a loving mother. The impression Rebecca gave off was of a woman unhappy with her current situation. Could that mean something insidious for her children?

Keelyn pondered the idea. Filicide wasn't an unknown social deviation but it was rare compared to other social ills. Keelyn's heart ached for the missing children. She didn't want to believe their mother could be responsible for their demise.

Sophia began to bang the blocks together. Keelyn smiled at the sound of her innocent play. Something terrible must have happened to Raven. She would never leave Sophia.

Keelyn started the movie and turned up the volume. Adults were clearing the picnic table. Bryce was dancing around his mother like a kangaroo on stimulants, begging to open his presents. The gentleman approached her and said something. Rebecca shook her head and cupped her hand behind her ear.

He spoke louder, but quiet enough not to turn the heads of the other partygoers. "We have some unfinished business."

Rebecca smiled coyly.

Keelyn's heart stammered to a stop.

It was the same phrase the man had uttered when he threw Rebecca to the ground at the park.

CHAPTER 24

Saturday's weather and Friday's blizzard were a dichotomy. The early morning sun was bright. Water dripped from the bare bones of sleeping trees. Rivers of melted ice coursed their way to the city's underground. The old catch phrase of Colorado weather flashed in Lee's mind. "If you don't like today's weather, just wait until tomorrow." Though a day was usually considered too long to wait for a change. Most often it occurred in about an hour.

Lee parked his car in front of Ryan's small home that sat near the border of Aurora and Denver. It was what Keelyn would call a quaint cottage, not befitting a young man but definitely a home with a magnetizing effect on the opposite sex.

And likely the rent was cheap.

After he closed the door to his vehicle, he made his way up the wet pavement. He'd asked the Zurchers for a key under the guise of bringing some of Ryan's belongings to the hospital. He inserted it into the lock.

He didn't divulge he was searching for clues regarding a possible attempted murder.

The door opened, the squeaky hinges breaking the silence of the quiet day. Lee tapped his boots on the bottom of the door frame to clear muddied slush and stepped inside, easing the door closed behind him.

It smelled sweet, like someone had baked sugar cookies. Lee walked a few paces down the hall and eyed a small office to the left and an extra tiny dining room to the right. A few more steps brought him to the main living room. Things were in order with the underpinnings of dirt usually overlooked. A turn to the right brought him to the single bedroom.

The bed was black veneered wood. Walls painted a near-turquoise blue made the room feel like a cave. Lee opened the nightstand drawers. A few fiction books. Glasses. A remote for the television that hung on the opposite wall.

A small bathroom was off to the right side of the bed. He opened the mirrored medicine chest. Every pharmaceutical looked benign enough. Most were over-the-counter analgesics, cold and allergy medicine. One prescription bottle for steroids filled over two years ago. Lee opened the bottle and counted the pills. Only two missing.

No syringes or vials.

Lee made his way to the kitchen and grabbed a kitchen-sized trash bag. On the counter stood several glasses. He examined the rim of each one.

No lipstick prints mired the edges. He sniffed them. They smelled like sweet tea.

Returning to the bathroom, he grabbed Ryan's toothbrush and toothpaste. In the bedroom, he packed clean shorts and several pairs of sweats.

None of these items mattered if Ryan didn't recover.

It was more for the benefit of the parents.

What was lacking was any evidence a woman had visited. Was it intentional? Someone purposefully trying to hide her fingerprints?

The backup beep of a dump truck tapped at Lee's mind. His heart hammered as he raced out the front door to the street, the white bag slapping against the back of his legs as he ran. Trash pickup had been delayed one day due to the storm. It was possible that if someone had ill intentions toward Ryan, he or she had placed incriminating evidence in the trash.

Lee raced to the street waving his hands and yelling for the trash man to stop. Ryan's heavy green roadside bin was up in the air, when the arm ground to a halt. The man leaned out the window, his massive eyebrows pulled together.

"Lose something in there?"

Lee sighed heavily as the lie slipped out of his mouth. "Yeah, I think I threw away my wallet along with the bathroom trash. Just go ahead and leave everything. I'll just put it out again next week."

The garbage man grinned. "Happens all the time. Just be glad you caught it now instead of after I'd dumped it."

Lee waved as the man drove off. Flipping the lid open, he saw one large black trash bag and a smaller white one. He put a finger through the loop of the smaller bag and lifted it out.

He set the bag on the ground and untied the knot.

IV equipment and several syringes.

He grabbed the bag and stood.

It wasn't likely he could get the police involved in Ryan's case at this point. After all, everything seemed to point to a medical malady. No one else seemed suspicious of foul play. And if this syringe contained some weird drug cocktail, he didn't want Ryan's name dragged through the mud before he could figure out what really happened. Going back to his friend's lab seemed the best solution. Of course, he didn't mind charging Lee a fee, a heavy one, for doing the work fast.

Unfortunately, Ryan's toothbrush was not going to make it to the hospital today. He'd need it to see if it matched any DNA on the syringe.

CHAPTER 25

Keelyn sat outside the interview room and peered at Rebecca Hanson through the two-way mirror. Keelyn's notepad rested on her lap, a stopwatch in her left hand. She leaned forward and clicked the top of the time-piece. For one minute, she counted certain mannerisms as the woman sat, her pale green eyes looking about her confined space. A curl of red hair circled around her index finger. Her children were missing and her facade was calm. Even being in a police interrogation room didn't faze her boredom. The detective framed this interview as simple inquiry and therefore she had not been read her rights. When they offered her a phone to call an attorney, she scooted it back across the table, emphatically stating she didn't have anything to hide.

We'll see.

Keelyn stopped after sixty seconds. Blink rate twelve times per minute. Gum chewed at a relaxed pace. These mannerisms were close to her baseline as observed in the multiple recordings Keelyn had watched of Rebecca's life. Rebecca was reclined in the chair, her head rested on the back. She swayed lazily side to side.

Louis Hernandez and Oliver Southway were the Boulder detectives charged with the interview. Louis would take lead inside the room. He busied himself with one final review of his notes; his olive-skinned index finger roved down the list of questions he wanted to ask. He adjusted his earpiece.

"Check?" Southway asked.

"Got you loud and clear."

Oliver brushed his long sandy hair from his gray-brown eyes. The color was akin to what Keelyn imagined the rough stone of British castles might look like. Had any of Oliver's relatives graced those ancient homes? Keelyn's eyes teased at sleep. Louis's Spanish accent coupled with Oliver's British one seemed odd for western America.

Though Boulder, Colorado, was known for its odd pairings.

"Are we ready?" Oliver asked.

Louis folded his notes. Keelyn stood and straightened his tie. Too late, she realized the gesture might be misconstrued. She backed up a step.

"Sorry. I can't seem to help myself these days since I've been taking care of my niece."

"No problem." He winked at her. "Always good to look your best for a murder suspect."

Keelyn smiled at his attempt to set her at ease. It would play well with Rebecca. "Remember, try to mimic her movements. It will make her more comfortable."

"I don't think she can get much more comfortable. She already looks like she might fall into a coma," Oliver noted as he made adjustments to the recording equipment.

"Won't that make me come across as feminine?" The cop machismo threatened.

"You want the truth, right? The best thing will be to convince her you think she's innocent until you're convinced it's a good time to push her to a confession. If she's really guilty."

"You think she's innocent?" Oliver eyed Keelyn evenly.

Keelyn scraped her teeth over her lip. "From watching hours of her life, I'd say she and her husband were definitely having trouble and maybe she wasn't thrilled with being a mother at times. But after being around a little one, I just find it hard to believe any mother could harm her children."

Louis snorted. "It's always the naive ones that fall the hardest." He entered the room. Rebecca stood. They shook hands briefly.

"What does he mean?" Keelyn asked.

"Parents are most often the ones who harm their children. It's a tough hurdle for law enforcement to get people to believe it. It's what makes prosecuting these cases so hard. No one wants to believe the one person on earth designed to give unconditional love would be the one to put a knife to a baby's throat and slit it."

Keelyn froze as the image stuck in her mind. Men had something in them, a violent streak. Not always actualized but genetically woven into their DNA. Could women be the same? A mother?

"He's starting."

Oliver turned on the intercom. Keelyn sat.

The first thirty minutes were about building rapport. Louis established how she and her husband met. When their children were born.

Rebecca rarely looked at the detective. She busied herself with picking lint off her clothes. At one point she reached into her purse to get her mirror and powdered her nose. She pulled off her glasses and rubbed them clean with her cotton shirt, examined the results in the light, and put them back in place using her middle finger to secure their position.

Though Rebecca likely didn't realize the micro gesture, Keelyn tilted in her chair at the sight.

"What is it?" Oliver asked.

"She has no respect for Louis at all. Self preening is dismissive behavior. You know what it means when someone displays the middle finger."

"Usually unhappiness."

"Well, she just did it to your partner when she put her glasses back on."

Keelyn stopped commenting at Louis's next question. "How did you feel the first time you held Sadie?"

During most of the interview, Rebecca had lazily swung her crossed right leg. Now it stilled. She interlaced her fingers and settled them on her lap. Blink rate up. Jaw muscles tight.

"What?" Rebecca asked.

"How did you feel when Sadie was born? The first time you held her in your arms. What was it like?"

She rolled her eyes at Louis. "What does that have to do with anything?"

"It's not a hard question, Mrs. Hanson. Most mothers can easily talk about these types of emotions."

"Look, everything wasn't hunky-dory when Sadie was born."

"Did you want the pregnancy?"

At that moment, Rebecca rested her hand over her sternal notch. A sign of discomfort. "Wanted? More my husband than me."

"You got pregnant for your husband's sake."

"Let's just say it was a failure of medication."

"So you didn't want Sadie."

"It's not a matter of wanting. I got pregnant. My husband wanted the child. I supported his decision and carried the pregnancy."

"Did you love her?"

"She wasn't the easiest baby. Cried a lot, especially at night. I couldn't even work because she wouldn't take a bottle for Steven. He'd call me at my job and beg me to come home."

Louis mirrored her position. "Must have been a terribly hard time."

"You. Have. No. Idea."

"But, did you love your daughter? Aren't you concerned about her whereabouts?"

The question hung in the air.

Oliver turned Keelyn's way. "See what I mean?"

Keelyn swallowed heavily. Rebecca was showing signs of discomfort but there was an underlying disdain surrounding the children. The sneer from the video supported this. Was it more with Rebecca than just feeling put out by her children's existence?

"What about Bryce?" Louis asked.

Another tense smile. "What about him?"

"Did you feel differently about him than you did about Sadie?"

"I was never really fond of the idea of having boys."

"But you didn't really love Sadie, either."

"I'm not sure I was made to be a mother." Rebecca crossed her arms in a self-imposed body hug and ran her hands up and down.

Keelyn's heart ached at the thought of those children as they grew up in a house with such open disdain. "Have him ask her about her photo albums, the videos. Who made them?"

"Why?"

"I don't know if I can explain it quickly . . . just have him ask for me."

A few moments passed as Oliver communicated the information.

"I noticed you kept a lot of photo albums

295

of the children. Was that your handiwork?"

"My mother is crazy about taking their pictures. She's the one who makes them."

"Satisfied?" Oliver asked Keelyn.

Keelyn closed her eyes against the thought. The one piece of evidence Keelyn held onto as proof of a loving mother fell to the wayside. What emotional connection did Rebecca show for her children? She looked back at Oliver. "Sadly, yes and no."

Detective Hernandez pulled a photograph out from his folder and slid it across the table. "Do you recognize this man?"

"Should I?" Rebecca hooked her ankles at the floor. This sudden interlocking a tell for discomfort.

"You don't know him?"

Rebecca raised one shoulder and left it there. "Doesn't look familiar."

"Is she lying?" Oliver asked.

"She's not committed to that answer. He needs to explore this further."

Oliver spoke into his mike and Louis passed a finger over his ear.

"Yes, but is it a lie?"

Keelyn swiveled her chair toward Oliver. "It's very difficult to pick up deception. I look for clusters of discomfort and pacifying behavior. Her blink rate is up, she's chewing her gum like a starved cow, and her palms ought to be chapped with as much as she's smoothing them over her legs."

"Interesting." Oliver's chair squeaked as he turned. "That's the photo of the chap at the picnic table from the birthday party. The one you pointed out uttered the same phrase when she was dropped off at the park."

Louis's tinned voice pulled her back to the interview. "We had someone review all those disks you gave us. Hours and hours she watched you. Want to know what she saw?"

"So now the police are into cheap parlor tricks?"

He thumbed his nose.

Careful, Louis.

"What she noticed is that you seem very comfortable with this man" — he pointed to the picture — "and not so comfortable with your husband."

"And how could she tell? I love my husband."

Louis fingered the picture. "As you sit next to him, you might as well be a stranger. Your body is turned away. Your arm is inches away from his. At one point, he brushes against you and you act as if you've been stung."

"So from this you conclude what?"

"What she also noticed was your attraction to this man." Louis pointed at the photo.

"He's an acquaintance."

Incongruent with her previous statement. She admitted knowledge whereas before she had denied knowing him.

"Well, what she noticed about this acquaintance of yours is that you're outright flirting with him."

Rebecca closed her eyes at the statement. "Really?"

Louis softened his voice and slowly twirled the photo on the table. "You lean into him. Playfully swing your shoe on your toes when you talk with him. Movement attracts attention. You want him to notice you."

"All that from a short video of a birthday party."

Hernandez curled his hand into a fist. "Who is this man, Rebecca?"

"I don't know his name. He's a friend of Steven's."

"That's funny. We asked your husband about this man, and he said he was a family friend but that you'd invited him to the party."

She pressed her lips together to the point of concealment. She smoothed her hands over her legs. "Of course he would say that."

"Why?"

"Because he's trying to insinuate I know something when actually I'm the victim. My children are victims."

"All I've seen is him defending you."

"In front of the cameras he's a different man."

"You seem relatively unconcerned about Bryce and Sadie. Most mothers will demand we do something to find their missing children. You've not asked me once what I'm doing to bring them home safely."

"What are you doing?"

Louis let the question fall unanswered, a swift dismissal of a hollow inquiry. "The woman who viewed your DVDs is the same woman you met at the park. Perhaps you don't remember her, but she says that the man who dropped you off said a phrase to her he also says in the birthday video."

Keelyn watched Rebecca's neck as she tried to surreptitiously swallow a lump in her throat.

"Can you explain that?" Louis pressed.

She leaned forward and buried her face in her hands.

"Who is this man, and where are your children, Rebecca?"

Rebecca looked up. There were no tears

in her eyes. An icy glaze settled on her face. "I want to talk to a lawyer."

"Are they dead?"

The smile that spread over Rebecca's face convinced Keelyn that what she first believed was no longer true. At that moment, she knew there was no hope for the children. Keelyn blinked away the vision of her bleeding siblings. It wasn't just fathers who killed their children; this mother had, too.

Chapter 26

The widow of Sheriff Benson would be available only during her knitting group. After the two-hour drive to get to the remote church in Teller County, Lee found the group of older women in a basement room, sitting at several tables. It was easy to spot her as she was the only African American woman there. He waved, and she motioned him to her seat.

Noreen Benson stood and enveloped Lee in a warm hug as she pulled his head down into her bosom like a grandmother to a grandson. He eased away, and her firm grip on his shoulder guided him into a rickety metal chair.

"Ladies, this here is Lee Watson. He was there that day when George was on that awful call where all those people died."

"Nice to meet you all." He turned to Noreen. "I was very sorry to hear about George."

"Thanks for the condolences." She motioned for him to set his arms wide and he complied. She tied a knot of bright pink yarn from the beginning of a skein to one thumb.

"I must say I miss George a lot for this very reason." After the knot was secure, she circled the yarn around his forearms. "So much easier to untangle yarn this way. He was a strong man and could stay in this position for hours."

The women nodded in agreement. Noreen motioned with her head. "That's Beatrice." The slight, older woman gave a friendly toodle-oo with her fingers. "And Gertrude."

"What brings you to our fine knitting group? We don't get many men in attendance," Beatrice asked, knitting with confetti-colored yarn in hues of blue and green. Only a few rows were completed, so Lee couldn't make out the final project.

"Actually, I wanted to talk to Noreen about George."

Gertrude clicked her tongue. "Such an awful thing that happened."

Noreen pushed Lee's arms to keep the yarn taught. He straightened in his seat. "What did happen, Noreen? I was shocked when I called and found out he'd died."

Beatrice shook her head, her eyes heavy

302

with sadness. Was she a widow as well? "So unexpected. He was strong as an ox."

"They make 'em strong in the South." Noreen began to wrap the yarn in quick fashion. Lee was surprised her shaky hands could be so accurate.

"Is that where you met?"

Noreen tilted her head toward Gertrude. "South Carolina."

"So he hadn't been sick?" Lee asked.

Her shoulders sagged. "I don't know if I can say that. He hadn't been physically ill. That call did something to him. Messed up his head. He retired from the department within the year."

"Did he do any other work?"

"He'd just sit there for hours on end, watching television. I got so tired of the history channel I wanted to throw up." She pushed Lee's arms up again.

"What did he die of?" Lee asked.

"They say a heart attack, but they never checked for sure."

"You mean an autopsy."

"Exactly. I sort of pushed for one but they said the evidence medically was clear that his heart sort of blew up. All this medical language about cardiac enzymes and trip levels." She motioned her hand in front of her face. "I don't even know if those are the right words."

"What made you want to ask for one if they seemed clear on his cause of death?"

Another gray-haired matron rounded the table with a tray of cookies. Lee's stomach grumbled a request at the sight. He gave a sheepish grin and tossed his hands up a few inches. She smiled back and laid several different varieties on the table and then ruffled her hand through his hair. These women definitely needed a few more visits from their grandchildren.

"Venus, you could at least get the man a napkin and show him we're not uncivilized." The woman obediently rearranged the cookies on top of a blue-and-white floral napkin.

There seemed to be a pecking order among the ladies.

Noreen continued. "Just something in my head said somethin' wasn't right. He'd had a physical about six months before he died. Even did one of those stress tests and whatnot, and they said he was the picture of good health."

"Did anything odd happen right before he died?"

Noreen tossed the paper skein cover into the trash and began to form a ball with the yarn, her tiny fingers blanched as she tightened her grip on the threads. "Like what?"

"Anything. A letter? A phone call? A strange visitor? Something that wasn't part of his watching TV all the time."

Her eyes drifted off as she wrapped, then zeroed right on his chest. "There was one thing."

"On the day he died?"

"Yes, he met with someone."

"Do you know who it was?"

"He was real secretive about giving full details. I was just happy he was finally getting off his rump and doing something."

"There was nothing he said," Lee clarified.

"He did say it was about that event. That he was meeting an old friend. Someone he could talk to, to clear his mind about it."

"Did he say whether it was a man or a woman?"

"He didn't specify who it was exactly, but I have a hunch as to who it was."

Gertrude patted Lee's knee. "Noreen's always one for the dramatics. Watches those murder shows all the time."

"*Dateline, 48 hours.* The Bio ID channel is her favorite."

"Ladies," Lee interrupted. "I'm interested in her theory."

"Do you remember the oldest girl who

survived? Not the one who was his step-daughter. The other one. Her real name was something you would never remember, but the hostage negotiator gave her a nickname — Raven."

Lee shifted uneasily in his seat. "Yes, I remember her."

"George became obsessed with her life. He would follow every news piece and TV story about her."

"And you think that's who he was going to meet?"

"Mm-hmm." Noreen nodded gravely.

"What makes you think they met?"

"There was something about him. Hard to put my finger on. It was the most emotional I'd seen him since he left the force."

"Happiness?" Lee asked.

"Expectation, I guess. But more than that. Sadness, fear . . ."

"Fear?"

"I don't know. Like I said . . . something I couldn't quite put a finger on."

"Do you think he went to ask for forgiveness?"

"Did he need to?" The look in her eyes tore at his heart. Sherriff Benson had done what he needed to do.

Lee inhaled deeply. "Mrs. Benson, I was there that day. There's nothing your husband did he should be ashamed of. He called in the experts. We're the ones who failed him."

She clucked her tongue. Her eyes glistened. "So dry here in this state, my eyes tear up all the time for no good reason. Should move back South." The ball of yarn grew larger in her hands. The last wisp fell from Lee's arms, and she pulled the knotted loop from his thumb. He leaned forward and drew her into an embrace as she began to weep.

CHAPTER 27

Sunday

Keelyn's boots sloshed through the melting snow. She was alternating placing Lucent's "wanted" poster and Raven's "missing" flyer on the telephone poles that lined the street. The muscles in her hand shook in fatigue as she squeezed the heavy-duty staple gun for the hundredth time. She pulled up onto her toes to ease the tension in the arches of her feet.

Her tired body began to match her drained spirit. Where was Lee? He wasn't even returning her phone calls. At least Mrs. Linwood was available to watch Sophia.

The sensation of being watched pulled at her subconscious, and she turned to look behind her. A man in a black leather jacket stood off in the distance and looked for something in the trash. Seemed a bit too well dressed for that.

She continued on to the next pole but

angled herself so she had a better view of the sidewalk from her peripheral vision. Next flier up, stabbed by the metal prongs into the wood. The man straightened and looked into the street. Keelyn walked to the next dead tree.

It wasn't unusual for Lee to be out of touch. Sometimes, SWAT assignments could carry over for a few days. But he wasn't with SWAT now. He'd had a few scheduled days off. Normally they would be together. And he had not returned one phone message.

She raised her arms and pierced the next piece of paper. The man had closed the gap by several feet and now leaned against a lime green Volkswagen Bug crusted with dirty snow.

A police officer doing foot patrol happened by her on the sidewalk. She signaled for him. As soon as he angled in her direction, the man behind her disappeared.

"Can I help you?"

Now what to say?

"Sorry to bother you. I just thought I saw someone following me, but he's gone now."

He glanced down the sidewalk behind her. "You know, this isn't the safest part of the city. Can I walk you back to your car?"

"No, I'll be fine. I need to finish hanging these."

"All right, but definitely get home before nightfall."

"I will. I promise."

"I don't want to see your face on one of these posters my next shift."

He bowed his head and continued on.

Keelyn walked another few steps and pulled more pictures from her tote. At the next pole, she had to pull down several advertisements for less than high end establishments to make room for Raven's picture. She fingered her lost sister's face. Black ink collected on the tip of her index finger.

Where are you? Did you leave Sophia on purpose? Are you even alive?

The next few steps brought her to the corner. Steam rose from the vented city underground. She unbuttoned the top end of her coat. To her right was an alley where several homeless individuals gathered, their hands held over a large metal canister for warmth. Black smoke curled from the cracked crevices.

What can it hurt?

She approached the group at a slow pace. Her hands held up in small surrender in front of her so it was obvious she wasn't carrying any weapons. The tote slid off her shoulder into the crook of her elbow. She reached in with the other hand and pulled out two fliers.

"Excuse me."

The first man angled away from her, his head tilted up as he poured heavy gulps of a cheap, rank alcohol into his throat. The street smelled thick of urine and feces. Keelyn covered her mouth and nose to quell the bile that rose from her stomach.

She inhaled deeply the scent of her fabric softener. It did little to replace the stench. A man approached her from the side. Startled, she jumped a step away from him.

"Doesn't look like you belong here."

A voice from the back of the group. "Hey, you don't need to treat a lady that way."

Keelyn squeezed her hand tight on the paper to stop it from shaking. "I'm sorry to disturb you. I just need a few of you to look at these photos." She pulled the pages apart and held them up like party favors. "Do you know either of these individuals?"

There was something there. It was quick. A hint of acknowledgment. His tongue worked a loose tooth in this lower jaw. "Sorry, can't help you."

Her shoulders dropped. "Are you sure?"

"Ain't safe for you here."

Someone tapped her shoulder. She turned.

An older white male was inches from her face. His gray hair hung in clumped, oily sections through the holes of his purple-and-once-white ski cap. The camel coat was several sizes too large and almost fell from his shoulders. He greeted her with a blackened smile of several missing teeth and his inflamed gums oozed white pus.

The people converged on her. Her mind tossed red warning flags at the invasion of her personal space and she started hyperventilating, feeling the telltale tingle in her extremeties. The muscles in Keelyn's thighs tightened in preparation for escape. She eased back a step.

"Let me see." His voice like stones scraped over glass. The odor of his breath a mixture of alcohol and cigarettes.

Keelyn raised her arms again. The papers rustled from the uncontrolled quivering in her hands. Her voice thin as she asked, "Do you know them?"

Unexpectedly, the man thrust his hand into the center of her chest and pushed her back into a brick wall. The sheets fell from her fingers and drifted in the breeze as her back slammed into brick. Her lungs seized, her breath gone. The loss of oxygen at the blow caused her vision to dim. Shouts of protest echoed throughout the group, but no one stepped forward to lend a hand.

"Why are you looking for them?"

She gulped. Tears streamed from her eyes. "She's my sister."

He leaned in. "They don't want to be found."

"Please," Keelyn pleaded, both for her sister and her own life.

A glint caught her eye. She turned her head. The bad side of a blade hovered by her neck. "What will you pay?"

She pressed herself further into the wall. "I have money . . ."

Then he was away from her. She blinked several times, clearing the haze. He was on the ground, another man on top of him, the hand with the knife held against the cement. He was yelling.

"Hector! I see you treat a woman like that again and I will come and kill you myself." He pulled the knife away, lifted himself off, and backed up. "Get outta here!"

The crowd drifted off. The man turned and all Keelyn could see was a kaleidoscope of tattooed skin. She recoiled, but he grabbed her by the arm and hustled her from the alley. They rounded the corner, and he propelled her into a local coffee shop. Finding a nearby table, he pulled at a chair and tossed her into it.

"What are you doing?" he yelled.

At first she withered, but then anger overtook her terror. She stood up. "Who are you?"

"Why are you down here without Lee? Are you trying to get yourself killed?"

She paused open-mouthed and clamped her teeth, accidentally biting the tip of her tongue. A salty, metallic taste filled her mouth. She swallowed to clear it. "What are you talking about?"

The tattoo man yanked her bag from the crook of her elbow and pulled out a small sheaf of papers. He snapped the sheets at her face so close that Lucent's image fuzzed in her vision. "These, Keelyn! Doesn't Lee think I can find his brother on my own?"

Brother?

A tremor overtook her stress-weakened legs, and she slumped back in the chair.

Lucent was Conner?

Lee knew Lucent was Conner?

Lee knew Lucent was Conner.

This is what he's been keeping from me.

The man looked at her quizzically, his breath quick in his chest. He set the papers on the table and sat down. He placed his hands over Keelyn's to still her trembling.

"Perhaps I should introduce myself. I'm Drew Stipman."

"I don't understand."

"I'm not sure what I should share since it seems Lee didn't tell you what he asked me to do."

"Please, tell me."

He shook his head. "This is really something you need to talk with Lee about. I've probably said too much as it is."

"Are you a private investigator?"

Drew inhaled and pulled his hands off hers. "Of sorts. Until my new life as a paramedic starts in a few months. Sometimes I help the police. Do you know Detective Nathan Long and his wife, Lilly?"

Keelyn pulled the sheets toward her in a daze. "Yes, I know who they are."

"I helped Nathan with Lilly's case. Since then, I assist the police in finding people who don't want to be found."

"You blend in well."

That brought a chuckle. "My gift, I guess." He leaned toward her. "Do you need a ride home?"

She tapped the picture. "Have you found him?"

"Keelyn, please. It's not right for me to say anything. I have a reputation to uphold."

She crumpled the papers back into her

tote and stood, shoving the chair into the table. "Thank you for saving my life."

He stood as well. "Keelyn — let me walk you to your car."

"I'm fine. It's just around the corner."

"Then I'll follow a safe distance behind. Lee would kill me if anything happened to you."

Those words were meaningless.

If Lee wanted her safe, why didn't he tell her his brother was the one who'd threatened it?

She gathered up her things, buttoned her coat, and tightened her scarf around her neck. It was hard to differentiate if it was the fabric or the plan brewing in her mind that lent to the constricted feeling.

"Fine."

She pushed through the door and stomped into the snow. Door chimes slammed against the glass as she exited. A few seconds later the jingled bells sounded again as Drew pushed through the door. Images of Christmas flashed through her mind. What would Christmas look like this year?

Concrete buildings, the boiled brew of sewer sludge venting from manhole covers, and the shredded souls that lined the sidewalk brought her back to reality. After she turned the corner and found her car, she unlocked the door and plopped into the driver's seat. After she threw her belongings onto the passenger's seat she slammed the door before another car ran into it.

In the side-view mirror, she could see Drew standing at the corner. Her hand stayed on the edge of the door's handle with her car keys in her palm. A curious standoff developed between them.

Drew settled his shoulder into the wall and picked at his teeth.

Moving the keys into her right hand, she inserted the car's key into the ignition. She pressed her foot into the gas pedal and turned the car over. Shifting from Park, she waited to let a car pass, then eased from the curb. In the mirror, Drew was gone.

Keelyn slammed the car back into Park, pulled her keys out, and exited the vehicle. As she neared the corner, she shuffled along the building and peered around the edge to check for Drew's location.

He was one block ahead, turning the corner to the right into the alley.

She ran to narrow the distance and eased up at the building's edge. Looking around the corner, she saw him disappear into a doorway three buildings down. As she stepped into the alley, the sky above her darkened and shadows spilled into the tight space as if the angel of death had come to hunt for victims. Street noise disappeared as the sound of her boots against the broken pavement echoed in her ears, her heart an anxious accompaniment to the pace. At the door, she laid her hand on the knob and opened it.

There was no one at the entry. The smell was a mixture of charred wood and human secretions. Keelyn covered her nose with her arm. Broken glass pipes with blackened bulbs littered the floor. She scooted an exposed needle to the edge of the floorboards. A staircase stood immediately to her left.

Soft, classical music played above her. The eerie sense of a haunted funeral parlor caused the hair on her arms to tug at her skin. She ascended the staircase, her hand gripping the sticky wood as she went, and she was thankful for the gloves that provided a barrier against the vermin living in the gooey substance.

A scream, so loud and sorrowful, washed over her in a concussive wave. She involuntarily backed down one step.

Again, a scream like nothing she'd ever heard.

Someone was killing Drew.

She looked around her. A broken lattice

from the staircase was three steps ahead. Racing up the rotted boards, she grabbed the wooden stick as she passed by.

The screaming came from the end of the long hall. As she neared the door, the stick raised above her head, Drew crashed into the hall, his arms bear hugged another man's chest.

Keelyn dropped the stick as her mind matched the face with her computer image.

Lucent.

No, Lee's brother, Conner.

Drew struggled to stay on his feet as the man continued to scream. At first, Keelyn thought he was clawing at Drew, but as she neared the twosome, she realized it was his own arms he scratched.

It was then Drew caught a glimpse of her. He swung Conner against the wall. The man momentarily slumped like a marionette with severed strings. In the end, the force of the hit did little to slow him down, and he writhed and screamed in the corner.

"Call 911!"

Keelyn reached to her side then realized the only thing she had was her keys clenched in one hand. "I don't have my cell."

Drew placed his boot on the man's back to pin him where he was as he opened his coat for his own phone.

"What's wrong with him?"

Drew pressed three numbers into his keypad. "I thought I told you to leave."

"You didn't answer my question."

He raised his phone to the window. "You didn't do what I asked you to do!" He threw the phone against the wall. "I can't get a signal in this forsaken slum hole."

Keelyn covered her ears as another set of screams peeled from the man's lips. He swatted at his legs like they were on fire. Drew kneeled next to the man and turned him on his back.

"You're going to have to help me."

"What?"

"Come on, Keelyn! You wanted to play with the big boys. Now's your chance."

Words of objection sat at the tip of her tongue. She shoved her teeth into them to keep them at bay.

"Grab his legs! We have to get him out of here."

"And take him where?"

"Don't you think the hospital would be a good idea?"

Chapter 28

Lee sat in his truck across the road from John Samuals's old property. It looked uninhabited. Considering the violence that happened here and the economy, it looked like the bank wasn't making efforts to resell it. Most of the government protest signs sat askew off the fence, the metal wire that hung them in place rusted and broken after seven years of wind, rain, and snow. All except one.

Always love your country. Never trust your government.

He pulled his truck through the gate, his tracks a mixture of melted snow and dirt, and rounded to the back end of the barn. He consulted the list of individuals who'd been there that day. About twenty law enforcement officers from two counties had been involved. In the past six months, four were dead.

Clay Timmons, Sherriff Benson. Then

there were two other individuals gone as well. One from a suspected drug overdose. The other had quit the police department but had been reported missing by her family about four months ago. Colorado Springs police had been kind enough to let him review the details of what they had so far regarding the missing officer, Melissa LaGrange.

Her parents had reported she'd expressed that law enforcement didn't feel like the right career path for her. After doing an Explorers program during high school, she'd been attracted to the adrenaline rush associated with putting the guilty and evil away. Once the reality of the job hit her, like abused women continually going back to those who'd inflicted violence on them, she'd lost her idealistic view of what she'd hoped to accomplish and started thinking of other careers. Nursing was her next choice, and she started taking classes at Colorado Christian University. She'd been doing well in school and had just applied to the school of nursing and developed some new friendships among her female classmates.

The predominantly male police department hadn't provided those opportunities, so her parents were glad for her to have the female camaraderie.

Except for one friend.

One they'd only met one time.

Who fit the description of Raven Samuals.

A death rate of twenty percent in such a short time span seemed unusually high. Suspicious to say the least.

He checked his phone. A message from Keelyn. Another from the lab.

He called the lab back.

"There's DNA matching the toothbrush and the blood found in the needle of the syringe."

"Any other DNA?"

"There are fingerprints on the syringe itself. Do you want me to submit them? No DNA after swabbing."

A memory pulled at his conscious reasoning. The medical team as they worked on Lucy Freeman.

"Hold those prints for now. Did you check the cap?"

"The cap to the needle?"

"Yes."

"Yeah, no fingerprints on the cap."

"Did you swab it?"

"No. Why?"

"Have you ever watched medical people when they work? Some will pull the cap off with their teeth. Might be saliva on there.

Check it for me?"

"All right, fine. Just because you're a good friend."

"And I'm paying you a lot of money."

"Okay, that too."

Lee disconnected. He ran his fingers over the keypad. He ached to talk with Keelyn. There was a distance widening between them. His worry over her safety was pushing her away. His concern showed as anger. His secret like rat poison on her trust. He knew in his heart she'd picked up his deception.

I want to fix it but I don't know how.

He put the phone back in its case at his side.

Samuals's decrepit house sat on two hundred acres of wild, untamed land. There were areas of prairie grass where dried winter shoots poked through the sheath of newly fallen snow. Some acres were heavily forested with pine and aspen trees. Lee withdrew the bound property maps from his back pocket to orient himself to the marked section that sat to the north of the almost fallen structure.

He was blessed that an old coworker of his was good friends with the county clerk. Under his close observation, Lee had been allowed to open up property files that detailed other structures present on the land.

The county clerk was an early Colorado history buff and was replete with stories about this property. He said there was rumored to be a house that was just an above-ground facade for an underground distillery and tunnel system. Since the land had been in long-term private ownership of gun-loving survivalists, few had ventured onto the property to determine if the legend was real. Several buildings existed on the property, and the clerk gave Lee a hint as to which two would be likely options for subversive activities.

John Samuals had not been the first antigovernment survivalist to call this land home. Teller County had a fairly decorative past. The Gold Rush hit in 1890 and the population ballooned to fifty thousand residents. In the early 1920s, prohibition drove distillation of alcohol underground. Teller County blossomed into bootlegger territory, and even now some residents struggled to return to normal, law-abiding ways.

Lee began to walk the land. Crystals of snow fell into the top of his boots. At times, he'd hit the base of a snow drift and sink his leg up to the knee. Finally, he came upon one structure hidden from plain view. The roof sagged in the middle of the simple, log cabin structure. The doorway and two side windows were open-mouthed, and the stone chimney lilted to one side. From a distance, it might resemble a simple jack-o'-lantern with its gaping holes and shifted stem.

Dirt floors remained, and Lee saw no wooden doors indicating a cellar below. Outside the small structure, the snow would cover any evidence of a tunnel system, so he surmised it might be best to look for the other structure.

Walking east, he hit the largest forested section of the property. This included the back fifty acres. Lodge pole pine trees stood as silent sentries, killed by a plague of tiny black beetles. The snow was not as heavy in this area, and soon Lee could make out a river rock stone-lined path. It wove through the property, building into a higher wall. Then, the trees seemed to line up on either side of the path until he came to a small clearing where the lane gave way to a generous-sized home.

It was two stories. Dark gray wood with thick strips of lighter gray mortar gave it a prison-striped appearance. Lee walked up the steps. The glass was intact in the door.

He brushed away the dirt and took in sheet-covered furniture and an old stone mantel, the same stone that lined the path. The knob broke in his hand when he tested it. He pushed the other side of the knob onto the interior floor and eased the door open; the squeaky hinges set his teeth on edge.

He stepped inside.

In the kitchen, he rolled up the rug. Plumes of dust filled the calm air in the slant of light from the window. He found what he was looking for. A door cut into the floor. Just the tufted edges of a knotted rope teased through the hole at one end, and he was unable to grab enough of the line to hoist the door open. In one of the old cabinets, he found a rusted knife sturdy enough to pry up one corner. He eased his fingers underneath and heaved up with both hands. Wood cracking against wood rang out like a gun shot.

A few moments after the dust settled, he grabbed his flashlight and waved it into the darkness. His phone vibrated. He grabbed it.

Another text.

Keelyn again.

What's going on? She wouldn't say why she wanted to get in touch.

He texted back. *What's up?*

He placed the phone in the breast pocket of his canvas shirt and took the crude wooden steps down. As he descended into the darkness, he brushed cobwebs off to the side. The sticky fibers clung to his clothes. One shiny black spider fell on his cuff and raced up his arm. He flicked it off with the snap of his fingers. A familiar anxiety began to creep over him. Pulses of dread clawed at his calm.

At the bottom of the steps, a tunnel loomed, the end of which he could not see. It was large enough for him to walk upright. It wasn't the confinement of the tunnel that had him standing frozen at the center, but the myriad of spiderwebs. He rubbed at his neck. His skin prickled as he imagined hundreds of spiders preparing to sink their fangs into open skin.

Shining the light forward again, he thought he could see an area where there might be a room to one side. Five steps would get him there. Holding his breath, he stomped in that direction, his arm in front of him as a shield to knock away the webs.

He turned left and shone his light into the dark interior. Tables were filled with lab equipment and bookcases held medical texts. He entered the room, knocking down more eight-legged homes and annihilating a few of their residents with his steel-toed boots. Slowly, his heart rate calmed and his vision cleared. He neared the shelving and took in some of the volumes.

Books on toxins, poisons, and neurological disorders. A refrigerator was in one corner. Lee stepped to it and opened it. Inside were stacks of Petri dishes, the red gel crystallized. He closed the door quickly, hoping time had killed off any virulent pathogens. How was it possible to get electricity down here?

With the flashlight, he peered behind the old appliance. A cord snaked into an outlet. What struck him was that these items did not appear to be circa 1920. More like artifacts from the past twenty years.

He neared the tables. They were metal desks from the '90s. Lee yanked open the cabinet and pulled out several file folders. His posture stiffened as his eyes widened in the low light. After he adjusted the narrowness of his flashlight beam, an insignia solidified on the front of the report.

An hourglass in front of an eight-pointed star, the celestial body like one a young child would draw from simple stick shapes.

Like the ring Lucent wore.

Like the mark carved into Ryan's skin.

Was it also like the partial mark found on

Clay Timmons?

NeuroEnterprises was the company. Lee hadn't heard of it before, but there were several firms located in the Colorado Springs area known to provide services to the government. Several had gone defunct in recent years in the vacuum created by dwindling defense contracts.

He leafed through the first several sheets. Pages upon pages of chemical diagrams. He flipped it closed as visions of his high school chemistry teacher berating him in front of the class for his lack of problem-solving skills played back in his mind.

He pulled out the next folder. What resembled a personnel file. He found several letters on company letterhead. Refusal of severance pay. Refusal of health benefits. A letter of termination for "grievous acts resulting in the death of L. E. Donnely."

Dust from the ceiling dropped onto the paper in a steady rhythm of heavy boots on the ceiling above him. Lee gathered the files up in the crook of his elbow and entered the tunnel. His arms felt weak. He edged farther into the darkness. The sticky silk hugged close to his face and tickled the inside of his nostrils at each quickened inhalation. He flipped off his flashlight and returned it to his utility belt. He drew his sidearm, pointed it at the base of the stairs and waited.

The sound of tiny appendages scratched at his ear drums. He sidestepped to one side of the tunnel and willed himself to believe it was the roots of trees poking through his shirt rather than the exposed fangs of poisonous spiders.

A circular beam of light hit the base of the steps. Dirt cascaded at each thump of the brown canvas shoes. The stranger was dark behind the light. Lee backed up several more steps to keep out of the iridescent scope. The man was now fully inside the tunnel. Lee held his breath as his heartbeat pulsed wildly.

Lee's phone vibrated against his chest, the light from the cover shone through his shirt, a beacon to his position.

The man also raised a gun and aimed it down the tunnel.

"I know someone is here. I followed your footsteps to the house."

The voice. He knew it instantly.

Why is he here?

Lee dropped his weapon and pressed himself to the side of the tunnel in case the sound of his voice spooked the man into firing before he realized he was a friend and not a foe.

Well, maybe friendly foe would be a more accurate description.

"Nathan, it's Lee."

Nathan raised the flashlight higher. Lee secured his gun and stepped fully into the light with his arms raised. Nathan mirrored his movements. Lee clicked his light back on.

"What are you doing down here?" Nathan walked slowly in his direction.

They met at the doorway. "I should ask the same about you."

Nathan rustled the dirt out of his hair. "This place seems to be the epicenter of all our current difficulties. I called El Paso County, wanting the run sheet, and they said you'd already asked for it."

"How did you find the house?"

"It was easy with all your footprints."

"Could have called it in."

Nathan brushed dirt off his coat with a floral embroidered hankie. "I didn't want anyone to know I was coming here, either."

Lee smiled. "I think I may have found something." He motioned Nathan into the small room.

Nathan ducked in, a low whistle escaped from his lips. "We knew John Samuals was somewhat of a mad scientist. That's why he was charged with domestic terrorism."

332

"Scary we never found this."

"Anything interesting?"

Lee set down the reports. "How are you with chemistry?"

"Let's just say I'm a cop for a reason."

"Ever hear of a company called Neuro-Enterprises?"

Nathan scratched his head. "Rings a bell. John had worked there, but the company had gone out of business a couple of years before he took his family hostage. There wasn't a lot of public material available, and what we tried to get was housed under the guise of protecting national security."

"It's hard for me to tell so far what they were into. The interesting thing is the reason John was fired was for involvement in a fatal injury to another worker."

"How'd he die?"

"It's not clear from the documents. However, the guy's last name was Donnely."

"As in Gavin?"

"Think there's a relation?"

"We better find out for sure."

Nathan grabbed his phone from the inner part of his coat just as Lee's vibrated against his chest. He cursed under his breath at forgetting to check the previous call.

The lab.

"It's a text from Lilly. I'm going to head

up for better reception. See what's up."

Lee nodded. His phone seemed good on bars so he dialed the lab as Nathan climbed the stairs.

Lee heard the lab tech pick up the line. "What's up?"

"I'm beginning to have newfound respect for you, Lee."

"Why do you say that?"

"There's DNA on the cap."

Lee chewed the inside of his cheek. "Male?"

"Funny you should ask. Happens to be female."

An ache spread through Lee's gut. "Do me a favor?"

"Another one? You're cashing in heavy today."

"Remember the DNA tests you ran to determine if Keelyn was related to the child found at the diner?"

"Yes."

"Still have a sample of those?"

"All three?"

"Particularly the one questioned as the mother for the child."

"Yes, why?"

"I need you to test it against the sample on the cap."

"You think Keelyn's half sister is the one

who handled this syringe?"

"Guess we'll find out."

The tech was silent for several moments. "All right, I'll check it out."

If the DNA from Raven matched the DNA on the syringe, it proved Raven was involved in these mishaps. How would he tell Keelyn of his suspicions?

Lee raced up the steps. Nathan turned from where he stood in the kitchen. "We've got problems."

"What is it?"

"Lilly's at the hospital."

Again, Lee's phone signaled. He grabbed it. Two missed calls.

Drew and Keelyn. Not a good combination.

CHAPTER 29

Keelyn's panicked call summoned Lilly to the ER Sunday evening. Nathan was MIA. As was Lee. With someone screaming in the background, she could barely make out Keelyn's words as she tried to explain the patient they were bringing in.

Now she stood alongside Keelyn outside the glass as the medical team on duty worked on the young man, his blond hair dirty and matted to his face. They'd placed him in four-point leather restraints just to keep him on the bed.

The screaming alarmed her the most.

He writhed so much the nurses couldn't get IV access. Then two needles slammed into each thigh.

A short few moments and the screams died as the man stilled. His clothes cut off, a quick examination of his skin, a sheet draped over, a calm washed over the scene.

Lilly eased Keelyn into a chair as Dr.

Tucker came through the door. The two doctors stepped a few paces down the hall.

"Do you know this guy?"

"Conner Watson?" Lilly asked to verify.

"That's what his ID says. This is one of the strangest cases I've ever seen."

"High blood pressure? Sweating all over? Severe muscle cramping?"

Tucker ran his hands through his hair. "How did you know?"

"It's just like Ryan Zurcher."

He glanced back at his patient. Still quiet. "The SWAT officer?"

"Exactly."

"What was wrong with him?"

Lilly glanced at Keelyn who was furiously texting. "They don't know yet. What we know more is what's not wrong with him. He hasn't had a heart attack. There was nothing in his belly even though his abdomen was hard as a rock."

"This guy's is, too."

She turned back to her coworker. "Zurcher's major vessels looked good. He didn't have a dissecting aorta or anything fitting those symptoms."

"Sepsis?"

"Initial cultures from Ryan's blood show a gram negative bacteria. Final culture and sensitivity reports are still pending but he's not responding as he should to the antibiotics, either."

Tucker pushed his hands into the pockets of his lab coat. "Then we're in the toxin category."

"Exactly."

"What about Zurcher's drug screen?"

"Nothing illegal. No cocaine. No pot. Nothing."

"Not surprising, though. Considering his profession, he's probably marked for random drug screens."

Lilly shrugged her shoulders. "Did you find any marks on him?"

"He's clearly using. He's got track marks. Heroin maybe. We'll send off a drug screen to check for sure."

"What did you give him to knock him out?"

"Ketamine."

Lilly walked closer to the window. "It's not going to last very long."

"I just need him still long enough for the nurses to get their lines in, get him cathed, and get everything sent off."

"Anything else?"

He eyed her suspiciously. "As far as marks?"

"Anything unusual?"

"Is there something you're not telling me?"

"Ryan had some strange markings on him. An hourglass."

"Haven't seen anything like that."

Lilly leaned against the wall and pointed to Conner. "Their presentations are so similar. What is affecting one is probably a clue as to what is affecting the other."

"A drug addict and an upstanding police officer?"

"They live in the same vicinity," Lilly offered.

"Yes, but totally different circles. Do you know if this patient has any family?"

"I know who his brother is . . . Lee Watson. He and Nathan are — were working together. He was with Ryan when he became ill."

"What you should do is have a talk with the brother after we fill him in on Conner's condition. See if he has any suspicions about Ryan not being on the up and up. Maybe he was earning a little extra cash on the side. Someone from the upper echelon possibly didn't like what the two of them were doing. Decided to take both of them out."

Lilly shook her head. "That's quite a theory."

"Isn't life stranger than fiction?"
That was one thing Lilly knew to be true.

CHAPTER 30

Lee stood with Lilly outside the door of his brother's room in the ICU at Blue Ridge. Nathan was inside with a member of the CSI team collecting Conner's prints to compare with the weapon found at the Freeman murder scene. Conner's face was a bloodless land of slackened muscle. His lips were parted by a large plastic tube connected to a breathing machine. A man in ceil blue scrubs adjusted the dial. Conner's chest rose and fell at the steady beat of the machine's desire. Lilly laid a soft hand on his shoulder.

The anxiety that tore at his soul was unbearable. Where was Keelyn? He'd called her several times on the two-hour drive back to the city. Either she wouldn't answer or she couldn't answer.

He didn't know which he dreaded more.

"What wrong with him?" Lee asked.

Lilly dropped her hand. "We're not

sure yet."

"Why's he on the ventilator?"

"He started to seize in the ER. After they loaded him with drugs to stop the seizure, he stopped breathing."

"What caused the seizure?"

"He had a lot of illegal substances on his drug screen. They're not sure if it's that mixture or some sort of toxin."

Nathan neared the bedside. He'd instructed Lee to stay in the hall until they were done collecting Conner's fingerprints.

Lilly cleared her throat. "Keelyn was following Drew when he found Conner. She knows Conner's the one who approached her in the diner. She knows he's Lucent."

"I'm sure Nathan told you he suspected that."

She didn't disagree.

"Were you here when he came in?" Lee asked.

Lilly nodded. "Shortly after."

"Did he say anything?"

"Screaming mostly. A nurse found a note in his pocket when they were looking for identification."

"From?"

"Someone named *Ariana.*"

Lee unbuttoned his collar and closed his eyes. Icy dread zinged along his nerves.

"Do you know this name?" Lilly asked.

"What did the note say?"

"That she wasn't done. Everyone needed to die who knew her by that name."

Lee pressed his thumb and forefinger across his cheeks and down his jaw line. "It's a message to me. Anything else?"

"Do you recognize the name, Lee?"

Nathan exited the room. To Lilly, "I've got to go."

"What's up?" Lilly asked.

He eyed Lee. "I got a call from Derrick Vanhise."

"Who's he?" Lee asked.

"The psychiatric consultant I hired to look through all the mental health files for Raven."

"And?"

Nathan shrugged. "He wouldn't specify over the phone. All he says is there're big issues he's uncovered with her treatment."

Lee's phone vibrated.

The lab. He touched the screen to answer. His breath heavy in his chest, his head light.

"Lee?"

"Yes."

"You know something I don't know?"

"Probably."

"The DNA from the syringe cap. It's a match."

He remained silent.

"There's one more thing."

"Still here."

"The substance inside one syringe was spider venom. Another syringe held Benadryl."

What should he say with Nathan and Lilly staring at him? Should he tell Nathan everything?

The voice in his ear filled the void. "Do you want me to notify anyone of these findings?"

"I'll get back to you." Lee disconnected the call. "Lilly, what does Benadryl do if given IV?"

"We give it that route for a lot of different reasons."

"Could it knock someone out?"

"It does have a side effect of drowsiness. Most patients fall asleep after an IV dose, particularly if given quickly."

Lee turned to Nathan. "I'm going with you."

Nathan surprisingly acquiesced. "Okay, but you're looking into the situation with the officers who have fallen ill in the last six months connected to the Samuals hostage situation. I'm on Freeman's death. Understand?"

"Fine. Whatever it takes."

"On one condition. You let me in on the phone call."

Lee pressed his lips. "I searched Ryan Zurcher's home on a hunch."

"And?"

Okay, he'd let him know partially.

"Found a plastic bag with some IV supplies in it. There was DNA on the syringe cap."

"Who did you test it against?"

"It was a match to the sample we presumed to be Raven's from the search of her house."

"Who's Ariana?" Lilly pressed.

Nathan looked knowingly at Lee. Was it his way to force him to start speaking the truth? Lee forced himself to look Lilly in the eyes.

"Ariana is Raven's legal name."

CHAPTER 31

Keelyn sat on her loveseat after she settled Sophia into bed. She picked up the mug of steaming tea, drinking the hot liquid and not caring that the first few sips deadened the end of her tongue. The lick of the gas flames fueled her rising anger. She kicked her crossed leg furiously and watched as the liquid sloshed over the side of the cup and circles of fluid dotted her black pants. The wind howled at her window and shook the panes against the wood.

Her mind was a jumbled mess of incoherent thinking.

One thing she detested was secrecy. A relationship could only be built on trust. At the very least, Lee had lied to her. He'd suspected Conner was the elusive Lucent. Hired Drew to find him.

To shelter him?

Isn't that what a good brother would do? Keep a family member from feeling the full weight of the police breathing down his neck? What about her safety? Sophia's safety?

The lights blanked out, and the house was draped in darkness. Her heart froze. Only the low flames of the fireplace provided any light. Keelyn set her coffee cup to the side and clicked her nails against the porcelain. It did little to dissipate the tightness in her neck. She rubbed at her muscles. The incoming snowstorm aggravated the un-settled feeling that crept into her mind. *It's just the power. Probably a transformer blew.*

Someone knocked on her door.

Had she heard that right?

Not at the front door, but the back door.

Several times.

Keelyn stood on shaky legs and considered bringing a weapon with her. The spoon in her tea seemed an inadequate choice. She mentally cursed the lack of fireplace utensils or anything large enough or heavy enough to use against an intruder. She walked with trepidation to the back of her home. As she neared the French doors that led to her gray, flagstone patio, vapors of snow whipped into the moonlight.

Why were her neighbor's lights on if the power had gone out?

Had someone cut her power?

She drew a bit of confidence from the fact that the dark house would allow her to see out more clearly than it would allow others to see in. Through the glass, she could see footprints up to the door. She pressed her nose into the cool glass and looked as far as she could to either side.

Was that just a figure running along the back fence?

Keelyn considered her options. Her hand rested on the lock. Wasn't this the mistake of every horror movie heroine? Actually opening the door to the ax-wielding psychotic man waiting just out of sight?

Keelyn eased her phone from her pocket and dialed the non-emergency number for police dispatch. Faint relief washed over her at hearing a familiar voice on the other end.

"Gloria. Thank heavens it's you."

"Keelyn? Looking for Lee?"

Dread pulled at her heart. "Lee's tied up at the hospital. Say, is there a car close by? Someone who could swing by and check my house?"

Through the phone, Keelyn heard the rattle of her typing. "Need them emergent?"

Wind fanned a sheet of snow and her sight of the backyard faded briefly. "It's probably just me being silly but my power is out. Only one on the street. Footprints up to my back door. I think I saw someone running back there."

The silence on the phone caused her heart to stutter. Keelyn's fingers ached as she held on to the device tighter.

"I'm sending someone your way. Lee said you'd been having some strange experiences."

"To say the least."

"It's going to be fine —"

"Gloria?" Keelyn glanced at the phone.

The call dropped. She dialed again. Busy signal.

How long before they arrived?

Chucking the phone to the counter, she grabbed a large knife from her butcher block, returned to the door, turned the lock, and swung the door open. Snow blasted her face. The icy crystals momentarily blinded her. After wiping them clear, she stepped onto the back porch, snow up to her mid calf. She leaned out.

"Hello? Raven?"

She noticed a rake knocked over onto a wooden bench. Could that have been the sound she heard? That would explain one knock but not several. Plus, it dropped away from the door. The snow seeped into her slippers as she walked the few steps to set the rake up against the siding. She turned back to the house, went inside, and locked the door.

She leaned against the frame and watched the yard. A fallen rake didn't explain footprints that stopped just outside her door. Sometime since the storm had started. The inside of the shoe impressions were barely dusted with crystals of fallen ice.

As she turned back toward the living room, she noticed something different about the front door. When locked, the deadbolt was in a twelve-six position. Now it sat at three-nine.

The door was not secured.

Her lungs burned for oxygen because she'd held her breath so long. The knife fell from her hand and clattered to the floor. Her knees shook as she walked. The door was ajar. Wind whistled through the crack as she neared it. A thin line of snow formed on the carpet.

Shoe prints. Inside her home. She followed their path with her eyes. They faded as they advanced to her staircase. Only small fragments of snow were visible on the bottom two risers. On the third step sat the smoke infested rabbit she'd thrown away a few days ago. A cool vibration swept through Keelyn's body.

Sophia screamed.

Keelyn's heart slammed against her ribs, and she leapt toward the stairs and jolted up them two at a time. The normally closed door was open. Sophia stood in her bed, hands clenched around the slatted headboard as she bounced up and down, screaming.

Wary to approach, Keelyn eyed either side of the room before nearing the terrified child.

Sophia continued to scream. A shrill so high it pained Keelyn's ears. "Sophia, shh, it's all right."

As she went to scoop the child up, she noticed several shiny orbs crawling on the mattress. She leaned forward.

Spiders.

Keelyn yanked Sophia up. One of the arachnids dropped from the child's neck onto Keelyn's hand. In one motion, she pivoted Sophia to one arm and slapped the back of her hand on her thigh to kill the vile creature. Dropping to the floor, she laid Sophia down and unzipped her sleeper and more spiders crawled from the opening. Quickly, she worked to remove the garment as more creatures scampered over her.

Several red welts rose from Sophia's fair skin.

In throes of pain, Sophia flipped side to

side and rolled away from her. Keelyn grabbed her leg to pull her back onto her lap. Tears welled in Keelyn's eyes. Her heart tore at the child's screams of agony.

"Sophia!"

The bedroom door slammed behind Keelyn. She jumped to her feet and tried the knob. It opened only a crack.

Something held the door closed from the outside.

She pulled with all her might. "Let me out!"

Again and again. Over and over. Nothing would give.

Keelyn grabbed Sophia from the floor and clutched her to her chest. It was like holding a crazed animal. Every effort Keelyn made to calm her screaming only seemed to intensify the effects of the venom.

Was the intruder still out there? Why did he want to hurt Sophia?

Keelyn groped for her cell. Her stomach plummeted. She'd thrown it on the kitchen counter.

Clearly, a nest of spiders didn't appear out of thin air on a child's bed. Someone had deliberately placed the creatures there.

Keelyn tried rocking Sophia to calm her. The child pushed and squirmed to be set free, her skin drenched, her face blanched.

Keelyn held her tighter and buried her face in her neck and wept. There was no phone in Sophia's room. How could she call for help?

If I stay in this room, Sophia is going to die.

Keelyn eyed the sippy cup left on the dresser. She set Sophia down and grabbed the future prison for the wayward spiders. Taking the top off, she scooped several up, including her homicide victim that lay eight legs up on the carpet, and screwed the lid in place. Once some of the venomous bunch were secured, she placed Sophia back in the bed and double-checked to ensure there weren't any stragglers still remaining in the sheets. The girl sat and banged her back against her headboard. Her screams caused Keelyn's body to shake with desperate anxiety.

At the window, she saw a car drive fast down her street and fishtail as it rounded the corner. Her knuckles knocked against the glass as she released the lock. Now free, the window slid up. She pulled the pins to release the screen, pushed it out, and watched it cartwheel down the roof and off the ledge.

The wind grabbed and knotted her hair as she stepped out onto the roof into the biting wind and snow. Keelyn eased onto her belly, slid to the edge, and let her legs fall off the side.

Now she dangled from the side of the roof.

Sophia's screams echoed like a wild banshee through the night air, even louder than the howling wind. Keelyn's pulse pounded at her fingertips, and she imagined each wave pushed at her apprehension, a steady drum of encouragement to let go.

Oh, God, please . . .

Keelyn released her grip.

She landed flat on her back onto the uneven ground, air exploding from her lungs. A sharp rock cut into her left side. Her initial breaths were weak and ineffective. Her vision clouded at the periphery.

Through the tunnel, she saw an aperture of light dance like a wayward fairy across her yard and illuminate her chest. In great pain, Keelyn rolled over onto her stomach and ducked her head down, trying to coax the frigid air back into her vacant lungs.

It was then she saw the blood that dripped onto her hands. She brought up her fingers and felt the warm stickiness at the tips. Her breath coalesced in staggered puffs.

She fisted her hand into her chest and forced herself to inhale deeply. It was as if a ball with hidden spikes suddenly released inside her lungs. Her teeth clenched against the pain.

"Help me!"

No voice. Just steps crunched toward her.

Looking up Keelyn saw the ghostly outline of a person walking, a pinpoint of light bouncing toward her. As she squinted into the moonlit snow, Keelyn could see the outline of a gun aimed at her.

Instinctively, she covered her head with her hands. Through one squinted eye, she could see the eerie glow of another flashlight dance beside her, flickering over the snow until it found its target.

The man who stood in front of her had his weapon raised.

But his face was suddenly lit up like a beacon, and his armed hand rose up to shield his eyes from the onslaught of blinding light in the darkness.

A fine whine raced passed Keelyn's left ear, and then tree bark splintered into the air just at her attacker's side. He turned and ran.

Keelyn pulled herself to her knees and looked behind her for her savior. The other figure had disappeared. Blood dripped into her eyes. She set one foot onto the snowy turf and heaved up then trudged around to the corner of her house. The pain in her chest was so great she couldn't bear to stand, and she dropped back down to the ground.

In desperation, she began to pray. The words spilled from her lips in silence. She closed her eyes and turned her face up. *Lord, I need you to give me the strength to stand, to get back into my house, to help Sophia.* Her fingers tingled as the wind sapped her strength. *I know you are here. You haven't deserted me. Please . . .*

Keelyn opened her eyes. The front door to her home remained open. She settled back onto her knees and fought to cull air into her lungs, her hand rubbed at the sharp pains, and she dared again to inhale as deeply as she could. A racking cough swelled up, and the more she hacked, the more it felt like a hot poker stabbed between her left ribs.

Red and blue lights pulsated against the facade of her neighbor's home. Someone nosed a curtain aside to peek at the mayhem, but no one stepped out to offer any help.

Keelyn bit her lips to suppress the cough. The move did little to stop the paroxysms. As she leaned on all fours, the unrelenting spasms spewed fine red mist into the snow and she wiped her mouth with the back of her hand.

A strange, yellow glow pulsated from her home. The crackle of wood snapped from inside and confusion clouded her mind as to what these elements could possibly mean.

She looked up just as her curtains were consumed in a ball of fire.

A squeal of air breaks behind her split the night. She grappled in the snow to get some traction.

Keelyn half crawled, half stumbled up the concrete porch.

Heavy boots on her walkway thumped in her ears. Fright for Sophia's life overrode any anxiety for her own.

A claw-like grasp on her calves yanked her off the step. Keelyn screamed as the pain flared in her side. She flipped onto her back and began to kick to break free.

A firefighter pulled her closer. "Who's in there?"

Keelyn inhaled with all her might. She needed her voice to be strong to break through his helmet and breathing apparatus. "My niece is trapped!"

"Where?"

She pointed up.

"Second floor?"

She nodded desperately. "There's something . . . blocking the door."

"What?"

Two EMS workers were at her side. "Was she in the fire?"

"Dave! We've got a child inside!"

A rush of three men tore through the open door. Glass exploded from the second floor and rained like hail down onto the front lawn. One of the men pushed her down and lay on top of her to shield her body. Pain seared through her chest and her vision blackened. A sharp scream hung light and airy above the roar of the fire, and Keelyn prayed it was from Sophia.

At least it would mean she was alive.

The paramedic eased off her chest. A red-lit probe was slapped onto her finger. The fast beep of her heart was echoed by the machine.

"Pulse ox 88 percent."

The oxygen mask over her face felt more like a smothering hand than a lifesaving measure, and she reached to pull it off.

"Keep it on. I need to listen to your chest."

The cool metal ring of the stethoscope further chilled her bones. Her teeth rattled.

He shook his head. "We've got problems. I can't hear anything on her left side."

"Her head is bleeding," the other remarked.

"Bad?"

"She'll need staples."

"Lung's going to be a bigger problem." He waved to another firefighter for the gurney, then turned back to her. "Were you in the fire?"

Keelyn shook her head.

"What happened?"

"I jumped . . . off the roof."

"To get away from the fire?"

Again, no! How could she make them understand what was really happening? Someone was trying to kill her and Sophia.

Just then, Sophia emerged in the protective grasp of the firefighter. Two additional EMS workers ran to meet him as soon as he cleared to a safe distance. Plumes of water shot up and added to the flying snow as the sprays iced in the frigid air.

Keelyn yanked the oxygen mask off her face, shoved at the two firefighters, and stood, staggering her way across the yard. She fell just short of Sophia.

The fireman yanked off his breathing apparatus and threw it to the side. He laid Sophia in her arms.

"She's okay. She's not burned."

The pressure in Keelyn's chest intensified. She reached into her pocket and pulled the sippy cup out.

The fireman pushed it away. "She shouldn't have anything to drink right now.

Not until the doctors take a look at her."

"Crying . . ."

"She's just scared."

"She was bitten." Keelyn shook the cup in front of the paramedic who listened to Sophia's heart. She leaned forward. Sophia tumbled off her lap into the snow. A strong hand gripped her wrist as she pushed the cup into the man's stomach.

"Inside. These . . . made . . ."

The pressure was too great. She could feel death groping for her.

"her . . . sick."

Keelyn tried to pull Sophia from the snow but she didn't have the strength to lift her. She held her face in her shaky hands, trying to burn the image of her features into her mind.

Strong hands clasped her shoulders. "I need you to lie down so I can help you."

Keelyn shook her head as she began to cry, the tears freezing and sticking her lashes together. It wasn't the fear of death that consumed her. Heaven would be a welcome relief from the pain that racked her body. What plagued her spirit was the sense of loss at not being there for Sophia. Of the life she could have had with Lee. Of the love she was letting slip away.

Hot fire exploded in her chest.

Her body fell beside Sophia.
A flash of bright light.
Then darkness.

CHAPTER 32

Derrick's office was the picture of East Coast Ivy League prestige, if you discounted the set of skis and surfboard in the corner.

"Where do you even use that?" Lee asked, pointing to the over-decorated piece of fiberglass.

"Sometimes on the west coast. Don't get to travel very much these days."

"Boulder keeping you busy?" Lee asked.

"Something like that."

Lee and Nathan settled into chairs across from the psychiatrist. Vanhise pulled his manila folder open.

Nathan thumbed for a clear page in his notebook. "Not like you to call me so late, on a Sunday even, for a psych consult."

"I knew I wasn't going to sleep unless we chatted. Are you familiar with how brainwashing works?"

Lee's elbow slid off the arm of his chair. "Brainwashing?"

"They don't let us use that anymore." Nathan poised a pen.

"Always the one with the dry sense of humor."

"Isn't that fairly controversial? Whether or not you can truly brainwash someone?"

"You're right, Lee. Theories abound as to whether or not you can forcibly impart a belief on an unwilling participant."

"Why bring this up in relation to Gavin Donnely?" Nathan asked.

"Let me just say that, at first, Donnely's treatment seemed to be on the up-and-up. Very standard cognitive-behavioral therapeutic approach to Raven's complaints. Early in her treatment, she suffered from basically depressive-type symptoms related to her feelings of abandonment by her remaining family members."

Lee squirmed in his seat. There was only one who was old enough to have cared for the orphaned child.

"Keelyn," Nathan said.

Vanhise nodded and turned his attention to Lee. "Nathan has told me you have a relationship with this woman. As I'm talking, I want you to be aware these are mainly Raven's feelings. We all know from our work that feelings can be significantly based on an individual's distorted view of reality.

They are just subjective impressions."

"When did that standard treatment change?"

"In Gavin's notes, there came a time when Raven began to question the larger picture, which is very therapeutic for the patient to see beyond themselves. Why did these terrible things happen to her? Was there some reason for it?"

"Why is this notable?" Nathan asked.

"It's notable for two reasons. One, Raven was actually improving under Gavin's therapy at this point."

"And the other reason?" Lee pressed.

"Gavin doesn't seem to like it."

"How can you tell?" Lee followed.

"It's more in the tone of his notes. Something to the effect that though Raven is seeing things in a healthy way, Gavin suggests he's failing in his mission."

Nathan flipped a page in his notebook. "But he doesn't spell out what that might be."

"Any psychiatrist wants his patients to be mentally healthy and self-sufficient. That's our ultimate goal. Much like a parent wants to produce a healthy, functioning adult. We should always be trying to work ourselves out of a job."

"But he doesn't do that," Nathan added.

"No, a far cry from 'Do no harm.' This is when he begins to use hypnosis. It's his process that's very suspect. It's very important we don't project our personal beliefs onto the patient as far as religion and values might be concerned. We should work within their framework to allow them to maintain autonomy."

"When did this begin to happen?" Lee asked.

Vanhise leafed through a couple pages of penciled notes. "It seems a few months before Raven began to volunteer at the church."

Lee thought through the tenets of his faith. Would he be able, under mental duress, to protect his belief in Christ as his Savior if someone in a position of trust tried to undo it? Was his faith strong enough? "He has something against religion?"

Vanhise tapped his tablet. "What I know is, he tried to remove these ideals from Raven. During hypnosis — there's a thing called hypnoscript. It's *generally* agreed upon by the patient and the therapist as to what will be said while the patient is under."

"Then Raven must have been on board," Nathan said.

Vanhise shook his head. "I don't think there's any patient who would have agreed to have something said to them like this. I'm actually shocked he wrote down what he was doing."

"Sociopaths are like that," Lee chimed in.

"What I see as I read through his notes on his hypnosis sessions with Raven is a process akin to brainwashing. When attempting to insert your own ideology, there are several points you hit upon. First, assault their identity. Make them feel guilty. You want to get them to a breaking point and then grant them leniency. Now, you're the only one who can help them out of the horrible situation you actually created. At this point, you can attempt to instill what you want them to believe into their fractured minds."

It amazed Lee how a person could allow a false savior as substitution for the real one. "Okay, let's say I buy all this. Raven was brainwashed during hypnosis. I'm not sure I'm even on board with this theory. But what belief was he trying to instill in her?"

"Ever hear the name Lucent?"

Lee looked to Nathan. "You gave him the items from Lucy Freeman's mother, right?"

Nathan nodded. "Of course."

Vanhise shuffled notes. "I haven't gotten to them yet."

"Samuals claimed Lucent was the one

who egged him on into killing his whole family," Lee said.

"Interesting. Keep in mind, anything resembling brainwashing is completely unethical, and at the very least, your Dr. Donnely should be investigated by the Board of Healing Arts. I'll be placing a call myself on Monday."

Lee leaned forward. "Derrick, you're driving me a little nuts here."

"Okay. He begins to tear down her belief in Christianity." He flipped back a few sections. "According to his notes, this was around the time of her church involvement. It was something she was finding comfort in."

"What's next?" Lee prompted.

"Well, it's the hypnoscript that's problematic. Basically, it's a mantra: The God she believes in is dead. The pain she feels is a result of all the people who have abandoned her. The police failed her when they didn't stop her father. Keelyn failed her when she didn't provide a home. Then he begins to, for ease of terms, *plant* the idea this persona, Lucent, can aid her in seeking revenge. And that revenge is the best way to get past her trouble."

Lee absorbed the implications of Vanhise's assessment. "Seriously? It's that blatant?"

367

"Of course not. That would open him up to even greater liability. Gavin's first issue of liability is, without substantial medical basis, changing Raven from a course of treatment that was working to one where she worsened. Unfortunately, it's the language of the hypnoscript he will hide under. It talks a lot about empowerment. Righting the wrongs in her life. Having this empowerment, where she has corrected all the wrongdoings, will ease her depression."

"That doesn't sound all bad," Lee said.

"The language is subtle. I'll grant you that. It's certainly possible he chose to exclude more overt prompts from his notes. But he does slip a few times. For instance, saying the responsible parties must be eliminated."

"But murdered?" Nathan asked.

"My guess is, were he ever to be questioned about this, he would say he meant from her mind. Really, he's set up the perfect crime. He could simply say he was attempting to empower her. Get her to move forward from a stagnant position. Raven, actually murdering someone, would be her misunderstanding of what he'd said. In which case, it would be the word of a respected psychiatrist versus a mentally ill patient."

"So you think it's possible she could murder someone?"

"She and Lucent have been set up as a team. Lucent is someone she could rely on for strength."

"But really they are a killing team," Nathan posed.

"Yes, you could say that."

Lee nearly doubled over in pain. How could his brother have gotten so mixed up in this?

"Were you aware my brother, Conner, is likely this person she terms Lucent?"

"Yes." He bowed his head toward Nathan. "We talked about that."

"Any idea how Conner and Raven could have met?" Lee asked.

Vanhise closed the folder and interlaced his fingers on top. "I think they likely met innocently enough through her work with the church. He was a homeless drug addict. Gavin speaks of an attraction between them. Raven convinces Conner to get into treatment."

"That's a good thing," Lee said.

"Not under Gavin's care. My guess is Gavin thought he'd be the perfect scapegoat. It would be better to have a real person as the fall guy, someone who could assume the identity. Then Donnely could just say these two mentally ill individuals teamed up on a murderous spree, and he was only trying to help them."

Lee's mind spun with the motivation for Conner to do such things. Did Gavin supply him with drugs as incentive?

"Do you know who the father of Raven's child is?" Vanhise asked.

Lee and Nathan glanced at one another. Lee's throat was too tight to speak.

Nathan took the lead. "You think Conner is the father?"

Vanhise leaned back into his chair. "Doubtful."

"Then who?"

Vanhise tapped at his folder. "What I see here is a doctor running amok. For some reason, he is bent on destroying this girl's life. To do that, he instills this character, Lucent, into her mind as the way to solve her problems — if the two of them can get rid of every person in her life that's let her down."

"But what does this have to do with Conner?" Lee asked.

"Once Gavin sees a budding romance between the two of them, he knows he needs to annihilate Conner as well because he is becoming a glimmer of light in Raven's life. What would be better than to set him

370

up for murder?"

Lee straightened in his chair. "You can prove that?"

"That's not my job; it's yours."

Nathan continued. "If the father isn't Conner, then who?"

"When you read through Gavin's notes there are moments of infatuation with Raven. I think you need to consider the possibility that Gavin Donnely is the father of her child."

"She would have been . . . what? Under the age of seventeen at the time she conceived?"

"Exactly."

"He could go to jail," Nathan followed.

"That's something I don't think he's considered as a possibility. He believes himself to be above the law."

Lee's phone vibrated against his hip. His checked the number. "It's the hospital. Excuse me," he said, as he took the call.

He listened and shook his head, closing his eyes against what he was hearing. "I'll be there as soon as I can." He ended the call.

"What's going on?" Nathan asked.

"Keelyn and Sophia are in the hospital."

Nathan stood up. "What's wrong?"

"They said Keelyn is in critical condition.

371

Sophia's sick as well. Something about an attack."

Lee fisted his hand tight around his cell. His secret really could kill Keelyn.

CHAPTER 33

Things never seemed to go well when Lilly was going off duty. At first she was unconcerned with the EMS reports from the field. The child was apparently stable, though obviously still in distress. The other victim, a young woman, was more critical, but her injuries were nothing the current pace of the emergency department couldn't handle.

The story could easily capture the evening news. Supposedly, a mother jumped from the roof of her home to get help for an ill child. Why jumping from the roof was necessary remained a mystery. Reports were fuzzy. There'd probably be something on the ten o'clock news by the time she got home.

It was the woman passing her in the hall on the gurney that caused her to stop, return to the workroom to set her bag down, and pull her stethoscope from it.

Dr. Tucker was at Keelyn's side. Her

oxygen level was low. She was in C-spine precautions and the rad techs were quickly snapping films to detect her injuries. He glanced Lilly's way.

"Hey, do me a favor! Take this dang sippy cup." He chucked it at her chest and in her surprise she deflected it to the floor. "She keeps saying it's why the little girl is sick. I can't make sense out of it and I need to stay here with her. Look into it for me?"

Lilly picked the cup up and unscrewed the lid and then jumped as if it were loaded with a half-dozen springy snakes.

Unfortunately, these were not a prank.

Inside, were four shiny black spiders. Three had met their demise but one struggled at the bottom of the plastic, swimming in a shallow pool of spoiled milk. She screwed the top back in place.

From the hall, she could hear the child's screaming. She stepped inside as two nurses attempted to settle her. There wasn't any consoling to be had. She writhed, and the agonizing nature of her shrills pierced Lilly's eardrums. Her small body was bathed in a fine sheath of sweat, her lips pale. At one point, she arched her back so violently she almost slipped from the nurse's grasp.

"Unwrap her. I need to look at her skin."

Through the screaming and fighting, they

wrestled her out of the blanket. Lilly counted at least six raised, reddened mounds of angry flesh. In at least three, she could make out the characteristic pale center with two small marks.

"We're going to need an IV placed."

"I'll stay with her." Jen motioned to her partner. "Go get the tray."

Lilly grabbed a few paper towels from the dispenser. Jen sat with the child in the recliner and swaddled her back into the blanket to get her to calm. "What do you think it is?"

After Lilly unscrewed the top of the lid, she tapped out the three dead arachnids. She noted the shiny black bodies and large, globular thoraxes. Using her hemostats, she turned one over on its backside.

The characteristic red hourglass was there but faded, like the eyes turned gray after death made its claim.

Lee burst through the door and couldn't help pulling his hands up to his ears at Sophia's cries.

Lilly looked to the nurse. "She's been bitten by this lot of black widow spiders."

Lee stopped short. "What?"

Lilly turned to Lee. "I think Sophia is suffering from the effects of the venom. I'm going to give her the antidote. It will cure her pain — better than any narcotic we could give her. We'll have to watch her closely, but she's going to be okay. Have you checked on Keelyn?"

He shook his head at the scene before him. "She's stabilized. Tucker said one of her lungs collapsed and pushed everything over. She almost . . ." Two more steps and he pulled the child from the nurse and clutched her tightly, rocking her from side to side.

Lilly stepped closer. The nurse eased from the recliner and Lilly nudged Lee into it.

His eyes glistened as his voice cracked. "What's happening?"

Lilly kneeled next to him. "They're going to be all right."

"Who would do this?"

"Is Nathan here?"

"He's talking to fire. They think it's arson."

Tears fled down his cheeks. He clutched Sophia tighter as she whimpered. "How did she come into contact with so many?"

"That's the question, isn't it?"

"I couldn't bear it, to lose either one of them. What's happening to her?"

The effects of venom on a human body had always been an area of fascination for Lilly. In some species, a single, almost invisible drop of a natural defense mechanism could incapacitate, possibly kill something infinitely larger in a matter of minutes.

Lilly turned back to the young girl. "There's a lot of venom in her system."

The ear-piercing screams and severe pain were out of the bounds of what was normally seen.

"She's acting just like Ryan did," Lee said.

Lilly's mind faltered as she remembered the two other patients who presented similarly. This tiny spider could hold the medical answer, not only for Sophia, but for a few other patients as well. The poison brewing in the young child's body initiated a nasty chemical cascade within her. Currently, the venom was causing a massive release of the neurotransmitter acetylcholine, which caused all of her muscles to painfully contract.

Hence, the explanation for the pain.

Lilly slowed Lee from rocking Sophia so vigorously. "The venom is making all of her muscles spasm."

This systemic effect targeted large muscle groups like the legs, abdomen, and back. It could mimic a surgical abdomen.

Like Ryan Zurcher.

There wouldn't be any explanation warranted from a drug tox screen.

Like Conner Watson.

Could it be that simple? Could one tiny insect cause such deadly illness?

Understandably, it wouldn't be hard to conceptualize why the little girl was so sick. With the number of bites and her relative size, the dose of venom coursing through her could induce a dramatic effect.

Lilly turned to the nurse who stood watch by the door. "Make contact with the pharmacy and tell them we're going to need enough anti-venom for one child and two adults."

The issue at hand was how could two adults without evidence of multiple spider bites become so violently ill?

Lilly turned to Lee. "How do you think Ryan and Conner came into contact with the spiders?"

"I don't think they came into contact with the spiders. Just the venom. Those marks were injection sites."

It was a probable explanation for their symptoms if they'd been inoculated with a massive amount of the venom directly into their tissues.

Or veins.

"But who gave it to them? Venom in that amount has to be harvested."

Lee closed his eyes and shook his head as

if unwilling to speak his thoughts out loud. As if saying them would expose a truth he didn't want to face.

"I found syringes in Raven's home. I think she's doing this. Keelyn's sister. I think Raven is trying to kill everyone who failed to save her family."

"But could she want Keelyn dead?"

Lee turned his head away from her.

"Lee, where do you think she got venom in this amount? Enough to make a large male seriously ill."

He held Sophia tighter as she battled against him. "I know where she's getting it."

CHAPTER 34

Intense pain in her left side woke Keelyn up. The stench of fire lingered in her nostrils. She opened her eyes and brought her hand up against the bright lights. There was an annoying beep to her right. A firm hand brought her arm down gently. Soft lips placed a kiss on her cheek.

Lee.

She pulled her hand from his and shifted her body away. The frown on his face tore at her heart. His eyes pleaded for something she couldn't quite discern. Questions piled in her mind. She was about to begin her interrogation, but upon taking a deep breath to ask her first question, her side lit up in pain. A cry escaped her lips.

Lee stood and jostled her bed. She bit her lip against the motion. "Can't you get her something?"

Lilly Reeves came into her view and sweetly nudged Lee to the side and took his seat. "Keelyn, do you remember what happened?"

Keelyn surveyed the room. Why was there a police officer she didn't know standing in the corner? And a fire captain?

She jolted up in bed. Something tugged at her side like she'd been hooked by an industrial size fishing lure. She groped with a shaky hand to her left and felt the garden hose that fed into her chest.

"Sophia?"

Lilly eased her shoulders back into the cushion of pillows. "She's doing okay. We gave her antivenom, and she had a little reaction. We're helping her. Let's talk about you." Lilly motioned to Keelyn's side. "When you jumped off the roof, you fractured a rib and it punctured your lung. That thing in your side is a chest tube. It's going to reinflate your lung." She pulled up a cord with a button. "This is your pain medication. It's giving you some right now, but when you feel you need more, you need to press it. Try it."

Keelyn took the button that resembled a miniature *Jeopardy* buzzer and thumbed the switch.

"Good. You can do that every ten minutes or so. Don't worry about giving yourself too much because the machine won't let you overdose. Now, about Sophia. She wasn't burned. A little bit of smoke inhalation we're watching closely, but she's not requiring oxygen or anything at this point."

A flood of heaviness began to wash over her. The pain medicine dulled her senses. Her eyes grew heavy. "Good."

Lee had walked around to the other side of the bed. He placed a reassuring hand over hers. Conflict stirred. The need she felt to have him hold her battled against her desire to confront the secrets he hid.

"That's probably the morphine you're feeling. Tell us about the spiders," Lee said as he rubbed her hand between his.

There were too many words she needed to say to make them understand. Right now, she'd have to muster the short version. The medication warmed her body and lulled her to sleep. "Someone broke in. Put the spiders there."

"Do you know who?"

"Whoever left the rabbit in the car."

The officer stepped closer to the bed. "What rabbit?"

Keelyn inhaled the cool oxygen flowing through the small tubes in her nose. "It was on the stairs."

"It probably burned in the fire," the captain stated as he neared the bed as well.

"I'll catch you up to speed on that issue," Lee said.

"This man, did he trap you in the bedroom?" the officer asked.

Lilly put her hand up. "Guys, she's not coherent enough to answer all this right now." She turned back to Keelyn. "Sophia was bitten several times by these spiders. That's why she was in so much pain."

Keelyn nodded. "She'll be all right?"

"She's not out of the woods yet. We need to watch her closely. Right now, she's on the peds unit. All the nurses are falling over themselves to take care of her."

"How many days?" Keelyn pointed to her side.

"For the chest tube? Depends on how much your lung decides to behave. Once it looks good on a chest film, we have to watch it for a few days on water seal. Then you can have it out if that goes well. It may be only a couple of days. Maybe longer."

Her eyes slipped closed. "I want to see — Sophia."

"Tomorrow," Lee whispered through her drug-hazed sleep.

CHAPTER 35

Monday

One week since Lucent's visit to Keelyn in the diner, and Lee bent under the knowledge that nothing in his world would ever be the same. Like a body count in a horror movie, his sum of who'd he'd failed was growing large. Most significantly, Keelyn. Conner. Withholding his past may have hindered the case. May have aided and abetted a criminal in the commission of a crime. Should he add Ryan Zurcher to the list? Had he put Sophia's and Keelyn's lives on the line in order to shelter his secret? His stomach lurched at the thought, and he clenched his jaw to keep the bile at bay.

Nathan sat down beside him. He took a small bottle of Tums out of his coat pocket and shook a few into his hand. Lee held his hand out for a few of the chalky discs.

"This case is turning into one big, sticky mess."

"Don't they all?" Lee crushed the tablets between his teeth.

"Not like this."

Lee dropped his head into his hands. Could he confess to Nathan what was really going on? They watched outside Conner's room as he worked with the sketch artist. The purpose was to identify the woman who'd given him the "drug" that caused his illness. The medical team had concluded that Ryan's, Conner's, and Sophia's illnesses were the result of envenomation with black widow spider venom. In two cases, their pain had completely resolved shortly after being given the antivenom. Ryan was the outlier who remained critically ill in the ICU.

Nathan returned the bottle and grabbed a tri-folded piece of paper from his inner coat pocket. "Fingerprint report came back for the prints on the gun we found at the scene of Lucy Freeman's murder."

Lee's chest tightened. The ripples of his actions were beginning to erode the foundation of his life.

"They're Conner's."

Lee nodded, his mind sucked into the black hole threatening to consume everything in his life he held close.

"I'm going to need to question him."

"I know."

"He'll be booked into jail once he's been medically cleared."

"Can I talk to him?"

Nathan shuffled his hands. "If I'm present and you promise no funny business. Remember, you've got a career at stake. Don't make the chief feel like there's any collusion going on."

The artist shook hands with Conner and exited the room. Lee recognized him as the same officer who had worked with Keelyn.

"Can I take a look?" Nathan asked.

It made sense. Nathan was the only one who'd had a close relationship with Raven after her family had fractured at the tip of her father's knife.

Nathan smoothed his fingers over the picture with heavy sadness in his eyes. "No need to post it. I can make the ID. It's Raven Samuals. Let's get a warrant out for her arrest."

Lee walked into Conner's room, with Nathan following close behind. Lee placed a firm hand on Conner's shoulder. "Feeling better today?"

"Yes. That pain was crazy." He pulled the sheets tight. "I can't go back to that ever again. I'm giving it all up. The drugs. The crazy life. I wouldn't have been exposed to

386

the venom if I wasn't so anxious to get a needle in my arm for a high."

Lee swallowed hard. Why did it have to be the moment Conner turned his life around he was going to be placed under arrest for murder?

Actions have consequences.

"That makes me one happy big brother." Nathan stepped closer.

"Conner, this is Nathan. He's a detective with the police department. He needs to go over a few things with you, all right?"

"Yeah, sure."

Lee stepped back.

"Conner, I'm going to read you your rights. You're being placed under arrest for the murder of Dr. Lucy Freeman."

Conner's face paled. "What? I didn't kill anyone!"

"I understand and you'll be able to tell your side of the story. The problem is your fingerprints were on the weapon found at the murder scene."

"That's not possible. The gun —"

"Conner!" Lee held a hand up.

Nathan lowered his voice as he went through the Miranda warnings. No need to strong-arm a man who was weak and clearly nonthreatening.

"Do you want an attorney?" Nathan asked.

Conner looked to Lee like a young boy lost on the street. "I'll find someone for you. Just don't say anything until you talk with the lawyer."

"No, there is something I want to say."

"Conner, please." Lee stepped closer to the bed. "I know as far as you're concerned I've not been a good influence on you. I'm telling you right now it's going to be best for you to keep your mouth shut until we get everything sorted out."

Conner's muscles wilted, and he flopped back into the bed. "Please, just let me say this one thing."

"He's an adult, Lee. He can make these choices for himself."

The crossroad of Lee's buried past and his current life careened toward one another like two fast-moving cars. The explosions of these worlds colliding were imminent. Could he save those he loved?

Conner eyed Lee with tired, lifeless eyes. "I did take the gun from your house. When I was heavy into using, I needed protection."

"Okay, Conner. That's good enough. I'm glad you told me. You don't need to say anything else."

"I didn't shoot her."

"I'm relieved to hear that."

"Dr. Donnely asked me for a gun. I brought it to one of our sessions. I haven't seen it since."

"How did you meet him?" Nathan asked. Lee could see his eyes ticking, tying loose threads of the case together. It seemed Gavin Donnely was consistently at the center of all these mishaps. Was he the spider at the center of this sticky web?

"Raven introduced me. She thought he could help me get off drugs."

"How long had you been seeing him?"

"A few months."

"Why did he want you to bring the gun?"

"He said he was going to use it in another person's therapy."

Lee eyed Nathan. "Conner, why did you pose as this character, Lucent, when you met with Keelyn in the diner?"

Conner smoothed the sheet over his legs.

Lee could hear Keelyn's voice in his mind. A pacifying gesture.

"Raven and I wanted to be together, but she didn't want the kid around. She said her sister owed her and if I acted like this person was real, it would freak Keelyn out enough she wouldn't turn Sophia away."

"Keelyn said you had a weapon."

Conner's hands stilled. "It was a fake. I swear. I would never hurt her."

Nathan crossed his arms over his chest. "Did you drive Dr. Freeman's SUV to the diner?"

Conner shook his head. "We were just supposed to be there at a certain time. Raven said she'd be sure Sophia was there. I think she called that doctor and set up the meeting."

"Raven was with you?" Nathan asked.

Nathan made eye contact with Lee, his eyebrows slightly raised. It began to gel in Lee's mind how it played out. Sophia had been in the care of Lucy Freeman. Who would a woman trust to meet? The mother of the child or a complete stranger? There was also evidence in Raven's home that Clay Timmons had been there. Add to that her DNA on the cap of a syringe that likely introduced venom into Ryan Zurcher and the odd markings on Clay not clearly identified.

Lee sat on the edge of the bed. "Conner, where is Raven?"

"I don't know."

Or, he wouldn't say?

Nathan motioned to Lee. They stepped out into the hall.

Lee faced Nathan in the hall. "I know

what you're going to say."

"You have to warn her."

"That her sister is a budding sociopath?"

"Past that. She is one. Keelyn shouldn't put any trust in anything Raven says if she tries to make contact."

"I know. I'm going to stop and see Keelyn before I leave."

"Do you still want to leave for the Springs and see what we can dig up on John Samuals's old company?"

"Give me thirty minutes."

Nathan returned to Conner's bedside, and Lee stopped by the gift shop then took the elevator to Keelyn's floor. He stood outside her hospital room, a vase of vibrant pink gerbera daisies clutched in one hand. He watched as she played with Sophia. The child was back to her exuberant self. Within fifteen minutes of receiving the antivenom, Sophia's pain had disappeared. For Conner, the effect had been equally as dramatic, though it had taken a bit longer.

Unfortunately, Ryan developed blood-borne sepsis. He'd been unstable through the night and died early this morning. Now Lee was determined to prove it was murder . . . and Keelyn's sister was responsible for it.

He swallowed into the tight space his

throat had become and nudged the door open. At first, Keelyn offered a gentle smile and his heart thumped at the look of tenderness in her eyes.

It was still there. Her love for him somehow survived. It was a relief, but he knew rough water loomed directly ahead. Keelyn handed Sophia back to the aide and asked if she wouldn't mind taking her back to her room in pediatrics.

Lee hugged Sophia on her way out the door. Raven's crimes would certainly put her behind bars, and Keelyn would become Sophia's legal guardian.

His stomach flipped at the implications of instant fatherhood, but his heart loved Sophia more than he ever considered possible and the thought of the three of them as a family eased his apprehension.

Lee settled the flowers on Keelyn's bedside table. He leaned over, and she wrapped her hands around his neck, brushing her soft cheek against his whiskers. Her breath against his neck weakened his knees.

For moments he held her until she pulled away and motioned for him to sit.

"You look amazing."

She blushed and tugged at her hospital gown. "Nothing like a girl in a sack gown to turn a guy on."

Something in her voice . . . A steely edge to the usually lilted words.

"How do you feel?"

It didn't take long for the tears to flow. She wiped at her eyes quickly.

"I'm glad you and Sophia are okay." Lee gently rubbed the back of his hand across her cheek.

"Are you?" Her hazel eyes, normally soft and inviting, stared directly into his with cold accusation.

"Of course. I would have died if anything happened to you."

"Something did."

"I know, but —"

"Explain to me right now why you never" — her voice broke — "t-told me it was Conner who came up to me in the diner. Threatened me and my family."

"I didn't know for sure."

She shook her head. "Please, I can't take it. Tell me everything. I can't be with you if you lie to me."

The line in the sand.

"Keelyn —"

"What is it?" She shouted. Never before had he heard her voice rise in anger against him. "Why do you never say anything about your brother?"

The muscles in his neck knotted painfully.

"You're not exactly forthright, either."

"This is not about me right now. This is about you and what you've hidden and how it almost killed me and Sophia."

His hands clenched his legs. "I know Conner didn't do this."

Keelyn eyed the gesture. "How can you be sure?"

His heart rate skyrocketed. Panic at what Keelyn's reaction would be. He inhaled and paused, the pressure in his chest like a bomb ready to give way. The words, once out, could never be taken back. "Because I'm pretty sure it was Raven."

"What?" Keelyn struggled to sit and move away from him in one movement.

He leaned back and rubbed his hands to ease his inner turbulence. How could he make her understand the evidence? What he believed in his heart to be true? That Raven was under the influence of an individual who seemed to be using her in some unseemly revenge plot.

"I don't necessarily think it's her fault."

Keelyn clenched her eyes and gave her head several shakes to ward off the accusation. "She's a murderess, but it's not her fault." Her voice taut with sarcasm.

Lee smoothed his palms over his legs. "Something like that."

"What are you talking about? My sister could never harm another individual."

"That's not necessarily true."

"What are you talking about?" Keelyn's nostrils flared.

"The stories you shared with me about when she was younger."

Keelyn's mouth dropped. She splayed her fingers wide on the sheet. "That's different."

"Beheading Barbie dolls?"

Keelyn's face reddened. "Lee . . ." A warning.

"Blowing them up with firecrackers?" Why did he push?

"That's enough," she fumed. "They were hardly live animals."

"Let me just say it's unusual for a girl to have a penchant to do such things."

"Girls can be just as destructive as boys. It doesn't mean they're psychopaths."

"What I mean to say is maybe there was a little something there Gavin Donnely fed on."

She couldn't look at him. "How?"

"Our psychiatry expert thinks Donnely put Raven under hypnosis and then suggested that using Lucent to seek revenge could solve all of her mental health issues."

Keelyn laughed out loud. A mocking

outburst of disdain.

His face flamed at her dismissal. "What's so funny?"

"Do you hear yourself?" She swept her hand through the air. "You're so quick to move suspicion away from your own brother that you're buying into this story — what, did Nathan invent this? He's known for being a little out there."

"It's not Nathan. A licensed psychiatrist feels this way."

She pressed her fingers over her scalp then winced seemingly forgetting the staples. "Did you tell this psychiatrist about Conner? That he was the one in the vicinity of two dead bodies and a kidnapped child and that in all of this, Raven hasn't even been seen?"

"That's not true."

Keelyn's eyes popped. "It is unless there's something else you haven't told me." His silence drew a daggered question. "What are you hiding now?"

"You remember Ryan Zurcher?"

"Absolutely."

"I searched his apartment. Found a bag with some IV supplies. I took it to a private lab for DNA testing."

"Did they find anything?"

"Raven's DNA was on the cap."

"How do you know it was hers?"

"I had it tested against the sample we submitted to them when we were trying to determine if Sophia was your niece."

Keelyn folded her arms against her chest. "You did this without asking me?"

"It wasn't for you to decide. It's a police matter."

"Then why didn't you submit it as evidence?" Her talent as a body language expert was going to waste. She should have been a prosecuting attorney.

He gritted his teeth. Throwing his decisions back in his face was making it hard for him to prove his case — a criminal on the defense stand. "The issue is what was in the syringe."

"What?"

"Spider venom."

Keelyn closed her eyes. He could sense the retreat. The anger. The denial. The suggestion that her sister was involved in something as heinous as murder was building a wall between them.

"Who left the spiders?" Lee asked.

She shook her head. Her eyes remained closed. "Now you're insinuating Raven tried to kill Sophia?"

"What I know is Conner, Ryan, and Sophia have all suffered the effects of this venom. What I know is Raven's DNA was on the syringe with a mixture of Ryan's blood and the venom inside."

Finally, she looked at him. "And where do you presume a nineteen-year-old obtained pure spider venom?"

"From Gavin. He has a whole cache. Does research. I'm telling you, Keelyn. This is the evidence."

Keelyn pulled the covers up to her neck and tightened them like she wanted to strangle herself. Almost as surrender, her shoulders relaxed. "That's the problem with you, Lee. You never think with your heart. Everything is not so cut-and-dried."

"What's that supposed to mean?"

Keelyn shrugged her shoulders. "Maybe I shouldn't say that. After all, you've been blinded by what your brother may have done. Even if Raven is involved in the things you say — at least no one has died at her hand."

Lee opened his mouth. Was it wise to point out Raven's actions had ultimately killed Ryan? He pressed his lips closed.

Keelyn continued. "That's not true with your brother."

The torrent of emotion within Lee collided like hot and cold air and the resulting thunder and lightning.

In his frustration, he lashed out at her. "You may want to rethink that theory."

She edged back into her bank of pillows. "What are you talking about?"

"Conner is claiming it was Raven who lured Freeman to the diner. That she's the one who killed everyone. His role was just to make sure you took Sophia."

"You told me Conner could have stolen that gun from you. Have they checked his prints against the weapon found at the murder scene?"

His answering silence fostered her conclusion. "You're going to believe that when it's his prints on the weapon? You're a police officer! Think logically about what you're saying."

He could see the pain in her eyes at his suggestion. Everything within him wanted to reach out to her, to hold her, to take her and Sophia away from this place . . . to hide them where no one could hurt them.

The light Keelyn brought to his life was like sunlight to a plant. He knew he couldn't live without it. Yet his anger at her accusation darkened that lifeline. Could they overcome this wedge their troubled siblings had pounded between them?

He stood, leaned down, and placed his cheek against hers. "I love you, and we are going to get this figured out." He cupped her head closer. "Just, please, don't trust Raven right now."

Tears fell from her eyes and his heart slumped. She pushed him back and pulled his engagement ring off her finger.

"Keelyn, no."

She held it up to him, between her thumb and forefinger, the light cast off from the diamond a mocking blow to the reality of the moment. "I always told you I wouldn't live with a lie."

"I haven't lied to you."

She dropped her hand onto her lap. "Lee, don't patronize me. Something unspoken is just as dangerous as an overt lie. You are hiding something from me. Something that has to do with your brother. About your relationship. Whatever that is, it's at the center of this whole mess." She grabbed his hand.

He clenched it into a fist. "I'm not taking your ring back. We're going to work through this."

Tears fled from her eyes down her cheeks. "When you tell me the truth, I'll consider taking it back." She pried at his fingers. "Until then, know that I love you, but I can't be with you. I'll not live with another man who can lie to my face and turn around and destroy my life."

"That was your father — not me. I love you —"

"That's the last thing he said, too. Take the ring!"

CHAPTER 36

The quiet hum of the tires against the road and Nathan's calm presence did little to ease Lee's distress over Keelyn. He stared at the barren fields as the sun hovered over withered weeds poking like skinny skeletons through melting snow. Keelyn's ring burned through the breast pocket of his shirt directly over his heart. He drummed his fingers against his face as he contemplated what his next move should be. How was he going to get her back?

"We have to find Raven," Lee said, keeping his eyes focused on the horizon.

"I know."

"I think she's going to come after Keelyn."

"I guess we better find her before that happens." A short silence. "Did something happen between the two of you?"

He felt the familiar cloak hovering, his desire to hide what had really happened. To protect himself against Nathan's insight.

"She broke off our engagement."

Instead what he felt was faint relief at having spoken the truth to Nathan about his situation. A tiny bit of weight fell off his shoulders. Was living in truth easier than hiding in deception?

"I'm sorry," Nathan said.

"I have to get her back."

"You will."

"I need to figure out what Gavin's stake is in all this. Why did he want to plant the idea of a nefarious character in Raven's mind? Just to see if he could do it?"

"Gavin doesn't strike me as a psychopath. You've been around men who are. It's the vacant look in their eyes that's always the dead giveaway. No feeling there. No compassion. Just a dead, soulless killing machine."

"And you don't think that describes Gavin?" Lee asked.

"No, I get the feeling of something different from him. Almost the opposite. Something extreme is bottled up inside. It's this all-consuming fire. Like he's feeling too much and he doesn't know what to do about it."

Lee pivoted, turned to the front. "When did you know you loved Lilly?"

Nathan chuckled. "It was probably the

first time I saw her. She'd planted her fist in my chest and told me to leave her patient alone."

Lee watched the yellow divider stripe flash by. "It was slower with Keelyn."

"Nothing's wrong with that. She's younger — wounded."

"Was there ever a time when you doubted . . . you know . . . that you and Lilly would make it?"

Nathan sighed. "It was complicated with Lilly. I knew I loved her long before she reciprocated. There was another man involved who had feelings for her. I was the detective on her case, so there was an obvious conflict of interest."

Lee drummed his fingers against his knees. "Those are normal complications of being in relationships. I mean, did you think there was a time when you wouldn't be together?"

He could see Nathan's smirk. Normal relationship bumps for cops were extraordinary for others. It was the circumstances of the job that added a unique aspect to the regular progression.

Things came up most couples never had to deal with.

"I think the thing that finally convinced Lilly of my love for her was I never wavered in my belief in what she said, even though it meant the possibility of losing my job. Now there was a point when I didn't think I could prove her case, and that's when she left for Las Vegas to do her own research."

"I think Keelyn thinks I'm not protecting her . . . that I'm trying to hurt her."

"You are hurting her though, right?"

"By wanting to keep some things private?"

"Lee, honestly, you've been kidding yourself for a while now, and I think you're beginning to realize that. They say honesty is the best policy for a reason. That Bible I've seen you with mentions that, you know."

Lee saw Nathan smile slightly. He knew Nathan was trying to soften the words, but his heart still crushed under the weight of his past actions and the ripple effects of those choices in his life.

Nathan checked the driver's mirror before changing lanes. "Also, the issue with Keelyn is that she feels guilty about not being there for Raven. There is a debt she feels needs to be paid back. If Raven is involved in causing these illnesses and possibly murdering these individuals, it may be something Keelyn is going to have to see for herself. Your job will be to catch her when she falls."

"You don't think she'd do anything that would put her life at risk?"

"You know her better than I do. What's your gut say?"

"That I better keep close tabs on her even though she doesn't want me around anymore."

Nathan's phone rang. He checked the face. "It's Vanhise." He slapped the phone to his ear. Lee watched as his nonchalant face contorted into concern. "What can we do about it?"

Dark clouds formed over the Rockies. Heaviness settled into the air. Nathan disconnected the call.

"Well, we may have more of an explanation for the friction between Lucy and Gavin."

"What's that?"

"He's had several complaints filed against him with the Colorado Board of Healing Arts and one was from Dr. Freeman."

"What did the other complaints entail?"

"Some were improper sexual advances during therapy."

"So Lucy did follow through." Lee's head pounded. "We need to look back over Dr. Freeman's notes. See if she knew of these other complaints. It would be another possible motive for him to take out his partner. She was going to kick him out of the practice."

CHAPTER 37

Keelyn sat in her hospital bed with Sophia cradled in her arms, trying to interest her in a coloring book. Normally, Sophia loved to sit and doodle, but Keelyn's coaxing did little to bring a smile to her face.

Something was wrong with her.

Keelyn stroked Sophia's cheek, and her niece's dark brown eyes lingered on hers like those of a wounded animal. Under Keelyn's fingers, she could feel her temperature rising, a faint pink flush set into her cheeks. Keelyn cupped her small hand to her face when she reached up.

"What wrong, little one? Aren't you feeling well?"

It was then she noticed the faint purple spots blooming under her skin. She pressed her thumb against them, and they didn't blanch into her skin. Small bruises? Not a rash? Keelyn pushed the call light for her nurse. Sophia whimpered at the movement.

The indicator light on her phone blinked. A text.

How is Sophia? Is she sick? Raven.

A sharp pain stabbed at Keelyn's gut. She smoothed her hand over the glass face.

Why do you ask? Keelyn typed.

Message sent.

She tapped her nail against the phone — waited everlasting seconds.

Fever? Weird Rash?

Keelyn's mouth dried. Sophia limp and hot in her arms. Her thumbs flew over the small keys nearly as fast as her heart sped in her chest.

What's wrong with her?

Sophia began to cry and pulled at Keelyn's hair.

I did more than just leave spiders in her pajamas.

Keelyn's body froze. What had Raven done?

Meet me at the ER entrance in one hour. It's the only way to save Sophia.

The pulmonologist following Keelyn's case stepped into the room with another nurse. Her hair was Wynona Judd red, and she had a devious twinkle in her eye.

Keelyn waved the nurse over. "Can you check my niece? I think she might have a fever — and there's this strange rash."

When the nurse scooped Sophia up, the child's foot caught and yanked at the chest tube. Keelyn's breath ceased at the pain as she clasped her side with her hand.

"So sorry about that," the nurse said. "Let me just check her temperature real quick, and I'll be right back."

Keelyn watched her leave.

"How are you feeling this afternoon?" the doctor asked. "Other than that little tug there."

Keelyn exhaled slowly. "Better."

"Any chest pain? Trouble breathing?"

"No, things are good. Any chance I can get this thing out today?"

"Well, you're definitely moving in the right direction. The lung, surprisingly, was fully inflated on your morning chest film. That's good. However, we can't just take the chest tube out right away. We're going to place it to water seal. If the X-ray is still good tomorrow, we can probably remove it, but then would need to watch you another day or so to make sure your lung doesn't collapse again."

"That's the soonest?"

"I'm afraid so. You had a significant injury. Not something to play around with."

"But the lung is back as it should be?"

"Yes."

"So, it wouldn't hurt to take the tube out now?"

He patted her knee like a wayward child. "We're not going to risk it, Keelyn. Three days, okay? Not too much to ask, is it?"

He left. The door clicked in his wake.

Wynona returned.

Sophia was not with her.

"Where's my niece?"

The nurse placed a blood pressure cuff on Keelyn's arm. "You were right. Sophia does have a fever of 104. Not something to play around with. The rash is concerning. I took her back to the peds unit. Her nurse is going to touch base with the pediatrician."

The pressure of the cuff around her arm matched the pressure squeezing her heart.

"What does a rash like that mean?"

"Well, sometimes it can mean there's a bacteria growing in the blood."

The cuff released. "That's dangerous, right?"

Velcro ripped as the nurse removed the cuff. "It can be."

Keelyn's mouth dried. Could she bear to ask it? It would confirm Raven had done something dreadful.

To her own daughter.

"Could she die?"

Keelyn's breath paused as she keyed on

the nurse's body language. There was a fleeting pass of widened eyes. A longer-than-normal eye closure. A deep breath to lengthen the moment as the woman thought of reassuring words. Tells for hiding serious news from another person. The woman wrung her hands. A sign of concern. She smoothed her hand at her neck. A pacifying gesture.

Her nurse pulled a tooth over her lower lip. "Don't you worry. It could be a lot of other things, too."

Keelyn swallowed hard. "How do they take these things out, anyway?"

The woman's tone dropped lower as if her knowledge of Sophia's true condition weighed her down. "You think it would be complicated, but it's not too bad. We'll give you some medication before so the pain won't be quite as severe."

"I mean the actual process."

"Oh, dear. I don't want to trouble you with such details today." Her wink an implication that the step-by-step details would be too horrid for her. "Let's go over it more when the time comes. I think the more people think about things, the more they begin to worry over it."

The nurse motioned Keelyn forward and untied the back of her gown, her fingers lightly pressed at the edges of her bandage. "Dressing looks good."

As soon as the nurse left, Keelyn grabbed her phone. Tears welled up in her eyes. Would she see Sophia again? Alive?

Keelyn knew she couldn't leave the hospital dragging a big, square plastic box and an IV pump. Somehow, she'd have to disconnect these things and hope Nurse Busybody left her alone with enough time to do it in.

Forty-five minutes remained.

The YouTube video of a doctor taking out a chest tube caused bile to burn the back of her throat. Nervous sweat escaped her pores. She fanned herself with a stack of papers to get the feelings to subside. Through the soft breeze she wielded, her eyes landed on her PCA pump. She began to push at the button relentlessly to open the floodgate of morphine back into her system. The familiar warmth washed over her and began to calm her nerves.

She dumped the contents of her purse onto the bed. Shiny metal signaled her nail clippers. She could use those to clip the sutures. The video mentioned a special dressing. Vaseline gauze. A close-up of the item resembled gauze caked with something yellow and sticky.

Maybe she could make something like it.

She leaned from the side of her bed and grabbed the large yellow basin that held personal grooming items. There it was in white and blue.

A tube of Vaseline. Keelyn held the hose at her side, stood, and swayed. The medication made her dizzy. After the fuzziness cleared, she rifled through the cabinets looking for gauze. Behind a stack of towels, she found a box of four-by-fours. The next cabinet over, she found wide, cloth tape. She tossed the items back onto the bed and crawled back under the covers and pressed the pain button again.

Last dose.

Thirty minutes left.

She began to shake.

There was a fine line between treating pain and still being able to walk out and leave the facility. Keelyn leaned back into the pillows and took slow, steady breaths. Her mind tried to convince her of the utter insanity of what she planned. Her heart spoke otherwise.

She had to do this — to save Sophia's life.

It'll be fine. He said the lung was okay. It's just like ripping a weed from the ground.

That's how the video made it look.

Five minutes passed. Twenty-five minutes left.

She pulled three large sections of tape and stuck the ends on her bed rail. After the packages of large square gauze were opened, she smothered them with the full tube of petroleum jelly and worked it into the fibers with her fingers. Supposedly, this oily jelly would keep air from entering back into her chest. Another few packages of dry gauze and her stack was complete.

She pulled up the side of her gown and began to undo the dressing. She paled at the look of the clear plastic hose wedged into her side. Blue string circled around the tube and into her skin near the insertion site. The nail clippers shook in her fingers as she clipped the string. Her heartbeat quickened as she pulled the sutures from her skin.

That was the easy part.

With her right hand, she took the pile of gauze and held it tightly over the site. With her left hand, she grabbed the large plastic tube, and took several deep breaths to settle her nerves.

And yanked — hard.

The pain was more than she expected and she screamed through closed lips, fell against her pillows and panted through the

414

pain like a woman giving birth. She held the stack of gauze tight against the open hole to prevent air from sneaking its way back in. Eventually, the pain quieted to a dull ache and she was able to secure the tape over the dressing. From her purse, she grabbed four pills of ibuprofen and swallowed them with the warm water from her bedside cup.

She sat in her bed for a good ten minutes, testing her breathing.

Was it easy? Any pain? Was she getting enough air?

Ten minutes left.

All systems good. At least for now.

Taking out the IV was a small task in comparison to the chest tube. She left the pumps on and running, the ends of the lines in the bed. She didn't want any beeping to alert the nursing staff.

After she eased out of bed, she opened the closet. One waft of her smoke-infested clothes caused her to cough and a sharp pain tinged at her side.

Did that mean air was getting back in?

She pushed the thought from her mind and wiggled into the clothes, then placed all the items back into her purse. With the door open, she peeked into the hall. The door to the staircase was close to her room, and she hurried over the linoleum until she was safely hidden behind the door. She ripped her patient ID bracelet off and let it fall to the floor.

Raven should be out front.

When she exited the hospital, she didn't have a jacket and only red, fuzzy slippers for her feet. She watched as people passed her by to get inside the building, curious looks on their faces followed by a dismissive shrug.

It paid to be waiting outside the emergency room entrance. People questioned odd clothing less.

A car waited. Keelyn bent forward to look as the window rolled down, the fine whine of electricity like static in the air.

"Hey, Sis."

She was beautiful. Dark red highlights wove through her black hair, its loose curls framing her flawless ivory skin. Red lipstick against plump pink cheeks. It was a strange greeting considering the distance of their relationship. Raven patted at the passenger seat.

Keelyn held her left side. "Tell me now what you did to Sophia!"

Raven leaned over and opened the passenger door. Her dark chocolate eyes held a welcome invitation. "Get in the car and I'll tell you. You can call her doctor after we're on our way."

"You would really let Sophia die if I didn't go with you?"

Raven tilted her head, a soft sadness washed over her face. "For now, it's more important you come with me."

The wind rustled through Keelyn's hair. "You need to turn yourself in. Get your life straightened out. The police think you're involved in Dr. Freeman's murder."

"The only way you're going to learn the truth about everything, Keelyn, is by getting in this car. Now get in!"

"Tell me first!"

Raven drummed her fingers against the seat with an expectant stare set in her eyes, the others clenched tightly around the wheel. "She's been infected with meningococcus."

Keelyn heard the faint swoosh of the sliding glass doors open behind her. A rush of warm air caused her flesh to tingle in the cool day. She turned to look.

In the gap stood Rebecca's kidnapper in a black leather jacket.

Her heart jumped. As he closed the gap between them, her mind culled an image from her recent past.

Closer up, it was obvious what she'd

missed before. He was the man who had followed her downtown when she hung the fliers.

He eyed her devilishly. Keelyn lunged for Raven's car door, but in two short steps the man grabbed her and secured his arm around her neck, the open barrel of a gun at her temple, and he pulled her up and back.

"You're a hard woman to track down." He walked her back toward a pickup truck. The same one that had dropped Rebecca off at the park.

Raven scrambled out of her car. "Let her go!"

A hospital security guard stepped out of the main doors. "Hey!"

Keelyn reached up and gripped her hands on the man's arms to ease the pressure on her neck. The guard's radio squawked. If she didn't break free from him in the next few seconds, Raven would be gone, and so would be her chance to set things right.

The man continued to pull her back.

Keelyn shifted her weight up. "You know Rebecca is going to put all this on you."

That stopped his motion. He leaned his mouth close to her ear. "It was all her idea. So we could be together."

Keelyn struggled to stay upright. "I know,

but you're the fall guy. You need to stop now. Tell your side. Show them where Bryce and Sadie are."

Every muscle in his body tightened.

"Are they alive?" Keelyn whispered.

"She killed them. In front of me . . ."

"Why do this for her then?"

The Taser aimed at the man behind her caught Keelyn's gaze. It was held by the guard, his stance firm, a determined look in his eye.

Keelyn raised her hands in surrender. "I'm too close!"

Adrenaline raced through her veins. She remembered Lee saying a Taser shouldn't be fired at someone holding a gun. The muscle contraction could cause the weapon to fire.

And the gun was pointed right at her brain.

"Please, stop!"

The guard's arm tensed as he yanked the trigger back. Keelyn dropped like dead weight to get her head out of her kidnapper's line of fire. The pop of the weapon firing was louder than Keelyn would have imagined. A small harpooned dart hit her arm and all her muscles painfully seized up like they'd been flash frozen into ice.

She fell to the ground and pulled the man

with her.

Her muscles tingled as if her whole body had fallen asleep. She could hear footsteps racing toward her. Raven hovered in her vision. A knife in her hand.

The guard approached as well. Raven waved the hunting blade in his direction.

"Back off!"

Raven yanked the probes from Keelyn's skin. The man began to get up and Raven stabbed at him to keep him down.

Suddenly there was red everywhere. Keelyn turned to see his hand at his throat, a look of panic set in his eyes as the blood flowed between his fingers. She tried feebly to offer aid but her muscles couldn't coordinate any useful movement. Raven's fist bunched up her shirt at her back and pulled her away from the injured man and dragged her on the sidewalk to her waiting car.

"Come on! We're leaving."

She looked up and saw the amber globe covering a security camera and mouthed a message for Lee.

CHAPTER 38

Getting background information on an extinct company had proved difficult. After brainstorming during the hour-plus drive down to Colorado Springs, Lee and Nathan surmised it would be best to approach the government agency responsible for employee background checks. All defense contractors required government clearance.

That meant contacting someone at the Department of Defense or FBI. Considering Nathan had worked as a hostage negotiator with the FBI during the Samuals incident, he called an old friend to see if he knew of anyone still around who worked at NeuroEnterprises.

That contact led them — with a stern warning about his paranoia — to the home of Charles Burns.

The home was in an older section of the Springs. The small cottage was tucked into a sheet of dead ivy, dried from the temperature drop of late autumn. Nathan's contact wove a tale of a widowed, lonely man but one who had been in the upper ranks of the NeuroEnterprises board.

They were warned he always approached the door with a rifle.

A loaded one.

Lee knocked and edged to one side. Nathan had a hand on his service weapon as they waited for a response. The sound of shuffling feet carried through the door. Its hinges squealed like a haunted house in the dead of night, and through the open crack eased the bad end of a long-arm rifle.

"Who's there?"

Lee drew his weapon but kept it at his side. "Mr. Burns. My name's Captain Lee Watson, and this here's Detective Nathan Long. We work for Aurora Police. We'd like to ask you a few questions about a company you used to work for."

"You're a long way from home base. Why do you want to talk to me?" The man neared the screen and pushed his face up against it so hard Lee could imagine his skin oozing through like Play-Doh.

Lee stepped a little closer to the door and waved with his hand. "Mind putting your gun down?"

"Not until you clarify your business."

Nathan gave a quick wave. "We're concerned that some of the technology you developed is possibly being used in a string of murders."

The statement caused the man to ease back from the door, the waffled impression from the screen red against his paled face.

Lee returned his weapon and placed his body in full view of the door. "Sir, someone is trying to kill my fiancée. If you could give us any information, I would be forever indebted to you."

He lowered the weapon. "You know, my Martha died a couple years back."

"I'm sorry to hear that, sir."

"Wish she were still here."

"I know."

He lowered his gun and set it next to the door. "Because of her I'm going to talk to you. She always said there would come a day when I'd have to tell the truth about that awful company. I guess today is it."

Nathan arched his eyebrows. Lee shrugged as he followed the man inside.

The house spoke of love suspended. Several pictures showed the couple throughout their life together. Children and grandchildren. One floral armchair sat empty, an unfinished quilt with a wooden hoop placed on the seat, apparently where Mrs. Burns had last left it.

Lee glanced around the small living room for another place to sit. Nathan leaned against the doorway leading into the small kitchen.

"What is it you want to know?" Burns eased himself onto the sofa, his joints crackled with the movement.

Lee pulled a small footstool from the nearby sofa and sat a few feet away from the older gentleman.

Burns was bald with intense hazel eyes. They were chameleonlike in the way they roved between his two guests.

A quiet suspicion.

"Would you mind giving us some background on the company? What position did you hold?" Lee asked.

He cleared his throat and reached for a water glass. "I was head of research and development." He gulped too quickly and the liquid dribbled down his chin. He wiped it with a forward swipe of his index finger. "What do you want to know?"

"What kind of research did they do?"

"Medical research."

"Narrow it down a little?"

"We were looking into ways spider venom could be used for medical purposes."

The scar at Lee's side tingled. "There's a

good use for spider venom?"

"Absolutely. A couple of areas under investigation were based on spider venom's affinity for ion channels. One was using it to prevent a particular arrhythmia after a patient had a heart attack. Another was as a coating over implanted medical devices. Even looked into its use as a pain killer and cancer treatment."

"That's amazing," Lee said.

"You see the news in the last couple of days?" Burns asked.

Lee shook his head.

"Spider silk as the mesh to grow skin grafts. The creatures really are amazing. Those fine threads are proportionally stronger than steel. Can you imagine? A lot of the work we did at NeuroEnterprises was the basis of what's being done today."

"But no one is using any of those therapies."

"The company stopped looking at medical applications once the government got involved. All good things are eventually used for evil."

Something disturbed Lee. He couldn't place his finger on whether it was the paranoid man or his worry over Keelyn doing something desperate.

"That's an interesting perspective."

"Can you deny it?" The man's eyes roved to meet Lee's and pinned him where he sat.

Lee shuffled his hands together. "You mentioned something about a day you'd have to tell the truth. Want to tell me about that?"

The man withered into his chair. And his eyelids drooped, as if burdened with a secret he didn't want to tell.

Lee understood the man's dread of openly confessing his sin. "We're not here about you. We just think it could help save some lives today."

Mr. Burns inhaled and sat silent for several seconds, then exhaled slowly. Fine beads of dread spotted his forehead, and he pulled a handkerchief from his pocket to sop up the betrayal. "Once we took a government contract, nothing was the same. It wasn't about helping people anymore. It was about finding ways to efficiently kill them."

"Were you . . . successful?"

The man swallowed heavily. "Depends on how you look at it. Have you ever seen the consequences of a spider bite? 'Round here something like the brown recluse or black widow could get you."

"We've seen a few recent examples."

"Most often, the effect is local. The brown

recluse venom rarely goes systemic. It will just stay in one spot and liquefy the tissue it's deposited in."

Lee's stomach protested and the remnants of his encounter with the little tyrant seemed to bubble up and boil at his side. "What about the black widow?" he asked.

"She tends to be a little more interesting. Most often, her bites have just local effects as well. However, more often than the brown recluse, her venom will cause a system-wide cluster of symptoms to develop on the victim. The side effects are distinct. Massive, uncontrollable pain. Sweating. Hysteria."

"What were the defense applications?"

"One: could the venom kill? Two: if not kill, could it be used as an instrument of torture?"

Why did the case have to center around this minute nefarious foe? He was infinitely larger. A single stomp of his heavy boot would annihilate his enemy. He needed to stay to know how the existence of this company set into motion the slew of events that cost so many lives.

He rubbed at his forehead. "You must have discovered something."

"The problem with any biological weapon is how you transmit it. Aerosolized delivery systems are favorable because of the potential to expose and kill a large number of individuals. You can potentially keep your troops safe while everyone else is dying if you know how to protect them. Anything where you have to come into close contact is less favorable."

"There was an accident?"

"I had two researchers focused on these different applications. Torture device and biological weapon. Both were trying to atomize black widow spider venom. It was a race between them. They were in constant competition with one another."

There was healthy competition between men, and then there was unhealthy one-upmanship with deadly results. This seemed to be leaning toward the latter.

"Due to the nature of the work, they were required to wear biohazard suits. One researcher was successful in aerosolizing a mass quantity. Once the compound misted into the air, every creature in the room keeled over. The effects were immediate. The heart just stopped beating. Death was instantaneous."

"Seems like a successful experiment. Goal accomplished."

"Trouble is, somehow it leaked into the building. First place it leaked was the rival researcher's lab. His whole staff succumbed. Several people died."

"Why didn't everyone die?"

"Fortunately, the compound broke down quickly. Had a really short half-life. That's what spared everyone else."

Lee found it hard to speak. "Is it still out there? This weapon?"

"That researcher had tremendous guilt. Inherently, he knew the implications. The government wouldn't be able to keep their hands off something like that. He knew they'd want him to continue his work. Then there was the boy."

"What boy?"

"I should say young man — just out of college. The other researcher had a son. At the funeral, the researcher responsible broke down at seeing that young man without his father. The lab had been shut down to investigate the accident so his notes had remained locked up. Right after the funeral, the whole site was torched. It was speculated he'd done it to prevent the formula from becoming known but we couldn't ever prove it."

"What were the researchers' names?"

"John Samuals and Lucent Donnely."

There it was. A connection. A motive. These two families had tangled long ago, and the residual effects were bleeding down the generations.

Gavin wanted revenge on the man who'd killed his father. It was one of the most basic motives. Maybe Keelyn was right. Could it be that Raven was the victim? That, somehow, she'd been consumed by the suggestions implanted by Gavin? Was there a more perfect way to exact revenge on someone other than to victimize his own child?

Lee jolted as his phone vibrated. He pulled it from his coat and his hand shook as he took the call.

Keelyn was gone.

CHAPTER 39

At first, all Keelyn could do was stare at Raven, at the sister who had been absent from her life. At the ghost who had haunted her every waking moment. The constant wonder about how she was, where she was.

Slowly, her elation at being near her lost sister was replaced with a cloying apprehension. She sensed going with Raven to save Sophia's life could have disastrous consequences for her own. There was a look of destruction in Raven's eyes. A maniacal lilt to her voice as if she were coming to the close of something she'd long hoped to accomplish.

A physical ache spread through Keelyn's chest. At first it was grief at having left Sophia behind. She questioned her wisdom at having broken off her engagement with Lee. The emotional distance between them now translated into a physical one. She fed on the moments of tenderness they had

431

together as a way to set her resolve, hoping to edge away her isolation.

In reality, she was lost and not sure where to go for help. She'd asked God for help before, and she had been forced to take care of things on her own. She didn't have the strength to do it again.

Night was coming fast, even though it was early evening. Dark clouds threatened snow. The car was cold despite the tepid air spewing from the vents. Keelyn huddled in her thin sweater that reeked of charred wood and shivered. Her teeth chattered like an annoying child's toy. She tried not to keep checking the knife Raven held against her leg.

"Where are you taking me?"

"A place where Lee can find you."

Her heart leapt with hope and fear at the same time; then the sneer of Raven's lip froze over the good feeling of Lee coming for her.

The house was a small, run-down hovel at the end of a long, rutted dirt road. Keelyn knew they'd driven south of the metro for a couple of hours. But once thin country road led to a thinner country road, which dead-ended into a grove of anemic, dried forest desiccated by pine beetles, she'd given up trying to determine their location.

How could Lee possibly find her?

Raven pulled up to the front and parked the car. After she climbed out, she pulled a heavy coat from the backseat and threw it onto Keelyn's lap. Lazy white flakes drifted onto the car and clung before their last gasps drizzled like tears down the windshield. Was it snowing in the city? Did Lee wonder if she was warm enough? Was he warm enough?

Keelyn opened the door and climbed out. "You couldn't have given this to me earlier?" Keelyn pulled the coat on. It reeked of cigarette smoke.

"Sometimes suffering builds strength. Isn't that something you wanted me to believe?"

Keelyn mulled over the statement. What was Raven's ultimate goal in bringing her here? She'd seemingly confessed to two goals already. To make her suffer. To draw Lee.

"Help me carry these."

Raven tossed a grocery sack her way, and Keelyn caught it on the fly. A few apples made a suicidal leap to the ground and rolled toward the front stoop. "Where are we?"

"Mom's childhood home."

Keelyn stood stock-still before the tilted

structure.

One thing tied them together. Their mother's DNA.

But why here?

"Are you coming?"

As Keelyn followed Raven up the path to the small home, she reminded herself how young Raven was, yet how old she portrayed herself. Regardless of age, wasn't there always a longing to be cared for?

Raven allowed Keelyn to enter first. The interior reminded Keelyn of an old miner's haunt. The wood floors were shredded. The kitchen and living room one combined place. The two offshoots of the main area included a small bathroom and a bedroom with metal cots and thin mattresses for slumber.

The door banged behind Keelyn, and her shoulders crunched into her neck at the sound.

"You never knew about this place?" Raven asked.

Keelyn set the groceries on the table. "How did you find it?"

"John Samuals has a lot of secrets."

Raven set a heavy duffel bag on the floor with a resonant thud and kneeled next to it. As the zipper opened, the high-pitched whine of metal against metal caused Keelyn's spine to tingle and set her teeth on edge.

Raven brandished her knife as she stood up, dried blood on the blade. "I'm going to need you to sit down."

CHAPTER 40

The stars twinkled merrily, mocking Lee's panic as the two men sped back to the hospital. He arrived a little over an hour and a half after the phone call. On his way, he scrutinized every car he passed, wondering if Keelyn were captive inside.

When they reached the medical center, they left the vehicle running in the loading zone and took the stairs up to the third floor. Keelyn's nurse shook as she explained her last moments with her patient. That Keelyn had asked how they removed chest tubes. That Keelyn had apparently yanked that plastic hose from her side, dressed the wound, and left the hospital with ease until the security guard found her being held hostage at the ER entrance.

Lee wanted to run and view the security tapes but it was better to start at ground zero. It seemed clear that Keelyn had made the decision to leave of her own accord before whatever had transpired outside. That reason could lead them in the right direction of finding her.

Most of Keelyn's personal items were missing. She'd dressed and taken her purse with her. Her phone was found on the floor next to the bed. Dropped in the haste of her leaving? Lee scrolled through the text messages. One instructed Keelyn to be by the ER entrance of the hospital in one hour. He dialed it back. Nothing.

Nathan mirrored his growing concern. "We're going to find her."

"She's not safe with Raven. She has a major injury."

Nathan rubbed his hands across the back of his neck and took a deep breath. "We'll work fast. We'll find her."

Security tapes showed Keelyn speaking to someone in a navy-blue Camaro that had been sitting in the drive for a couple minutes before she emerged. Keelyn's uncertainty reflected in the patchy screen.

The remainder of the scene was surreal. A man came from the hospital entrance behind Keelyn and grabbed her, pulling her back, presumably to the truck that remained unclaimed at the front. They were running plates now. Nathan identified Raven as the woman who popped from the Camaro and

437

came to Keelyn's aid. Taser fired by security. Keelyn dropped from the surge of electricity. Raven stabbed the man in the neck and then reached for Keelyn, grabbing her by the shirt and pulling her toward the car. Keelyn's eyes in the surveillance camera as Raven pulled her back.

Silent words mouthed with emphasis.

Lee peered closer. "Play it back. What is she saying?"

Nathan spoke to another officer. "The plates are registered to an Evan Richter. They match the partial plates Keelyn gave to police about the man who dropped Rebecca off at the park. He's currently in surgery for the knife wound to his neck."

Lee pointed at the video screen. "Back it up again." He motioned for Nathan. "You read lips?"

"Not that well."

"I know who can," the security guard offered, and he picked up the phone.

"Who's that?" Lee asked.

"My wife. She works in ICU. Has to read lips all the time. She'll be down in two minutes."

Lee stood. "I think these two events are likely unrelated."

"I agree. Raven sent the text and then did pick her up."

"The other is happenstance. This guy's vendetta against Keelyn catching up with her on the wrong day."

The security guard walked to the door and in came a slight woman with platinum blond hair cut in a pixie style. "Honey, the police are here. A patient's been taken from the hospital. Can you tell what she's saying?"

The woman sat in front of the screen as her husband played the footage several times.

"I can clearly see the word *sick*. That's easy. Someone is sick."

Lee remembered the string of texts and the mention of Sophia being ill. "Could it be Sophia?"

After a few more playbacks, the woman nodded her head. "Yes, that could definitely be it."

"What else?" Lee asked.

She neared the screen, mimicking with her lips what Keelyn said to the camera. "It's like she's saying *men*. Then i-n-g. Like mening with a hard g."

"Could something like that make a child sick?" Lee asked.

She leaned her head into her palm, her eyes vacant in thought. "Meningitis? There's a bacteria that causes meningitis and blood-borne sepsis that can be very scary — meningococcus."

Lee turned to Nathan. "Is Lilly here today? Can she check on Sophia?"

Nathan nodded. "Yeah, I'll see if she can run up there." He grabbed a nearby phone.

The woman's voice brought Lee's focus back to the screen. "Rice and Sa . . . something."

Lee straightened. "The two missing kids. She's saying Bryce and Sadie?"

The woman paled. "Are dead. She's saying they're dead!"

Lee laid a supportive hand on her shoulder. "Anything else?"

"Becca?" She bit her lip and peered back at the screen. "Last part is — *don't come after me.* I'm sorry. That's all I can make out."

Lee pulled her to a standing position. "I can't tell you how much you've helped. I'm really grateful. How'd you get so good at that?"

"From watching people trying to talk to me when they're on the ventilator. I've been in ICU for twenty years. I've got to get back to the unit now."

Her husband gave her a quick hug. "Told you lipreading would come in handy someday."

Lee waved as she exited the office.

Nathan turned to a fellow detective. "We need to issue a warrant for Rebecca Hanson's arrest. If that man makes it, we need to question him immediately." He turned back to Lee. "You're right. I think they're unrelated but transpired on the same day."

"We need to find Keelyn first," Lee said.

Nathan smoothed his hand over his face. "Trouble is — we don't know where to look. Where would Raven take her?"

"I don't know." Lee leaned with both hands on the desk. The still image of Keelyn being dragged by the scruff fueled his anger. "I can't just stay here!" He slammed his fist on the desk.

Nathan crossed his arms over his chest. "We have to be smart about this. We don't know what Raven intends to do with her. We have to start from the inciting incident, even before John Samuals took his family hostage. The death of Lucent Donnely and the boy he left behind. It's time to bring Gavin in and get this thing figured out."

The good doctor wasn't hard to find. He'd been lapping up liquor for several hours at his home.

While Gavin sat in the drunk tank sobering up, Nathan and Lee went back to the doctor's office, searching for clues in a not

441

so genteel fashion. They'd moved furniture aside and were ripping up the carpet looking for hidden compartments. Lee yanked drawers open and shattered the thin wood of the doctor's locked cabinet. But it was ultimately the cases that housed Lee's nemesis that hid what they were looking for. Lee's heart quickened as he moved the cases aside.

Behind the shelving was a compartment holding fifty or so disks.

Video of Gavin's sessions with Raven and Connor.

Lee and Nathan found a player in the conference room and sat to watch video. After two hours, Lee's eyes were burning, and he rubbed at them when he felt a subtle nudge at his shoulder. Bringing his head up, he glanced to his right where Nathan offered a witch's brew of microwave-heated coffee dregs. Lee accepted the cup but pointed to Nathan's jacket where he knew he hid his antacids.

Nathan shook a few into his hand.

They'd distributed disks to a few more officers who helped flag material for them to review. Vanhise had joined them and scratched copious notes onto his yellow legal pad. Lee looked several times to the stacked cases to make sure the sound was not eight tiny legs as they escaped. Disgust shadowed Vanhise's face as Gavin toyed with Raven.

At first, the seduction Donnely used to erode Raven's foundation was subtle but obvious to the three of them. It was clear Gavin had a physical attraction toward Raven. At first, it was flirtatious comments about her hair, her dress, her naïveté. Then it progressed to simple touching. A shoulder caress. A gentle hug. A finger brushing away a tear instead of offering a tissue.

Then a kiss on her lips.

Vanhise squirmed in his seat. "This is outright criminal. My blood is boiling."

At first, there were constant questions about her belief system. Why God? Why Christ? Did she really believe in all that personal-relationship mumbo jumbo?

Then slowly, session after session, never with more than a hint, he introduced the idea of revenge. Of assuming a character. Of exacting justice against those who had abandoned her and left her to raise herself.

Of murder.

Vanhise flipped through his notes. "You know, he never outright says the words. There's the undertone that taking revenge will help her overcome her depression and anxiety, but he could merely say these were therapeutic strategies and not a call to arms per se."

Lee tossed his crushed Styrofoam cup into the trash. "We're going to need more. Isn't there something you see you think we could use?"

"Trust me; there is plenty to get Gavin on. What these tapes show is his interest in an underage girl and obvious crossing of ethical boundaries. I imagine this alone could carry legal penalties. I'm sure the police could come up with all sorts of things. How about conspiring to commit murder?"

"One thing strikes me as funny as we've watched these tapes," Lee said.

"What's that?" Nathan asked.

"Gavin isn't a smoker. Nothing in this office reeks of smoke."

"What does that matter?" Nathan asked.

"Before the fire, Keelyn had been having some strange things happen to her — things being left at her home for Sophia. Four separate instances. A package of diapers. A basket of toys with a strange note. A bag with diaper cream someone handed to her in a drugstore. In one case, this rabbit showed up. She threw it away because it reeked of smoke. Cigarette smoke."

"So?"

"The next time she saw it was the night of the fire. Same rabbit. It terrified her because someone dragged that thing out of her trash and kept it, then tormented her by leaving it there for her to find after they broke in."

Vanhise began to flip back through his notes. "That would be unusual unless someone had an emotional connection to the object."

"Like a parent?" Lee asked.

"Someone who was holding onto it to make sure Sophia got it back because it was a cherished toy," Nathan offered as an alternative.

"But the note left on the rabbit was threatening. When it was left at the house, someone tried to kill them."

"I reviewed a few of these sessions while the two of you stepped out to get food." Vanhise scoured through the cases and inserted a disk. "Three gifts — the diapers, cream, and the toys — would have been left by someone who cared about Sophia's welfare. What did the note in the basket say?"

"Something like, 'your friend is really your enemy.' "

Images popped up. Vanhise fast forwarded through several scenes. "Here."

It was an interaction between Gavin and Raven.

"How long ago was this?" Lee asked.

"Early in her visits. Over two years ago."

There was no sound for this particular session. That was inconsistent with the other tapes, a deviation from his pattern. Did Gavin know what was going to be said and wanted to hide it? Did he still want the memory but no proof to hold any charge against him?

"We seriously need to start bringing lip-readers with us," Nathan said.

Lee leaned toward the screen. The teen kept a protective hand over her abdomen. Guarding? Protective?

Gavin reached to his side, placed his palm over his heart, and pulled a stuffed rabbit from a bag that sat next to his chair.

"That's it," Lee confirmed. "The same animal."

"So we know where it came from," Nathan verified.

Lee motioned for Vanhise to stop the scene. "I think two people were leaving things for Keelyn. There is a distinct difference in the items that were left. Some were helpful — toys and diapers. Then there are the instances of this smoky stuffed animal that creeped Keelyn out."

446

Vanhise followed Lee's logic. "Each parent is leaving something for the child."

"Yes, exactly. I think this session is their first meeting after Raven has told Gavin of her pregnancy. Why else would he have this stuffed animal unless he already knew?"

"Okay," Vanhise agreed.

"But there's no evidence Gavin is a smoker. Whoever has been holding onto that rabbit is a smoker. That's fact."

"Where is all this going, Lee?" Nathan asked.

There was a puzzle here and a few pieces left to put back in place. Was his suspicion of Raven clouding his judgment? Was Gavin really the only guilty one who'd influenced Raven to do all these horrible acts?

"I want to know if Gavin is Sophia's father."

Nathan turned the screen off. "Okay, fine. But what will that accomplish?"

"The night Keelyn was attacked, she said someone was ready to shoot her when she came down off the roof, but her attacker was then chased off by another individual. Keelyn even thinks that individual may have injured her assailant in the arm. The police on scene state it wasn't any of them who fired." Lee pressed his palms together. "If Gavin is the father, I think he's been trying to keep tabs on Sophia by offering these gifts."

"What makes you think it wouldn't be Raven, her mother?"

Lee closed his eyes at visions of Keelyn caring for Sophia. "Because to me, Raven hasn't done one motherly thing. My gut says the child became a pawn for her to get what she wants."

"So your feeling is Gavin is the victim? That a teenage girl persuaded an older man to do . . . what?" Nathan asked.

Lee shook his head. "I don't know. Something is not fitting right. We need to find out who Sophia's father is."

"And if it's Gavin?" Vanhise asked.

"He could be brought up on a whole other level of charges," Nathan offered.

Lee's phone vibrated. "What I'm suggesting is that possibly Raven caught wind of what Gavin planned to do to her, and played the gullible victim to carry out what she really desired."

"And blame Gavin in the end?"

"Exactly."

"In the morning, we'll interrogate the good doctor." Nathan checked his watch. "He should be sobered up by then."

Lee scrolled through the text message, and

then froze as fear cascaded through his body.

Keelyn dies in 48 hours. Come find me. Raven.

Chapter 41

Keelyn sat mesmerized in an old rocker as she watched the embers of tobacco burn at the end of Raven's cigarette. Keelyn's leg was secured at the ankle and chained around the base of an old metal stove. A butcher knife sat poised on the table. One easy move and it could be in Raven's hand.

The lit tobacco was the only item that provided any illumination in the decrepit home, and the hypnotic motion of Raven drawing poisoned breath culled at the edges of Keelyn's mind. A gentle nudge at something she should remember. Piece together. The gleam from Raven's phone faded.

She'd texted someone.

Keelyn rocked at a slow pace intentionally to ease the tension in the room. "When did you pick up that habit?"

Raven flicked ashes onto the floor. "Does it bother you?"

Keelyn inhaled, the stench of nicotine

burning her nose. Sharp pain poked at her left side in protest. "I'm just wondering if you miss her."

At first there was just a hint of a smile. Not a real smile. The fake one reserved for polite social interaction. Then it faded into a sneer. Just as she'd seen on Rebecca's face.

Contempt.

Keelyn swallowed heavily. "Did you ever love her?"

"Why would you even ask such a question? Of course I love her."

"Why did you try to kill us?"

"Who says I did?"

Keelyn drummed her fingers to quell the jitters.

"Who is her father?"

Raven crushed the tip of the cancer stick into her chair. "Some things are better left unsaid."

"What is your point in bringing me here? For keeping me prisoner?"

"You would be so surprised that I'd want to spend time with you? The chains are so you'll listen."

"And the knife?"

"Insurance."

Raven's cold demeanor fed Keelyn's alarm. "We haven't talked for almost two years. Why now?"

"Everything has its time. Isn't that what your Good Book says?"

Primal instinct kicked in, and Keelyn began to weigh her options. Whatever Raven's point was in bringing her to this dismal structure, it wasn't a good one.

Convincing Raven to release her meant gaining her trust. Finding equal ground.

Time to backtrack.

"I was curious about something."

"Just one thing?"

It was hard seeing Raven as a woman, a mother, when Keelyn remembered the lanky twelve-year-old girl from that horrible day. Raven at one time had been the peacemaker. The one who would make light of tense moments. Defuse situations. That was the point of her drawings and connecting with Nathan through the windows. She'd made a game out of seeing which person she could get the attention of first.

"The Bibles in your garage. Why so many?"

Raven folded her hands, a shadowy figure in the moonlight.

"Do you believe all that book says?"

"The Bible?" Keelyn rocked. "What do you believe?"

Keelyn's eyes adjusted to the dark. Raven's facial features were blurry, and her feet were

452

tucked under her body. It hindered Keelyn's ability to read her.

Silence.

"Was there anything that spoke to you? There must have been if you were out on the streets trying to convince others about its message."

"Do you think I'm crazy?"

Keelyn pulled herself tighter into the coat Raven had given her. Between the lingering cigarette smoke and the burned ash from her home that clung to her clothes, she preferred the latter.

She couldn't knock the chill. "Troubled, maybe."

"Then possibly you don't believe what you read in that book."

A shiver took hold of Keelyn, and she clenched her teeth to keep them from cracking against each other.

Raven stood and opened an old iron stove. Already prepared inside was balled up newspaper and kindling. She pulled a small match case from her pocket and lit the pile. At first the sight of the fire kicked Keelyn's heart into overdrive. Her head ached at the memory of Sophia trapped in the flames.

Raven blew at the structure's base, and the flames danced as they consumed her breath. She grabbed a small log and placed

453

it gently on the pyre.

The chains slid over the wood in eerie musical notes as Keelyn pulled her feet away. Would the heat translate up the metal links and burn her? "When did you start to have trouble?"

"Living with John Samuals was never easy."

Interesting. Not using the word *father*. She'd distanced herself from any emotional connection.

"I'm sorry."

"Are you?"

"Raven —" She stopped. The words of an unspoken promise left unsaid.

She added a few more logs onto the growing flames and closed the door. "You were the only joyful thing. I craved your visits. The loneliness was never ending."

Keelyn's mind tumbled. For what purpose had she been brought here? Was Raven just trying to reestablish their relationship in a way her sick mind thought reasonable? By force? How could Keelyn convince Raven to set her free?

"I loved our times spent down by the water," Keelyn said.

Raven returned to her chair and lit another cigarette.

Keelyn continued. "The water was so

cold. Looking for minnows. Catching frogs."

"Every visit you dressed more girly, but you still always acted like a boy," Raven said.

The glow from the stove warmed Keelyn's face. To her relief, the metal around her ankle remained cool. "When did you notice Mom getting sick?"

"Something happened with John at work. Eventually, the fences went up. He bought weapons. He had all this lab work he was doing. It seemed to suck the life right out of her. She began to just exist day after day."

Raven brushed away a fallen tear. Keelyn's heart hoped the emotional expression was something she could work with to build rapport. "I noticed that, too."

"At least you had an out." She flicked the filter to the floor.

Could those embers light the brittle wood?

As they faded, Keelyn felt relief. "I did like to come and see you. When I was with my dad, I was often alone. I understand that kind of loneliness and I loved being with you. I did want to always be with you." Even in the darkness, she could see the hint of a faint smile cross Raven's face and her shoulders dropped a little as they relaxed. An emotional opening? "Raven, we can have that friendship again. You haven't gone too far. Let me go. I'll say I came willingly. That you saved my life."

For a moment, Raven seemed to relent. She pulled her legs out from underneath her chair and leaned forward. Then, a faint tremble took hold. Her head dropped into her palms, and her fingers slid up her skull and clenched tufts of her hair so tightly it pulled the skin up from her face.

A futile attempt to hide significant emotional pain.

"Did John hurt you?"

"It depends on what you're really asking." She pulled her face up and dropped her hands back into her lap. Another cigarette plucked from the package. "What is it you really want to know?"

"Were you physically abused?"

The embers flared as she inhaled. She raised her head up, the smoke funneled through her nostrils. "There are things worse than that."

Keelyn's heart grew heavy. "Like what?"

"Whatever happened at work with John began to haunt him. We'd hear him wake up in the night screaming. We'd hardly see him in the day, and when he came back to the house, he would rant and rave about the government."

"When did he start to hallucinate?"

"Some things begin so slowly you never

really know when the beginning is."

"Didn't he get better?"

"Life was hard for all of us. After he lost his job, we were fine for a year. He was in his cave most of the time. We tried to make do. Mom halfheartedly homeschooled us but was never consistent about making sure the work was done."

"I thought you were going to school."

"Believe me, it would have been a welcome break." She tapped more ash onto the floor, and then was motionless as she watched the end sizzle. "We barely made it the next four years. A few months before John took us hostage, the electricity was turned off. The cops were coming by. He was finding more weapons. He taught those of us who could hold a gun how to shoot."

"I remember the Christmas tree replaced with rifles."

Raven pointed the cigarette at her like a mother warning her child to back off. Her other hand settled on the knife. "None of you get it."

"What do you mean?"

"The reason John Samuals killed half our family. Tried to murder me . . ."

Keelyn paused her rocking. "You're saying it wasn't because he was hallucinating?"

"That's what I'm saying."

"Then what was the reason?"

"Whatever secret he held, he figured if he was in prison, they'd stop hunting him for it."

"Sounds like a conspiracy theory."

"Only if it's not true." Raven twirled the knife on the tabletop. "And to answer your earlier question — I'm not letting you go."

Keelyn's eyes settled on the spinning blade as it counted off her remaining hours like a fast moving clock hand.

CHAPTER 42

Tuesday

"This isn't going to work if you can't keep your cool. He's not under arrest right now. Let's just try to build the strongest case possible," Nathan said.

Lee leaned against the two-way mirror. "I know you're the expert here. You can keep me on track, but I need to take the lead."

"Don't give away too much too early."

"I know what I'm doing. It's not my first suspect interview."

Donnely was a shell of the man he'd met earlier in the week. His skin was pale. A short, scraggly beard was matted with food particles. Though sober this morning, his physical demeanor was slow and uncoordinated. Streams from the water he'd spilled still dripped off the table.

Lee took the towel from Nathan and both headed into the room. Nathan hovered in the corner. Lee began to mop up the water.

"Things don't seem to be going so well for you, doctor."

The man sagged into the chair, his eyes downcast, hands limp at his sides. "This is all a misunderstanding."

Lee tossed the sodden towel into the corner. "Or maybe I shouldn't use the term *doctor,* since you crossed so many ethical lines with Raven that you must have burned the Hippocratic Oath as soon as you got your license."

The slow deflation continued, and Lee thought the man might slide onto the floor like Salvador Dali's liquid clocks. "I never did anything improper with Raven."

"That's why Lucy Freeman filed a complaint against you, right?"

Donnely clenched his hands tightly. "What is it you're accusing me of?"

"Well, the easy stuff would be serious ethical violations. The medical board is going to be more interested in that. Coming from us as law enforcers could be sex with a minor, arson, and murder. That carries jail time — hard-core jail time. It all depends on what you say. How honest you are."

His face grayed, and Lee saw the tremble take hold. From the corner, Nathan signaled to back off. Too much too soon and the man would disengage.

460

Lee folded his hands on the table. "Let me ask you a few background questions. What was your father's name?"

Donnely clipped his feet around the legs of the chair, clutched his stomach, and swooned forward.

Nathan took two steps from the corner to steady him at his shoulder. "You all right?"

"I'm going to be sick."

Nathan pulled a handkerchief from his pocket and wiped the sheen from Gavin's face. "You're going to have to settle down. If you're just truthful about what's happened, it's going to be better for everyone."

He nodded minutely and eased back.

"Your father's name is Lucent, correct?"

Another affirmation.

"He and John Samuals were coworkers."

"Yes."

"Your father died at that company."

Donnely's eyes darkened as his brow furrowed. Sometimes affirmation of the truth didn't come from the spoken word. Lee saw the traces of motivation for what had happened in that look.

"Did you hold Samuals responsible?"

A dark flash. "He was and has never suffered any real consequences."

Lee leaned back. "That must bother you terribly."

461

Gavin folded his arms across his chest. "Of course."

"So you can see why we're having some difficulty here. You insinuated yourself into Raven Samuals's psychiatric care; you used some therapeutic techniques that deviate from standard treatment. Then Raven begins to suffer some striking hallucinations, which she names after your father. The same hallucination her father said instructed him to kill his family."

"You think I created Lucent?"

"Didn't you? The psychiatrist we have reviewing your records states it is possible to create pseudo memories under hypnosis."

"That may be true — but hallucinations?"

Lee eased back. "We found all your tapes. We've been watching how you interacted with Raven."

"Good. Those will actually work for my defense."

Lee tapped at the desk with his fingernails. "How do you imagine?"

Gavin leaned forward. "Have you ever watched those stage shows with people being hypnotized?"

Lee shrugged. "Once or twice."

"The first thing a stage performer must differentiate between is the low and high hypnotizable. A low hypnotizable is not

462

really under their suggestion."

"Nice fact. How does this pertain to Raven?"

"Even before the show, the hypnotist must ferret out those who are most susceptible to hypnosis. He'll weed out those who don't seem to be responding, typically these low hypnotizables. He wants to put on the best show possible."

"And how does this relate to your case?" Lee asked.

"The audience can't really tell the difference between those who are truly hypnotized and those who choose to voluntarily participate for the good of the show."

"I don't see how this helps you."

"I'm trying to point out that a professional can tell the difference. There are certain mannerisms a low hypnotizable will perform to try to convince the hypnotist they're really under their influence when the truth is they are not."

"Like what?"

"Well, if you watch the tapes closely, early in our sessions when I ask Raven to walk around the room, she bumps into the furniture."

"So?"

"Just because you're hypnotized doesn't mean you're blind. If you review tapes of people under hypnosis, they don't run themselves into things. So this behavior is a ploy or a lie a low hypnotizable puts forth in order to convince the hypnotist they are under their suggestion."

"Again, how does this help you?"

"It will be proof Raven was never under my influence. That these choices she made were of her own volition. She's truly a murderer and not in any way by doing something I told her to do."

"Doctor, your own theory is working against you. If you knew she wasn't being hypnotized — then why did you keep doing it?" Lee pressed his palm into the table. "It doesn't make logical sense unless it was *your* ruse to frame Raven for the murders. That's what an expert witness for the prosecution is going to say, and the jury will eat it up."

"You know this because you're a lawyer?" Donnely sneered.

"No, but I know people, and I've been involved with a lot of jury trials. What you're doing is setting up an implausible scenario. You're stating Raven wasn't under your influence because she exhibited these mannerisms proving she wasn't hypnotized. Raven will say she was hypnotized because she exhibited those same symptoms. All the prosecution will need is one tape of a hypnotized individual running into some-thing, and your defense is out the window."

Donnely blew out through puffed cheeks. "Listen, you don't understand what's been going on with her."

"Why don't you let us in on that."

"She's a disturbed girl."

"And your professional basis for that as-sessment is what exactly?"

"One, the things I already stated. Raven was never hypnotized. Two, surely you can see how her mind became deluded living on that isolated property with a psychotic chemist who'd created a particularly viru-lent bioweapon. She was schooled in living as an isolationist. Taught how to use weap-ons — like knives — at close range. And three, Raven's confession of what happened the day her father took her family hostage."

Lee gave a warm smile. "We appreciate that but Nathan and I are fully aware of what happened. We were there."

Gavin turned around and looked directly at Nathan. "I know you had a special relationship with Raven. She spoke very fondly of you."

Nathan shrugged off the compliment. "How does that bear on what you're going to say? I was trying to help her. It seems you were doing the opposite."

"You were with the FBI then. You're likely familiar with all the evidence in the case."

"Where are you going with this, Donnely?" Lee asked.

Gavin continued to skewer Nathan with his gaze. "Weren't you confused by the two sets of fingerprints on the knife?"

Nathan eased off the wall. "It's not unusual to find more than one set of prints on a knife in a household full of people."

"Maybe a butter knife. But a hunting knife?"

Lee tried to pull Gavin's focus away from Nathan. "If you're claiming Raven held that weapon, you just said yourself John was teaching Raven to use them."

Donnely kept an even stare on Nathan. "You're right, he was. But the position of the prints will be different if you're stabbing someone rather than if you're holding it to draw the blade over someone's throat." He took his index finger and mimicked the movement across his neck.

"That's enough," Lee warned. "This isn't helping you."

"What I suggest to Nathan is that he fess up about the position of those smaller prints on the knife which he never disclosed to the public."

"Why does this matter?" Lee asked.

"Because Raven confessed to me that John told her if she just killed one sibling all the rest would live. He just didn't keep his promise in the end and came for her next."

Nathan's jaw clenched. Without a word, he turned and stormed from the room. Lee followed.

"What's going on here?" Lee asked.

Nathan rustled his hand through his hair. "He's right about those prints."

"You think Raven actually murdered one of her family members?"

"We asked John about the position of those prints. He confessed he'd been teaching Raven to use the knife. He didn't say she'd been complicit in the murders."

"Maybe John was protecting her."

Nathan rubbed his neck. "Even if what Donnely says is true, I doubt Raven would have faced jail time. Imagine the duress she was under. Did Keelyn ever mention anything like that? Confess to seeing any of it happen?"

"No, but remember, she wasn't in the house the whole time. She and the other two came out before the killing started."

Nathan paced. "Raven was only twelve. Would she have had the strength to cause that kind of injury?"

Lee's heart skipped a few beats. "If I

remember correctly, the girl that died was younger than Raven by a couple of years . . . smaller in size." He turned and watched Gavin through the glass.

Nathan stood next to him at the window. "It gives Raven a stronger motive to want to annihilate all of us. We'd already saved three of her siblings. But we left her alone, and she was forced to do that."

"So you think Gavin is right?" Lee asked.

"I'm saying it could be a possibility we need to consider."

"Now you're thinking like me. I've suspected Raven is not an innocent victim. And now Keelyn is alone with a full-fledged killer, and we're running out of time to find her."

CHAPTER 43

Keelyn felt like she was being broiled in an oven with the rack positioned at the highest grooves. She threw her covers off and felt the coolness lap at her right side while her left continued to bake in the fire. The chain remained around her ankle. A hypnotic hammer pounding at her temples matched the elevated thrum of her heartbeat. Cigarette smoke invaded her lungs as she inhaled the frigid air. She coughed, her left side racked with pain. As she opened her eyes to the cobwebbed hovel, she was hit with a moment of stark clarity, and her subconscious was able to snap all the connections and seemingly random events into place.

Raven was a smoker. The stench-filled rabbit left for Sophia was orchestrated by Raven. Raven was the one who trapped her in the house and tried to kill her and Sophia. She was probably the one in the vehicle that had sped off.

Then who were the other two in the yard?

"Wake, wake, Sleeping Beauty," Raven chided, again blowing smoke at her face. Keelyn dispersed the fumes with several quick waves of her hand.

What was meant to be a charmed reference to how her mother used to arouse them in the morning came across as vile teasing. Keelyn eased herself to a sitting position, guarding her left side with a firm hand to act as a counter pressure to the pain. Raven had pulled a moldy, thin mattress onto the floor next to the wood stove for Keelyn where she'd spent the night sleeping. The pain, being chained, and being held at knifepoint had sapped every bit of strength. She pulled up the cuff of her coat. Her watch was gone.

Why would Raven take it?

"How long have I been out?" Keelyn asked.

"It's late morning. How's your side feeling?"

Keelyn's injuries from jumping off the roof had been a subject of conversation on their drive to the house. She lightly touched the staples that closed the cut on her head. There was still a big bump. "Hurts a lot."

Raven grabbed two pills and a plastic cup filled with water and motioned for Keelyn to open up her palm.

She waved her off. "No thanks."

"It's just Tylenol. You can trust me."

Odd word choice but Raven's countenance seemed sincere. Keelyn accepted the pills and examined them. Characteristic manufacturer's markings were evident on the white tablets, and she swallowed them. Her stomach gnawed at the pills as if she hadn't eaten anything in days.

"Can I have my watch back?"

"Does it have some special meaning? I was going to take your ring but I noticed it wasn't on your left hand anymore. Want to talk about it?"

A mentally unstable sibling offering advice. Cue the *Twilight Zone* music.

Sorrow pulled at Keelyn's spirit. The ache of being separated from the man she loved, both physically and emotionally, hurt her spirit more than the battering her body had taken. She'd take the pain of her bruised body first. "I ended our engagement."

Raven's eyes bulged. It was the first time Keelyn noticed true panic nip at her facade. Why would she care about that? It certainly wasn't for Keelyn's welfare. Could she use it to her advantage somehow?

"Why?" Raven asked.

Keelyn picked at the shredded wood

471

boards that covered the floor. "He was hiding something from me. When my father committed suicide, I decided I couldn't be with someone who lied. I could tell there was something he was hiding from me about Conner. He refused to tell me what it was, so I broke things off."

"Everyone lies."

"It doesn't have to be that way. A marriage shouldn't be that way."

"What do you think he was keeping from you?" Raven asked.

Keelyn pulled the sleeping bag tighter over her shoulders. "Lee knew Conner had approached me in the diner, posing as Lucent. He even hired someone to find Conner. Never told me it was his brother."

"It's because Lee's responsible for his brother's current state."

"How? What happened between them?"

"Conner would never be where he is if it wasn't for his big brother." The contempt in her voice as she referred to Lee's relationship with Conner was clear, but there was something else there — a wistful look in her eyes when Conner's name played on her lips. She tapped cigarette ash onto the floor. "You're better off without him, anyway."

"Did you meet Conner while working for the church?"

Raven snubbed the orange glow into an old wooden cable holder that served as the kitchen table. "Yes."

"You never answered my question from before. Why did you have so many Bibles?"

"I was going to give them away."

"You were witnessing to people?"

She remained silent. Keelyn looked closely. It was there, a small quiver in her lower lip. Raven brushed a tear off to the side. This limbic leaking indicated a line of questioning she could pursue to garner the truth. "What was it about the Bible that drew you in?"

Raven pressed her lips together. "It's just a book of old tales."

"I don't believe that. I don't think you do, either."

Raven bit into her lip. "It was the pursuit."

"What pursuit?"

"Of God for us. The Bible is the romance story every girl should read. What every girl aches for."

Keelyn's heart sank at her sister's admission. She'd had that ideal with Lee and shoved it away. Could she get it back? Wasn't that the hidden desire of all people? To feel singularly pursued to the ends of the earth? The romanticized vision of someone laying down their life for another was woven into the human DNA by God as an imprinted map to find the way back to him. Raven's earthly examples had betrayed her terribly, yet she was still able to find ultimate hope in an ancient book.

"What changed?" Keelyn asked.

"I realized how silly it all was."

"Why silly?"

Her voice barely a whisper. "To believe someone would actually do that for me."

Keelyn's spirit broke. She'd remembered someone quoting a study to her once that if a girl had a poor relationship with her father, it was harder for her to believe in God. An earthly example was needed to imagine the spiritual Father doing the same. In that absence, it took great imagination to believe it was possible. Some overcame it. Some didn't.

Raven was one of those who hadn't.

"Did you read the whole book?"

"Every word — more than once."

"What did Conner think when you would talk with him about it?"

Her face softened. A faint smile played on her lips. "I don't think I've ever heard of another beginning like the one Conner and I had. Meeting the way we did. He was open to what I had to say."

"You were a couple?"

Raven slumped back in her chair. "I saw something in Conner I saw in myself. He'd been abandoned by his family, too. His brother kicked him out of his house. Did you know that about your fiancé?"

Keelyn frowned. "Yes, he told me."

"Ever wonder about that before all of these things happened?"

"I think we were both at fault for agreeing to keep the past buried. But now I know secrets are destructive. Lies are destructive."

"Then why do we tell so many? White lies? Which lies are good and bad?"

Keelyn drew up her knees. "That's why I wondered if you read the whole Bible. If you knew about the father of lies."

"Of course I read about him."

"Then you should see how you've fallen victim to the lies he's been whispering to you: That God doesn't exist. That he's not there for you. That the only way to conquer your depression is to seek revenge on those you hold responsible. What deception has bought you, ultimately, is a prison term."

Raven closed her eyes and folded her arms over her chest. "Yet you did the same."

"What?"

Raven locked eyes with Keelyn. "Fell in love with a liar."

Keelyn's heart seized. She hoped Raven

wasn't alluding to falling in love with evil and the perceived benefits that ended in destruction. How far had Raven gone? Was Raven the killer Lee painted her as?

Raven rocked slowly in the chair. "Why did you fall in love with Lee? Why did it have to be him out of all the men in all the world?" Raven threw her arms wide and then slammed them onto the table. "The man who failed to save our family? How could you do that!"

The burst of anger shocked Keelyn. It was there, the smoldering resolute determination of a fully bought lie. She fiddled with the clumps of dirt on the wooden floor as she thought about the question. The fire crackled behind her.

"We met at Ruby's Diner. Do you remember going there with Mom sometimes? Those days she'd take us away from John's, drive a couple of hours to that place way up north."

Raven held her silence.

Keelyn sighed and pulled the chain through her fingers. "At first, it was just friendship. We'd both been through this terrible experience. There was something comforting about not having to talk about it, but knowing the other knew."

"Doesn't seem like enough."

"That wasn't all there was. He's handsome. Eccentric for a guy. It's crazy to see him in his SWAT uniform with C. S. Lewis's *The Screwtape Letters* tucked under his arm. Ever read that book?"

"I know the gist."

Keelyn let the comment slide. "Above all, he had this presence. An air of confidence. I always felt safe and loved. I knew he'd do anything for me."

"Except be truthful."

Keelyn's stomach turned. "Can you tell me the truth about why we're here?"

No response.

"Why did you leave those spiders? Infect Sophia with the bacteria? Why did you set fire to my house?"

Raven looked genuinely shocked. "I'm going to claim responsibility for the things that happened to Sophia. I trapped you in her room. I wanted you to be stuck long enough with her so you'd know it was the venom that made her sick, but what fire?"

"You didn't set my house on fire?"

"I wanted to help someone, not kill you."

"Help someone? What about Sophia — you nearly killed her! I still don't know she's okay."

"Death by black widow envenomation is rare. Has to be done the right way. And the bacteria is treatable with antibiotics."

Keelyn's heart skipped a beat. The right way? What was Raven alluding to?

"How were you trying to help me?"

"Not you, Conner."

Keelyn dropped her forehead into her knees. None of this made sense. She eased her eyes up, her voiced pleaded. "Raven . . ."

She leaned forward and lit another cigarette. Inhaled deeply and held the cancerous smoke in her lungs for several long seconds. Keelyn waited for her lips to turn blue. She exhaled slowly. "I knew the only way to save Conner was to get him into the hospital. Otherwise, he was going to kill himself on the streets with all those things he was putting into his body."

"I still —"

"I injected the spider venom into his veins. A good healthy dose. I'd tipped off Drew on where Conner was so he'd find him and take him in."

"Then Sophia?"

"I needed a way to show the medical team what was making Conner sick so they could give him the antivenom."

Keelyn's mouth gaped open. Sophia as a guinea pig? Her hope that Raven had an iota of mothering instinct evaporated.

"How could you do that?"

"It worked, didn't it?"

The end justifying the means. Another purchased deception with her niece's life as the currency.

"You were depending a lot on people making connections in an unclear situation. Have you seen what that venom does to people?"

Raven flicked the edge of her cigarette and then lazily rolled the shortened stump between her thumb and index finger. Unruffled. Controlled.

No evidence of disharmony between her thoughts and actions.

Raven smiled. "Absolutely. It's quite amazing, actually."

CHAPTER 44

After Donnely's interview, Lee spent hours combing through Raven's personal records to find possible locations of where she could have taken Keelyn. They'd made a list of every store from which there was a receipt and every friend she'd called.

Four hours into the day, their bellies crying to be fed lunch, Lee and Nathan turned into a highway offshoot where a food truck sat. Lee ordered three grease-dripping tacos fully loaded, a Dr. Pepper, and two churros. After devouring each morsel and resisting the urge to lick the greasy wax paper, Lee felt the hunger pangs ease.

Was Keelyn cold and hungry? Guilt-induced bile bubbled in his full stomach and he held his hand out for Nathan's medicine.

Nathan popped a few Tums as well. "I'm going to regret this in a few hours."

"Sometimes you act like you're fifty."

"I'll be glad to make it to fifty. Retire from this job and find something less stressful, like skydiving."

"That's crazy."

"This coming from someone who begs to be shot at on a daily basis."

"That's what Kevlar is for."

Nathan took another couple of bites of his burrito. "We're going to need to start thinking outside the box. Nothing from Raven's house has led to any new clues as to where Raven might have taken her."

Lee balled up the remnants of his lunch for the trash. "We might be making it too hard. Raven wants us to find her. In her mind, she can't just deliver the address. Wants us to sweat it out a little. But ultimately, she's setting this up as a showdown so it has to be something we'd be able to figure out."

"But what is that thing?"

"We've searched all of Raven's known whereabouts and her father's. Raven's other siblings are minors and those properties didn't lead anywhere." Lee arced his trash into a nearby wastebasket. "We need to focus on Gavin."

"He's not exactly been a well of forthright information."

"Let's make some calls to see if we can

481

find the locations of where he grew up. Maybe we need to look into the company where everything started. Check into Gavin's real estate."

"Thought you might say that. I've already got a few officers working on Gavin's holdings."

"Might as well throw his father into it as well."

"Right, good idea."

Lee's phone chimed. He held a finger up to Nathan. The information nearly knocked him off his chair. He set the phone down with a hard thud and wondered if he shattered the glass.

"What's that about?" Nathan asked as he folded the wax paper remnants.

"Gavin isn't Sophia's father."

"Interesting. I think he believes he is."

"Raven led him to believe it."

"Then who is the father and how will it help us find Keelyn?"

Lee stood from the small orange table. "We should split up. I'll run you back to your vehicle. You stick with real estate holdings. I need to go to the DNA lab, and I think we better talk with Gavin again if my hunch pans out."

Nathan stood as well. "Okay. Maybe Vanhise will have something more by then, too.

Four hours tops. Is that enough time?"

Lee squared his shoulders. "It'll have to be. We're more than sixteen hours down."

CHAPTER 45

Keelyn watched as Raven lifted the pot of warmed pork and beans off the top of the wood stove. Cut-up hot dogs had been cooked in the thick mixture. What was the point of her making a meal they'd loved as youngsters? To gain favor with Keelyn? To poison her?

Raven handed Keelyn a bowl of the mixture. She'd placed Keelyn in the rocker a safe distance away from her position at the table. Reading Raven's body language was akin to reading different sides of the same coin. At times, Raven seemed to reminisce and crave their conversations, and Keelyn wanted to stay in those moments forever. Forget about the pain of Lee's kept secret. Reacquaint herself with the sister she'd lost to circumstance. Those instances convinced Keelyn that Raven was not the murderess Lee claimed she was.

But at other times, a darkness shadowed

her face and flattened her eyes, making Keelyn shudder at the possibility Lee's cop instinct was dead-on and she was in the presence of a sociopath.

Keelyn brought a spoonful of the stew to her lips. Though it was hot enough to scald her tongue, she took several bites to quell the grumbling of her stomach. The water she drank to cool her mouth did little to stop the burn. She scraped her tongue with her teeth, and the deadened nerves were dull against the pressure.

"They say a blizzard is coming." Raven sat at the table.

Great. Keelyn glanced out the window. It was late afternoon, but the sun began its descent earlier in the day and aspen trees marred its orange glow. In the distance, thinned edges of black, smoky clouds wafted closer like the Angel of Death, their increasing density a cover for the storm that grew in their bellies. The air seemed heavier, colder. Inside the cabin Raven was sitting farther away from the wood stove, and her breath was visible coming from her nose. Keelyn pulled the sleeping bag tighter. Her fingers numb as she stirred her food.

"Do you think Lee will come for you?"

Keelyn paused, the spoon halfway between the bowl and her mouth. She set the utensil down, momentarily mesmerized by the three votive candles Raven had lit. Unfortunately, they did little to add to the interior temperature of the cabin.

"What if he doesn't?" Keelyn asked.

The wind howled through the holes where the mortar had chipped and fallen to the ground. Raven tapped at the wood with her knuckles. Small threads of melted wax tumbled down the edges of the half-eaten candles.

Keelyn shrugged. "I don't know if he'll come. I want to believe he will."

Raven stroked her neck below her ear lobe then grabbed the fourth cigarette in what seemed the same amount of minutes. The food Keelyn had eaten began to tear at her insides. Raven's bowl sat untouched. These cues signaled to Keelyn that Raven truly didn't have a game plan if Lee didn't show up. Her limbic system was in a state of discontent. The fact that Raven questioned whether or not Lee would come meant she'd been communicating with him somehow.

That there was a deadline.

What would it mean for Keelyn if Lee didn't show up? What was her sister's ultimate plan?

"Why do you want him to come?" The

words came out thin through her constricted vocal chords.

"To feel pain like I feel pain."

Keelyn swiped at the fluid that dripped from her nose. "Is that why those other men died?"

"What other men?"

Keelyn nearly tipped off her chair. "Clay Timmons? Ryan Zurcher?"

Raven almost spoke and then clamped her lips closed. She rose from the table and made her way into the small bedroom, lay down, and began to cry.

In her distress, she'd left her phone on the table.

CHAPTER 46

Lee's visit to the DNA lab had proved his hunch correct. His body ached with tension and his head throbbed. How did the new puzzle piece help him figure out what was really going on?

How could he use it to save Keelyn?

Then came the emergency phone call from Lilly Reeves, who'd happened upon quite a scene in the pediatric unit when she stopped to see Sophia. The hospital was discharging her. In Keelyn's absence, Sophia was headed back to foster care.

Lee couldn't take the thought of Sophia alone with people she didn't know, her sweet brown eyes full of dread in the arms of a stranger. He needed to protect her. No — wanted to protect her. He'd let Keelyn slip through his fingers. Lee wouldn't let the same happen to Sophia.

He rushed up the steps to Sophia's floor. As he crashed through the doors, he saw

Sophia wailing in the arms of a woman in a horrid purple suit. The pediatric nurse and Lilly Reeves followed her at a quick pace. A look of relief washed over Lilly.

He put his palms up to the woman before she could round the corner to the bank of elevators. "Please, wait. Lilly, I thought the pediatrician said she'd be several days in the hospital on antibiotics."

"Her cultures were negative. She didn't have the bacteria."

The social worker looked pensive.

Lee continued. "Then what caused the fever? The weird rash everyone freaked out about?"

"Serum sickness — from the antibiotic I gave her a week ago. The symptoms can be managed at home."

The woman began to push by Lee.

He stepped in front of her. "Can we talk about what you're doing? I'm here to take Sophia home."

She raised a questioning brow but tipped her head as she relented. "Why don't we discuss matters in her room."

Once they were back, Lilly eased the door closed. Sophia continued to cry in the stranger's grip, clawing at her arms and arching her back to be set free. Lee slowed his pace as he neared her.

He reached his arms out. "Please, can I hold her?"

The social worker eyed him suspiciously as he approached. Sophia leapt for him. He cuddled her close and rubbed her back as the racking sobs eased.

"And you are?" the woman asked, her nose rose to the ceiling. He knew most social workers were compassionate individuals. This one seemed to be lacking that trait.

"Lee Watson. I'm Keelyn's fiancé. I'm helping her take care of Sophia."

Lilly caught his eye. He swallowed heavily. Had Nathan told her about Keelyn breaking off their engagement?

"I haven't met you before."

Lee held out his hand. She took it limply. He released the strands of cold noodles. "Sorry. I've been working very hard to find this little girl's mother. Otherwise, I would have been happy to sit down and chat with you."

Her eyes narrowed in question. Is this how people felt when Keelyn observed them? His mind raced through the possibilities of things he could say to convince her she had to let him keep Sophia.

"I'm sorry, Mr. Watson. I'm not comfortable with this whole situation. You're not biologically related. The child hasn't been in an entirely safe environment. And considering that the circumstances of Keelyn leaving the hospital are suspicious at best, I think the child would be better off with another family for the short term." She took a step toward Lee. "Until we get everything figured out."

Lee backed up until the cool metal bars of the crib pressed through his clothes. The icy slats sent nervous shots up his spine. His heart hammered.

This was the beginning. The line in the sand. The starting point of his new life. If he was going to keep Sophia, get Keelyn back, now was the time to start telling the truth no matter what it meant for him in the long term.

"I am related to her."

The woman's eyebrows furrowed with doubt. Lilly leaned against the wall, her eyes wide.

"How exactly?" The woman asked, her voice a question of improbability.

"I'm her uncle. My brother, Conner Watson, is the father."

"And you can prove this?"

"Yes, ma'am, right here. I have the same type of DNA report that your agency considered when you allowed Keelyn to take Sophia. It shows I'm related to her."

He reached for the folded piece of paper from his back pocket. She took it from him and uncrumpled the page.

Lee felt lightheaded as he watched for her reaction. Sophia snuggled her face into his neck, her breath a peaceful whisper as she began to rub her small hand at the stubble on his face.

An image popped into his mind — of him, Keelyn, and Sophia together. He craved for it to come true. He wanted to be tied to them. He'd give up everything if telling the truth about his past would keep all of them together.

Her face softened. "And you think you can do this? Care for this young girl until Keelyn returns?"

"Absolutely."

"And your police work?"

Uncertainty jumbled his thoughts. How could he hold this all together? If he was with Sophia, it wouldn't help him find Keelyn, and she had twenty-eight hours before Raven's threat clock timed out.

Lilly cleared her throat. "Actually, Lee's made arrangements with me to watch her for the next several days."

"And you are?"

"Dr. Lilly Reeves." She neared Lee and placed a reassuring hand on Sophia's back.

"Sophia and I know each other pretty well. Keelyn had already spoken to me about this possibility. As you know, her home caught fire and is unsuitable right now to live in. They were coming to live with Nathan and me until other living arrangements could be found."

"And you have what you need to care for a young girl."

"Actually, yes. There are two very precious children that visit often, so I'm well stocked. They're actually close to Sophia's age. Sophia will be quite comfortable, I can assure you."

Lee put on his best charismatic smile. "See, we're all set."

The woman pressed her lips.

Lee held his breath.

"Fine."

Lee's spirits soared in welcomed relief.

"Dr. Reeves, I'll need your address, and I'll be stopping by tomorrow to ensure this arrangement is truly on the up-and-up."

"Fabulous."

It was then Nathan burst through the door, mindless of the situation. "What is it with you two?" He glared at Lee and Lilly.

Lilly stepped quickly beside him and slid her arm around his. "Nathan," she said, as a woman would calm a child. "Sophia will

493

be staying with us until Keelyn and Lee figure out what to do."

His mouth dropped. Lee shook his head slightly at Nathan, and silently prayed he wouldn't say anything that would cause the woman to reconsider.

Nathan stammered over his first few words. "Wha— that's great." He stepped away from Lilly, his annoyance plastered back on his face. "Why don't the two of you have your phones on?"

Lilly stepped to Lee and took Sophia. "I left mine in the ER. I'm off shift, anyway. I'll stop by and get it. What's the problem?"

Lee grabbed his phone from his pocket as Lilly eased Sophia from his arms. It was powered down.

He tried to turn it on. "It's dead."

Dread filled his mind.

"Evan Richter is asking to speak to you."

"Who's that?"

"The man who was involved with Rebecca Hanson. He wants to make a confession, but he says he'll only give it to you."

Anger fueled Lee's disbelief. "He can wait until Keelyn is found. Or convince him to give it to another officer."

Nathan shook his head. "He says he has information about Keelyn. Something you'll want to know."

CHAPTER 47

The weather through the rotted curtains was on the verge of calamity. Raven had been truthful about the threat of oncoming snow. At first when her sister had fled to the small bedroom, Keelyn's thoughts were on escape. She'd scanned the room for where Raven might have placed the key for the lock to her chain. The dark clouds and hazy sheets in the distance caused her survival instinct to kick in. But even if she broke free, which was better? Alone on the mountain with few clothes and no food and water, or stuck in a hovel with a potential killer?

Then there was the added heaviness in her chest. Keelyn reached under her clothes and felt the edges of the dressing on her left side. Under her skin was what felt like air bubbles and they popped like Rice Krispies when she pressed. She inhaled deeply but the pain at her side stopped her mid-breath.

Had her lung collapsed again? Her heart

quickened at the thought of running. Her injury along with the weather was as good a restraint as the shackle on her leg.

Raven's reaction to learning of the young men's deaths perplexed Keelyn. Her body language spoke of betrayal and confusion. Nothing made sense anymore, and Keelyn's usual confidence about her ability to read people began to waver. Then again, psychosis wasn't supposed to make sense.

Her heart ached for Lee. For his calm presence. For the warmth of his body to take this bone-chilling cold away. In her mind, she pictured his blue eyes, his tousled blond hair, and the ease of his smile.

Keelyn stood from the rocker. Within one step, the chain was taut. When she leaned toward the table, her imprisoned leg in the air as she stretched the length of her body toward her lifeline, her fingers reached the edge but were still too far away to grab the phone. She eased back to think.

The phone sat at the opposite edge.

It was a circular table.

Just spin it.

Keelyn leaned out again, nothing as graceful as a ballerina but effective enough for the task at hand. Slowly, she turned the table and kept an eye on Raven for any movement. Through the door, Raven's crying had ceased, and Keelyn wondered if she had fallen asleep.

A few pulls and Keelyn was able to finger the phone into her palm.

She eased back into the rocker. The phone was turned off. Likely the reason they hadn't been able to ping her location if Raven sent a few texts then powered it down. The search radius would be large, anyway.

Keelyn turned the phone on, and her heart sank when the four frames came up to insert the access code. What could it possibly be? Keelyn didn't know Sophia's birthday. Considering Raven's feelings about motherhood, the odds of it having anything to do with Sophia would be unlikely.

She'd keyed in Raven's birthday.

Wrong passcode.

She marched through all the children in Raven's family, alive and dead.

Try Again.

Parents.

Phone Disabled. Try again in one minute.

Keelyn tapped her fingers on the glass.

What held significance for Raven? When did all her trouble start? It was that day when their father held them hostage. She'd insinuated something unspeakable had happened in the house after Keelyn was rescued.

She keyed in the year.

No.

The date.

Yes.

Anxious energy pulsed through her nerves. She silently fist-pumped her success. Glancing back to the phone, she checked the signal.

One measly bar.

She pulled the phone close and through quick trial and error was able to access the text messages. There were several between Lee and Raven.

There seemed to be a countdown looming. Raven had texted him originally 48 hours. She was malicious with her threats. Taunting Lee to find her. She kept referencing the beginning. The beginning of everything.

How could Lee possibly determine that meant her mother's childhood home?

Keelyn brought up the keyboard and with numb fingers began to key her location to Lee.

She hit send.

Message not delivered.

Tears broached her lower eyelids. She keyed the message in again.

Message sent.

Relief flooded over her. Accessing the system again, she deleted evidence of her attempts to reach Lee in case it angered Raven. She waited several minutes for Lee to text back. Something to reassure her he'd received her location. That he was on his way.

Nothing.

She dialed 911.

The call dropped.

Raven stirred in the bed. Keelyn powered off the phone and stood. More movement from the small bedroom. Keelyn's heart fluttered as she reached out and slid the phone across the table.

It teetered close to the edge and threatened to fall off.

Keelyn sat down.

The phone stayed put. Raven turned in her direction.

Their eyes met.

And as the sun finally set and darkness filled the small home, it appeared Keelyn had one day left to live.

CHAPTER 48

The man was pale with a thick bandage on the side of his neck. The respiratory therapist rolled out the ventilator as the ICU nurse tidied up things at the bedside. She set a cup of ice on his bedside tray and harangued him to take just a few chips at a time. She approached Lee and Nathan, a warning look in her eyes.

"He hasn't been off the ventilator very long. His voice is weak, and he's pretty tired. Take it easy on him."

Lee nodded affirmation and approached the bed, with Nathan a few steps behind. He held out his hand. The man took it with a surprisingly strong grip. Nathan and Lee each took a chair at either side, trailed by a fellow member of the police department who was going to record the confession for evidence.

After all the formalities had been completed, the man signaled to Lee the recording was active.

Lee turned to the figure in the bed. His brown eyes were dark and weary. His black hair slicked with greasy buildup. A hot shower seemed in order.

"Mr. Richter, I understand you want to make a full confession of your crime."

He nodded. Lee tapped his heels into the floor. He could sense Nathan's admonishment to take it slow but could hardly stay still knowing this man could have information that would help them find Keelyn.

He wanted to throttle him to get it out.

"When did you first meet Rebecca Hanson?" Lee asked.

"We met a couple years ago." His voice was hoarse. Richter brought a hand to his neck, the pain evident in his eyes. "I was a client of her husband's. I eventually got to know them and became a friend of the family."

Lee looked at the videographer for a sound check. The man gave a thumbs-up. Lee turned back to Evan. "When did the affair start?"

Evan took a couple of ice chips, letting them melt slowly on his tongue. Lee sat on the edge of his chair. He felt like a lion ready to pounce. Was he torturing him on purpose?

"About a year later."

"Who developed the plot?"

More ice. Evan smoothed his fingers over his Adam's apple to coax his muscles to swallow the fluid. "It was Rebecca. She wanted to be free of her family. Liked what we had together."

"Her husband took out the life insurance plans on the children," Nathan interjected.

"At Rebecca's insistence. Ask him. One million dollars on each."

"What did Rebecca want you to do?" Lee asked.

"Pose a kidnapping of the three of them. Drop her off at the shelter so it would look like she wasn't involved. I was supposed to find a place down in Mexico where we would later meet." The ice seemed to be helping the flow of words. Lee discarded the thought of wanting to chuck it against the wall.

"Are the children alive?" Lee followed.

A shadow passed over the man's face. He choked on his words and sank his head into the pillow and simply affirmed what they already knew with a shake of his head.

"We're going to need a verbal answer," Nathan said.

"No, they're dead."

"Who killed them?" Lee asked.

"She did. I swear it. Drowned them in a bathtub at this sleazy motel where we were staying."

Evan began to shake. Lee eased the cup of ice from his hand. "Where are the bodies?"

The man gave an address for a local storage facility. Nathan signaled to the two waiting officers to go and get it checked out.

"When did the plan start to fall apart?" Lee asked.

"When Keelyn Blake helped with her interview. Rebecca felt like she was getting too close to the truth and it wouldn't be long before they'd arrest her. She thought if we took her out, the problem would be solved."

"That's what you were trying to do at the hospital yesterday?"

His eyes widened at Lee. Incredulous. "Don't you keep an eye out for her at all?" He grabbed the cup back from Lee, took more ice, and chewed.

Lee's anger began to lay gasoline over his nerves. "What are you talking about?"

"I've been following Keelyn for almost a week. I couldn't believe my luck when she got in a tussle with those homeless people downtown. Then, some weird tattooed guy saves her life. Who has luck like that?"

"So the hospital was your second attempt," Nathan clarified.

"The third actually."

Lee's stomach turned violently. He clenched his hands so tightly the muscles in his arms began to shake. "Would you mind moving this along?"

"You know how on the news there's the story of that young missing woman, Raven?"

Nathan sat up straighter. "Yes."

"Such a weird name."

"Your point?" Lee asked.

"Well, that story stuck with me because of all the things I was caught up in. I was watching the news every moment for any information to see if the police were on to what we were doing."

"Go on."

"Then Rebecca tells me this woman is related to Keelyn — who she just despises. She keeps commenting on and on about how Keelyn should just disappear. Really pressuring me to take care of business." Evan went for the call light, his cup of ice empty.

Lee slid it out of his reach. "And?"

"I really struggled."

"Really. That doesn't sound very sincere."

"I obsessed over watching what the news said. Then there was a picture of her sister's

504

psychiatrist and he'd been taken by police for questioning."

"Evan, I don't see the point of how your story relates —"

Nathan waved a hand to cut him off. Lee tapped at his watch.

"My second attempt was the night her house burned down."

He couldn't hide his anger. "You set her house on fire?"

"No — no. Something was already happening when I got there. A woman came bolting out of the front door. Left it wide open. Got in her car and sped off down the street."

"Did you get a good look at her?" Nathan asked.

"Mostly. She was pretty. Black, curled hair. Fair skinned. Bright red lipstick."

Nathan shifted. His gaze locked with Lee's. *Raven.*

"What did you do next?" Lee prompted, attempting to keep the man on track.

"I slowly got out of my car. I was trying to figure out how to go about what I needed to do. I'd brought a gun with me to get the job done."

Lee waited for the man to gather his thoughts. He was sure if he glanced in the mirror, his hair would look like he'd set his finger into an electrical outlet, the amount his nerves zinged in his efforts not to quickly beat the information out of this weasel.

"I stood at the front door and just listened."

"What did you see and hear?" Nathan asked.

"I could hear a child screaming. It was horrible. Like she was being tortured or something."

"Yeah, I guess kids can't scream when they're drowning."

"Lee, back off." Nathan warned.

Maybe Evan would take it as a ruse. The maddening pulse at Lee's temple spoke otherwise.

"Then someone was banging on the door and yelling to be let out. Then there was the smell of something burning. I peeked in the doorway and noticed these candles from the coffee table had fallen onto the carpet, and it had caught fire."

Lee stood up to ease the pressure building in his chest. How could he not have been there for her? His secret was a prison that kept him from keeping her safe.

Keelyn had been right.

"Again, I was thinking what blind luck I'm having. She's trapped. The house is on fire.

506

I'll just back off and let nature take its course."

"You're sure you weren't the one who killed Bryce and Sadie?"

"No, I told you. It was all Rebecca. You don't believe me?"

Lee leaned forward and pressed his palm into the man's chest, his fingers crawled up the side toward the dressing on his neck. His threat of pain widened the man's eyes.

Nathan stood and gripped his wrist to ease him off. "Lee, this isn't going to help."

"It's just that you sound very cavalier about waiting for a woman and a child to burn to death." Lee sneered and pushed off.

Richter took in several gulps of air. "I'm sorry. You don't know what Rebecca drove me to. The power she had over me."

"You're weak!" Lee yelled.

"Aren't we all? Haven't you ever been?"

Was he any different?

Nathan paced to the end of the bed. "We're getting off track here. Mr. Richter, why don't you continue on with what happened next."

Evan rubbed at the reddened imprint of Lee's hand. "Then I heard something fall. I walked around the side of the house. I saw her in the snow." He began to tear at the sheet over his body. "Now, I know I have to do something. She's going to live. Get help. I walked near her to shoot her in the head."

Lee stood and took several steps back to prevent himself from taking another shot at the puny man who sat in the bed. He folded his arms and leaned into the corner.

Nathan took the signal that it was better for him to lead. "What stopped you from shooting her?"

"Well, this man came out from the woods. He shot me first. Winged me." Evan ripped open the snaps that formed the sleeve of his gown. A scabbed line slashed through a bruise that covered his shoulder. "It wasn't bad so I never went to the doctor." Spoken proudly.

"But what does this have to do with Keelyn Blake?" Lee asked.

Nathan leaned in. "Look, Evan. You better answer the fine officer's question. He's with SWAT. That means he can shoot from a distance and never be seen. You could be in hell in the next breath and never know it was coming."

The man swallowed hard. "The man who took a shot at me was Gavin Donnely. The man they questioned when the psychiatrist turned up dead and Keelyn's sister went missing."

"Why do you think he was there?" Nathan asked.

"Why else? To kill Keelyn, too."

Nathan looked at Lee. "We need to bring him in. No more messing around. He's got to know where they are."

Overhead, the paging system alarmed. "Code blue, room 325."

Lee's vision flamed white.

Conner's room.

CHAPTER 49

Lee scurried from Evan's ICU suite, knocked the sliding glass door as he exited, and ran full tilt down the hall. Seeing the group of people gathered at the elevator, he rounded the next corner and slammed through the stairwell door, taking the stairs two at a time. His boots echoed like flash-bang grenades. Nathan's footsteps followed in his wake.

The hallway outside Conner's room was chaos. Two security guards wrestled with a man on the ground as the medical team tried to push the red, stainless steel code cart into Conner's room. Where was the officer who was supposed to be watching him? When Lee was a mere five steps away, the man broke free and ran off.

"What's going on?" Lee shouted.

His heart caved as he looked sideways into the room. His brother a limp, pale shell as a linebacker-built tech pumped at his sternum to supply oxygen to his body. They slapped large electrical patches on his chest.

"The nurses claim that man did something to this patient."

"Get this place locked down!"

Lee exploded past the fatigued guards to follow the unknown man. Nathan stayed close on his heels, the sound of his coat flapping like a flock of angry birds. Lee heard the other stairwell door on the far end of the hall bang open.

He kicked his speed up. Three short flights down and the man would be out in the open and not as easily detained.

As Lee and Nathan piled into the stairway, the man was just one flight ahead of them. His hand visible on the metal railing as he swung around for the next half-flight.

Lee drew his weapon. "Stop! Police!"

As Lee hit the first-floor landing, cool air rushed up the well. The man had reached the ground floor and was now outside. When Lee came through the heavy fire door, a quick look right and left confirmed the man to be running away from the hospital toward the right.

Lee's SWAT training stemmed his anxiety over Conner. He broke out at a sprinter's pace after the man. Quickly, he began to close the gap. The only thing he heard was his footsteps as they pounded after this villain and the scrawling wind as it rushed over his body. He returned his weapon to his holster without breaking stride and pumped his legs harder.

Mere feet away, he reached up, his hands brushed against the collar of the man. Two more steps and he leapt like a runner taking a hurdle and clamped his target in his arms. They both rolled through the mixture of snow and mud.

The man tried to elbow him in the gut to break free. Lee grappled his neck and pressed it into the ground. Nathan joined him. Lee grabbed a pair of handcuffs and secured the man and pulled him up by the arms, yanked him around, and tossed him up against a nearby tree.

Lee stumbled back.

Gavin Donnely.

"Mr. Donnely." Nathan paused to catch his breath. "You saved us some time in trying to find you for questioning. Now it seems we'll be able to hold you for attempted murder."

Lee's breath heaved in his chest as his muscles released acid into his veins. He raised his fist. "You better tell me right now what you did to Conner. If he dies, I'll make sure you get the death penalty."

Gavin shrugged like an insolent teen. "Who says I gave him anything?"

Lee's fist was swift as it connected with Gavin's face, and Gavin slumped to the ground. Nathan seemed to sense what was on Lee's mind, and they began to turn out the doctor's pockets, looking for any evidence that might suggest what the offending drug had been. Lee felt the lumps of two glass vials in one front pocket and pulled them out.

Valium and potassium chloride.

Potassium chloride was part of the lethal injection used to kill death-row inmates.

Lee broke out in a run back to the hospital.

CHAPTER 50

Wednesday

Soft winter light seeped through the decayed curtains and playfully tugged at Keelyn's eyelids. Another morning in hell. Raven had moved her into the tiny bedroom. As she turned on the cot, a puff of dust shot up into the shaft of gold, and she watched the particles dance in joy at being released from their musty prison.

Something was wrong.

The crunchy air had increased in the tissue in her left side. She could only draw breath to a point before the pain caused her teeth to clench as her vision faded. Short and shallow was all she could muster, which left her with perpetual light-headedness.

Something was missing.

Keelyn shuffled her feet together. The chain was gone.

She eased up from the thin mattress. The room rippled, and she closed her eyes against the nausea. The weak metal hinges creaked as she rose. When she left the small room, she found Raven sitting at the table, eating through a box of powdered sugar doughnuts with an open container of orange juice next to her.

Raven pushed the box in her direction. "Your favorite, right?"

Keelyn pulled the metal folding chair from the table and sat. Raven set a napkin down with two doughnuts and sloppily poured juice from the container into a plastic cup. Keelyn brushed the pulpy fluid from her pants, then wondered what a few speckles of juice really mattered in the scheme of things.

The juice was warm, and the doughnuts stale. She pushed them away after a few bites. "Why did you take the chain off?"

Raven ignored her question. "You don't look well."

Keelyn pulled the inside of her cheek between her teeth. Should she tell Raven she felt ill? Would it convince her to release her? "My side is hurting a lot."

"Why don't you take a walk?" Raven brushed the sticky white from her lips.

"You're fine if I leave?"

"You're not a prisoner."

"Why the change of heart?"

515

Again, no answer.

Keelyn pressed her lips together, the residual sugar created a sticky paste. She cleared the gluey mess with her tongue. Wasn't she still imprisoned? Even if she could willingly leave, she had no idea where she was, and common sense had taught her staying in one place was always the best way to be found.

"That's okay. I'd rather talk with you."

"Really, I think the fresh air will do you some good. It stopped snowing."

In Raven's eyes, there was a dare. A mischievous, deadly twinkle. They'd played this game often when they were young children. One of them would hide something in the woods and challenge the other to find it. Whoever had the best time won. On that desolate property, it would keep them entertained for hours. That's how they'd found one of the other houses on all those acres.

Was there something Raven wanted her to find in the woods?

"Are you going to come with me?"

"I'm going to finish breakfast."

Keelyn headed to the front door.

"The back might be more interesting." Raven closed the box of doughnuts.

She crossed in front of Raven and headed

516

out the back screen door. A well-worn path snaked through the trees leading off the back concrete step that crumbled at its edges.

Keelyn walked into the freshly fallen snow. In her normal life, she loved this time of day. Inhaling the cool, clean air helped Keelyn shed the light-headedness caused by fitful sleep. As she began at a slow pace down the path, Sophia and Lee came to mind. Tears gathered at the possibly she would never see them again. She curled her fists and swiped her eyes.

Keep it together.

Light danced as the leaves filtered its fall to the ground. The path was easy to follow, and the trepidation Keelyn initially felt at finding her way back slipped away. Another alternative began to take root in her mind.

Maybe it would be best to leave.

Keelyn stood in the middle of the alley and glanced behind her. The home was just out of view. The day was young. It gave her hours to find someone to help. Surely they couldn't be far from a road, another house. Better to take her last day and find help then wait for whatever Raven had planned.

She ran down the path, footstep after footstep, her toes curled tight into her slippers to keep them in place. The snow crunched at her feet. Each breath was a knife in her side. At first she held her hand over her wound to stifle the pain.

Keelyn only covered a short distance before coughs tore from her throat. Her head swam, her vision dimmed, and she fell forward. The heels of her hand bit through the snow to the gravel underneath, and she slid to a stop. She eased onto her right side, her breaths quick and short. A black halo formed around the hazy sun, and she blinked quickly to edge away her body's desire to succumb to unconsciousness.

Dread set into her mind. Inside her chest was a bomb with an unknown detonation. Exertion would accelerate her to that point.

There was no leaving the house. Tears ran down her cheeks, and she rested her head on her outstretched arm and prayed her short sprint hadn't already hastened her death.

Something caught her eye.

In her direct line of sight on one side of the path, Keelyn could see that the ground was different. Instead of wild undergrowth in the shadowed spaces of the trees, she noticed overturned earth where someone had dug through the snow and clay to expose underbelly.

She lay for several minutes on her side,

gulping for air like a fish out of water. A ghostly sensation lingered at her spine. The hairs at the base of her neck tingled as they stood on end. Eventually, the pain eased, though her breathing remained rapid.

Keelyn sat up. Denial attempted to block her mind against the truth of what she was actually seeing.

Then she spied something else.

After fifty or so steps, another area of rustled, uneven earth.

Keelyn stood and walked to the next area. Her knees weakened and she slumped to the ground near the second site. Moisture seeped into her clothing as her spirit struggled against what it was going to find. She began to shiver as she crawled out to pick up a thick stick. If felt like acid ate away the tissue at her left side with each forward motion. On her knees, she neared the site and sank the stick into the uneven dirt.

It gave easily. This ground had been loosened recently.

She slammed the stick into the crusty particles more toward the center.

A sick thud caused her to jump back. The stick sank inside something, making it stand perfectly straight, like a nail in a board. A sentry laying claim to what was underneath.

Keelyn's breath came in staggered shakes.

She pulled up on all fours, the tears freely falling as she edged toward the outer periphery. A blue hue tinged the ends of her fingers as their numbed tips danced over the dirt.

She began to dig.

Each motion of her upper body increased the pain in her side. Snot dripped from her nose as she pulled at the dirt with her deadened, cold hands. The last thing she wanted to do was yank the stick from whatever held its position. The ground gave away easily as she supported herself with one hand and scooped with the other.

A horrid smell drifted from the pile. Keelyn turned her head to the side and buried her nose in her coat to keep the wretched odor at bay. She turned back and dug more. The need to know overcame her fright.

A pale flesh tone appeared, marked with angry purple collections of blood. She brushed the particles away.

A male hand.

A left hand with a ring on the fourth finger.

A husband.

Keelyn pushed back from the site and wept. Streaks of dirt clung to her face as she wiped her tears. The truth of what all this meant yanked her soul into a well of despair she feared she would never climb out of.

What Lee had tried to get her to believe was true. Raven was the danger in her life. The one who posed the greatest threat.

Now she was stuck in some desolate forest with a serial murderer.

Keelyn froze as she heard footsteps come up the path. She scrambled to her feet and clenched her teeth against the pain. The remnants of the grave clung to her clothes, and she swatted at her legs to clear the dirt. Death clung to her like a lost child.

"I see you found them."

Keelyn's tongue was full and heavy. Her mind blank at what she should say.

"Didn't take you very long."

Keelyn closed her eyes, exhaled, and tried to slow the thrum of her heart inside her chest. This was a game she was going to have to survive. She needed her wits about her. If she was ever going to return to Lee and Sophia, she had to pull herself together and start thinking about what her options really were.

She opened her eyes. "Who are they?"

Raven neared her. Keelyn felt her mind plead with her to back away as Raven breached her personal space.

She stood firm.

"Some of the people who failed us."

"How many graves are there?"

"Not enough. Not everyone."

An understanding shone through the mire of confusion that gripped Keelyn since she'd been pulled into Raven's vehicle. What was the reason for bringing her here? To this place?

It was to draw Lee. Maybe even Nathan.

Raven beckoned them to their deaths.

And Keelyn was the worm at the end of a long, sharp hook.

But did she want the same for Keelyn?

"How could you kill them?"

Raven looked shocked. "What?"

"How could you *murder* them?"

"You think I did this?"

Keelyn almost toppled over. "How did you know they were here if you didn't put them here?"

Raven slapped her hands to her head. "I helped Gavin bury them. He's the one who killed them."

Understanding cleared the haze of Keelyn's malnourished, injured body. She knew why Raven had fallen prey to Gavin's enchantment.

He was the physical representation of what Raven ached for. He had relentlessly pursued her.

He'd used Raven to get his own revenge on John Samuals.

Better than murdering her body, Gavin had killed her spirit.

"Do you know how much trouble you're in? He's setting you up to take the fall" — Keelyn spread her arms wide — "for all of this."

"I know."

Keelyn's jaw dropped. "You do?"

"Last night I pieced it together. When you told me Ryan and Clay had died."

Faint warmth burned from Keelyn's heart. A shimmer of hope against the darkness. "Then you can stop all of this right now. You can turn yourself in and confess your side of things. You can put him in jail. You can still be there for Sophia."

The words, at first, seemed to pull Raven's will. And then it came, like death had laid its hand on her soul. A hint of resigned resolution. Of prey trapped in a cage.

"He won."

"Raven, what are you talking about?"

She fisted her hands and pushed them into her eyes. "You don't get any of this!"

Keelyn backed up a few steps. "Tell me."

She opened her arms to the sky. "I wanted to hurt them. I was so trapped in this despair, I wanted to hurt everyone who'd left me in that hellhole. For them to feel just a little bit of the pain I did. For them to realize how awful it was and just maybe say they were sorry."

"But, Raven —"

"That's why I started seeing Gavin. For the depression. I wanted it to go away. I wanted to be happy. I wanted to be whole —"

"Calm down —"

"That's what I found in the Bible. It's what I loved — God pursuing me. God loving me so much he actually died."

"Okay —"

Raven screamed into the forest, a high-pitched wail that silenced every living creature within hearing range. She clawed at her arms.

"Gavin said the only way to feel better was to make those people feel the pain I did. He said there was a way to do that — to get them to realize what they'd done. He gave me the spider venom to inject but he promised me it wouldn't hurt anyone."

"He lied to you."

"Now I'm going to die."

Keelyn's mind brewed with confusion. She pressed her fingers into her forehead. "You can still stop this. You can come clean.

I'll help you."

"It's too late! I'm going to finish it. In the beginning, I didn't want people to die. Now, I don't care anymore."

Keelyn's body felt heavy, the weight of Raven's choices like a straight-jacket around her. "I don't think that's true."

"Nothing can redeem me."

Keelyn prayed for wisdom. For a way to help Raven understand there was still hope. A way out of this mess her sister had been victimized into. "Remember what you read. You have to stop believing these lies."

"God would want me to be punished."

What could Keelyn say to turn this around?

"What will you do when you're done?"

Raven's eyes narrowed as the words sank in. Her mouth gaped open, yet no words were vocalized.

Keelyn stepped closer. Her breath puffed from her in rapid, thin vapors. "What will you do when this is over? You won't be going back to Sophia. You'll either rot in prison like your crazy father or be on the run your entire life!"

She'd lit the fuse.

Raven punched her left side where her dressing covered the tunnel into her chest. Keelyn's eyes widened in shock as she

525

struggled to breathe. She backpedaled several steps before gaining her balance. Anger flamed her vision white as the adrenaline surge muted the pain.

Keelyn charged back, hit Raven mid-chest with her forearm, and knocked her to the ground. Just as Keelyn went to hold her in place by pinning Raven's shoulders into the cold dirt, Raven sat up and pulled Keelyn's ankles out from under her.

Keelyn's back slammed into the earth. Air exploded from her mouth. Her side ruptured in fire. Terror flooded through her as she vainly tried to refill her lungs with icy air.

Raven scrambled and sat on top of her.

"What's the matter, Sis?" She placed her hand in the middle of Keelyn's chest. "Can't breathe?"

Her vision faded, and all went black.

CHAPTER 51

Lee slugged another hot cup of coal black coffee to shake the edges of fatigue that clouded his mind. Nathan had insisted he take a few short hours to sleep before they hit Gavin with this interview, and the torn couch in the detective's lounge offered little comfort. Neither did his tormented thoughts. Sleep came in fits of surrender.

Less than twelve hours left to ascertain Keelyn's location, develop a tactical plan, and try to get there in time to save her life. Coordinating between agencies was going to be a nightmare with such a short window.

Conner barely hung onto life. When Lee had returned with the drugs in hand, it gave the medical team the clues they needed so they could administer drugs to counteract the effects of the potassium on his heart. The ICU physician explained the massive dose of the electrolyte seized up the muscle so it couldn't beat.

Unfortunately, it had taken the medical team more than twenty minutes to stabilize Conner's heart rhythm. Now he lay in a comatose state.

He probably didn't even know he was Sophia's father.

Lee glanced at the text again.

I'm at Sophia's. My grandmother's house.

He was unsure of when the message was actually sent. The situation with Gavin and Conner had tied Lee up well into the early morning before he could get his dead phone into the charger. In the interim, they'd sent teams of police officers to try to find out where this location could be. Clearly Raven's phone was either turned off or out of power. Finding Keelyn's grandmother's home was mystifying the best detectives on the force. They'd sent additional officers to John Samuals's property to see if any remaining personal effects could offer a clue.

They'd found an old photo album. Some with sepia-toned pictures contained a young girl who appeared to be Keelyn's mother, Sophia. They were trying to track down a marriage license, anything.

So far, Keelyn's life fell like sand through his fingers.

He had to hit Gavin with everything he had.

Nathan approached the interview room. "You ready?"

Lee checked a few notes. "Absolutely. Has he been read his rights?"

"Yes, he's refusing a lawyer. Says he wants to get everything out in the open."

Lee smiled. "They're always their own worst enemy."

"I'll let you take the lead since you found the most damning piece of evidence. Just remember, you get him mad enough, and he may not tell you anything. It might be best to come across as a friend first. Like you admire him."

Lee's stomach twisted in pain. Befriend his enemy? "I'll do what I need to do to get Keelyn back."

He pushed through the door and pasted the best fake smile to his face he could muster.

"Dr. Donnely. Hope you were able to rest a little bit last night."

"Oh sure, sleeping in a fetid jail cell was just dandy."

Lee let the comment slide. He sat at the table. "There're a couple of issues we're going to need to clear up."

Nathan positioned himself behind Gavin so he was visible to Lee. His eyes deviated toward the ceiling.

"Can you explain what you were doing inside Conner's room?"

"It's simple. I was visiting a former patient. Checking on his welfare."

"And the drugs in your pocket?"

"Just some empty vials of medication."

"The doctors think you used the Valium to knock Conner out and the potassium to stop his heart from beating."

"Well, nice theory, but the trouble the hospital is going to have is they were already using these medications for Conner's treatment. The Valium to help ease his anxiety and the potassium chloride was a part of his maintenance IV solution. My being there when he arrested was merely happenstance. Unfortunately, I think your brother suffered a drug error caused by the hospital. Sadly, it isn't that rare."

Lee inhaled deeply to keep his fist from striking Gavin again. "I've got to hand it to you."

"How so?"

"You've really pulled yourself together over the last two days. Last time Nathan and I saw you, you looked like you were unraveling a bit."

Gavin nodded. "Things are clearer for me now."

"Speaking of former patients, I'd like to

talk about Raven. I have the sense there may have been more than a doctor-patient relationship going on."

"And your basis for that might be?"

"For one, the psychiatrist reviewing your medical care of Raven will testify, at the very least, you were overstepping your bounds by touching her inappropriately and may have gone as far as to enter a sexual relationship with a minor. In fact, you think you're Sophia's father."

Gavin shrugged.

"That's why you bought Raven the house she was living in. Why you were paying her bills."

He stilled.

"I was confused about several things happening to Keelyn. She got these mysterious gifts at times for the child. Toys — diaper cream. It was the ointment that confused me when I looked at it. Had to be special-ordered. When I talked to a local pharmacist about it, she said the only people who really knew about it were physicians."

"What does any of this matter?"

"I think you suspected Raven could be a danger to Sophia and were trying to warn Keelyn about it. To protect Sophia."

"If that's true, maybe I'm not such a bad guy, after all."

"The problem is, Sophia is not your child. She's actually Conner's."

Gavin's eyes widened slightly. He folded his hands on the table. "Looks like you're going to have trouble getting some of your accusations to stick. How can you prove Raven and I were ever together?"

"That statement leads me to believe you feel like you've got everything wrapped up with a nice little bow." Lee mimicked the motion with his hands.

Gavin chuckled. "You can think whatever you want."

"I'd like to talk a little bit about what you were like as a young man."

"That's been quite a few years."

"Nathan and I discovered an interesting thing. Your father was killed in a work-related accident caused by John Samuals."

Gavin bit into his lip, a small fracture in the facade. "That's true."

"In light of that, why would you want anything to do with the Samuals family?"

"Of course, I wasn't a fan of John Samuals. A year after I started medical school, he set up a meeting to talk about the accident. Said he was going to try to fix things."

"How?"

"By making sure there was an antidote for

the weapon he created."

"Why would he need to be worried about that when the evidence of his work was destroyed?"

"As long as John Samuals is alive, his work can be duplicated."

Lee put aside the conspiracy theory. He didn't have time to delve into it with Keelyn's time running out. "So you forgave him."

"Absolutely."

"Why did you insinuate yourself into Lucy Freeman's practice?"

"Truth be told, John Samuals was a fascinating character. I wanted to know more about him, and I knew Lucy Freeman had the most intimate information."

"But why did you stay?" Lee pressed.

"What do you mean?"

"Once you were in, I'm assuming you read through all of John's psychiatric notes. After you got all of those dirty little secrets on John, you could have walked away — should have walked away. I'm looking for the reason you stayed."

"You're right. I could have left, but then I met Raven. She was so troubled. I thought I could really help her."

"That's the only reason. A sense of altruism?"

"Well, the money was amazing, and I was using my salary to fund my other projects."

Lee shuffled through his notes. "Speaking of that, I've been curious about your fascination with spider venom. I almost wonder if you were trying to replicate John's work. Reformulate that bioweapon yourself. That would have been big bucks if you could have done it. Big defense contracts would come your way, I bet."

Gavin sat silent.

"But then there was the part of you that really wanted to avenge your father's death. What better way to do that than make John suffer by having one of his kids go down for murder."

"Really? That's what you think?"

"What I *know* is several people will testify that Raven worsened under your care. Why would you let that happen? If you really cared for her, if you weren't cutting it, why not let Dr. Freeman take over?"

"At best, Lucy Freeman was incompetent."

Lee's gaze locked on Gavin's eyes. "She caught on to you. Filed a complaint. Is that why she died?"

"You'll have to ask your dear brother about that."

"Oh, right. The gun with Conner's prints

on it and all."

"Exactly."

"Curious thing about those prints." Lee slammed a couple of DVDs onto the counter.

At first, a mild look of surprise quickly covered with a claim of contemptuous boredom. "What would those be?"

"Dr. Vanhise, an ethical, highly respected psychiatrist, has been reviewing these tapes of your patient sessions. My guess is these people didn't know they were being videoed without their permission, right?"

Gavin swallowed hard, the snake with a mouse caught in his throat.

Lee continued. "And we found your two secret stashes. One behind your spider friends and the other tucked up in the attic of your home. Those were pretty good hiding places, I have to say." Lee tapped the first silver disk. "This DVD shows you administering a sedative nasally to Conner, taking the gun you asked him to bring, and pressing his prints onto the weapon."

"That was part of his therapy."

"Of course it was. That's why you're wearing latex gloves while you do it. It wouldn't be because you were concerned your prints might get on the firearm."

"You still have Conner at the diner with

535

the dead doctor. Oh, and that nasty little interchange."

"Ah, yes. That's true. He was there."

"Fingered at the scene by your fiancée."

"We're not together anymore. I should thank you. She was getting on my nerves anyway. Her and that bratty kid. Good riddance." He waved at the air as if batting a mosquito. Lee's heart hammered at the lie. Was Gavin as good at reading body language as Keelyn?

Gavin smiled slightly. "Good to be free, right?"

Lee tapped the second disk. "This is footage from the front of the restaurant. You were smart to have Lucy park the SUV all the way into the corner of the lot so the actual shooting is not seen. You asked Raven to coordinate a lunch meeting, right? Then you show up. Tell her you want to talk. Maybe you were going to drive them off site and that's why Freeman was on the passenger's side."

No comment.

"Curious thing is there is footage of your vehicle coming and going from the lot. And the trunk seems weighted down when you enter — like maybe there's a body in it. Clay Timmons's body, perhaps." Lee pushed the case aside. "But forensics will sort that out now that your vehicle's been impounded. Regardless, footage puts you at the scene of the crime."

"Vicinity doesn't mean collusion."

"No, but Raven and Conner will testify you're the one who shot Lucy Freeman and put Clay in the back of that SUV. How you did that without people in the diner seeing you still amazes me."

Gavin fanned his fingers and pushed them into his chest. "I should be worried? As if the accusation of a drug addict and a mentally unstable missing woman will hold any water."

Lee shuffled the DVDs. Next hand. "For a long time, I couldn't get the symbol out of my head — the one we found on some of your victims. Then I discovered that it's the logo for the company where your father worked."

"That's not highly classified information."

"And then there're these . . ."

Lee slapped the baggie of syringes onto the table. The ones he'd recovered from Raven's house. "Recognize them?"

Gavin shrugged.

"Raven kept them in her house. I had a little testing done."

Gavin circled his finger in the air to signify his boredom. "Oh, golly gee, let me guess.

Spider venom on the inside?"

"Ding, ding, ding. Awesome answer. But unfortunately, no get-out-of-jail-free card."

"Now you know the real killer is Raven since they were found in her house."

"Another thing the lab found in the needle was a bacteria. Meningococcus. Medical examiner found the bacteria in Clay Timmons's blood-stream. Cultures from Ryan show he was infected as well." Lee stood and leaned on his fingertips. "That's what really stumped the doctors at the hospital. Why were these individuals so sick when black widow spider venom rarely kills?" He ran his hand over the baggie. "That was really the point for the symbol in those early victims. It was to inject the bacteria into multiple sites so hopefully sepsis would take hold. Plus, it was going to take time for you to teach Raven how to give it IV. And nothing like an homage to daddy dearest and the physical pain the vemon induces."

Gavin gave a few jaded claps. "Quite a theory."

"We found cultures for the bacteria in your office."

"Raven obviously had access to those. She was a patient."

"So she made these deadly syringes up all by herself?"

"That's what I'm guessing."

"Then why are your prints on these syringes?"

Gavin looked like he might topple over. "That's not possible."

"So either you were sloppy, or Raven didn't quite follow directions as you had asked." Lee slapped another DVD onto the desk. "Remember that secret stash in your attic? It held the biggest prize of all. This little home movie details the instructions you gave to her. How to use the venom and dispose of the evidence. Why you crazy creeps keep this stuff is amazing to me. Makes it so much easier to get that needle in your arm."

Gavin swallowed hard, then crossed his arms over his chest. "Detective, are you threatening me?"

Lee stood and hovered over him. "Consider it what you will. Now, if you want the death penalty off the table, you need to tell me where Raven took Keelyn."

CHAPTER 52

A sudden snowstorm had swooped over the Rockies and sat over Teller County like an obstinate child. Gavin Donnely had seen the light, or perhaps the potassium chloride, and shared the location of the home where Keelyn's mother had grown up. Due to the storm, Teller County officials were stretched thin and were quick to agree to a co-operative effort with Lee and Nathan at the lead.

Night shrouded the small structure. Little light shone from within. Voices cracked in Lee's earpiece as each officer sounded his position around the perimeter. Eight officers composed this group. Nathan served more as an observer, while the others narrowed in on the target. Lee made his team swear no entry unless he signaled or became incapacitated.

Lee edged around the front of the house and peered inside. Keelyn and Raven seemed to be arguing. Raven motioned several times to her phone. Lee hit the button for the light on his watch, and the eerie green glow matched the sick feeling in his gut.

Right at the deadline.

He had to get Keelyn out alive.

Lee dialed the phone number from which Raven had sent the last text and was surprised she answered.

"You were almost too late, Lee."

He inhaled icy air as his heart raced in his chest. "Raven, I'd like to end this peacefully. I want you to come out of the front door with your hands raised."

"That's not going to happen."

"Then send Keelyn out, and I'll come in and talk with you."

"You're not getting it, Lee. I thought you were smart."

He leaned into the house and looked at her face through the dirty glass. "I know you must want to see Sophia again. She misses you."

He could see her head tilt slightly as if reconsidering, but then she shook her head violently as if to prevent the reasonable solution from taking hold.

"Don't think you can bust in here with gas or flash grenades. I've dumped gasoline all over."

Raven was limiting their options and the chatter through his earpiece confirmed the rest of the team knew what that meant. Discharging something inside the small cabin could spark a fire if what Raven said was true.

They either had to go in or shoot Raven from the outside.

Through the window, Raven stood, threw the phone aside, and grabbed Keelyn's arm, brandishing a knife in her free hand.

Lee couldn't risk a bullet hitting Keelyn, so he punched through the door with his shoulder and immediately held up his hands so she could see he didn't have a weapon trained. He slowly closed the door behind him.

"Decided it was best to come in?" Raven swung the knife outward.

Lee looked around. What he didn't smell was gas. What he didn't see was fluid sloshed around or any evidence of a container that might have held the flammable liquid.

Raven had lied.

"Guess the gasoline was a ruse." In his ear, he could hear Nathan confirm flash-bang grenades were back on the table.

"Had to make sure you'd actually come in."

"I want to help you get this whole thing sorted out."

His heart stumbled as he searched Keelyn's hazel eyes. Definite relief and the spark of their attraction was still in her weary smile.

Lee maintained his position, his hands up in surrender. "You guys have been up here a few days. Are you thirsty? Hungry?"

Raven tightened her arm around Keelyn's chest. "We don't need anything."

"Okay. Can we sit?" Lee motioned to the table.

Keelyn coughed, her face stretched with pain. "Maybe you . . . could tell . . . Raven how . . . Sophia's been doing?"

What was wrong with her? Keelyn was having trouble breathing. Her chest heaved at an increased rate under Raven's hold. Sweat slid down her face. It was too cold to be from a simple rise in body temperature.

Unless she had a fever as well.

"Of course. I'm sure you've been very worried about her. She's great." He looked at Keelyn directly. "I've been taking care of her with Lilly's help. She's safe."

"And Conner?" Raven asked.

Lee set his hands on his hips. "Actually, Raven, I am forever in your debt. You helped save Conner's life by letting Keelyn know about the spiders." Did that come across as sincere?

"So he's okay?"

Lee closed his eyes. "He's still very sick."

"Is he dead?"

Lee shook his head.

Raven's body stiffened. "Gavin did something to him, didn't he?"

"Yes, he tried to kill him."

Tears coursed down Raven's cheeks. She sniffed hard. "It doesn't matter. It's time to finish all of this." She pointed with her knife to the table. "That's for you."

He broke his gaze from Keelyn to the circular, wooden table that sat in the middle of the room. A syringe sat at the center.

"I want you to inject yourself with what's inside."

Keelyn bit into her lip, pleaded with her eyes for him to refuse. He pulled out the metal chair and sat down.

"Why do you want me to do this?"

"It's the only way you can save Keelyn."

"There's got to be more to it, Raven. You just used Keelyn to get me here."

Lee began to remove his tactical gear. The Velcro as it ripped was like sharp nails against his spine. His teeth cringed.

"I need you to feel the pain I've felt over all these years."

Lee shrugged out of his vest and let it fall to the floor. He unbuttoned the cuff of his shirt. "Because of what John made you do to Cheyenne. The choice you had to make. There's a lot I would change about that day. I want them back, too."

Raven laid the knife against Keelyn's chest. "That's a lie."

Lee's muscles tightened. He began to roll the fabric of his sleeve up. "I can assure you it's not. I know a lot about lies and how destructive they can be." He patted the vest of his shirt and took out Keelyn's engagement ring. He set it on the table.

Keelyn visibly shook. Her mouth opened to speak but upon inhaling to form the words, her knees buckled and she dropped forward, the tip of the knife perilously close to her neck. Lee's heart slammed against his rib cage. He stood from the chair, nearly knocked the table over. Raven pulled Keelyn back toward a wall for leverage.

Lee raised a fist to keep the team from splitting apart the cabin.

"Sit back down!" Raven screamed.

With a clenched fist, Lee reached back to feel for the metal folding chair and eased himself down. Keelyn's face was full of abject fright. She reached toward her neck and smoothed her fingers in the hollow well

545

above her sternum feeling the blood that settled there.

Lee swallowed hard. In his life he never imagined he'd witness Keelyn held hostage again. His anguish at the thought of losing her threatened to overtake his years of training. "Raven, it doesn't have to be this way. If you could just set the knife down so we can talk. Let me have my medical guys take a look at Keelyn."

Raven shook her head and moved the knife closer to the side of Keelyn's neck.

Desperate thoughts flooded his mind — willed his muscles to move. "Gavin lied to you. We know he's framed you for murder. He's confessed. It's not too late for you to stop all of this."

Raven turned the edge of the knife into Keelyn's neck. A faint smile played on her lips.

Enjoyment.

Only rarely had he seen the manifestation of true evil. And here it was holding his loved one at the tip of a knife.

Keelyn winced as a small cut formed. Even in the darkness, he could see the dark red line flow down the curve of her neck. Keelyn reached up to ease the blade away.

Lee held up a hand. "Raven, stop! I'll do it. I'll do as you want. Just don't hurt,

546

Keelyn. It's the only thing I ask."

As part of his SWAT gear, Lee carried a tourniquet. He took it from the small patch of his belt, unfurled it, and wrapped it around his arm, the elastic as tight as the invisible hand around his throat. His movements were quick and sure as his muscles retained the memory of the maneuver from his horrid past. He flicked at the vein in the crook of his elbow until it popped up, a thick rope in his muscle.

Lee picked up the syringe and uncapped the needle with his teeth. He spit the cap to the floor.

"Before you die, are you going to tell her the truth about your past?" Raven chided. "Why it is you're so comfortable getting yourself ready to inject yourself with this poison . . . Gavin's special mixture."

Did the syringe contain the same drugs Donnely had given Conner? If so, the venom was the least of his worries.

The statement convinced Lee his options were running short. The look on Raven's face was maniacal — every animated evil clown rolled into one. She fed on his pain for her pleasure.

Wanted to see him suffer.

Wanted him to feel Keelyn's repudiation of what he had been.

That was the emotional pain that ruined Raven. That led her to believe every lie whispered in her ear.

Rejection.

Lee loosened the tourniquet slightly to ease the tingle in his hand. If left on too long, the vein would tense and rupture when he inserted the needle. He didn't want to fail Keelyn in his last opportunity to save her. He felt panic creep into his chest. Not at any concern about his need to fulfill what Raven asked, but at the fear of what Keelyn's face would betray when he told her the secret he'd longed to always keep buried. Would she still love him?

He rubbed at his arm, at the old scars he now told people were from donating blood.

"Tell her!"

Lee looked at Keelyn directly. "I was a drug addict. I'm the reason Conner became one. I gave him his first hit. I stuck the needle in his arm."

Keelyn's knees buckled. Her eyes narrowed with betrayal. Raven laughed and tightened her grip around Keelyn. The knife pressed tighter. Another stream of blood.

Lee's head pounded. He pressed his thumb and forefinger hard against his tear ducts to prevent them from exposing the self-hatred he'd carried for over a decade.

"After high school, I didn't really have a plan. I refused to go to college. My father said, 'Either get a job or enlist in the military.' I picked the latter. Flipping burgers just didn't appeal to me."

"Okay, Lee. It's enough —"

The smile on Raven's face unnerved him.

"No, Keelyn. I'm going to tell you everything with the hope you'll pick this ring back up and put it on your finger." His bones sucked in the chill from the cabin like dry sponges. A tremor settled into his chest. "After a four-year stint and then my discharge, I started to dabble in things I shouldn't. Like drinking and smoking weed."

Keelyn stared at him, wide-eyed. He rubbed at the knotted muscles that threatened to pin his shoulders.

Stay calm. Be ready.

"That didn't quite come close to some of the thrills I had in the military. I started using IV drugs."

Lee inhaled and held his breath. It did little to stem his nerves. "Conner was sixteen at the time. He looked up to me. Wanted to do everything I did."

"Lee, I . . . understand —"

He waved her off. "Conner walked in on me one time when I was shooting up. Said he wanted to try it." Lee pressed his palm into his face and shoved it down over his chin. "He threatened to tell my secret if I didn't do as he asked and so I'm the one" — Lee picked up the syringe — "who put the needle in his arm and injected the poison that ended the potential life he could have had. After that day, I never shot up again. After that day, Conner couldn't stop." Lee smoothed his hand over his head, his neck tight with the noose of his confession. "I've been covering it up ever since. I knew I could never work in law enforcement if I disclosed it. I was amazed I passed the lie detector. Guess it showed what a practiced deceiver I was."

Lee studied Keelyn's face. Was there a hint of forgiveness? Keelyn broke his gaze, and his heart stalled. In his death, he wanted to know she didn't despise him. That would be hell. He leaned forward and dropped his head into his hands. It was what he feared. His actions had annihilated every relationship that had any meaning. There was no coming back.

The wind howled. Just under the turbulent gusts, he could hear Keelyn's staggered breaths.

"Lee . . ."

He raised his eyes.

"I love you," Keelyn whispered.

A flood of peace washed over him. Lightness filled his chest. His breath unhindered. The bonds of those lies on his life — broken. The words were like sweet salve to his open, dry soul.

"I forgive you."

Cool, fresh water filled the cracks.

He broke his gaze from Keelyn and centered it on Raven. "Now, I can die in peace. I'm fine with it."

Keelyn openly wept. His sorrow at her pain intensified.

"But, Raven, I want to say something to you before I do as you ask. That lie I held onto, the guilt cost me everything that's important. My family. Keelyn. Probably my job. I felt distant from God because of it. Isn't that how you feel? Lies pushed me away from the one thing I really wanted. God's love."

Raven pulled Keelyn closer to her chest, drew the blade back, and poked the tip at Keelyn's neck. Blood dripped slowly from the previous cuts onto Keelyn's collarbone.

Lee held Raven's gaze. "I know you read the Bible. You had to if you wanted to give them away to other people. What you didn't read closely enough was that the father of lies has convinced you of the same set of lies. That lying and revenge are the only way to end your sadness." Raven stiffened, and Lee tightened up the tourniquet. "Let me tell you, Raven, all it does is increase it. It's a prison you'll never break free from. Just like the lie I covered up imprisoned me until today."

"I don't care what you say!"

He looked at her gently. "When I do this — inject this venom into my body — I'm going to be praying for you. For your forgiveness. For the hope that the truth of what you read in that book will break through this lie you're living under and set you free."

He shoved the needle inside his vein. The sting barely registered. He drew the plunger back and his blood circled into and mixed with the toxin. "This is not what I want. I want to be married to Keelyn. I love her and Sophia. I'd like to help you, Raven, get your life back."

Raven's hand tightened around the blade, she pressed the knife into Keelyn's neck. The metal tip slid in. "Just do it!"

Before Raven could edge the knife deeper into Keelyn's neck, he shoved the plunger in.

CHAPTER 53

"Lee!"

Lee threw aside the syringe. He stood up from the table, staggered three steps, and crashed to the ground.

Keelyn reached for him, but Raven held fast. "Now, it's your turn."

She felt the knife slice further into her skin. An unfamiliar whistle pierced into the cabin, faster and higher than the wind. The sound stalled Raven's inward thrust of the blade, and the sound of windows breaking was followed by two concussive booms. It felt like the noise would level the tiny structure.

Keelyn felt Raven's arm drop, and she shoved her back. That one movement sapped her strength, and she felt her muscles strain to stay upright. Keelyn's ears rang from the explosions. Smoke filled the room. Muffled voices hung at the end of a long tunnel. Keelyn tried to walk toward

Lee, but her chest felt like lit gasoline, and she stumbled to her knees. She pressed her nose into her clothing to keep from inhaling additional smoke, but the stench proved too strong. Coughs seized her chest.

Slowly she crawled in the direction of where Lee had fallen, groping the floor like a blind person. Her fingers felt his warm flesh. She patted up his body till she felt his face. She pulled up his jutted chin and pressed her ear against his mouth and nose. His lips were warm against her cheek, but he didn't draw breath. She opened his lips and placed her mouth over his, their last kiss brought to mind as she blew hard into his mouth to fill his lungs.

She almost passed out from the pain of offering that one breath.

Tears streamed down her face. Her weakness could mean his death.

In the darkness and noise, she couldn't tell if it was her screaming or someone else.

Keelyn shook her head. *Try something else. Lee wouldn't give up this easily.*

She felt for the buttons on his shirt, estimated where the center of his chest was, and pushed with all her might. Each compression felt like ribs were shattering in her own chest. Pain shot down her left arm and up into her jaw. Sweat dripped from her face. Fatigue overtook her will, and Keelyn slumped over his body.

Flashlights lit up the darkness. Another officer knelt beside her.

"Help. Me."

A hand grabbed hers and eased her off Lee. Her vision tunneled. Lights welcomed her at the end.

"Keelyn, it's Joshua." The lead SWAT medic. "We're helping Lee. Trying to counteract what we think was in the syringe . . . probably potassium. Keelyn!" The light was bright in her eyes. A palm rested on her cheek. "Can you breathe?" His ear pressed close to her lips. A stethoscope snaked under her shirt.

She pushed it away. "Lee . . . first."

"Nathan! Need a set of hands over here!" A mask over her face. A fresh flow of clean air cooled the heat in her body. Joshua pulled her coat open and cut her shirt up the middle, exposing her chest.

Nathan's voice. Worried. "Is she alive?"

"She won't be in a minute."

"What's wrong with her?"

More light.

Keelyn looked beside her. An officer struggled to place a set of handcuffs on Raven.

Another medic team worked on Lee. One

performed CPR. There was an open trauma kit. The floor was littered with syringes and used boxes of medication. Another officer knelt beside him and readied a bag of IV fluids.

"Keelyn, this will be cold."

Her eyes stayed on Lee.

"What are you going to do?" Nathan again.

"Her left lung has collapsed, and putting this needle into her chest will buy us some time."

Another needle in Lee's arm. Clear fluids flowed. The medic shoved in what seemed an endless number of medications.

Keelyn reached for Lee's hand. Tears fell freely. Her soul crushed by the thought of losing him. He was a good man. He'd been trying to protect her. He'd given up his life to save hers.

In the end, Raven had forced a screenplay of what she couldn't understand in the Bible.

A man laying his life down for another.

Lee had willingly stepped into the role.

Keelyn prayed fervently. Raven screamed as the officers placed her in handcuffs and hauled her outside the shack. But Keelyn could barely hear it above the crazy humming in her ears. Warmth soothed her fatigued muscles.

"He's in v-tach."

"Let's shock him!"

The fine whine of a defibrillator as it charged.

The needle as it pierced her chest.

The pull of something as it beckoned her away.

CHAPTER 54

Christmas Eve

Keelyn stood before her mother's childhood home now a pile of ash, lit by a troubled soul that loved to watch things burn.

At least that's what the fire department was calling it . . . arson.

The charcoal gray particles had mixed and melted into a fresh layer of snow and the black dots looked like cancer in the clean, crisp crystals. Yellow crime tape could still be seen tied around some of the aspens where the fire had not melted the plastic and just as ribbons around trees often times marked something to remember . . . so did these.

Lives lost. Innocence captured. People murdered.

Almost.

In fact, Keelyn's lung had collapsed again. The SWAT medic saved her life by jamming the needle into her chest. It bought her enough time to make it to a hospital for another chest tube to be placed. This time, she did follow instructions and made no further attempts to take it out herself.

Conner had survived Donnely's attack but was currently in prison, along with Raven and Donnely. It was too soon to tell what myriad of charges would actually stick. Several trials loomed.

Lee also survived his brush with Gavin's toxic mixture that contained the same potent dose of potassium chloride he'd tried to kill Conner with and not any spider venom. Though Raven had almost gotten her wish to see him imprisoned under the earth with the other bodies they'd found along the path. He'd been in a coma for a week before his eyes had fluttered open, his blue eyes clearing in every second he held Keelyn's. The warmth of his fingers against her cheek was the seal of her resolve to mend what had broken between them.

And this was part of that process.

To find the ring.

His engagement ring.

Buried somewhere in this pile of broken dreams.

And so, she'd set to it. Bundled in her coat, a scarf tight around her nose and lips to keep the air from solidifying her face, she worked to sweep a metal detector over every inch of the rubble. Even in the quiet, she missed the footsteps approaching her from behind and she screamed as a hand rested upon her shoulder.

Keelyn whipped around and clipped the man's shins with the metal detector then raised it above her head for another hit when the man reached up to steady her hand.

A playful smile on his face.

"Lee!"

"Want to take it easy with that? They just let me out of rehab."

She dropped the contraption and rushed into his arms. "How did you find me?"

"Sophia's sitter let the secret out."

He held her for the longest time. The faint musical notes played by the wind as it rushed through the pines calmed her fluttering heart. She pressed her face into his chest and he smoothed his hand over her tangled hair.

Easing her back, he searched her eyes with his, his palm on her cheek. "Why would you come back here?"

Keelyn placed her hand over his. "To find your ring."

Lee pulled his hand down and took hers. "Any luck?"

She shook her head and began to cry. He draped his arm over her shoulder. "Keelyn, it's okay."

"I should never have given it back."

"Honestly, you had every right to." Heaviness settled into his face. "I'm not sure I'd want you to have it back."

An ache pulsed through her body. At that moment, she wanted the earth to swallow her up. The pain of living without him too much to think about.

He turned away from her. "Fire is an interesting force. So destructive yet it's also a purifier. When a forest burns — it brings renewal. Healthier trees grow."

"Lee —"

Taking her hand, he got down on one knee. "The reason I don't want you to have that particular ring back is it represents our old relationship. It's better it burned, hopefully melted away never to be found again" — he reached into his coat for a small, red velvet box — "so I could give you this."

He flipped the box open and the strength leached from Keelyn's knees. She felt light-headed.

A ring. A new ring. Brilliant against the winter light like the snow as it dazzled.

He gripped her hand tighter and locked her eyes with his. "Keelyn Blake. I pledge to

561

be the man I should have always been. To love you with my whole heart. To never hide anything from you. To be a father for Sophia . . . if you'll let me."

Keelyn's heart swelled with joy. She drop tackled him in a hug and pressed her lips against his.

After a long kiss, he eased her back. "That's a yes for sure, right?"

She nuzzled his nose. "Yes, absolutely. One hundred percent."

"Just one favor?"

"One?"

"Don't ever let the guys know you took me down."

CHAPTER 55

One year later

Keelyn had always wanted a winter wedding. Christmas Day couldn't be any better. The sanctuary was lit only by the red-and-white candles reminiscent of candy canes. Her drop-shouldered dress was lined with white fur at the neck and cuffs. She turned as she felt Sophia tugging on the long train.

"Soo pretty," the child cooed as she laced her fingers over the crystals. "It's shiny!"

Keelyn brought up the bouquet of red roses to her chest, and she leaned over to kiss Sophia's cheek. "You're so pretty." Keelyn fingered the red velvet dress. "Time to drop your petals."

"Now?"

"Yes. Go, sweet girl." Keelyn nudged at her back. Sophia had practiced this for weeks, dropping a handful of petals with each step.

Lilly Reeves glanced back at Keelyn. "Are

you ready?"

Keelyn looked over the sanctuary and thought about the people she wanted to have there. Her lost family members. Her mother and father.

The scent of cinnamon and vanilla calmed her nerves. "Ready."

Lilly winked and began her slow walk down the aisle.

Lee walked up to the altar. Keelyn held her breath. He was oh so handsome in his black tuxedo with red cummerbund. His blond hair a little longer than his former military style buzz cut. On his face was the sense of peace he'd been given as a gift, he'd said, from his brush with death — a struck match of clarity. Considering his commendable service to the police department and that his indiscretions had occurred before his hiring, he'd been allowed to keep his job. Even from this distance, his blue eyes were like sapphire pools of warm water. His smile a beacon that drew her feet forward.

"Were you going to leave without me?" Nathan took her hand and looped it through his arm. He rubbed at her fingers. "I'm so happy for the two of you."

"Thank you for doing this. Nothing like double duty."

"Best man and giver-awayer. I couldn't

think of a better way to spend my day."

They began to walk down the aisle to Pachelbel's *Canon,* the music as light and airy as Keelyn's spirit.

Her nerves tingled as Nathan took her hand and surrendered it to Lee. He kissed each of her fingers gently. Tears slid down her cheeks.

"I'm never letting go" — with his other hand, Lee reached for Sophia's chubby fingers — "of either of you."

ABOUT THE AUTHOR

Jordyn Redwood has served patients and their families for nearly twenty years and currently works as a pediatric ER nurse. As a self-professed medical nerd and trauma junkie, she was drawn to the controlled chaotic environments of critical care and emergency nursing. Her love of teaching developed early and she was among the youngest CPR instructors for the American Red Cross at the age of seventeen. Since then, she has continued to teach advanced resuscitation classes to participants ranging from first responders to MDs.

Her discovery that she also had a fondness for answering medical questions for authors led to the creation of Redwood's Medical Edge at http://jordynredwood.com. This blog is devoted to helping contemporary and historical authors write medically accurate fiction.

Jordyn lives in Colorado with her husband,

two daughters, and one crazy hound dog. In her spare time she also enjoys reading her favorite authors, quilting, and cross-stitching. Jordyn loves to hear from her readers and can be contacted at jredwood1@gmail.com.

The employees of Thorndike Press hope you have enjoyed this Large Print book. All our Thorndike, Wheeler, and Kennebec Large Print titles are designed for easy reading, and all our books are made to last. Other Thorndike Press Large Print books are available at your library, through selected bookstores, or directly from us.

For information about titles, please call:
  (800) 223-1244

or visit our Web site at:
  http://gale.cengage.com/thorndike

To share your comments, please write:
  Publisher
  Thorndike Press
  10 Water St., Suite 310
  Waterville, ME 04901